Stuck
With
Him

BOOKS BY DANIELLE OWEN-JONES

Stone Broke Heiress

Stuck With Him

Danielle Owen-Jones

Bookouture

Published by Bookouture in 2022

An imprint of Storyfire Ltd.
Carmelite House
50 Victoria Embankment
London EC4Y 0DZ

www.bookouture.com

ISBN: 978-1-80314-086-5
eBook ISBN: 978-1-80314-085-8

For Tom
I'd be happily 'stuck' with you anywhere

ONE

It's difficult to do urgent, career-defining work while hiding in the toilet of a rowdy beach club. My attempts to concentrate on the laptop that was precariously balanced on my sunburnt legs were constantly thwarted. Every few minutes, a gaggle of excitable, tipsy women would clatter in on their clunky stilettos, slurring and swapping ideas about how to catch the roving eye of the Premiership footballer spotted on the VIP daybed outside.

Cursing myself for forgetting my AirPods to block out the noise, I tried to ignore the high-pitched shrieks and the deafening house music beats pounding the walls from the DJ booth outside. Instead, I squinted my exhausted eyes and leant closer towards the screen as the laptop quietly whirred on the lacy kaftan pooled in my lap, covering my lobster-red thighs.

Once lipsticks had been swapped, shiny faces blotted and gossip exchanged, the toilets quieted again, and I embraced every moment of temporary tranquillity. Well, as tranquil as the busiest beach club in Marbella possibly could be. As soon as the ladies' room was empty, the muffled bellows of the perma-tanned, far-too-old-to-still-be-doing-this DJ echoed outside. His roars would then be met with the crowd's drunken hollers of delight to the starting beats of the next 'banger'.

I rubbed my eyes, forgetting that my eyelashes were coated in generous lashings of mascara. *Come on, concentrate, Lucy*, I mumbled to myself. The letters and numbers on the screen in front of me were jumbled. It could've been a result of the Pornstar Martini that had been thrust into my hand the minute I arrived at the beach club. Or it could've been the sheer exhaustion of trying to keep my interior design business afloat while club-hopping my way around the Costa del Sol in the name of my best friend's final hurrah with her 'Bride Tribe'.

The good thing about the widely encouraged and generally socially acceptable binge drinking of a hen party, at least, was the fact that my plan was working. I'd purposely brought a huge tote bag with me and feigned generosity in offering to carry everyone's beach towels. But really, my laptop was safely hidden inside. Ah-ha! And, although pushing the bride-to-be towards tequila shots at 10 a.m. wasn't my proudest moment, at least I knew that if she was a little sauced and not wondering about my whereabouts, then I'd be safe to get through my urgent work in the sanctity of the ladies' toilets. Plus, there's a limit to how many willy straws a woman can drink from in a lifetime, and I'd reached mine.

Grinning at my excellent plan, I worked my way through my emails. There were still eighty-seven that needed my immediate attention since I'd checked my inbox in the villa that morning. That's the thing about owning a business. People are always quick to tell you how hard it is – how twenty per cent of businesses fail in the first year and sixty per cent within three years. But I can handle hard work. That's who I am. However, it's the age-old cliché that's the real challenge – that there are *literally* not enough hours in the day, or the night (luckily, I'd figured out how to function on just four hours of sleep).

Flashes of fluorescent pink dashed across the keyboard as

my newly manicured, holiday-ready nails tapped urgently over the keys. I'd been working quickly and ploughing through every task, but time had blurred and I had no idea how long I'd been hiding in there. Worse comes to worst, I'd tell the rest of the hen party that it was the dodgy seafood we ate last night, and I'd been stuck on the loo – nobody could argue with that.

But then, the door to the ladies' swung open with force, filling the toilets with booming dance beats. My heart stopped in my chest when I heard the livid groans and moans, paired with the platform wedges, furiously stomping in like a pack of angry animals. I jumped as a fist thudded on the toilet door three times.

'We know you're in there, Lucy!'

I knew who the voice belonged to. But instead of answering, I remained silent, curling myself around my laptop, hugging it protectively, with the tassels of my white kimono nestled around my bare limbs.

'You need to come out!'

It was Emma, the sister of the bride. She didn't sound as happy as she had been last night when she was doing tequila shots from a barman's sun-kissed eight-pack.

'You've ruined everythinnnng,' another voice slurred, and I identified it as Hayley – the hen party's number one liability. There was always one, and she wore the title like a badge of honour. Literally. There were badges personalised with our identities that we were forced to answer to throughout the holiday. I was 'Loosey Lucy' which was ironic, given I'd been called tightly wound and highly strung my entire life.

'Lucy, seriously...' Emma's angry voice hissed again.

Despite the developing situation, and my acute awareness that my hen party badge should've read 'The Worst Best Friend/Bridesmaid in the World', I was distracted by the ping of my inbox – a noise that would wake me from the deepest sleep. The name in bold at the top of the folder immediately spasmed my stomach into knots. It was Lavinia. My most important, highest-paying client. I quickly scanned her words in the email, my heart pulsing in my throat. She was aware of the problem I was having with my luxury wallpaper supplier in Italy – the problem I'd hidden myself away to try and resolve.

There was no way I could leave now. This toilet was my new home. Hopefully someone could post my things here. If I painted the walls, built some rustic shelves for a couple of scented candles, threw around a scatter cushion or two, it might resemble my signature cosy but elegant personal style. It would certainly be a test of my skills as an interior designer, but hey, maybe I could make it work?

'I'm just a bit...' I coughed dramatically to disguise the sounds of my typing. 'Indisposed!' I shouted.

'We know you're in there working!' Emma bellowed.

Two pairs of pedicured feet, clad in high platform wedges, shuffled around outside the door.

'Yeah, we know,' Hayley mumbled.

'I'm *notttttt*...' I said, elongating my words to buy me more time so I could finish quietly typing my email. 'I had some dodgy seafood last night and I just need a bit of a quiet sit-down!'

'Oh, really?'

I shrieked as I heard Emma's voice from above, and looked up to see her face peering over one side of the cubicle. Hayley's face was propped above the opposite side, her eyes lazy and unfocused, but beautifully framed with feathery fake eyelashes.

'We see you.' Hayley pointed clumsily and tutted. '*Worky McWorkason*.' She wriggled a finger, her nails filed to a long, sharply pointed tip.

'Lucy, I'm not kidding,' Emma said, with an earnest tone in her voice that had so far been reserved for the rented villa's Prosecco supplies getting low, and the 'butler in the buff' who was terrible at timekeeping. 'You have the booking for the champagne spray, and now they're saying they won't do it because we've missed our allotted time!'

'No spray. No sparklers,' Hayley slurred, pouting like a child.

'Exactly, no *sparklers*!' Emma shot me a furious glare, to my confused expression. 'The sparklers in the champagne!' she said impatiently. 'You know, when the staff deliver the bottles filled with sparklers and they spell out your name with big boards. It was supposed to be the highlight of the holiday and you've ruined it, Lucy. You've *ruined* it!'

'Ruined it,' Hayley repeated, while sipping the dregs from a plastic flute.

'I'm sorry.' I looked from one to the other, feeling a lurch in my stomach. I genuinely was sorry. 'Seriously. I'm sorry. I'll go and talk to them now,' I garbled. 'I'm sure they'll still do it for us. It's just, I had an urgent work thing—'

'Yeah, yeah, we know.' Emma rolled her eyes dismissively. 'Lucy when do you *not* have "an urgent work thing"?' she air-quoted.

'When, Lucy, when?' Hayley's head lolled from side to side as she eyed me, or attempted to.

'I know, I know, I get it,' I said, with one eye still on the draft email. 'But honestly, this really is urgent.' I pleaded with them as I looked up, from one to the other. 'I wouldn't be doing this if it wasn't absolutely essential. There's a serious supplier crisis with my biggest client. Her wallpaper—'

'Wallpaper!' Emma's eyes were wide with indignation, her nostrils flaring. 'Wallpaper. Bloody *wallpaper*! Are you kidding me, Lucy?' She slammed a hand against the top of the separating wall and the entire cubicle shook. 'You know how important this is for Katie. It's her HEN PARTY. It's her LAST FLING BEFORE THE RING.'

'OK, OK.' I sighed, relenting. Katie was my best friend and she'd never forgive me if I ruined her hen party – I wouldn't forgive myself either. I pressed save on the draft reply that I'd been carefully crafting before raising my hands in surrender to the hen party police. Now wasn't the time. Maybe I could try and sneak out later when the naked butler was back again; the girls were always distracted then.

'I'm sorry, I'm coming.' I pushed my laptop lid shut, and Emma and Hayley nodded victoriously before climbing down from their positions standing on the toilets either side of me.

Pins and needles shot through my legs as I stood – a give-away for the fact I'd been sitting in that position on the toilet for much longer than I realised. I put my laptop in the tote bag and swivelled around to stretch out my back, feeling the tense muscle knots that were knitted between my shoulder blades.

I pulled the lock back and the door creaked open. Feeling like a naughty schoolkid, I slumped out of the cubicle to the still-furious glares of the two women dressed in matching pink bikinis, white sashes and elaborate headbands.

'I hope you still have your flower crown?' Emma whispered, with a subtle wrath that felt out of place when it was a question about headbands made from satin flowers. 'Seriously, Lucy. I'm kicking you out of the I Do Crew if you've lost it.'

'That'll mean you're not a Bridesbabe any more,' Hayley confirmed earnestly.

'Don't be silly, you two. *Of course* I still have my flower crown,' I said, losing a few petals as I pulled it roughly from my bag. I hastily plopped it on top of my frizzy hair, which had been ravaged by the humidity.

'It's a good job Katie didn't know that we'd booked a champagne spray and sparklers,' Emma said, in her subtle yet menacing tone. She grabbed my arm and paraded me through the ladies' room, like a police officer who'd just apprehended a criminal. 'She would *never* forgive you,' she added, with the same gravitas as if I'd been caught in bed with the groom-to-be.

'But I guess at least it was supposed to be a surprise and what she doesn't know can't hurt her.'

I was taken aback by the intensity from Emma, who ordinarily was a lovely girl. I knew her heart was in the right place, but the pressure of being a bridesmaid was getting to her – she just wanted everything to be perfect, and to give Katie the amazing hen party she deserved.

The sudden brightness and the immediate blast of heat hit me the second we stepped outside into the full impact of the blazing Spanish sun. My eyes watered as I tried to blink away the shock of the light – the contrast between the glaring sunshine and the dim bathroom I'd hidden myself away in.

Emma didn't loosen her grip on my arm, despite my whimper when her razor-sharp nails grazed my fresh sunburn. She was holding me as if I were a wild animal about to run away at any moment, which to be fair to her was partly correct. As terrible as I felt about the champagne spray, it was taking every fibre of my being not to make a run for it. The future of my business depended on it.

The gaggle of shrieks and giggles got louder and louder the closer we walked along the pool and towards the daybeds allocated for our party. There was a cluster of four-poster beds to share, each with gleaming white mattresses, pillows and sheer curtains that were billowing like sails in the wind. But a bride who was blushing – with fury rather than love – immediately distracted me.

'Where have you been?' Katie stomped over. Her hands were on her hips, off which hung the strings of a tiny white bikini.

'I was in the bathroom,' I said sheepishly.

'You were in the bathroom for two hours?' She crossed her tanned arms over her chest.

'No, not two hours!' I said, half laughing. 'Definitely not

two hours,' I added guiltily. Was I really in there for *two hours*? No wonder I couldn't feel my bum.

'What were you doing in there, Lucy?' Katie's eyes were covered, thanks to the big Prada sunglasses she'd snapped up in duty free, but I knew that underneath them those baby blues were seething with rage. 'Because unless you were getting friendly with a hot waiter, why would you have abandoned my hen party?'

Everyone around us stopped their conversations and turned to watch the drama unfolding. I felt a lump in my throat. I didn't have many friends, thanks to my workaholic lifestyle, and Katie was my oldest – ever since we got the same bus to school together and discovered a shared love of cheesy pop music. We spent our entire childhood and teenage years side by side, totally inseparable. I couldn't lose her, and I was already on thin ice.

Katie shook her head and let out a half-laugh as she looked up to the cloudless, cobalt sky. 'You were working, weren't you?' she said, shaking her beachy waves again.

I said nothing. My ridiculously high, totally inappropriate for the pool, platform wedges were rooted to the spot.

'You just can't stop, can you?' Katie said in disbelief. 'Not even for my hen party, not even for my *last margarita as a señorita.*'

Credit where credit's due, Emma had planned a plethora of phrases for the hen party. There was no doubt she'd been a much better bridesmaid than me. I felt sick as the thought struck me that perhaps this was the last straw for my long-suffering, patient best friend.

'I'm sorry,' I whispered, suddenly feeling small and vulnerable in the matching bikinis that showed off too much bum-cheek, but that all of us were too scared to refuse to wear.

'You're sorry?' Katie said. 'You're sorry?' She tapped her foot rhythmically as she placed her hands back on her hips again. There was complete silence as she stared at me until her foot stopped suddenly. 'OK, prove it to me, Lucy. Prove you're sorry.'

I hefted the tote bag further onto my shoulder. 'Of course,' I said diplomatically. 'I'll do anything. Anything you want. I'll do a truth or a dare. I'll go and persuade strangers to buy me a drink. I'll snog every man whose name begins with D in this place. Whatever you want,' I pleaded. And to my surprise, I genuinely meant it. I had to make it up to Katie.

'I'm really sorry, I lost perspective, but you know how much my work and my business means to me.'

'I do,' Katie said with a nod. 'But, Lucy, how many conversations have we had about how unhappy you are with your life? About how all you do is work? You can't remember the last time you had a decent night's sleep, a proper holiday, a good *shag*.' She emphasised the word and I blushed. 'How many bottles of wine have we polished off while you've cried over the pressure of living up to your high-achieving parents' standards, of running your own business? Or the quite frankly insane things you've had to do for your demanding clients?'

I guess that depended on what your idea of *insane* was. I mean, yes, I *was* nearly arrested in Thailand for accidentally smuggling a rare tortoise that had hidden itself inside a hand-woven rug. And, OK, *perhaps* the time I was almost hospitalised for dehydration when my car broke down in the Mojave Desert on the way to finish a fit-out for a client's new hotel in Las Vegas might've been a step too far for *some* people. But I said nothing. I was rooted to the spot.

'Say you're going to switch it off,' Katie said. 'Promise me you're going to switch your laptop off and live your life. At least for one night while we're here. Please.' Katie's collarbones moved up and down as she panted.

We stared at each other, not breaking eye contact.

'This isn't about me, or the hen party. This is about you. You're not living, and I'm worried about you.'

I shuffled from foot to foot. This felt like much too deep a conversation to be having when we were in little more than underwear, and the surroundings were adorned with signs saying things like: 'One tequila, two tequila, three tequila, floor!'

Internally, I decided that I'd agree for now and come up with a solution later. I guessed that was part of my problem and Katie's point – I couldn't sit back, and I couldn't let things go. I always needed a solution and I always had to solve a problem. I always needed to have control.

'OK.' I surrendered, holding my hands up. 'Fine, you win.'

'So, you're going to switch off?' Katie confirmed.

'I'm going to switch off,' I said through gritted teeth.

'Are you going to be Loosey Lucy?' Katie said slowly.

'I am.' I nodded.

'Say it…'

'I'm going to be Loosey Lucy.'

Katie beamed and the crowd started clapping. Before I knew it, they were all chanting 'Loosey Lucy'. The hen party girls came squealing towards me, thrusting a shot glass into each hand and surrounding me in a heady cloud of floral perfumes, sun cream and alcohol. I watched Katie stalking away with my laptop, but the crowd was blocking my view and clutching on to me. Unable to reach her or shout out to her, I realised that resistance was futile. I knew she wouldn't do anything to my laptop, not really. She'd probably just hide it from me.

So, I downed the shot of tequila in one hand, and the unidentifiable spirit in the other, and I accepted my fate as Loosey Lucy for the night. After all, what was the worst that could happen?

TWO

My head was on fire. My brain was pounding. I took a deep breath in and immediately felt bile burning in the back of my throat. My eyes were stuck together, and I couldn't prise them open until I peeled the fake eyelashes from my eyelids. The room was blurry. It was far too bright, as if somebody had decided to turn on every single light, which only emphasised the white walls, white floors and white bedding pooling around me. If I hadn't felt like I was dying, I probably would've enjoyed feeling like I was on a fluffy cloud.

But hang on. I wasn't alone. There was someone next to me. I yelped in panic as I clocked the warmth of the body next to me, hidden as a lump under the fluffy duvet. Oh no. Had I brought someone home with me? Had we...?

Holding my head in my hands, I tried to piece together what had happened last night, but the truth was that I couldn't. The memories wouldn't materialise, no matter how hard I tried to force them. The last thing I could remember was Katie threatening to drop my laptop into the pool at Ocean Club, and then some vague chanting of 'Loosey Lucy' and other various phrases perfectly personalised for Katie's impending nuptials. Then, nothing. Complete blackout.

Rubbing my eyes again, I tried to ignore the throbbing headache, the stomach-churning nausea and the smell of stale tequila seeping through every pore in my body. First things first, I needed to find out who the gentleman in my bed was. And then I needed to find my laptop. I wasn't sure I cared to know the details in between. I'd bury my head in the warm Spanish sand. Ignorance was bliss.

Feeling a surge of bravery thanks to my plan, I prodded him gently. No movement. Oh God, he was *alive*, wasn't he? I didn't kill a man for his laptop, *did I*? I mean, I wouldn't have put it past myself. Those emails were urgent.

'Excuse me,' I whispered.

What if he didn't speak English?

'Hola,' I said, shaking him gently. That was about as far as my Spanish went.

There was movement. A hand reached over the top of the duvet, pulling it down slowly to reveal a messy mop of hair, long eyelashes and pillowy lips. His eyes opened slowly. Then, a flood of recognition as he saw me.

'Ah, hola señorita,' he said sleepily. I sighed in relief at the handsome stranger in my bed. Well, it could've been much worse.

'Hi,' I said shyly.

'Good morning,' he replied, with the soft lilt of a Spanish accent. 'You feeling OK today?'

'Mm-hmm,' I lied. I needed to cut to the chase. Step two of my plan was more important than this awkward exchange. 'My memory is a little hazy though.'

'Yes, sí, I imagine it is.' He ran a hand through his bedhead.

'Did we...' I pushed my lips together and widened my eyes. 'You know.'

He giggled adorably. 'No, we didn't. You were very, very...

how you say in English...' He hesitated. 'Inebriated, pissed, hammered, legless—'

'Got it,' I interrupted.

'Drunk girls aren't my thing. Beautiful ones are – which you are, very much so. But not drunk.'

My cheeks flushed. He was flattering, but certainly lying. I was ninety-nine per cent sure that a clump of fake eyelashes was glued to my chin.

'So, if we didn't – you know – why are you here, in my bed?' I was grateful as I realised my pyjamas were intact, and as he pushed the covers off, he was practically fully dressed too.

'We had fun in the bar after Ocean Club. And you said you wanted to prove your friends wrong,' he explained with a nonchalant shrug. 'You mind if I take a shower?' He gestured to the en suite, and I nodded.

Although there were no memories, it made sense. I had to prove to Katie and the others that I could let loose and enjoy myself, even if it was only for a night.

But that just wasn't me.

'Good morning!' Katie bellowed, when I finally showed my face in the kitchen after bidding farewell to my new friend, Leo. 'Good night?' she winked.

'Great night,' I grunted as I rubbed my temples, my head still pounding.

Katie was tidying all the hen party paraphernalia from the open-plan lounge area of the rented villa. The floor-to-ceiling windows on one side revealed a sky so blue it looked like a painting instead of real life, and the ocean in the distance framed the scene perfectly.

Stifling a yawn, I poured coffee from the percolator on the stove into the nearest mug. I desperately needed caffeine and hangover food – the greasiest breakfast I could get my hands on, then I'd be fine. Or I'd be on my way to being fine. I could track down my laptop, answer my emails and deal with the crisis at work properly.

'What time is it?' I asked sleepily. I had no idea of the time – together with my laptop, Katie also confiscated my phone yesterday. It must be about 6 a.m., I reasoned. My internal body clock never let me down, and the villa was so quiet the girls must've still been sleeping off their hangovers.

Katie checked her watch. 'Two o'clock,' she announced breezily.

I spat out the coffee in my mouth and it blasted around me.

'Lucy!' Katie exclaimed as she jumped back. The brown liquid was splattered around the kitchen, leaving dark splashes and stains all over her immaculate, white 'Bride To Be' dressing gown.

'Two? In the afternoon?' I panted, wiping my mouth. 'Are you serious?'

'Yes, I'm serious.' She patted down her dressing gown dramatically with a damp cloth and eyed me angrily, even though I knew she had the same one in six other colours. 'The girls are at the beach,' she said. 'I told them I'd wait for you. Why? What's wrong?' I knew she was torn between annoyance and concern.

'I need my laptop, Katie. I didn't realise what time it was. I need to email Lavinia. I have to talk to the suppliers...' My head was spinning. My thoughts were spiralling, twisting and twirling, going round and round like a whirlpool – both from drinking my body weight in cocktails last night, and also from sheer, stomach-churning, vomit-inducing panic.

'Fine,' Katie groaned and relented. 'I guess you kept your promise yesterday. I'll get it.' She padded across the room in her flip-flops (which also said 'Bride To Be' on the soles) as I hastily wiped away the rest of the spilt coffee. My heart leapt as she opened a drawer and handed it to me. Yippee, I was reunited with my baby. Everything was going to be OK.

'Thank you,' I mouthed, breathing a sigh of relief. I flung open the laptop lid, almost accidentally ripping it off. The familiar sight of my email inbox illuminated the screen. It was still left open from my makeshift office in the Ocean Club ladies' toilets last night.

But the number of emails couldn't be right. It was triple what it was yesterday. Even though I always had a lot of emails, it was never this many. Immediately my stomach squeezed with dread at the sheer volume of them. Something was wrong.

I placed the laptop down on the kitchen island and hooked a stool leg closer with my foot so I could perch on it. My pulse quickened as I scanned the screen. Subject lines were written in shouty capitals. My biggest clients had sent multiple messages. Words like 'Urgent' and 'Immediate attention needed' and 'Termination of contract' and 'LUCY FOR GOD'S SAKE OPEN YOUR EMAILS!' filled the subject lines of my inbox. Something big – no, not big, something *catastrophic* – had happened.

Everything moved in slow motion around me as Katie chatted away, tidying up, totally oblivious to what was happening. I still couldn't piece it together as I scrolled through the inbox. My head was pounding from my hangover, my stomach was growling and unsettled. Everything felt hazy and unclear, as if my mind was surrounded by a thick cloud and an intense fog that wouldn't shift.

Then I checked my sent folder. And I saw it. An email sent at 3 a.m. That in itself was not a good sign. I felt my hand instinctively moving closer to my mouth as panic engulfed me.

'Katie,' I breathed, and she turned around to face me. 'Was my laptop in the drawer for the whole night?'

'Yes,' she answered casually. 'Although, actually, no.' She pushed her sunglasses further up her head. 'We did that exercise with Sally. Remember?'

I shook my head. My palm was still covering my lips, the final messy remnants of last night's lipstick smudged over my skin.

'Yeah, I suppose you wouldn't remember,' Katie said mischievously, with a sparkle in her eyes. 'Honestly, don't worry though. You shouldn't have beer fear or anything, you didn't make a tit out of yourself. And hey – you pulled a right fitty!' she winked.

'Katie,' I interrupted. 'What did we do with Sally? What exercise are you talking about?'

She leant over the counter, her generous cleavage pushed up against the top of her vest. 'Sally's training to be a counsellor, isn't she?' I nodded. Sally had been every girl's go-to agony aunt for the duration of the holiday. She'd listened to boyfriend problems, friendship troubles, and had offered advice over copious bottles of wine and tear-stained tissues.

'She wanted to help you last night,' Katie explained. 'You were relaxed, you were carefree. You actually were "Loosey Lucy" for once. It was the perfect time to do it.' She sipped from her steaming mug of peppermint tea.

'To do what?' I asked desperately.

The unopened email in my sent folder was still in front of me. It was an unexploded bomb.

'To say all the things to your clients that you could never actually say,' Katie said, eyeing me earnestly. 'To tell them exactly how many extra hours you work for them behind the scenes that they don't know about. How you exhaust yourself and regularly suffer burnout from trying to make their unrealistic visions for interior design come true. How you spend money from your own pocket sometimes when the budget is suddenly cut, but you want to finish the project and make it perfect...' Katie stopped for breath. 'Do they even have any idea of the time you went missing in South America because you were trying to find that remote alpaca farm for those wool cushions?'

I shook my head.

'Or when you were thrown out and nearly *arrested* at London Fashion Week for stealing a sample of the runway fabric that your client just *had* to have?'

I shook my head again.

'Or what about when you were temporarily held hostage by the antiques collector in Berlin who thought you were trying to steal that vintage clock?'

'It was a misunderstanding,' I pleaded. 'My German is... rusty.'

'See, all these insane things, all these situations you get yourself into...' Katie sighed. 'Not to mention that time you almost unknowingly took on the contract for that porn entrepreneur's new filming studio.'

We both shuddered as we remembered it. So much *leopard print*. So much *leather*. So much *latex*.

'Well, everything you could never say about your job, you finally said it.' Katie beamed. 'You got it all out and I'm so proud of you. You must feel amazing!'

'Did Sally write it down?' I asked desperately, ignoring Katie's praise of my drunken offloading. I felt anything *but* amazing right now.

Katie nodded. 'Yeah, she wrote it all down on your laptop to email it to herself, so she could help you if you needed it when we're back home. She's such a lovely girl—'

'Katie!' I shrieked. 'She's sent it. It's gone.'

Katie's brows knitted together in confusion. 'Gone to her email, you mean?'

'No!' I shrieked. 'It's in my sent folder and it's gone to...' I braced myself and clicked on the message, terrified of what I was going to find. My stomach felt like it was being weighed down with bricks.

'It's gone to everyone, Katie. It's been sent to *everyone*.' I felt the blood drain from my body. I knew I was pale without even looking in a mirror. I felt transparent – ghostly – like the life had just been sucked out of me.

Katie shuffled around and stood beside me. 'Oh shit,' she said. Her hand darted to her mouth. 'Is that your entire address book?'

I nodded, my head dizzy and light with the tiny movement.

'She must've clicked it by accident,' Katie said.

'My laptop has voice-activated control,' I murmured. 'If she or anyone else said "send to all" then it would've done it. It would've sent to all...'

The gravity of the situation dawned on me.

Katie squeezed my shoulder as she sensed my frozen body. 'I'm so sorry Lucy. We were all laughing and joking,' she said before she audibly gulped. 'We were saying imagine if you sent it to everyone in your address book... it might've picked up on it.'

It felt like my throat was closing. My heart pulsed hard against my chest. I couldn't move my limbs. I stared at the screen.

The most important thing in my life was ruined forever.

THREE

It was Katie's wedding day. Exactly two weeks after we had flown home from Spain, and my innermost thoughts and frustrations had been emailed to every single one of my clients. Damage control had been the theme of my fortnight, together with an average of two hours' sleep a night, and what I was convinced was still a lingering hangover. I'd grovelled, I'd persuaded and I'd begged. My tactics changed from my initial denial and insistence that it was a sophisticated virus, to what I thought was a perfect explanation: a competitor had hacked into my emails and sent it. Most clients didn't buy it – especially the ones who recognised the specific details that related to them on the email (at least nobody had been named directly). But a couple had seemingly given me the benefit of the doubt and had stuck by me.

Now, I was waiting for an answer from my biggest client: Lavinia Lawrence, a wealthy divorcée who had commissioned me for each of her homes around the world – a rustic villa in a Tuscan vineyard, a chic townhouse in Paris, a fabulous ski chalet in Austria. And her most recent, most exciting project: a Manhattan penthouse. The space was industrial and bare, bursting with potential – all exposed brick and high ceilings, with jaw-dropping views showcasing the City that Never Sleeps in all its glory. In short, it was my dream interiors project.

However, as well as being my highest paying client, Lavinia was also my most demanding and high-maintenance one. Luckily, she occasionally showed a glimmer of a sense of humour, depending on what mood she was in. And I was hoping she could appreciate the funny side of the whole ordeal, especially if she didn't recognise the jokes and quirks that were about her on the email.

Either way, today was the day I would find out whether she was going to keep working with me – and no doubt make me pay for my frustrations. Or if she was going to terminate my contract and move over to a competitor, which meant unless I could keep my other clients and win some new projects, I'd probably have to close my business and get a new job. I'd have to go back to working for a huge, faceless corporation with no freedom or creativity.

The only spanner in the works as I awaited my fate – a tiny, minuscule detail – was that today was Katie's wedding day. The luxurious bridal suite of the country house in the Sussex countryside was filled with flowery perfume and clouds of hairspray, as the bridal party, or 'Bride Tribe', all got ready together.

Katie was glowing (with love, but also a *lot* of Charlotte Tilbury highlighter) as she sat down at the makeshift make-up station beside the four-poster bed.

'Cheers, girls!' She grinned as we clinked our glasses of bubbly together. Her treacle-coloured locks were wrapped in cylindrical rollers and scattered around her head, ready for the hairdresser to undo after mine and Emma's half-up, half-down hairstyles were finished.

'Mrs Davies to be!' Emma said in a sing-song voice.

'To the future Mrs Katie Davies,' I said. I forced myself to smile, pushing my nerves and anxiety to the back of my mind. I couldn't remember the last time I'd slept more than a couple of hours or eaten a nutritious meal. My hands were shaking, I was nauseous. I couldn't think straight, and I had a constant dizzy feeling and ringing in my ears that I was pretty sure wasn't normal.

The surroundings were calming, at least, with big oak trees outside the window and luscious emerald lawns with tidy flower beds. Smartly dressed guests had started milling around the grounds. Some were already getting stuck into the free bar; others were looking up at the sky and debating whether it was going to rain.

It was my turn in the hairdressing chair next, and I tried so hard to switch off, to relax, to enjoy the day and not think about whether my phone was going to ring and what the answer would be. I tried to summon my inner zen, and then decided that if that didn't work, the bottomless champagne might help. Although it probably wasn't the best idea on an empty stomach. My appetite had disappeared since the day of my work crisis.

I took a sip from the crystal flute and nestled into the squidgy cushions on the chair while the hairdresser teased my locks into place. There's something so calming about someone playing with your hair, isn't there? I forced myself to sink back into the seat, to relax my stiff shoulders and calm my breathing. My curls were tousled and pinned, before the diamanté hair piece was clipped onto the loose knot at the back.

The morning passed in a blur of nervous anticipation. Emma and I were matching in our dusky rose, one-shoulder dresses. Katie was even more mesmerising than usual in her beaded ivory gown that hugged her curves in all the right places.

'Do I look OK?' Katie asked, glancing over one shoulder as she fixed her veil.

'Look *OK*? Are you kidding?' I answered, feeling tears wet my eyes. 'You look magnificent. Even more than you usually do.'

I carefully pressed my fingers against the corners of my eyes so I wouldn't ruin the smoky brown look the make-up artist had spent the best part of an hour perfecting.

A knock at the door signalled our cue to pick up the bouquets that were soaking up the last of the water.

'Time to go,' Emma said, clapping her hands together and passing me my beautiful blossoming bouquet.

The delicate sounds of the string quartet filled the grand reception area, with its milky pastel walls adorned with oil paintings. Emma and I walked ahead of Katie, down the stairs and through the opulent hallway, decorated with impressive antiques. We headed towards her dad, Mick, who was waiting outside the ceremony room where she and Matthew would soon say 'I do'.

Katie's dad's eyes were wet with tears as we approached him. He stood proudly as they embraced, before she offered him a tender kiss on his cheek. Even though the doors were closed, we could feel the excited anticipation in the air as the music drew to a close, and we heard the gentle thud of the one hundred and twenty guests taking to their feet under the instruction of the registrar.

Emma and I glanced at each other and grinned.

But then, the petals in my bouquet began trembling and the stems I held in my hand started vibrating. The sound of Darth Vader's theme boomed at full volume, the ringtone I'd chosen for Lavinia. I looked down and saw that as well as the bouquet, my hands had a death grip around my phone. I thought I'd put it away, I was *sure* I had put it away.

I looked up again sheepishly, and Katie and Emma were glaring at me.

'You brought your phone out?' Emma hissed.

'I'm so sorry, this is an accident,' I sniffed.

Emma's furious glare was unwavering.

'Lucy,' Katie said behind me. 'I know what you've been going through with work has been tough, and I know how important your job is to you, but this is my *wedding day*.' Her soft kohl-lined eyes were wide with impatience as she stared at me.

'What's going on, pet?' Katie's dad said, totally confused by the unfolding situation. 'Where's that music coming from? You're not walking down the aisle to this, are you? There's a time and a place, Katie love.'

'No, Dad, I'm not,' Katie snapped, before regaining her composure. 'Sorry,' she said. She closed her eyes, trying to muster up her patience. The music stopped and we all breathed a sigh of relief as the tension defused.

'Come on, let's go. Can you put that thing on silent?' Emma asked me frostily.

I looked at the phone again; it was still ringing. I knew I should've ignored it, and if it was anyone else, I would've done. But it was Lavinia. She was calling to give me her answer as to whether she was firing me. The answer that would tell me if my business, the one I'd built from scratch – the single most important thing in my whole life – would be OK. Everything was resting on her decision, and I knew she wouldn't ever leave a voicemail or a text. She was direct and old-fashioned. If I was ever going to convince her to keep me on, it had to be right now.

It felt like the room was in slow motion around me as I turned on my heel and looked pleadingly at Katie, arm in arm with her dad.

'If you take that call, you know what it means for our friendship, Lucy,' she said, her knuckles turning as white as her dress as she tightened her grip on her dad's suit-clad bicep.

I closed my eyes, took a deep breath, and made a choice.

FOUR

THREE MONTHS LATER

Walking through Liverpool city centre was like retracing the steps of my old life. It was teasing in its similarity, but it couldn't have been more different. A diet of ambition and adrenaline used to be my fuel. But the sleep deprivation and the high blood pressure had been worth it because then I had been at the top of my game in my career, living my dream. However, that was before my highest paying clients had all fired me.

Now, I was drinking acidic coffee from a polystyrene cup, while eating a pack of breakfast biscuits with an alarmingly faded expiry date. *This isn't where you're supposed to be*, a small and irritating voice in my head whispered as I stalked through the streets. *You've gone from having your own amazing office and jetting around the world visiting clients to eating stale biscuits and drinking terrible coffee.*

I tried to shake the voice off, to think about the positives. The cheap coffee wasn't *that* bad – not if you asked for it to be so piping hot that it numbed your taste buds, anyway. At least the coffee moistened the cardboard-like biscuits. And on the plus side, I still had a few clients, which meant I didn't have to close my business for good. I was incredibly grateful to those who had stuck by me after the mass email disaster (the ones who perhaps didn't recognise, or remember, any of the stories to be about them and their crazy demands).

For my own sanity, I couldn't allow myself to dwell on what had gone wrong with my interior design business. The painfully honest bulk email was just the tip of the iceberg. Before that, there had been cashflow issues, supplier problems, overdue invoices... the list went on. I was guilty of trying to grow too quickly, of doing all the things a fledgling business does before it's ready. Now I was facing the punishment of my ambition, and everything fell on my tense, knotted shoulders.

Instead of starting the day with my previous routine of a sunrise six-mile run, followed by early Zoom meetings to catch up with my international clients, my new, quieter work schedule paved the way for something a bit different. I'd committed to attending a weekly 'spiritual well-being course' for people battling demons of varying degrees (my demon was an inability to switch off, which I'd argued wasn't *that* bad, as far as demons go). Every session was a variant of either yoga or meditation, and throughout each one, I could think of a million other ways I could be spending my time.

However, my attendance at the class was non-negotiable if I wanted to save my friendship with Katie. Missing walking down the aisle at her wedding to take the most important phone call of my career was undoubtedly the final straw for her, and I regretted making that choice every single day. The only saving grace was that I had managed to sneak back in before they said 'I do', and I'd convinced Katie that my tears were of happiness for her special day, not from being fired by Lavinia. (And thankfully, a groomsman had overdone it on the morning whiskies and started snoring during their vows. So, luckily, he'd taken the heat off me.)

We were still on shaky ground though, and that last chance of friendship came with a friendship-saving list; number one was attending this weekly spiritual well-being course. I had to finally prove to Katie that I was listening to what she had been telling me over the years – and what most people I knew had told me frequently – that I needed to try and switch off, to learn how to relax and to re-evaluate my priorities.

I was willing to do anything to salvage the friendship I had with my long-suffering, best and only real friend. And I was trying to ignore my cynicism about the whole thing. What on earth did Katie think would happen if I agreed to this 'illuminating journey along the tranquil path of soul-soothing and heart-healing spiritual enlightenment' (so it said on the leaflet) – that I'd become an entirely new person? That a softly spoken man with impressive abdominals would fix me after a few hours of sitting in silence and trying to locate something called a core?

Still, despite my scepticism, I had to make it up to her and show her how much I regretted my erratic behaviour during what could only be described as burnout-meets-breakdown-meets-quarter-life-crisis – and perhaps a bit of leftover sunstroke and tequila poisoning too.

Pushing open the door to the yoga studio, I tried to calm myself; to let the dim lights and the incense sticks soothe my anxious mind. My entrance was met with a welcoming nod by the man sitting cross-legged in front of the women gathered on brightly coloured mats, in equally brightly coloured gym wear. Having missed the introductions at the first class thanks to oversleeping (I'd finally discovered the joy of eight hours a night), I was convinced our instructor's name was something hilariously hippy, like Ocean. Or perhaps Breeze. Maybe Peace, given he'd said the word enough times during the classes. 'Inner peace', 'find your peace', 'make peace with your past', 'peace and love', 'peace, peace, peace...'

Tiptoeing along the wooden floor, I took my usual spot at the back of the class, where I always tried to hide. Today was a meditation session, and as I sat in the cross-legged position, every attempt to clear my mind and follow the instructions that Ocean Breeze had given the class at the start was thwarted by my work worries. The minutes passed, and I kept shaking my head every time an uninvited thought found its way into my mind. If my eyes were open, I probably would've seen either the instructor or one of my classmates looking concernedly over at me and my erratic, twitching head.

Eventually, I allowed myself to open an eye. I surreptitiously lowered my gaze, forgetting there was only a pale band of skin and a scattering of freckles where my watch should've been. Watches and phones were banned during the classes, which irked me. Wasn't it enough that we had to sit in silence on the floor as if we were back in school – legs crossed and back straight – but we couldn't even know *how long* we'd been doing it? Probably an hour. It must've been. Couldn't have been less than an hour. Although the class was only forty-five minutes, so perhaps not.

Anyway. *Focus, Lucy. Focus.*

I allowed myself a sly smile, but tried not to audibly giggle as I remembered Ocean Breeze's job title: Yoga Teacher and *Breath Technician.* I mean, come on. Who needs technical guidance on the simple process of *breathing?* Of *inhaling* and *exhaling?* But the yummy mummies surrounding me were lapping it up and lapping *him* up. Give him his due, if regular meditation was responsible for his enviable physique and glowing skin, then perhaps I should've been taking it more seriously.

Bloody hell, Lucy, I admonished myself again, furrowing my brows in frustration. *Concentrate. Focus.*

Straightening my screaming back muscles, I tried to calm my mind. It felt like it always did – as if it was moving at 200mph when all I really wanted was a residential area limit of 30mph. I mean, I would've even settled for a 70mph motorway cruise. I breathed deeply through my nose, trying to feel every

extended inhalation in my core – I was still not 100 per cent
sure I knew exactly what or where my core was, but I nodded
along confidently whenever Ocean mentioned it. It was definitely somewhere in the stomach region.

Just as I thought I was making headway with this meditation malarkey – counting up an all-time record of three inhales
and exhales without my mind wandering to work or what I
fancied for breakfast – Ocean Breeze stopped the soft music.
He gently clasped his hands together, a quiet noise that made
me jump, even though it was as hushed as a leaf delicately
falling to the floor. Perhaps people were right when they told
me I was jittery.

I opened my eyes and self-consciously looked around to see
if anyone had heard or noticed my quiet gasp. They had. And I
was met, as always, with the rolling eyes of my fellow class-
goers. I didn't own anything from Lululemon, and I thought a
downward dog was a phrase for a sad puppy, so they hadn't
accepted me into their lycra-clad tribe of toned biceps, post-
class green smoothies and almond butter energy balls.

'Thank you, everyone,' Ocean whispered. 'Thank you for
being present physically.' He gestured around the room in a
sweeping motion. 'Mentally.' He tapped his head gently. 'And
spiritually.' He placed his hands in the prayer position at his
chest. 'Namaste,' he whispered. Then, he closed his eyes and
bent forward over his crossed legs. We all copied him, as a wave
of hushed tones murmuring 'namaste' filled the room. I added
'in bed' silently – it had gone down like a lead balloon that time
I said it out loud, and nobody had sat near me ever since.

Ocean Breeze pushed himself up from his spot at the front
of the room and shook out his limbs, the creases in his linen
clothes stubbornly remaining. I smiled at my second favourite
part of the session. The first was the moment it ended, and this
was the second. He pulled the cord at the side of the floor-to-

ceiling windows and there it was – a panoramic view of my city. Liverpool.

The Liver Birds were basking in the glory of the early morning sunshine and the Radio City Tower stood tall in the middle of the city centre, while water ebbed beside the Albert Dock and the silhouette of the cathedral loomed in the far distance. I felt a glimmer of hope in the bottom of my stomach at the day ahead – but the light went out as soon as I felt it shine. I was still feeling lost, even with the promise of the weekly spiritual well-being course to 'find yourself' through yoga and meditation.

'Before I forget,' Ocean said, addressing the class, 'there's a change to the schedule next week.' He tiptoed across the sunlight-speckled yoga studio. 'I have to make a last-minute trip to our venue in Spain. One of our teachers had a nasty injury in the advanced headstands course and they need me to take over,' he said nonchalantly. I smirked, feeling vindicated at the news. I always knew yoga was dangerous. 'So, there's a new teacher taking over this class for a few weeks.'

'Count me out then,' one woman purred. Her hair was the same bright silver as the chunky rings on each of her fingers.

'My replacement is an expert. He's one of the partners of the studio. I promise you'll like him.' Ocean Breeze winked, with a flirtatious grin. He knew how to play his audience. After all, he knew that he must, to keep the payments – to essentially sit in silence with him – coming in. 'I'll see you again next month.' He waved the class goodbye.

Clumsily, I rolled up my yoga mat. I'd managed a grand total of three inhales and three exhales – a new record for me. Maybe I was beginning to find my 'inner peace' after all?

FIVE

'You really don't have to do this, you know,' Katie said, mid-salad bite.

I ignored her and carried on. The table was wobbling with the force of the pencil on my sketchpad, as my eyes darted between the creamy paper and the interiors of the restaurant. I was soaking up every element of it and taking in every inch of the surroundings.

'Your food's going cold!' Katie cried with an eye-roll. 'Seriously, Lucy. Stop.' She put her cutlery down and placed her hand on mine.

'You know what I'm like when inspiration hits,' I said, almost gasping after holding my breath in. I offered my pencil in surrender. 'It's like someone else takes over my body.'

'Of course I know.' Katie sighed. 'At least it's me who's benefitting from your obsession this time,' she added cheekily. 'Come on. Eat.' She nudged my plate forward with her elbow.

My mouth watered as I surveyed my plate, loaded with my favourite dirty burger and equally dirty fries. Hopefully it was still warm. I always lost track of time when I was in the zone. However, the restaurant was Katie's dream interior and the exact style I wanted to replicate. Cosy, farmhouse chic, and just the right balance of contemporary with rustic touches. The table we were sitting at was distressed wood, in perfect symmetry with the reclaimed wood ceiling beams. Classic white walls and barn doors with whimsical accents and pops of colour made the room feel spacious but inviting. Antique picture frames and vintage prints decorated the walls, with hanging pendants, hurricane lanterns and flickering candles romantically lighting the space.

'If you can make my new house look exactly like this, I'll officially forgive you for not walking down the aisle with me.' Katie grinned and nicked a chip from my plate.

'I don't deserve your forgiveness for that,' I half garbled, unable to put down the deliciously dirty burger now it was in my hands – and my mouth. I'd discovered the joy of food again after my previous diet of caffeine and stress.

'Come on, Luce. I'm kidding. OK? We know now that you were insanely overworked, sleep deprived for years and not thinking straight. It was only a matter of time before you had a breakdown, and it all caught up with you. Plus, I know throwing yourself into your work is the way you deal with what happened to Dotty.' Katie bit her glossy lip, before deciding to change the subject. 'But you're ticking off my friendship-saving list rather nicely, aren't you?' She nicked another chip, and I playfully batted her hand away.

'If you're talking about attending that spiritual well-being cult – sorry, *course*...' I teased. 'Then yes, I suppose I am.'

'It'll be good for you,' Katie said, sitting back defiantly. She knew she had the upper hand; that I wasn't going to argue with her. 'You know I'm right. You know Dotty would think so too.'

A pang hit my heart at the thought of Dotty, my beloved grandmother. The woman who'd raised me while my success-obsessed parents travelled the world for work. Dotty was both my muse and my mentor. She taught me everything I knew about interior design and how a room should tell a story, not just look pretty. She was completely self-taught – though she could've been a designer if she'd had the opportunity, with her artistic flair, natural talent for crafts and incredible eye.

'Sorry, I didn't mean to upset you.' Katie looked at me worriedly as I felt my eyes watering with the beginnings of tears.

'I'm fine.' I cleared my throat. 'But yes, you're right. She would've lost her head over me replicating the workaholic ways of my absent parents.'

'Not as much as that time when we both pretended we'd got our noses pierced, and stuck on those temporary tattoos.'

'Falkner Avenue had never seen a pensioner run so fast.'

'I thought she was going to hit us with her rolling pin! I've never been so terrified!' Katie giggled.

'How were we so scared of someone hardly even five foot tall?' I wiped the happy tears away from my eyes as I recalled the memories, growing up with my spirited grandmother, and all those rebellious after-school adventures with Katie. I felt Katie's hand on mine. We didn't need to say what we were both thinking about those cherished days with Dotty.

'You just enjoy your honeymoon,' I said. 'I'll plan your fabulous house interiors, while also learning how to inhale and exhale.' I rolled my eyes. 'Then, you'll come home from your round-the-world trip with a new house and a new best friend to look forward to.'

'I don't want a new best friend, you know that.'

'You know what I mean.' I smiled, before taking a final bite of the burger loaded with decadent yumminess. 'Your old best friend – just minus the meltdown, and adding some new mental and physical flexibility.'

'Sounds good to me.' Katie grinned. 'Although, speaking of moving out, have you started thinking about maybe looking for another apartment yet?'

I winced and shook my head. My recent living situation was far from ideal, but it was temporary. I was living with Katie and her new husband, Matthew, before they jetted off on a globe-trotting honeymoon, arriving back home to move into their dream house that they'd designed and built from the ground up – and entrusted me with the interiors.

'Are you going to start looking soon?' Katie asked gingerly. I knew she felt bad about turfing me out when they sold their flat, but it wasn't her fault I had to move in with them when I could no longer afford the rent on my luxury penthouse apartment after losing my highest paying clients.

'Yep.' I nodded, trying to convince myself more than her. Katie was the only friend left who hadn't ghosted me after being fed up with me caring more about work than nourishing a friendship with brunch dates and wine nights.

It wasn't like I could move in with my parents. They called Sydney home now, where they both worked as architects. I hardly saw them except for the occasional Christmas, and our usual conversations were restricted to awkward, stilted Zoom calls and overly formal emails. They weren't exactly the under-standing type that you could lean on and call up for advice – I hadn't even told them about everything that had gone wrong lately.

'Anyway!' I said brightly, before taking a glug of the mock-tail next to me. Without getting too Freudian, I knew my obses-sive, workaholic attitude stemmed from the inner want of my parents' approval. 'Tell me more about which of my ideas you like best for the open-plan kitchen and dining area.'

I brushed the crumbs away, picked up a pencil and tapped my sketchpad again. I needed to steer the subject away from my absent family and my impending homelessness. I needed to get lost in my favourite world – the world of design.

SIX

Our new instructor was late, and every passing second was a waste of time. Something I couldn't stand in life was wasting time. The constant need to be productive was an intrinsic urge I struggled to fight, and one of the reasons why I'd been semi-forced into signing up for the spiritual well-being course.

Then, the door swung open. Ocean Breeze's replacement – probably named Blue Moon or Summer Sunshine – sauntered barefoot into the room with the same relaxed air of a man strolling along a Caribbean beach. He was wearing an identical uniform to the other teachers at the studio: loose linen trousers and a T-shirt that was just tight enough to reveal impressively muscular arms (which I was convinced they did on purpose).

Taking his place at the front of the class, he pulled off his khaki beanie hat, and chocolate-brown tresses tumbled over his shoulders – his perfect curls were enough to give Jonathan Van Ness a run for his money. He beamed at the group, revealing pearly white teeth.

'Hey, everyone, good morning.' He grinned, with sleepy eyes. 'Yeah, I'm sorry I'm late, guys.' He checked the time on his sports watch (annoyingly, the studio teachers were allowed the gift of time, unlike the attendees).

'Is that all you have to say?' one of the group admonished him, equally as annoyed as me. 'This would never happen with Nigel.'

Nigel? Ocean Breeze was actually called *Nigel*? I refused to believe our usual breathing technician went by the name of *Nigel*.

'Ah.' Our new meditation teacher smiled with an air of teenage awe. 'Good old Nige. No, you're right. He'd never be late; I need to work on my timekeeping.' He nodded solemnly, but followed it with a carefree shrug that boiled my blood, before rolling out his mat and grabbing a block to perch on. It was a yoga day.

I tried to shake off my annoyance and forced my limbs into the position that never got easier, no matter how many times I did it. One ankle over the other, back straight, chest and shoulders out. My posture had taken a hammering after years of stooping over a computer screen, together with lugging a heavy laptop and bursting portfolio around.

'Let me introduce myself,' our new instructor said, each hand resting on opposite knees. 'My name is Ziggy – well, my spiritual name, that is.'

That was more like it; a much more appropriate name than Nigel. I grunted and everyone turned to look at me. 'Sorry,' I whispered and rubbed my nose. 'Hay fever.'

He smiled patiently and continued. 'But you can all call me Zack. I'll be taking this class for the foreseeable future, and we'll be doing a calming and relaxing combination of meditation and yoga. It sounds like Nigel's going to be taking the reins at our Spanish venue for a little longer than we initially thought. But I can assure you, you're in expert hands, if I do say so myself. As a partner here, I've worked at our different studios around the world; however, lovely Liverpool is now my home. I've lived here for the last few years.'

'What brought you to Liverpool then, love?' another woman asked flirtily. 'Why did you leave the Maldives or Mykonos for Merseyside?'

'Please, ladies.' He gave a bashful grin, but the cynic in me wasn't convinced he didn't know exactly what he looked like. After all, the studio was ninety per cent mirrors. He pressed his hands together in a prayer position at his chest. 'There will be plenty of time for questions at the end of the session. Let's not waste any more time on me when we could be awakening our bodies, nourishing our souls and soothing our minds.' He clicked play on the remote and the usual sounds of birdsong and babbling brooks echoed from the speakers, bouncing off the wooden floors and plain white walls. 'We'll begin with our grounding breathwork, to be present and to invite awareness of both breath and body.'

Just like Nigel (the name was still distracting me), Zack began to gently guide us through our 'conscious breathing' exercises. He held a hand to his chest as he urged us to breathe in slowly and deeply, hold the breath, and then exhale as slowly as we could.

'*Shanti, shanti, shanti,*' he chanted, before closing his eyes and inviting us all to do the same with a smooth hand motion.

After a few minutes of the guided breathwork, I sneaked a peek at him. He was smiling with his eyes closed as he sat at the front of the class, perching with perfect posture on the yoga block. His eyelashes fluttered and he opened one eye, catching my stare at the same time. I quickly closed mine again, feeling like the naughty kid in school.

'Great start, everyone,' Zack said, after a few silent minutes. He pushed himself to his feet. 'I'm going to show you the yoga sequence we're going to do this session, with different options for advanced, intermediate and beginners.' He flashed a subtle smirk at me. Why did he assume I was a beginner? 'I'll go through the advanced sequence first,' he said.

I sat back and crossed my arms. Little did he know, I was always a top student in everything I did. I was going to prove him and his *beginner* assumption wrong. I was going to master the advanced poses. This was yoga, after all – wasn't it supposed to be stretching and balancing? How hard could it be?

'First, we're going to stretch down into *padangusthasana*, also known as big toe pose.' Zack eased himself forward and slowly bent his body down, so his torso was parallel to his straight legs and his palms were flat on his feet. *Easy peasy*, I thought as I watched him.

'Next, we'll do a plank.' Zack planted his big hands down on the mat as he easily stretched his legs out backwards. His strong arms held his weight as if he were a feather, without even a tremble – just his T-shirt tightening distractedly against his biceps. I guffawed silently again. A plank was fine; even *I* could manage a plank. Was this really the *advanced* sequence?

'Then we're going to push our feet down, lift our bodies upwards at an angle and go straight into downward dog.' He manoeuvred his body backwards and his T-shirt fell up his torso, revealing his tanned stomach and dark snail trail. Unintentionally, because this guy was *so* not my type, I was surprised to feel my head tilt to the side to get a better look (and glimpsed Barbara next to me doing the same thing). But Zack was on to his next move before I could shake myself from my gazing back to the present moment (ironically what I was supposed to be concentrating on doing in the class, anyway).

'After downward dog, we'll go into dolphin, and then head-stand prep.' Zack placed his head down onto the mat between his arms, and leant forward on his tiptoes. 'Then one leg tucked.' He smoothly pulled one leg in without even a quiver of his arms that were supporting his body. 'And both legs tucked.' He pulled his second leg in, so only his forearms and his head were on the floor. 'Into full headstand,' he announced, slowly pushing his legs up and balancing perfectly on his head in front of the class – their silent nods and prying eyes were distracted by the effect gravity had on his T-shirt once again.

I've got this, I reassured myself, psyching myself up. *I can totally do it.* I ignored the instinctual feelings of hesitation, as I still hadn't mastered the basic moves in the classes I'd attended so far. However, I must've located my core by now. It was probably just a subconscious thing that you learnt to do without knowing it for definite. And surely I had to try some *advanced* moves in order to *advance* in the class? It made perfect sense. Katie would be so proud of me. I was really committing to the course and pushing myself out of my comfort zone – not being at all competitive, just *enthusiastic.*

Zack ran through the other sequences for intermediates and beginners, but I only half watched. I was too busy giving myself internal pep talks for my forthcoming headstand, and was hardly paying attention. (Apart from frustratingly getting distracted by his nimbleness – he made it all look so easy, and he did it with a smug smile too.)

'So, if we could have all the advanced members of the class over here, please.' Zack directed the group to the far side of the studio. 'The intermediate to the opposite side,' he said, as he pointed. 'And the beginners in the middle please, guys, so I can keep an eye on you.'

Wow. Could he sound any more *patronising*? I scoffed and looked around at my fellow class-goers in the hope of some solidarity. Perhaps we could stage a coup? Burn some sage and peacefully protest (in a nice and easy yoga pose – I couldn't hold 'Tree' or 'Dancer' for the duration of a *long* protest). We could chant affirmations together and insist on a different teacher. One who wasn't late for class, or who wasn't a condescending show-off, with his impressive headstands and equally impressive abdominals. I looked around to rally some allies, but all I saw was coquettish admiration and schoolgirl-like giggles as Zack smiled and chatted with the class, while they sorted themselves into the different levels of yogic know-how.

Noticing I was standing in the middle of the room with the beginners, I shifted over to the other side and joined the advanced group.

Zack looked at me and raised an eyebrow. 'Beginners are in the middle,' he said.

'I know,' I answered coolly.

'This is advanced.'

'I know,' I repeated, a little more impatiently. Who did he think he was? Making a judgement about me and my yoga skills? He didn't even know me. Well, I'd show him. I'd have the last laugh. Although, we were supposed to be quiet in the classes, so a victorious silent meditation instead.

Zack held his hands up defeatedly and mumbled a not-very-sincere-sounding apology. I looked at my reflection in the mirror. *You've got this, Lucy*, I told myself. I was relieved I was wearing my best yoga leggings. I knew I should've chosen some practical ones, but these had a subtle shimmer and made my bum look great. Though I hoped Zack didn't notice my feet were in desperate need of a pedicure. I crossed one foot over the other self-consciously, in the hope of hiding the flaking remnants of pink polish. Then I looked at him, with his great hair but self-satisfied smile. Why did I care what he thought about my feet?

'Excellent. Nice work, everyone.' Zack clasped his hands together from his position at the front of the class. 'So, do we all remember the sequence?'

I snorted. He only did it five minutes ago; did he really think we were that forgetful?

'Sorry, I haven't caught your name,' Zack said, locking eyes with me. Perhaps my snort was louder than I thought.

'Me?' I asked, feeling the eyes of the room on me.

'Yep. You.' Zack nodded, straightening his shoulders arrogantly. He was loving this, I could tell.

'I'm Lucy,' I said proudly, matching his stance – only I was about a foot smaller, and with a much less athletic frame.

'Lucy,' he repeated as he held my gaze, my name like silk on his lips.

'Seems like you remember the *advanced* sequence perfectly, Lucy.'

I nodded much more confidently than I was feeling, but I wasn't going to let him know that.

'Perhaps you could talk us through it? Or even better, maybe you could show us? Give everyone a very quick reminder of what we're doing?' He flashed a smirk, just for me, before turning and beaming charmingly at the rest of the class.

'Erm...' I hesitated, feeling my cheeks flush. 'I don't think everyone needs a reminder, do we? We've only just watched your demonstration, after all.' I looked around at the faces surrounding me. But my hopes for some sort of yogic solidarity were dashed (again!), as the only mutters were my fellow classmates saying they'd already forgotten and that a quick refresher of the sequence order would be helpful.

I gulped. I refused to meet Zack's eye as I focused on the floor in front of me and desperately tried to remember the sequence – while cursing myself for being so *enthusiastic* (note: not competitive) to be top of the class. And also admonishing myself for being so easily distracted by Zack and his remarkable flexibility (offset by his pompous attitude, naturally).

'OK.' I planted my feet down at the top of the yoga mat. 'The first in the sequence was...' I hesitated as I bent downwards. What was it? Definitely something to do with toes. Or maybe it was feet. 'Little feet pose!' I announced triumphantly, albeit with a smidge of doubt; it didn't sound *quite* right.

'*Padangusthasana*,' Zack confirmed haughtily to the group. 'Also known as *big toe* pose.' I knew my cheeks were flushed

scarlet with growing annoyance as I heard him and his tone.
Luckily, the room was dimly lit. *And* I was bent forwards, with
my head against my shins, so he couldn't see that he was getting
to me.

'That's what I meant,' I mumbled, feeling the blood rush to
my head, and likely making me look even more red-faced. *Not
to worry*, I told myself. I could do this without looking at him, I
just had to keep my head downwards. Oh, hurrah! A reminder
of the next move. 'Then we'll go into downward dog.' I clumsily
manoeuvred myself into the position, not helped by my
sweating hands and feet that kept slipping on the mat.

'You've missed plank, actually,' Zack said, and I tried to
ignore his know-it-all tone by focusing on not slipping off the
map entirely – otherwise very soon I was going to resemble
more of a squashed dog than a downward dog.

'Next, I'm going into dolphin... and then headstand prep...' I
breathed. My entire body was trembling, my speech peppered
with breathlessness. I felt like I had no strength, as if my bones
were turning to noodles. Where was my core when I needed it?

'I think that's enough,' Zack said. His feet appeared next to
me on the mat as I continued to inelegantly shift myself around.

'No. I can... I can do it,' I said, while trying to balance my
body weight on my head, which wasn't ideal, given how much
I loved carbohydrates. I pushed upwards and lifted my leg up.
Then I felt Zack's hand on my calf. My leg felt tiny in his
grip, and I gasped quietly at his unexpected touch. For a
second, I thought he was helping me get into the headstand
position that I could absolutely, definitely do. But instead, I
realised his hands were gently pushing me down, not helping
me up.

'Hey!' I shouted, as he carefully placed my wayward,
shaking limb back down on the mat. I could still feel the
warmth from his touch through my leggings, and I ignored that
weird, gaspy jolt I felt when he touched me. 'Hey!' I said again,

as I sat up quickly to look at him. 'Why did you do that? I was doing a headstand!'

'I don't think you were,' he said gently. We were face to face, thanks to his position on his knees, and me on mine. I was close enough to see the freckles that speckled his nose. My chest rose up and down with every huff I took – both in anger and also because I was painfully out of shape. Plus, my head felt dizzy after trying to balance my entire body on top of it – perhaps not the best idea, with hindsight.

'Top marks for trying though, Lucy,' he said, still pompously but also unexpectedly kindly. Before I could breathe a reply, Zack stood up and took his place at the front of the room, ready for the class to do the sequence together. Admitting my humiliating defeat, and after wiping the beads of sweat from my forehead, I subtly shifted my mat a few inches over to the right, into the beginners' group.

SEVEN

My fingers fiddled with the hem of the old T-shirt I'd thrown on in a tornado of stress from my awful morning. The last thing I wanted to be doing on a day that felt almost as bad as the round-robin email at Katie's hen party was to be in Zack's company. My blood pressure was rising with every minute that he was late for the class – *again*. I ground my teeth as I glared towards the studio door in frustration. My day had started off so well-intentioned, but then it quickly went downhill. I'd been trying this new idea that a wellness influencer had been talking about online. The core of it was to 'reclaim your morning'. For me, it translated to:

1. Don't look at your phone when you haven't even properly opened your eyes.
2. Don't also press snooze eighteen times before rolling out of bed.
3. Leftover pad thai does not constitute a healthy breakfast.
4. A good skincare regime should consist of more than

       haphazardly slapping on some free magazine
       samples and hoping for the best.
5. Scrawling a shopping list isn't the same as mindful
      journaling.
6. Running like a maniac to move your car before the
      parking limit kicks in doesn't count as meaningful
      cardio.

My morning had included all the habits I was trying to break free from. But still, I tried. I tried to *reclaim my morning*. I gave myself a pep talk. Then, I drank the horrible lemon and fresh ginger concoction that the wellness guru swore by, before meditating for approximately twelve seconds.

Trying to ignore my state of feeling utterly frazzled, I'd then sat down to check my emails properly. My heart sank as I clocked the subject line of the first email in my inbox: Notice of Contract Termination. I was losing another client. I scrolled down with my heart racing; the second email was an overdue invoice I'd forgotten about, and the third was a pitch I'd been unsuccessful in winning. To make it even worse, Katie then called to say that the buyers of their flat were threatening to pull out of the sale if we didn't move out earlier. So, my lack of home was feeling even more real, and looming closer.

Every day, I felt like I was starting all over again and trying to hold it together. And every wasted minute of the class that passed by, thanks to Zack's lateness, riled me up even more. Why did he think his time was more valuable than everyone else's? I chewed my fingernails to try and alleviate some of my frustrations. And I stopped myself from fantasising about accidentally-on-purpose giving him a little kick during Warrior pose. Then my mind wandered to all the poses that would be best for accidentally-on-purpose kicking him, which would probably be frowned on, given the idea of the course was to find inner peace and tranquillity.

Interrupting my daydream, the door swung open and Zack strolled in. 'Hey, everyone,' he mumbled. 'Sorry I'm late again, guys.' It was an exact repeat of his first class. Only this time, nobody admonished him for not being as good at timekeeping as Ocean – sorry, Nigel. Wow, I was surprised at how much I missed dear Nigel, now that we were left with Zack. I hoped he wasn't doing too many extreme yoga moves in Spain and would be back again soon.

I glared at Zack as he casually pulled off his beanie, followed by his hoodie. He didn't meet my eye as he perched on the yoga block in front of the class. What could possibly be so important that he was late again? Or was he just naturally rude and unpunctual?

'Grounding breathwork to begin with,' he said nonchalantly.

'Hmph,' I grumbled quietly, but secretly hoping he'd hear, so he knew at least *someone* in the class respected the idea of punctuality.

After a couple of minutes of his chanting, I opened one eye to look at him. I couldn't understand how he managed to tangle his long limbs around so perfectly. My spine felt as though it was curling forward like a prawn, and my feet always slipped on my leggings whenever I sat cross-legged. He must've sensed me looking because he opened an eye and stole a glance at me. I quickly shut my eyes as soon as he did. It was exactly what had happened in our first class together.

'You're less likely to be able to mediate if you keep opening your eyes,' he said quietly to the group, but the message was obviously directed at me. 'Every master was once a beginner.' There it was again – him and his condescending tone, belittling me when I was trying my best, as a *beginner*.

My breathing quickened as my annoyance started to take hold.

'Whatever you're feeling, just let it go...' he whispered, and again, I knew it was directed at me.

Easy for him to say, I thought; he didn't look like he had a care in the world. I couldn't imagine him having the same restless sleep that I had every night. Tossing and turning while worrying about my job, money, and now, where I was going to live.

'Find your inner peace...'

I swallowed hard and tried again to calm myself. If only it was that easy.

'Trust the universe. You're exactly where you need to be.'

That was the phrase that made me snap. My eyes flew open as my blood bubbled. 'How the hell do you know that I'm exactly where I need to be?' The words were tumbling out before I could stop them.

'I'm sorry?' Zack replied calmly, but with just a hint of annoyance, and only one eye open.

'How can you say things like "trust the universe" and "you're exactly where you need to be" and all the other bullshit phrases in this class when you have absolutely no idea what's going on in our lives?' I panted, forcing myself to stop for breath.

'You must trust the process; you must trust yourself,' Zack answered softly, somewhere between emotionless robot and patronising teacher – his standard role.

'I did trust myself, and it all went wrong!' The words spat out of my mouth. My whole body felt hot and tingly, and there was a bead of sweat trickling down the back of my neck.

'Of course, there's an aspect of being accountable for your own actions. You can't simply run away from situations you've put yourself into.' He said it in his pompous tone, with his superior attitude that had grated me to my core ever since meeting him.

Barbara, to my right, turned to look at me, awaiting my

response. The group was divided between being drawn into what was happening and trying to stay focused on their mediation. My chest felt heavy, and it moved up and down with every furious breath I took.

'I'm sorry, I can't do this,' I mumbled. I admitted defeat and pushed myself shakily to my feet. I felt uneasy; my limbs were so wobbly that I was struggling to put one foot in front of the other. I cut my losses and left my yoga mat where it was, tiptoeing through the sea of my classmates.

'The first stage of being present in yourself and your body is accepting that you can't change the past,' Zack said breezily, as I walked past him. 'You have to embrace the present. Simply let go of the past.'

I turned to respond, but internally I was waving a white flag. I needed to get out of there and get some air, away from him and his unrealistic, supercilious and simplistic attitude to life. I stomped through the door, shoved my feet into my old trainers and stormed down the street.

EIGHT

'Lucy, you can't just leave like that.' Katie rubbed her fingers across her temples as we sat opposite each other in the kitchen.

'Why not?'

'Are you even *allowed* to leave?'

'It isn't prison, Katie. It's a weekly yoga and meditation course. They don't exactly lock you in.'

'Maybe they should, if you're going to be a flight risk.' Katie tapped the spoon against the side of the mug, shaking off any dripping remnants of the Yorkshire Gold tea. 'And I thought to get the full benefits you had to commit to every session—'

'Please,' I interrupted, my head resting on top of my favourite interiors magazine on the table. 'I don't want to talk about it.'

'Come on. A brew will help.' She placed the steaming mug in front of me and shuffled into the chair opposite. 'A cup of tea solves everything.' It was our beloved phrase – one my grandmother would always use when we were growing up and her house was my home, and practically Katie's second home. No matter what was going on, whether we'd failed a school test or had our hearts broken, a cup of tea (preferably Yorkshire Gold) always solved everything.

'I don't know what came over me, Katie,' I mumbled with my head down, feeling the glossy pages sticking to the tears on my damp cheek. 'I was just so angry, I had to get out of there. I couldn't listen to another second of that ridiculous man's simplistic spiel about solving all your problems with peace and love.'

'Is that really what he was saying?' Katie stroked my hair gently.

'He might as well have been,' I grunted. 'If only it was that simple.'

'But you've always been such a positive thinker, Luce. You have the most amazing can-do attitude I've ever known. Don't let what happened with your business harden you.'

'I just don't understand.' I sniffed, trying to fight back the tears stinging my eyes. 'I did everything right. I worked hard at school. I finished my design qualifications and intense training with flying colours. I earned my stripes in those awful, soulless corporate jobs, and I worked my arse off to start my own business. And it *still* all went wrong.'

'You've just had a bit of bad luck, that's all,' she said soothingly. 'It probably happens to everyone when they're starting out in business. You're still only young. You're at the start of your career, not the end.'

I lifted my head up and peeled back the paper stuck to my cheek. 'But what's the point?' I took a sip from the steaming tea, the colour a perfect builder's brew. 'Literally, what's the point when it could all just go wrong *again*? I don't even recognise who I am any more.'

'Your work doesn't define you, Lucy.' Katie rested her hand over mine.

'That's the thing, Katie. It does. It always has, and it probably always will. It's how my parents are. Being a workaholic is in my genetic make-up. All I've done is try and keep up with their impossibly high standards and achievements. I'm nothing without my work.' My head felt heavy, my brain bursting with stress. I rested it sulkily on my hand and took another gulp from the RuPaul mug.

'Don't be so hard on yourself,' Katie said. 'And stop trying to live up to your parents' quite frankly *ridiculous* expectations. Were they the ones who raised you, Lucy Clark?'

I shook my head sulkily.

'Were they the ones who helped you with your homework? Or helped you discover your passion for interior design? Who let you have free rein of the house, to splash paint on the walls and make your own wallpaper? Who taught you how to sew, to sketch, to walk into a room and see things differently to everyone else?'

I shook my head again.

'Exactly. Dotty did all of that. And she'd be so proud of you, Lucy. You know she would be.' Katie held her hand over mine on the table. I was so grateful that she understood me, probably better than I even understood myself. 'Except the whole working yourself into the ground thing – she definitely wouldn't approve of that. You know she was the complete opposite to your parents. She recognised that life was for living, not for working.'

'I know,' I whispered.

'Life throws curveballs sometimes, it's just how it is,' Katie said gently. 'There's always a lesson to be learnt. You have to try and let go of the past and look towards the future.'

'Oh, bloomin' heck, Katie. You sound like him now.' I half giggled, wiping my face and realising I had magazine print all over my tear-blotched cheek.

'Who?'

'Him, "Ziggy",' I mocked with a grimace. 'Zack, I mean. Ziggy is his *spiritual name*.'

Katie eyed me puzzledly.

'The new breathing technician at the class – the reason why I walked out.' I rolled my eyes.

'Ziggy?' Katie said, her blue eyes wide. 'As in Ziggy Stardust? David Bowie?'

I shrugged petulantly.

'Sounds like he has good taste in music if it is.'

'It's probably more because the name starts with a Z and I bet he's secretly all about the catchy branding – I wouldn't be surprised if his middle name was "Zen",' I mumbled cynically. 'Plus, I can't imagine him listening to any music except the nature sounds on the studio's soundtrack.'

'Is he hot?' Katie raised a perfectly shaped eyebrow.

Instinctively, I made a face. 'Not really. I mean, maybe if that kind of look is your thing.'

'Like what?'

'I don't know – like Harry Styles, but if he backpacked around the world, slept in a tent and didn't wash for a while.'

'Mmm,' Katie said dreamily. 'Sounds good to me.' She grabbed my mug from me, even though I still had a couple of mouthfuls left. 'Come on. That's enough of a pity party for now.'

'You're right.' I groaned and wrinkled my nose as I checked my watch. 'I need to go.'

Katie eyed me kindly. 'Are you sure that's a good idea? Today?'

'Mm-hmm,' I answered. 'It's Thursday, I always go on a Thursday.'

'OK. If you're sure.' Katie nibbled her brightly painted thumbnail. 'Ooh, I know!' she shrieked suddenly, making me jump as she clapped her hands together.

'What?'

'How about a cocktail night when you get home?' Katie shimmied her shoulders excitedly. She always knew how to cheer me up, and it usually involved cocktails or chocolate, or both – she made a mean chocolate espresso martini. 'Why don't we watch *Drag Race* and I'll make a themed drink for each of the queens?'

'You always have to be a bit extra, don't you? But yes, let's do it.' I laughed while I sloped out of the room, leaving her throwing open the cupboards to check if we had sparklers, edible glitter or sugar flamingos left over from her last birthday party.

My tiny bedroom was the opposite to the place I used to call home – a chic and spacious penthouse apartment on the Liverpool waterfront. Still, at least I struck lucky when Katie let me move into her place last month while I found my feet.

Throwing myself onto my bed, I checked the clock and debated not going, but I knew I couldn't cancel. This long-standing weekly appointment was a non-negotiable part of my week, even if I wasn't in the mood. There was no doubt I was still reeling from the class. Perhaps I'd overreacted and been overly sensitive. But it once felt like anything in life was possible and that everything was excitedly ahead of me. How did it all go wrong when I thought I'd done everything right? And how did Zack know *exactly* how to get under my skin?

I pushed my head into the soft pillow, and tried to resist the urge to throw my phone in my laundry basket when I heard its high-pitched ping informing me I had a new email. Given the luck of my day, it was surely going to be something terrible, even though I felt too drained to care.

The letters and words jumbled together at first, as I blinked my tired eyes to life. My stomach plunged when I read the email properly. But this time, it wasn't plunging in a bad way, as a natural reaction to awful news. It was good news. *Really* good news. It was the glimmer of hope I'd been waiting for. And coincidentally, it'd come on a Thursday – my favourite day of the week.

NINE

Zack and I had managed to avoid eye contact and any mention of my storming out of his last session. There was a slight awkwardness in the air but I wasn't going to let it get me down. Today was an exciting day. After the class, I was getting away – from the studio, from him and his overly simplistic attitude – and taking a step into my new life. I'd booked a viewing for a house! And not just any house, a very special house.

I strode purposefully through the glorious city centre, taking the route past the Liver Birds and breathing in the fresh air along the walkway by the River Mersey. There had been no doubt in my mind where I was going the next day, after the Rightmove alert popped up on my phone. As I headed towards the house, I walked through an area of Liverpool that was being redeveloped – the old warehouses and former factories transformed into fusion food restaurants and chic bars. I'd always loved this part of the city, where old meets new. Eventually, my footsteps led me to my favourite area – the Georgian Quarter, home to magnificent architecture and a fascinating heritage.

Turning the corner, I passed by Falkner Square, which looked just like Eaton Square in Belgravia (minus the seven-figure property prices), with its majestic townhouses surrounding a blossoming garden. Then, I saw it. Right at the end of the road. Number eight. The house with the sunshine yellow front door. The paintwork a little more faded than it once was, but still the same house.

It was then that I saw the big sign attached to a wooden stake outside. My heartbeat quickened at the same time as my pace. Feeling grateful that I was wearing trainers, I sprinted towards the building that was so familiar to me. The sign said exactly what I assumed it would – 'For Sale' – and it was outside my house. Well, not *my* house, exactly. I didn't own it. But it owned a piece of my heart. It was my grandmother's old house – the house I'd grown up in.

A visceral rush of memories flooded through me as I stood outside, taking in the familiar sight of the beech tree on the pavement that was uncharacteristically large and dominating for the street, where the townhouses were nestled close together. That lovely tree used to block out the light from the bay window in the lounge, but it was so beautiful that it'd be a sin to chop it down. I moved closer to the house and touched the red-brick pillar on one side of the small driveway, felt the gravel under my feet.

The urge to rush up to the front door, swing it open and run inside was burning like a fire inside my body. However, I knew the old, rusty key I still kept in my purse after all these years wouldn't work. Gingerly, I forced my leg forward to take another step closer. But at the same moment, the brass handle on the yellow door turned. I quickly sidestepped and hid behind the pillar.

'You're lucky you acted quickly. We've had a few viewings already and the sign's only been up for a couple of days,' a voice said. The door closed again to the sound of bunches of keys jingling together. 'Although the amount of refurbishment work involved is putting people off.'

My throat felt raw and my mouth was dry. This was *my* house. It had been sold and bought by strangers once, maybe even twice, but it couldn't happen again. I leant my head against the red bricks and looked up at the cotton-like clouds in the sky.

This was my happy place. It was where my grandmother lived and where she raised me, saving me from a life of boarding schools while my parents travelled and worked throughout my childhood. The kitchen was where she'd taught me how to cook her legendary recipes – something I'd forgotten when life got in the way over the last few years. The garden was the place where we'd sit together, drinking fresh lemonade under fluffy clouds, and she'd tell me that I could do anything I wanted in life if I put my mind to it.

It was where I called home, the place where I was truly happy. My memories were ingrained in the bricks, as solid as the cement that held them together. A stranger couldn't buy the house, not again. It was mine. I had to buy it. Everything going wrong in my life would be better if I could just get back here again, where life was easier and everything was possible.

Practically shivering with zeal and determination, I stepped out from my hiding place behind the pillar and onto the tiny driveway.

'Crikey Moses,' the first man, an estate agent, said. He clutched his chest. 'Sorry, love, you gave me a fright.'

But it was the man next to him I was puzzled about.

'You?' I said, unable to stop the instinctual wrinkling of my nose in surprise and disdain at seeing him again.

'Me,' he said freely. It was Zack. My meditation-loving, deep breath teaching, yogi nemesis.

'What are *you* doing here?' I folded my arms across my chest. I'd only seen him half an hour earlier at the class.

He opened his mouth to reply, but instead kept quiet and just rolled on his heels with his hands in his pockets. If he'd skipped a class, perhaps I could tell on him and get him in trouble, I thought mischievously. That'd serve him and his patronising attitude right.

The estate agent, sensing the frosty atmosphere, raised his eyebrows. 'I'll, er, leave you to it,' he said.

'No, please don't,' I interrupted. 'I'm here for my viewing I booked online. This is my h—' I stopped myself from finishing the sentence. 'This house is very special to me.'

'Sorry, but you're a bit late for that, love,' he answered, straightening out his tie. 'You'll have to take it up with the new owner.'

My stomach plunged as if I was on a rollercoaster.

'What?' I whimpered. 'But it can't be. I booked a viewing on your website last night.'

The estate agent shrugged apologetically. 'Sorry, love, it mustn't have gone through. Did you get a confirmation email?'

'I'm not sure. I don't know,' I whispered. My voice hushed to a stop and my hands shot to my flaming cheeks. 'Could I speak to the new owner? Maybe if they knew about this house then they'd understand?'

'Well,' the man said. 'He's standing right there.' He gestured to Zack, and I felt my mouth drop open.

'You?' I said again.

'Me.' He smiled, pulling his woolly hoodie closer around his body.

'You can't be.' I felt my lip trembling. 'This is *my* house.'

'Your house?' His eyebrows knitted together. 'Why is it for sale then?'

I bit my lip. Every word he spoke managed to get under my skin. I pushed my hair back from my face. No. He wasn't going to win this one.

'Is it definitely too late?' I asked the estate agent, who'd been looking from me to Zack and back again, as if he was watching a tense tennis match.

'Well, no, not really. But he's put an offer in. A very generous offer.' He shuffled from one foot to the other, his shiny shoes gleaming in the sunshine. 'I'd be surprised if the current owners don't accept it.'

'And do you have a mortgage in principle agreed? A deposit?' I eyed Zack sternly. Surely this guy didn't know the first thing about buying a house. I hadn't known him for long – we'd only met a handful of times, but he acted as though there were butterflies floating where his brain should be.

'Technicalities,' Zack said dismissively, waving my question away with a brush of his hand. 'I'll be sorting that out later with my formal offer. Not that it's any of your business,' he added quietly.

'Are you serious?' I laughed, feeling victorious. I had my answer. Clearly, this man knew nothing about buying a house. However, there was just the small matter of... No, never mind. That was just a technicality too. I'd figure it out. I'd come up with a solution, like I always did.

I turned to the agent. 'I'd like to put an offer on the table too, please.'

'Hey!' Zack said, and the agent and I both jumped at the sudden volume of his usually soft voice. 'You can't do that.' Zack straightened his posture arrogantly. I smirked at his reaction. I just *knew* he couldn't have been in that permanent state of zen, like he made out.

'I can.' I nodded. 'Can't I?' I turned to the estate agent for confirmation.

'Well...' He pulled a face that screamed he'd rather be anywhere else than here. 'You haven't even looked inside – wouldn't it be wise to arrange a viewing, perhaps?'

'I don't need to. I know this house like the back of my hand,' I answered firmly, while choosing to ignore the state of the neglected exterior.

'Sorry, Zack.' The estate agent held his hands out in a

gesture of defeat. 'She's entitled to put an offer forward, just as you have.'

'She can't know what *my* offer is though, can she?' Zack asked.

'No, that's confidential.'

'So, if she can't match it or go higher, then the house will be mine.' He held his chin in his hand, a cute dimple peeking out over his short fingernail.

'I can match it.' I straightened my shoulders, feigning confidence.

'With all due respect, miss,' the estate agent said, pushing his glasses further up his nose, 'you don't know how much it's listed for.'

'Remind me?' I tried to sound as casual as possible, flicking a piece of fluff from my shoulder.

Dipping into his briefcase, he pulled out a glossy A4 leaflet about the house. He pointed to the price printed in bold as he handed it to me. 'It needs a hell of a lot of work doing to it,' he grunted. 'The owners aren't exactly what you'd call house proud.'

My heart dipped at his words. My grandmother would've been devastated to have seen the house fall into disrepair. She took great pride in her home, especially the garden she'd spend hours carefully tending to, wearing her flowery wellies and carrying pink shears in her hands. It would've broken her heart to see it left unloved and overgrown after it was sold.

'I'd like to put forward an offer for consideration,' I said again, without hesitation. The idea of owning the house again overruled me; it was like a spark that ignited a fire inside me – I couldn't ignore it.

Zack's green eyes felt like they were burning a hole in the side of my head.

Clenching my fists together, I winced as I did the sums in

my head. 'I'd like to offer...' My brain was spinning at the speed of my thoughts.

'Write it down here, please,' the agent said. He handed me a leather-bound notebook. 'And also, your details, miss...'

'Clark,' I replied. 'Lucy Clark.'

I glanced at Zack and he pursed his lips, giving away nothing except annoyance.

For dramatic effect, I underlined the figure confidently, before passing the notebook and pen back.

'OK,' the agent said objectively, glancing at the page and closing it. 'I'll be putting both your offers to the owners, and I'll let you know in due course. Out of interest, Miss Clark, do *you* have a mortgage in principle agreed? Or a deposit?' he added, surveying me like a schoolteacher admonishing a naughty pupil. 'You'll also need to send over your proof of funds before the offer can be officially submitted.'

'If you haven't asked him that before now, then I don't see why you're asking me?' I folded my arms over my chest stubbornly. Was he acting like some of the men I'd encountered throughout my years in business? Patronising me because I'm a woman? Or was I being overly defensive?

'Well then,' he replied defeatedly. 'I'll bid you both farewell.' He sighed, forced a smile, and pretended to raise an imaginary hat in a gesture of goodbye.

I felt Zack's gaze turn towards me. Instead of looking back in his direction, where I could feel the burning glare of his eyes, I looked up at the house. It was so familiar, yet so different. The paintwork, once immaculate, peeled off the walls in thick, messy strips. There were cracks in at least two of the front windows, and there was a bird's nest in one of the alcoves. The neglected front door, while still the bright yellow it had always been, was pale and peeling. There were no hanging baskets filled with blossoming flowers in the hooks either side of the door, and no welcome mat that was lined with muddy wellies.

'May the best offer win,' Zack said. His words shattered my trip down memory lane, while also interrupting my thought that perhaps I should've booked a viewing before putting forward an offer, considering the state the outside was in. But I brushed the thought away, together with the worry of what the inside must look like. Zack held out his hand for me to shake; his wrist was covered in stacks of distressed leather and beaded bracelets.

'May the best offer win,' I repeated as I held his gaze, and we sealed it with a handshake.

TEN

The following week passed, and I felt a wave of nerves hitting me like a slap to the face every time my phone lit up. I kept waiting and waiting for the estate agent's name to illuminate the screen. Instead, it was just another urgent work email or client phone call to deal with – the story of my life.

The clock struck 7 p.m. that Friday after another torturous day of clock-watching, and I headed out of a newly opened co-working space to meet Katie for drinks, hoping it would be the perfect distraction. But then my phone started ringing. It was Brian – listed as Slightly Unfriendly Estate Agent in my phone.

'Hello,' I breathed, answering it after just two rings. 'Did I get it? Did they accept my offer?' My competitive nature and desperation to outdo Zack took hold before Brian could even answer my greeting.

'Well, it's a little complicated, Miss Clark,' he replied.

'What does that mean?' I stopped and leant against the wall of the bar I was standing outside.

'It's a bit of a coincidence, but you and Zack both put forward exactly the same offer.'

'Oh...'

'I know,' he replied. 'Great minds think alike, eh?'

Pfft. What an insult. Mine and Zack's minds were totally not in the same category.

'So, the owners have been taking their time mulling over it.' Brian filled the silence when I didn't answer his offensive statement. 'But they want to see who's going to be the easiest buyer. They want to act fast; they don't want to get stuck in a chain.'

'I see.' I felt a lurch deep down.

'Do you have anything to sell?'

'No, I'm living with a friend at the moment.'

Katie waved manically at me through the window of the bar. I waved back and pointed at the phone. She gestured for me to hurry up and pretended to drink my drink. I laughed, but suddenly felt guilty. I hadn't even told my best friend and generous housemate/landlord about my elaborate plans to move out and buy my childhood home. Part of me didn't want to get my hopes up about it.

'That's a good start,' Brian said. I could practically feel him nodding down the phone. 'Just another thing, Miss Clark – you never did confirm whether you have an agreement in principle?'

'What?' I stalled, pressing the phone against my ear.

'An agreement in principle, Miss Clark,' Brian repeated. 'It's essentially a way for the bank to find out if you can borrow the amount you need to buy the house.'

'I know what it is.' I bit my lip. 'Of course I do,' I lied.

'Excellent. You'll need to send that over as soon as possible, please. And a deposit?'

'Yes, I do have a deposit.' I grinned. At least that was the truth. And I knew it was exactly what my grandmother would've wanted when she set it aside for me, under the strict instruction that it could only be used to buy my own home. I'd tried to persuade my parents that I should've been allowed to invest it in my business – or *save* my business – more times than

I cared to admit. Now, I was glad they'd stood their ground about my grandmother's wishes.

'It sounds like you have a good chance then, Miss Clark.'

'What about Zack?' I said, before immediately feeling puzzled as to why I cared.

'I'm calling him after you to ask him the same questions.'

'OK, great.'

'I'll keep you updated, take care,' Brian said chirpily, before hanging up. It was amazing how much his attitude had changed now that I was a serious potential buyer.

My phone dropped into the pocket of my jacket, and I felt conflicted emotions. From one side I could breathe a sigh of relief – at least I had a deposit. But an agreement in principle? I knew the bank would question my finances. Mortgages are hard enough to secure when you're self-employed, but my accounts weren't the healthiest after everything that had happened. I doubted a bank manager would be impressed by the recent drop in my profits. Not to mention going from being forecast to turn over £1 million in my second year in business – and hailed as the next big name in interior design – to barely keeping my head above water and relying on the good graces of a few forgiving clients.

I pushed open the door to the bar and headed over to Katie. I'd tell her tonight, I decided. Then tomorrow morning, I was heading straight to the bank. I couldn't let Zack of all people take my house – anyone but him, with his arrogant ways (but rather beautiful, shiny hair). Nope, I was going to fight for 8 Falkner Avenue.

———

I was treating the meeting like a new business pitch – something I'd done more times than I could count. I was feeling cool, calm and collected. My outfit was fabulous: a beautifully tailored suit, which had been my gift to myself when I won my first big client, paired with my favourite Osprey briefcase. I looked professional and trustworthy. I looked like someone who was responsible enough for a mortgage. At least, I hoped I did.

My nerves, though, were certainly more intense than they'd ever been for a new business pitch. I tried to use the skills I'd learnt on the well-being course so far. (After all, I thought, I might as well get *something* out of enforced time with Zack.) I kept reminding myself to take deep breaths, while trying to ignore the images of Zack that kept sneaking into my head. But I couldn't stop drumming my long nails on my briefcase or tapping the stiletto heel of my shoe on the shiny floor.

'Ms Clark?'

Finally, the nervous spell was broken. I waved at the woman who'd stepped out from the door of her office and called my name into the waiting room.

Standing up, I brushed down my suit and strode confidently into the small office, taking a seat on the chair opposite her, where she sat at a desk behind a big computer monitor. The lights were bright and the walls were covered in framed posters with big, bold statistics about mortgages and interest rates, together with happy-looking homeowners. Hopefully I'd be smiling as much as them when I left this meeting.

'I believe you're looking for an agreement in principle, Ms Clark?' the woman, whose name badge read Annie, said.

I nodded nervously. 'Yes, I am.'

'That's great,' she replied, clicking the mouse. 'We can certainly help you with that today. Let me just get your file up and we'll see what we can do for you.'

My nails started tapping again, as if they had a mind of their own. These nerves were new to me recently. I wasn't a naturally nervous person. When you've presented in front of five thousand people about the benefits of recycled glass at the annual Interior Design Show in Monaco, or pitched to design the interiors of a pop superstar's new London home, it eradicates any public speaking fears for good.

'I believe you've found a house you're interested in buying?' Annie asked without taking her eyes off the monitor, clearly reading the online form I'd filled out when I booked the appointment.

'I have,' I said, proudly straightening my shoulders. 'It was actually my childhood home.'

'Oh, wow,' Annie replied. 'That's amazing. Let's look at how we can get you set up then. It might feel like we're going into a lot of detail, but just think of this as a bit of an advice session so we can get to know your situation and offer the most appropriate mortgage for your needs and circumstances.'

I nodded nervously.

'I believe you're self-employed?'

I nodded again.

'Have you brought your company accounts and self-assessment tax return?'

'I have,' I replied confidently, flipping open my briefcase. It was stuffed with the papers I'd asked my accountant to print off for me. Usually in a situation like this, I'd proudly organise them into a colour-coded file, but time was of the essence, so I sheepishly placed the creased papers onto the desk.

Annie pulled the wad of documents towards her. 'I also need to verify your identity and address – do you have your passport or driving licence? And a council tax statement or credit card statement from the last three months?'

'I do,' I said with glee. Maybe this was going to be easier than I thought. 'And I also have confirmation of my deposit that I can put towards the house.'

'Excellent,' Annie said, as she shuffled through the pages. 'Give me a few minutes to look through all this and then we'll go over the questions together.'

I smiled at her in agreement, hoping that if I showed I was

reliable and responsible, maybe she'd take it easy on me and help make my dream a reality. There was *no way* Zack was going to be a better buyer than I was. I didn't know him well, but from what I did know, I could safely assume he wouldn't recognise responsibility or organisation if they hit him in the face. I just hoped the mortgage advisor he was seeing didn't get swept away by his charm offensive, or enchanting green eyes, or adorable dimples, or perfectly curly hair...

'Oh,' Annie said. Her tone jolted me from my unnervingly swoony daydream about my number one enemy and house rival. She squinted as she held my papers closer to her face and read them carefully.

'Is there something wrong?' I said, as nonchalantly as I could manage.

'It's just that you only have two years' worth of company accounts. We usually want to see at least three years and, well, these are a little—'

'Yes, things have been a bit *challenging* lately.' I cut her off and tried to summon a confident tone. 'However, my revenue is getting much better now. I'm working every hour of the day to get the business back to where it was, and I still have some great, loyal clients who—'

'Your cashflow is all over the place,' Annie said, matter-of-factly. She examined the accounts closely, running the nib of her biro over the printed words and numbers.

'Mm-hmm,' I mumbled. 'I mean, I wouldn't say *all over the place*, per se.' I held my hands out pleadingly. 'It's just a bit... well, it's all part and parcel of running a business.' I could feel a light film of sweat forming delicately over my face.

'What happened here? There's a bit of a dip.' Annie placed the paper on the desk and pushed it towards me with one finger as she gestured to the number.

I subtly wiped my brow. 'To be completely honest with you, I tried to grow the business too quickly, before I was ready, I guess...' I leant closer to the desk. 'It was so exciting at first, all this money coming in,' I explained. 'I signed a lease on an expensive office in the city centre, but I hadn't streamlined the business enough...' I shook my head. There was no point in revisiting it; I was already beating myself up about it enough.

'It all sounds like it was going where you wanted it to go,' Annie said sympathetically, as if she were a counsellor instead of a mortgage advisor.

'I guess I was a bit naive and trusting,' I replied with a sigh. 'All of a sudden, these huge projects were coming in from clients. I trusted they'd pay their bills at the end of their contracts, and I wouldn't want to seem rude to pester them when the money didn't land in my account. So, I'd do the work and engage the suppliers that we worked with to provide the goods, but then sometimes the clients would either take months and months to pay, or refuse to pay altogether, even though they were happy with the work.'

I felt a tear sting my eye and I almost wished this *was* a counselling session so that Annie could, at this point, pass a box of tissues over to me. I looked around the small office and couldn't see any, though. Just stacks of files and paperwork, and pots of pens.

'Sometimes you feel like you do all the right things, but everything just goes wrong,' I whispered, as I distracted myself by fiddling with the hem of my blazer sleeve. 'It's been hard, but then it got worse.'

'Worse? As in, at this point?' Annie pointed to the most recent accounts, where my income dipped after I'd lost the bulk of my clients thanks to the disastrous round-robin email from the Marbella hen party.

'Mm-hmm.' I nodded. I didn't fancy going into detail with Annie about the infamous email and why I'd lost all but a handful of clients. I was still torturing myself about it. Not to mention almost losing my best friend over how I'd handled it, and feeling like I was losing my mind from the stress of the entire situation.

Annie sighed as she gathered the papers neatly again. Once they were in a pile, she tapped the bottom of them on the desk and placed them down in front of me, smoothing over them with her long, manicured fingernails.

'I'm genuinely really sorry to tell you this, Ms Clark, but with these accounts, we can't offer you a mortgage.'

'But wait,' I said, ignoring what she was saying. I lurched forward and grabbed the documents. Flicking through the pages, I found the one I needed. 'This is my deposit. It's a good chunk of money and it's more than ten per cent of the property's value. Surely this will help?' I clutched it desperately.

'I'm sorry,' she said kindly. 'That deposit is great, but we can't give you a mortgage on that alone. You need to show consistency in your company accounts, ideally over at least three years.'

'But...' I leant back into the squidgy chair. 'The house is for sale now. I need to buy it *now*, otherwise I might lose it again, forever.'

'I'm really sorry,' she said again, holding her hands out. 'I'm sure there will be other great houses that you could consider when your accounts are a little more stable. And you could always try other lenders? Although, if you want my honest advice, I do think they'll come to the same conclusion.'

'Oh,' I said resignedly. 'OK,' I murmured, as I gathered the papers defeatedly.

'Off the record,' Annie said when I stood, my high heels suddenly feeling like a terrible idea in my wobbly state. 'What you've done with your business is impressive. Even with the things that have gone wrong. It's clear to see that you have ambition, determination, and that you're hard-working. I'm sure things will get better again.'

They would if I could just get back to that house, I replied in my head. When would the opportunity to buy it come up again? If ever? Instead of asking her those questions, I managed a weak nod and a half-smile. Thanking her for her time, I headed out of the door and tried to hold my tears back as I walked out into the bustling high street.

ELEVEN

Hi Lucy, I know this is a little weird. I hope you don't mind me texting you. I've 100% broken the rules by using your contact details from your booking on the course, but please don't get me fired. Listen, I know Brian called you about the house already. He called me too because I can't buy it either. But I have an idea. Would you like to meet, and we can talk about it? (It's Zack by the way) *hands together emoji*

The words of the text message danced around the screen as I squinted at it, rereading it again and again. What did he mean? Why didn't he win the house fair and square, if I couldn't buy it? And could I really get him fired? It was tempting...

'Who is it?' Katie said, as she threw a tangled bunch of string bikinis into the open suitcase on her bed.

'It's Zack...'

'The hot hippy?'

'Yeah,' I said absent-mindedly. 'Wait, no!'

Katie smirked.

'Not hot. Just hippy. Anyway, he wants to meet.' I frowned as I read the message again.

'Why?' Katie said. She placed her collection of sunglasses into the increasingly full suitcase, nestling them between about twelve pairs of flip-flops and a deflated unicorn pool float.

'I don't know.' My brows wrinkled together as I read the message for the third time, trying to figure out what his idea could be, and how I should respond. 'He says he has an idea about the house.'

'Well, you should go.'

'Really?' I looked up at Katie, realising that, weirdly, I actually did want to go and meet him. But surely that was because of the house. Nothing to do with him.

'Why not?' Katie said. She sat on her bursting suitcase, willing it to close as she pulled the zips around. 'What have you got to lose?'

It was true. What did I have to lose?

———

Zack was late – twenty-five minutes late and counting. Of course he was. So far, there had been no occasion in our short time of knowing each other when this man hadn't been late.

I checked the time on my phone again and audibly huffed in a gesture of pointless frustration. My coffee was long gone, and I was on the verge of walking out. Was he really so arrogant to think that his time was more precious than mine?

That was it, I decided. I was leaving. I'd had enough and I wasn't waiting a minute longer. I turned and yanked my jacket from the back of my chair, just as the soft thud of a bag hit the table, and the chair opposite was pulled from its position. The legs screeched against the floor, making me wince.

'Sorry I'm late!' Zack announced. He pushed his thick hair back from his face and smiled innocently, as if nothing had happened. As if he'd just rolled out of bed following ten hours of blissful, deep, uninterrupted sleep. Which he probably had.

'You're not *just* late,' I vented. 'You're practically *half an hour* late. I was about to leave.' I eyed him furiously. 'What makes you think your time is more important than mine? I'm really busy, you know. But I set aside the time to meet you, and you just waltz in here, all bright and breezy...'

'Hey, hey.' Zack held his hands out. His wrists were almost entirely covered in bracelets and old festival wristbands – a pet peeve of mine. Totally unhygienic. 'I'm really sorry I'm late, Lucy, but you need to chill out a bit. It's Sunday, a day of rest.'

'Pfft,' I huffed. 'For you, maybe. I bet every day is a day of rest for you,' I said snippily.

Zack was unfazed by my annoyance, which only riled me more.

I leant back into the seat with my arms crossed defensively over my chest. Copying my movement, he also reclined in his seat. His white cotton T-shirt rode up as he placed his hands behind his head, revealing the dark snail trail creeping up his stomach, from the button on his trousers to the hem of his top.

It was a stalemate, a tense stand-off between us. Neither of us moved an inch. I narrowed my eyes into a glare, but he just smiled back in response before wiggling his eyebrows. A part of me was determined not to give in, but then I realised we'd be here all day if I didn't – clearly, he had nothing to do, whereas I had *everything* to do.

'Anyway, what did you want to talk to me about? What's so desperate?'

'Fancy a coffee?' he said, smiling gleefully at his victory.

'No, I don't want—'

'Sure you do,' he interrupted, ignoring me and pointing towards my empty mug. 'I'll get you a coffee. You want food too? Shall I grab a menu?'

'Fine,' I said, admitting defeat. 'Thanks,' I added quietly.

It was clear he'd been here before from the way the staff reacted to him, smiling and laughing as he picked up the menus and pointed to our table. The most I'd got from them when I arrived was a groan and a huff.

'The food looks great here.' He sat down opposite me, his scent – wood, sea salt, lemon – filling the space around us. For a minute I was taken back to the only time in my life when I knew what it was like to be carefree. Zack smelt like the holidays I remembered as a child – the rare ones my parents would occasionally take when work would allow them, when they weren't sub-contracted out to design a new skyscraper in Singapore or Tokyo, where they had both lived for long periods of my childhood.

'Have you been here before?' I asked out of curiosity, wanting to stop thinking about my strained relationship with my parents. There was no doubt that I had lingering resentment about their absence in my childhood, salvaged only by my close relationship with my grandmother.

'Never.' He shook his head.

So the staff must've simply fallen under his charming spell and warm energy – or *positive vibes*, in his words.

'What are you fancying? I'm going to have an Americano, although do they make it fresh? I can't see.' I squinted towards the barista before continuing to ramble. Why was I nervous to have a meal with him? 'Anyway, if you want to get food, then I'll go for the avocado toast with crispy bacon and a poached egg. I know it's boring and I could make it at home, but it's exactly what I'm in the mood for. Although I can't see what type of bread it is, is it sourdough? Or is it—'

'Woah, woah, woah, slow down. I haven't even decided on a drink yet.' Zack glanced at me cheekily over the laminated menu.

'I've had more time to sit here and think about it, haven't I?' I retorted, to his subtle, yet mocking, eye-roll.

'Do you always live life at one hundred miles per hour?' he asked, tracing the edges of the menu with his fingers.

'I wouldn't say that.' I crossed my arms defensively again. It was my typical stance whenever I was near Zack.

He raised an eyebrow before his eyes travelled back to the menu, which offered all the best bits of brunch – although I couldn't remember the last time I'd gone for brunch. My Saturdays, and my Sundays for that matter, would typically be spent getting through work while it was quiet. That was one of the best things about working at the weekend – usually nobody emailed or called you. Most people had lives outside work.

'Pancakes!' Zack said decisively. His eyes were wide with childlike enthusiasm, his smile sparkling as he beamed. 'I'm going for the vegan pancake stack. Extra blueberries, extra strawberries.' He slapped the menu down triumphantly.

'What a surprise, you're going for the only vegan option on the menu,' I mumbled under my breath.

'I'll go and order, then we can talk about why I asked you here.' He stood up from the table and stretched out his limbs with a sleepy yawn. He'd *definitely* just rolled out of bed.

I reached into my handbag and opened my leather purse, pulling a crisp twenty-pound note from inside and presenting it to him as he went to walk towards the till.

'Absolutely not.' He waved it away. 'My treat.'

'Please,' I said firmly, shaking the note in front of him. 'I don't need you to buy me brunch. I'm an independent woman, I can pay for myself.'

He looked taken aback at my words. 'I'm sorry, I didn't mean to offend you. I thought I was being chivalrous.'

'Yeah, well,' I replied, unsure why I was being so stubborn and prickly about it. Surely I could let a man innocently buy me a meal. It had been so long since one offered that perhaps I was out of practice. The last date I went on, the guy asked to share an Uber ride home that dropped him outside a strip club, so maybe I just wasn't used to gentlemanly gestures. Not to mention my ex-boyfriend, who'd cheated on me with his personal trainer, and then again with his PA when I gave him another chance. *It's better to be independent and look after yourself*, I nodded. You could always rely on yourself.

'I insist,' I said to Zack firmly.

He reached forward and tentatively took the note from my hand. 'OK,' he replied, his expression still a little puzzled. 'If you insist.'

I watched as Zack again befriended every person he met in the short time it took to order our food – from the woman he let go ahead of him in the queue because she seemed in a rush, to the staff behind the counter who revelled in telling him the recipe for their banana bread, and the elderly lady whose coffee and cake he ended up carrying to the table for, as her hands were shaky.

Zack's natural ease and confidence with his place in the world amazed me. Just watching him in the cafe, I saw that he breezed through life with a natural optimism and carefree attitude – something utterly alien to me. I frequently felt like I lived my life in a hurricane of stress and worry. Well, when I stopped working for long enough to actually think about it.

'Here we are.' The gentle clink of the coffee cups on the table and the announcement that he was back in his position in the chair opposite me shook me from my daydream. 'An Americano, and you'll be pleased to know it's super fresh. They ground the beans right in front of me,' he said triumphantly.

'Good.' I pulled the steaming cup towards me. 'What on earth did you go for?' I peered across at the fluorescent green liquid in his mug.

'Matcha latte with vanilla almond milk.' He beamed. 'Want some?'

'I'm all right, thanks.' I couldn't help wrinkling my nose with disgust as he took a sip of what looked like blended sprouts.

'It's good for you,' he added, clocking my expression. 'High in antioxidants, loaded with vitamins...'

I shook my head. 'I'll stick with my coffee, thanks.'

'Suit yourself,' he said with a smile before leaning over the table, his hands clasped together. 'So, before the food gets here, the reason why I texted you.'

'Go on,' I said.

'I take it Brian told you that you were unsuccessful with the offer on the house?'

I nodded. It was the only thing I'd been thinking about since I heard. 'How do you know?'

'Of course he couldn't say it directly – client confidentiality and all that – but he pretty much said the house was still on the market, so I put two and two together.'

'I can't lose that house. It's my childhood home,' I murmured, before sipping my coffee to distract myself from the second lump forming in my throat.

'It is?' Zack raised his eyebrows. 'Now it all makes sense.' He leant back in his chair, nodding as if he'd just figured out the answer to a maths equation. 'That's why you were so crazy about it when we bumped into each other.'

'Crazy? I wasn't crazy.'

'You so were. Your eyes went all wide and bulgy.' He did a frog-like impression that half made me giggle, half made me mad again.

'Anyway. Yes, it's a special house,' I said, changing the subject. 'A really, really special house.'

'Why don't you live in it any more? If it was your childhood home?'

'It's a long story,' I replied, running a finger over the rim of the empty coffee mug. 'It wasn't technically *my* childhood home. It was where my grandmother lived. She looked after me a lot. My parents... Well, that's another story.' I shook my head. 'They sold the house when my grandmother's health deteriorated after a stroke. I always said if it ever came up for sale then I'd buy it. I've had the Rightmove alert set up for years.' I half chuckled, remembering the heart-stopping moment the email had landed in my inbox. 'My deposit is money set aside from my grandmother. Although, of course, she didn't think I'd necessarily be able to buy that exact house, she knew how much I wanted my own home one day and she wanted me to have that security. It was something she never had when she was growing up.' I blinked away the beginning of a tear in my eye, before shaking myself back to reality. 'Gosh, sorry. That was probably information overload.'

'Not at all,' Zack said. His bottle-green eyes didn't break contact with mine for a moment. His ease at listening explained why he was so good at his job. He had a way of making you want to open up and spill your secrets, without even saying a word. It made a difference from my past relationships, with guys who only ever wanted to talk about themselves.

'Well, you won't lose that house. It isn't going on the market. I mean, yes, technically it is. But I have a plan that means it won't be for long. And I think you'll be interested.'

I took another gulp of coffee, holding the steaming mug that was like a hot water bottle shaped just for my hands. 'I'm listening.'

'Be honest with me,' Zack said, holding eye contact. 'Do you have an agreement in principle for a mortgage?'

I hesitated stubbornly, before shaking my head. There was no point lying. 'I went to the bank for an appointment with an advisor. I was sure I'd be fine getting one. I don't know how I missed it, to be honest. But basically, because I'm self-employed and I've had some... cashflow issues' – I kept it vague; I didn't know him well enough to offload all my problems – 'they turned me down. Bloody typical when all I've done is work hard, put my career first, and I can't even get a mortgage. It's laughable. It's totally ridiculous, so unfair. In fact, I feel like writing to...'

He held up his hands to politely stop me as I felt the words tumble out of my mouth – as he'd say, at one hundred miles per hour. 'And you have that deposit?' he asked, before chewing his thumbnail.

'Yep.' I nodded. 'It isn't massive, but it's decent – it was more than enough for the offer I put forward for the house.'

A smile slowly formed over Zack's face, his lips rising upwards, emphasising the adorable dimple in his chin.

'What? Why are you smiling like that?'

He leant in closer to me, and the fresh cotton scent of his T-shirt rose over the smell of coffee in the small space between us. Everything about him smelt incredible. 'I'm employed, have been for years. My job is safe.'

'Well, woopty bloody do, good for you. Want a medal?' I joked, but the delivery was a little snarkier than I'd intended it to be.

'I don't mean it like that.' He shook off my attitude with an amused laugh. 'I mean, I have the monthly repayments.'

I felt my brows furrow as I eyed him curiously.

'We could buy it together.' His smile revealed his flawless teeth. He must've had a brace when he was younger; they were too perfect to be natural. Hang on – what did he just say?

'Buy it together? Are you mad? We don't even know each other.' I gulped my Americano, grateful that he didn't announce his absurd idea when I had taken a mouthful of the fresh coffee. I would've been at risk of spluttering it all over his white T-shirt.

'And?' he asked casually, as if it was no big deal and not the craziest idea I'd ever heard.

'And? Are you actually being serious?'

'Well, why not? We'll be housemates.'

'We'd end up killing each other, that's why not.' Just the thought of living with this man, this *stranger*, was giving me heart palpitations. I could feel my pulse quicken, but then perhaps it was because the double-shot Americano was the fourth and fifth shot of espresso I'd consumed that morning, and maybe my body had finally decided to reject caffeine.

'The avo, bacon and egg?' a voice next to me asked politely.

'Here,' I answered, raising a hand but not moving from my position, rubbing the tension in my head.

'And the vegan pancakes for you. I hope you enjoy,' the giggly voice added flirtatiously as the second plate was placed on the table.

'I'm sure I will,' he replied, equally flirtatiously, which annoyed me, and I wasn't sure why.

'Delicious!' he announced after his first bite. 'Here, you have to try some.' He moved his cutlery to cut a chunk of pancake for me.

I looked up at him as I rubbed my temples and considered how I could get out of this situation, which was clearly going to be a waste of my Sunday. 'I'm OK. Thanks.'

'These pancakes are seriously in-*credible*. Holy moly.' He loaded a forkful and put it in his mouth, his eyes closed in delight. 'Mwah!' He did an exaggerated chef's kiss. I tried my hardest to stifle my amusement at his enthusiasm for the simplicity of perfect pancakes.

'Your food's going cold.' He used his fork to point towards my plate.

I picked up my knife and fork and tucked in. The dish was brunch perfection. Sourdough bread that was fluffy in the middle, with crispy brown edges. An egg that offered a golden, gooey eruption the minute my knife tapped the yolk. Green and ripe avocado, complemented perfectly by the crispy bacon. Oh my God, it was amazing. I'd forgotten how great brunch was – I'd forgotten how hungry I was. I shovelled it into my mouth, each taste more delicious than the last. Gosh, was it too late to order extra avocado? Or another—

'Erm, Lucy?'

I looked up and Zack was staring at me, his eyes wide with alarm.

'Yeah?' I said, politely trying to dab away the avocado chunk I could feel on the side of my lip.

'Do you always eat so fast?' he asked timidly, as though he was uncertain of how I would react.

'What do you mean? I don't eat fast,' I guffawed. Although, judging by my almost-empty plate compared to his – still filled with the juicy blueberries and ruby-red strawberries scattered over thick and fluffy pancakes – perhaps I did.

'Talking, eating, drinking...' He gestured at my now-empty coffee mug. 'Do you always do *everything* so fast?' He laughed before avoiding my eye, looking back down at his plate.

'I guess so.' I sighed. 'I don't know, I suppose I haven't really thought about it.' I lied; it was what everyone was always saying to me – the story of my life. I moved my cutlery over my plate, purposely trying to slow down, to savour each bite and prove Zack wrong. I could move slowly, I could relax.

'Anyway, this has been nice,' I said. 'It was good to have brunch and I'll obviously see you at the next class.'

'If you don't throw a strop and walk out again,' he said cheekily.

'I didn't throw a strop!' I replied.

'So, it's a no to the house idea?' Zack swiftly changed the subject with a sad undertone to his voice.

'It just doesn't work.' I shook my head. 'It doesn't make sense.' I leant my elbows on the table and rubbed my temples, feeling Zack watching me.

'Hear me out,' he said, placing his cutlery down. His plate still looked full, as if he hadn't taken a single bite. 'We both want this house, right?'

I nodded.

'You want it because it was your childhood home and there's sentimental value.'

'It isn't just the sentimental value,' I cut in. 'I mean, yes, it is. I don't know, it probably sounds silly...'

'Go on.'

I sighed and took in my surroundings. I didn't expect to be pouring my heart out to Zack, of all people. 'I just know things will be OK if I get that house back. I know it's only a house, but it's so special to me and it meant everything to my grandmother. It was the place where we lived together, and it was where I truly learnt my passion in life. She taught me everything I know about interior design.' The memories poured back. 'I just know if I don't get it back now, I'll probably never be able to again.'

'I understand that,' Zack replied, considering his words carefully. 'Family is everything.' He shook his head ever so slightly – so subtly that I might've missed it. 'Although, you still haven't seen inside the house, have you?' He swiftly changed the subject. 'It probably looks a little different—'

'It doesn't matter to me,' I interrupted. 'I'd love that house no matter what it looked like. I know those walls – I've painted them, wallpapered them, I've hung pictures on them. I've made curtains to hang from the windows. I've rearranged furniture in every possible combination.' I laughed at my childhood memories of a teenage me driving my grandmother mad because the rooms would look completely different every few days. And she'd tell me off, only half seriously, when she had to try for the hundredth time to get paint out of my school jumper, or wallpaper paste from my bunches.

Zack's locks fell in perfect bouncy curls around his face as he nodded, listening carefully and giving me the space to talk. He rubbed his mouth with a napkin and set the cutlery down, the fork crossed over the knife, declaring his meal finished, even though there was still plenty left.

'But why do *you* want it so badly?' I said, moving to sip my coffee but forgetting my mug was empty again. 'And were you viewing it during studio hours? I know you were joking in your text, but that paired with pinching my contact details and I probably could get you fired, you know.' I popped a mouthful of bacon into my mouth rebelliously.

'You wouldn't dare, Clark.' He said it with a twinkling glint in his eye, which was far sexier than it should've been. 'It's the vibes I get there,' he said.

'Oh God.' I rolled my eyes. 'Of course. It's all about the "vibes" with you, isn't it?' I air-quoted.

Zack didn't seem to take offence as he brushed off my cynicism with a smile. 'What can I say? It's true. I live my life going off my vibes – *my instinct* – and it hasn't let me down so far.'

I rolled my eyes again. 'You were really going to go up against me – and potentially take my childhood home away from me – just because you liked the *vibes*?'

'I've walked past that house every day for years, ever since I moved back to Liverpool,' Zack said. 'I love everything about it. I love the beech tree outside that feels far too big for the road. I love the bright yellow door, when all the other doors are black or white. I love the etchings on the bay window frames in the front,' he said dreamily. 'I don't know. Even though the paint is peeling and the garden is overgrown, I've just always really loved that house and its potential.'

I checked my cynicism for a moment; I was captivated by the way he talked about the house, and the passion he had for it even though he didn't know it apart from walking past every day. 'Tell me more about you, *Ziggy Zack*. You know my situation, it's only fair that we talk about you as well. So, you have the monthly repayments – why don't you have a deposit? I take it that's why you were turned down by the bank?'

Zack's expression turned from warm to cold in seconds. His smile froze as his jaw tensed and he locked his fingers together. 'I didn't realise the time,' he said, looking at his watch.

'Oh,' I replied, taken aback by his sudden uncharacteristic abruptness. Then I immediately felt silly and foolish at how much information I'd just divulged to a stranger – not even a stranger, but someone I actively disliked.

'Look, erm...' He scratched his head and looked around. 'I've persuaded Brian to give us forty-eight hours to see if the plan can work. The offer's there if you want to go away and think about it, but I understand if you think living with a stranger is too much. Brian says we need to act quickly as there's been other interest and the sellers want to move fast.'

Zack stood up and picked up his tote bag, which was filled with yoga mats, blocks and other stretching paraphernalia. A hairbrush with blonde hair wound around it fell onto the table. I looked at it and then up at his mahogany locks. Obviously, that shiny platinum hair belonged to a significant other. My stomach did a weird wobble, but then, if we were seriously considering this, perhaps it was a safer bet if he was attached.

'Think about it, yeah?' Zack said, shoving the hairbrush back into his bag. 'We can figure it out. We can set boundaries, or rules or whatever, if we live together. Of course, financially, we'd have to work something out too. We can make sure it's fair and square. But if you want that house and I want that house, this could be the only way.'

I nodded my head.

'I have to run; I have a class to teach. Think about it and call me, OK? Let me know whatever you decide.'

I nodded my head again and he offered a guarded smile before striding through the cafe, waving goodbye to the adoring staff as he did. I watched through the window as he walked down the busy street, quickly getting lost in the hustle and bustle of the crowds.

Was this something I could do? Could I really buy a house with a stranger – with *Zack*? It might've been my only chance to get that house back, but was it worth it?

TWELVE

'What do you think about this?' I picked up a wooden chair. Its faded cushions were haggard and ripped, and the beautiful wooden frame was peppered with chips and dents. To me, it was like looking at a sad, adorable puppy – the last one to be picked for a new home. But I knew I could give it the love and TLC it deserved. 'Katie!' I shouted again, showing her my amazing find.

Katie made a face, her nose wrinkling as she scowled. 'It looks like something a grandmother would have in a 1970s bungalow.'

'Exactly,' I whispered. I held it out in front of me, taking in all the details – the snags that could be easily fixed, the covers that could be re-upholstered, the easy DIY ways to mend wooden fixtures so nobody would ever know what it once looked like. Society was far too fast to throw things away these days.

'Bloody hell, Lucy. What do you mean, *exactly*? You'd better not be considering it for my new house.'

'You said you wanted farmhouse chic. This is it.' I carefully shook the chair at her. 'It's a spin on it – it's cottage-core.'

'Well, I don't mean *that*.' She waved her hand over it from a distance she deemed safe. 'I mean more like ethereal, romantic, Instagram-worthy farmhouse chic,' Katie breathed dreamily. 'As if a family of chickens might walk into the kitchen at any time!'

'You know that would be worrying if they did, given your house is on the outskirts of a busy city, not deep in the rolling hills of the Cotswolds countryside?'

Katie rolled her eyes and ran her fingernail over an antique French cabinet with elaborate etchings and timeworn velvet shelves. 'Well, they're more than welcome in my kitchen at any time. I'll save them from their fate as McChicken sandwiches.'

I'd dragged Katie out to my favourite vintage indoor market, even though she hadn't stopped complaining about the 'musty' smell the entire time we walked around, and vetoed nearly every idea I had for her house interiors. At least the day out was taking my mind off two things, I reasoned. The first was work, which was demanding, as always. I was doing things for free when I knew I shouldn't have been, but I was on the last strike with some of my clients and I needed to keep them happy. The second thought that dominated my mind at all times was Zack's idea – to buy my childhood home and live in it together, as strangers.

I wandered around what was my idea of paradise – swooning as I took in the vintage treasures, the vibrant colours, the luxurious fabrics, the striking textures, and the furniture that had been discarded without a second thought for how it could be refreshed and saved. However, I was weirdly distracted as I tried to concentrate on the task at hand and not think about Zack. Not the emerald curtains that reminded me of his eyes, nor the adorable dimple in his chin, or the way he looked at me like I was the only person in the room... For goodness' sake. *Focus, Lucy*, I admonished myself.

'Anyway, have you had any more thoughts about Ziggy Stardust's proposition?' Katie said, as she picked up an intricately detailed and heavily embellished wall hanging between two fingers and held it at arm's length, as if it was contaminated and only she knew about its hidden germs.

'Not really,' I mumbled, before pinching the work of art from her snobbish, unappreciative clutches. I still had twenty-four hours until Brian, the estate agent, needed an answer. But I was no closer to a decision than I was when Zack abruptly left the cafe after our brunch. 'I've been so busy with work. I guess I've pushed it to the back of my mind.' It was a bit of a lie. Although I was no closer to a decision, I still spent most of my time thinking about it.

'Come on. Let's make a decision once and for all – then you can move on, or move out. Either way. Plus, I'm going on my honeymoon tomorrow, and it'd be nice to know that you have a plan, and a home, before I go and you move out.'

That was why I loved Katie. Even if we bickered like siblings, she was always there for me when I needed her. Part of the reason why we acted like sisters was because we practically were. My grandmother's house – my childhood home – became her sanctuary when her parents divorced and she was being fought over like a rag doll. At least throughout her childhood, she knew she was always welcome at 8 Falkner Avenue. Well, apart from that one time she overdid it on her first taste of cheap vodka for her eighteenth birthday and threw up in Dotty's beloved rose bush. Dotty grounded her for a week, as if she were her own granddaughter.

'Let's start with the cons, the negatives.' Katie held out a hand as she began to count points on her fingers. 'Number one, you'd be living with a stranger.'

'Not just that,' I said. I opened my inspiration scrapbook to try and source matching patterns and fabrics for the pieces I'd cut out and glued in. A flurry of magazine cuttings and swatches fell out onto the floor. 'I'd own the house with him,' I explained, as I bent down to pick up my prized possessions that served as inspiration. 'It's not as simple as renting, which can easily be temporary. This is more permanent, this ties us together. It isn't like I can just up and leave if it doesn't work out. *And* he isn't just a stranger – I actively *don't like* him.'

'OK, so that's two cons then, yes? Owning a house together is complicated and you hate the man.' Katie tapped two pink-painted fingernails in confirmation. 'Any others?'

'I'd be putting up the deposit and he'd be making the monthly repayments, so I guess I'd be investing more, upfront at least, than him.'

Katie nodded. 'An excellent, practical point. You'd need to figure out the logistics of the finances, which isn't impossible to solve. But yeah. Let's pop it on cons for now.' She tapped a third finger as if it were a physical bullet point in a written list.

'There was just one other thing,' I said, before biting my lip.

'What?'

'He acted a bit weird when I asked him why he had the monthly repayments, but not the deposit.' I pursed my lips. 'Like, he was super sketchy about it.'

'But couldn't he say the same about you?'

I shook my head, tucking my hair behind my ear. 'No, I was pretty open with him. I told him my company accounts were a bit up and down, and that the bank needed to see three years' worth. I told him that the deposit was from my grandmother.'

'Maybe he's just a private person?' Katie offered.

'Perhaps.' I shrugged, running my hand over a gorgeous but neglected chesterfield-style armchair. It could easily be restored to its former glory if I could fix the button tufting and redo the nailhead trim. But I knew it wasn't Katie's style and I didn't have the spare cash to buy it for myself. Plus, I didn't techni-cally have a home to put it in. 'I think it feeds into the reason why I probably shouldn't live with him though. I hardly know the man. Who knows what secrets he's keeping?'

'I'm sure you're being dramatic about it,' Katie said. 'It's probably nothing. Everyone struggles to find a deposit for a house these days, especially without family help.'

'True,' I agreed.

'The only reason we can afford to build our own – and go on our honeymoon, in fact – is thanks to Matthew's grandfather's inheritance.'

'Yeah, fair point.' I nodded. 'Anyway, I think we're going to struggle with the pros of the situation. Literally the only one is getting that house back.'

'Isn't that a pretty big one? It's such a special house. And it's very serendipitous that it's up for sale when you're looking for somewhere to live. I'm so sad I can't visit it again before I fly out.'

'I know, me too,' I said as I squeezed her arm. I was going to miss her while she was away on her around-the-world adventure. 'But is it all worth it? The hassle, the risk? Putting up with Zack, day in and day out?'

'When have you ever been afraid of taking a risk?'

'Well, exactly – and look where that's got me.' I pulled a piece of floral chintz fabric over my face to hide myself, before I clocked what it was. 'Hey, do you like this?' I shuffled it in front of Katie. 'This is perfect for your rural-cottage-but-not-really-because-it's-in-a-city aesthetic.'

'Ooh, I do actually.' Katie brushed a hand over the blossoming floral pattern.

'Finally we're getting somewhere!' I nudged her playfully.

'Yes, but stop distracting me from the matter at hand,' Katie said. 'Tell me why you wouldn't at least take a risk and give it a go?'

'Excuse me for feeling a little risk-averse at the moment.' I sighed, as I held the fabric out to properly take it all in and envisage it going in the perfect place. 'I risked everything to start my own business and it's failed.' I took a photograph of the pattern.

'It hasn't failed, you're just going through a tricky patch,' Katie said kindly.

'A tricky patch indeed.'

'It happens to everyone,' Katie said gently, sensing my defeated tone. 'I'm sure all the best interiors experts went through this when they first started out. Can't you just call up Kelly Hoppen or Michelle Ogundehin and ask them?'

'Oh yeah, I'm sure.'

'So, in conclusion, we have three cons and one pro.' Katie slapped her hands together.

'Sounds like it's decision made,' I said resolutely. 'More cons than pros.'

'There's another pro we haven't talked about,' Katie added. 'It's an adventure, isn't it? Not only is it your old house, but it's the chance for a fresh start, a new beginning. Isn't that something you've been wanting? Plus, the small matter of you having to move out anyway.'

I sulked and exaggeratedly pouted my lips. 'You seem to be much more on the side of me doing this than not.'

'You know it's not like that,' she said. 'I just think it's a good opportunity that you shouldn't turn down if you're going to regret it later. Who knows when that house will come on the market again? Or *if* that house will ever come on the market again? This could literally be your only chance.'

'Jeez, when you put it like that...'

'You know what I mean,' Katie said. 'Worst case scenario, think of it as a waiting game – you can move in with him, save up and offer to buy him out eventually. He'll probably jump at the chance if you two hate each other as much as you say.'

'That's not a bad idea actually.' I nodded, feeling a glimmer of hope flickering.

'Let me go and pay for these bits you've collected.' Katie gestured at my bulging basket. 'I'm so excited to see my finished house when you're done!' She clapped her hands together and skipped away, towards the queue.

I stood back and looked up at the roof in the simple, industrial space. It reminded me of my dream project – the New York penthouse – that I'd missed out on when Lavinia dropped me.

My life right now felt like a whirlwind of decisions. I'd made the wrong choice when I let loose at the hen party. I'd made the wrong choice when I picked up my phone and almost missed the vows at my best friend's wedding. Would I be making the wrong choice with the house too? How could I trust myself when it came to decision-making with my track record?

Either way, I knew what I was going to do. I rooted around in my handbag, fished out my phone and clicked on my contacts. I inhaled a deep breath, just as the meditation sessions at the spiritual well-being course had taught me, and I tapped the name on the screen.

THIRTEEN

'Hello again,' Annie the friendly mortgage advisor said, as she beckoned Zack and me down the corridor at the bank. 'Nice to see you back here again so soon, Ms Clark. Is this your boyfriend?'

I held back a snort as I was about to erupt into a belly-shaking level of laughter, until Zack offered his hand to Annie. 'Yes, I am. Lovely to meet you, Annie,' he said in his usual charming (to strangers!) way.

Zack looked her straight in the eye as he gently gripped her petite fingers in his big hand. Annie shot me a glance with an impressed glint in her eye, which threw me. Was I the *only* person in the world he grated on? Who wouldn't be taken in by his charm? Why couldn't someone else live with him if he was so universally adored? Why was I the one who had to buy a house with him?

'My boyfriend? What the...' I murmured to Zack under my breath as we walked behind Annie. I was retracing the route towards her office for the second time, after my disastrous first visit and mortgage refusal.

'Just go with it,' Zack whispered back. 'I'm sure it'll be easier if we pretend that we're together.'

'We can't *lie*,' I hissed, as Annie turned around. I forced a beaming smile and Zack threw his arm around my shoulders.

'My lovely little Lucy's a bit nervous, that's all,' he said sympathetically to Annie.

I glared up at him; I hardly even reached his shoulder. He grinned down at me mischievously.

'No need to be nervous. This way, please.' Annie opened the door and motioned for us both to take the seats in front of her desk. It was a familiar sight to me, as I sat down next to Zack. I couldn't believe I was here. Again. This time with Zack – my fake boyfriend.

'Let's get started, shall we?' Annie asked, as she sat down in the chair behind the desk. She ordered the stack of papers and glanced over them.

Zack reached across his chair to hold my hand and I instinctively karate-chopped it away, as if it were an irritating fly. Annie looked up and I remembered – I quickly grabbed hold of his hand, participating in his plan. We were a happy couple. We didn't want to kill each other. My manic smile and eyes like saucepans must've surely cemented that fact to her, as we sat across from her desk together.

'This should be fairly straightforward,' Annie said. 'Of course, I've met with you, Ms Clark. And I've had your details sent over.' She nodded at Zack. 'So I know your individual circumstances. May I just ask, why didn't you decide to buy together at first? It might've made things a little easier, given your circumstances, both separately and together.'

'Erm.' I crossed my legs and uncrossed them again. 'Well...'

Was it hot in here? I felt as though I was burning up. The bright office lights were like a police interrogation room. And I realised we should've ironed out the details of our story before the meeting, which Zack was fifteen minutes late for, naturally.

'We didn't realise how much we liked each other,' Zack cut in, squeezing my hand. 'Until we realised that we were about to live apart, we just hadn't realised that we can't live without each other.'

He turned and smiled at me, and I dug my fingernails into the fleshy part of my palm.

'Oh, how lovely!' Annie said, her mouth widening to a bright smile. 'How romantic!'

'Mm-hmm.' I nodded, swallowing a gulp, and then chewing the side of my lip as if it were a gummy bear.

'How long have you two been together?' Annie asked politely.

'Erm.' I looked up and pretended to think about my answer. 'Well, it'd be about two...' I began. Luckily, I didn't have the chance to reveal the truth of how long we'd really known each other – two weeks – because Zack interrupted me.

'Three years,' he answered, then looked at me adoringly. 'Sorry to interrupt, honey bun.'

Honey bun? Eugh. My breakfast was beginning to make an appearance at the back of my throat.

'I know you were about to say two years, and I guess it is *technically* two years.' He shrugged apologetically. 'I just always count the year that you were chasing after me.' He chuckled.

'Chasing after you?' I said, open-mouthed.

'Oh, come on, you don't have to be shy about it.' Zack smiled and rolled his eyes jokingly at Annie.

I was furious. Every word he said sounded like nails on a chalkboard. I pulled my hand from his grip, pretending I had an itch on my ankle, which I then furiously scratched, to the point that I could've drawn blood if I'd carried on.

'How sweet! Sounds like it was love at first sight,' Annie said dreamily. 'Well, for you at least, Ms Clark.' She smiled at me. 'And how did you both meet?'

'At work,' I lied, almost shouting in an attempt to try and answer before Zack and his imaginary stories.

'Yes, at work.' Zack played along and leant back into the chair, his hands comfortably in his lap. 'Lucy came to my class. I'm a yoga teacher and meditation facilitator, you see,' he added smugly, straightening his shoulders. 'But my lovely Lucy thought it was a different kind of class and we bonded over her hilarious error.'

'What error? What happened?' Annie was leaning forward, hanging on his every word.

I stared at him. Yes, what error? What on *earth* was he talking about?

'Well, we're all friends here,' Zack said. 'I guess I can say – you don't mind, do you, princess?'

I physically shuddered at *princess*, which he took as a green light.

'She thought it was a tantric sex class.' He rolled his eyes amusedly. 'Our tantra yoga classes are still riding the wave of Sting and Trudie's enthusiasm for their seven-hour tantric sessions. Even though his claim turned out to be somewhat exaggerated, class bookings are still *very* good. And Lucy here was desperate to see what all the fuss was about.' Zack winked at me.

'I see.' Annie nodded, smiling politely but eyeing me with a not-so-subtle sprinkle of judgement. 'Quite the adventurous pair, you two are.'

'You wouldn't believe...' Zack nodded mischievously. *Surely* he could feel my furious gaze. *Surely* it must've been burning a hole in his perfectly chiselled cheekbones.

'Darling,' I added, patting him on the hand more aggressively than I intended. 'Annie doesn't want to hear about all that.'

'Twelve hours, we've managed,' he said, with a mix of glee and pride. 'Take that, Sting and Trudes.'

'Anyway!' I clapped my hands together as I felt my face glow pink with mortification.

Annie's eyes were wide with fascination – or horror, I wasn't sure which. She shook herself back to reality and cleared her throat. 'OK, well, on that note. I... erm... just need to take a few details,' she said, flustered and flappy. 'I'll add them to your file, Ms Clark, if you're the party offering the deposit.'

'Great,' Zack said with a smile.

'Brilliant,' I said through gritted teeth.

'Could I just take your full name, please, Mr...'

'Zack.' He answered with a cheeky glance my way, still revelling in my humiliation.

'Zack...?'

'Oh, my full name?'

Annie nodded with a hint of impatience at his slow-moving ways. Finally, someone was understanding just one aspect of my frustration with him.

'Zachariah Henry George Archibald Bamford.'

I turned to look at him. I expected his middle names to be along the lines of River Wild or Autumn Leaf.

He coughed quietly. 'The third.'

OK. *That* I didn't expect either. Was Mr Free-loving Hippy-doo-da actually a posh boy?

'Do you need my spiritual name too, or just my full name?' Zack added earnestly.

'Erm, just your full legal name for now, thanks.' Annie eyed him quizzically. 'And your birth date?'

'The twenty-seventh of September 1992. I'm a Libra,' he declared, wearing his star sign like a badge of honour.

'I think star signs are a load of rubbish,' I whispered, as Annie was temporarily distracted by her filing cabinets, where she was searching for a piece of paper.

'Let me guess what you are,' he said, his body leaning closer towards me, but his face still looking straight ahead. 'I bet I can get it in one.'

'Try me...'

'Leo.'

I stayed silent.

'I'm right, aren't I?' His voice hiked up a couple of notches in victorious glee. 'I knew it!'

'How?' I said, turning to face him. He shrugged nonchalantly, but with a hint of arrogance that irked me.

'We'll have to arrange a coffee or another brunch date to sort out all the details if we can go ahead with this,' Zack said.

Why did my stomach flip when he said the word 'date'? I ignored it. It was certainly to do with the word 'brunch' rather than 'date' – I did love brunch.

'When works for you this week?' He checked through the calendar on his phone, which was such an old model, I was surprised it even featured a calendar.

I picked up my phone, copying him as I scrolled through my busy day-to-day tasks of client meetings, supplier catch-ups and site visits. Peppered in between was shopping for hidden treasures at my favourite markets, antiques dealers and charity shops, together with some inspiration trips to the incredible museums and art galleries Liverpool has on its doorstep. Even just wandering around and soaking up the architecture of the city offered inspiration on a plate for me. That was always my favourite part of interior design – the research and the ideas. Although it was a close call with seeing the look on a client's face when they saw the finished project for the first time. That never failed to give me a real sense of accomplishment, and it was so special knowing that people were living in, working in or experiencing a space that I'd played a key part in creating – and that they were hopefully now in a much happier place because of it.

'Hmm,' Zack murmured, as he peered into his phone

screen. I stole a glance and noticed that his wallpaper was a photo of him and a beautiful woman, cuddling a dog at the top of a mountain, surrounded by stunning scenery. Her bright blonde hair looked exactly like the platinum strands wound around the brush that had fallen out of his bag.

'I can do Thursday evening?' he offered.

'I can't,' I said. It was an instinctual reaction. My Thursday evenings were booked up indefinitely with an immovable, important appointment. But there was an agitated tone to my voice as I looked at the beaming faces on his phone wallpaper – even the cute dog looked like it was smiling.

Zack opened his mouth to reply, when Annie returned to her desk with a wad of papers that she bundled into a plastic folder.

'OK, guys, we're all set!' she announced. 'This is everything you need to know about your agreement in principle. There's enough detail in there for you both to go ahead with the formal offer on the house.'

'Oh, wow,' I replied. The reality was suddenly hitting me. 'It's really happening,' I said, a little dazed. On one hand, I was ecstatic that I'd hopefully be able to buy the house that meant so much to me. On the other, I was buying it with Zack.

'It's really happening.' He grinned at me. And something in his smile told me that wasn't the end of his plans to wind me up.

FOURTEEN

The day had arrived. I was moving into my dream house! Katie and I had toasted the news during a very excitable FaceTime call when I told her. I tried to ignore how envious I was when she showed me her overwater villa in the Maldives, while I battled the freezing breeze from the River Mersey as I walked to my car.

A decade had passed since I'd walked out of the door of 8 Falkner Avenue for the last time, literally kicking and screaming, because I didn't want my parents to sell it. But very soon I'd be walking back in there again, with a new key in one hand and the deeds in the other. Of course, there was also a ninety-nine per cent chance of some more kicking and screaming, given I was going to live there with Zack. Zachariah. Ziggy. Whatever his stupid name was.

A quick Google search after that meeting at the bank had informed me there was no reason for us to pretend that we were a couple. There was no rule about relationships for a mortgage – you could get one with a group of friends, if you wanted. Although we might've had to blag that we weren't basically complete strangers, we could've been a bit more honest and said we'd be tenants in common – with no ridiculous stories about tantric sex marathons. I shuddered at the thought.

We made the deadline just in time, and I was practically skipping with glee as I headed towards the house that would soon be my home. I told Zack I'd meet him that morning so we could figure out formalities (claim the bedrooms we wanted) and then I was moving my stuff in later. Not that I had a lot – I'd sold most of my nice things to try and free up some money.

Rounding the corner by Falkner Square, I saw the yellow door of number eight in the distance. The sign that had read 'For Sale' last time I was there now had another strip of text over it: 'Sold!' I was fizzing with excitement. I didn't even care that I had to live with Zack. It was a price worth paying to be able to call this house my home again. And there was always Katie's idea to annoy him as much as I could, then buy him out eventually, when the business picked up and I was in a financial position to do so. I reassured myself it was bound to happen because I'd spent every waking hour working my bottom off for my clients, and pitching for new ones.

Striding purposefully down the road, I headed for the open front door. The gravel was a little sparse in the small front garden, more so than it was when Dotty lived there. As I got closer, I noticed properly for the first time that in fact, everything was different. There were no tidy flower beds or potted plants with flowers and herbs growing, their branches winding neatly along the walls. I'd been so distracted by the prospect of buying the house when I last stood there with Zack and Brian that I hadn't looked too closely at it. My attention had been sidetracked by trying to find a speedy solution for how I could buy it when Zack and I were pitted against each other. I hadn't taken it all in – and there was a lot to take in.

'Hello!' I shouted through the ajar front door. The doorbell was hanging off and there were exposed wires where it should've been. A chunk of wood and flaking paint fell into my hand as I opened the door further so I could explore inside. There was no answer to my greeting, but I supposed it was mine – *ours* – now. So, I let myself inside.

My heart throbbed in my chest, quickening with every breath I took as I looked around the hallway. This couldn't be 8 Falkner Avenue. No way. It must've been some sort of time capsule, or perhaps a portal like in *The Lion, the Witch and the Wardrobe*, except instead of Narnia, the wardrobe took you to an abandoned, scary house in Merseyside.

A vile smell hit my nostrils and I winced as it stung my eyes. Covering my nose, and feeling tempted to cover my eyes too, I tiptoed around. I fully expected to see a family of rats scuttle beside my feet – and not the nice, friendly ones in Disney films that sing catchy songs and welcome you to a new, magical land.

The wallpaper, stained brown by cigarette smoke and goodness knew what else, was peeling off the walls. Underneath my feet were either stained carpets or wood that looked like it was rotting from the inside out. Remnants of the previous owners were scattered around the hallway: white envelopes with bold red letters spelling 'Final Warning' emblazoned across them. Bottles of wine and beer with liquid leftovers sitting inside. Cigarette stumps and stained tissues. The state of the place explained why they wanted a speedy sale.

Carefully, watching my feet, I stepped towards the lounge. I needed to see some of the things that would remind me of what the house used to look like. The beautiful bay window and the grand fireplace – at least those original features would remind me of how it used to be. I pushed the door open and screamed as something flew into me. At first, I thought it was a bat. (OK, full disclosure: at first I thought it might've been a ghost.) But then I realised it was a bird, and it swooped over my head as it made its hasty exit. I almost wanted to join it in flying away as I took in the sight of the living room.

The windows were covered in black sheets that looked like

they were superglued to the wall and the ceiling, blocking out all the light. It gave the room an eerie, haunted house atmosphere. The only stream of light hit an abandoned rocking chair, which reminded me of the beautiful one my grandmother used to sit in. The timeworn chair was next to a dirty sofa with the cushions cut open; the cushion padding was strewn around the room, but the dampness and mildew had made it mouldy and yellowing. A damp, earthy smell filled my nostrils and hit the back of my throat.

'Lucy?' I heard a voice in the hallway, and for the first time in my life, I was happy to know Zack was nearby.

'Hey!' I shouted, as I darted from the lounge back into the hallway.

'Welcome home!' he said, as sunnily as if we'd just moved into a magnificent mansion, complete with a swimming pool and tennis courts.

I parted my mouth to reply, but I was still too shell-shocked. Instead, I covered my nose and squeezed my nostrils together again. What *was* that vile smell?

'Are you OK?' he asked gently, stepping closer to me.

'Mm-hmm.' I nodded, my voice sounding squeaky and high-pitched, thanks to the tight clutch of my nostrils. 'I'm just surprised...' I motioned around.

'Is it a bit different from when you lived here?' he said jokingly.

'Just a tad. I can't believe the state of it, especially the lounge.'

'The lounge?' he said, his long, thick eyelashes drawing together as he blinked rapidly. 'Are you kidding? That's the tamest room. You haven't seen the kitchen yet.'

I gulped.

Zack batted it away like it was no big deal. 'Don't worry. The potential was what drew me to this house. The mess is just superficial. We'll have it fixed up in no time.'

Something heavy fell behind us, making us both jump and flinch.

'Why on earth did you want to live here? I mean, you viewed it, I didn't!'

'I told you,' Zack said patiently, running a hand over the walls. 'It's the vibes of the place.'

'I'm not getting good vibes.' I shook my head. 'I'm getting *The Haunting of Hill House* meets Stephen King's next best-seller vibes.'

'Pah.' Zack laughed as he leant against the wooden banister, which began to tilt and creak with his weight. He straightened up again, pretending it hadn't happened. 'Just think of the potential. You're an interior designer, use your imagination.'

I whimpered. Potential to be the setting of a Netflix horror series, yes. New home potential? I wasn't seeing any – and it was my job to visualise homes. Eight Falkner Avenue was completely unrecognisable as the home I grew up in. My memories were covered in mould, and other unidentifiable growths.

'Come on, it'll be fine,' Zack pleaded.

'I can't move in here, not when it's like this. I don't think we'll get out alive. And what *is* that smell?' I pinched my nostrils together firmly again.

'There's some sort of sewage issue apparently,' Zack offered casually. 'No biggie. We can use the outside toilet until it's sorted.'

'The outside toilet? The *outside toilet*?' I put my hands on my hips as I eyed him indignantly. 'I am *not* using an outside toilet. I forgot this place even had one.'

'Suit yourself.' Zack shrugged.

'Argh!' I wailed and stamped my feet in frustration, feeling the floorboard give way underneath my shoes.

'If you're going to be such a princess about it, why don't you hold off moving in for a bit while I sort it out?' Zack said.

'A princess? I'm not being a princess...' I shook my head.

There was no point arguing with him. 'And what would you do if I go away? Make it your own? Push me out?'

'No,' he said, perplexed. 'Of course not. Why would I do that? We own this place together. And you're the interiors guru, anyway. You'll know how to transform it back to its former glory.'

The look on his face made me feel immediately guilty for always thinking the worst of him. The fact I naturally leant towards pessimism now (after once being such a 'Positive Pollyanna'), combined with my bad experience of my toxic, cheating ex-boyfriend, meant I didn't always think the best of men and their intentions.

'I'm just saying,' Zack continued, surveying the mess, 'I cleared my schedule for a bit, I have no classes. If it's going to bother you so much, why don't you leave me to it? You give me some guidance about what you want. I'll get it fixed up so it's a little less *lived in*.'

I raised my eyebrows at the understatement of the century.

'And then we can work on the rest of it together. The sewage issue will be sorted by then too.'

I held my chin between my fingers, sensing the cogs turning in my mind. This was what I was good at: solutions. This was simply a problem that needed solving. Although perhaps Zack had come up with the best solution already.

'You're sure you won't mind being here on your own?' I asked. 'And the smell… it won't bother you?'

'Ha!' he chortled. 'I spent years backpacking around the world. No smell will ever be worse than a shared dorm room with sixty other men in the heat and humidity of a Bangkok summer, while the majority of them have food poisoning or hangovers.'

'Fair enough,' I said, shuddering at the thought. 'And you won't be… scared?' I glanced around again and swore I saw a dark shadow in the reflection of the broken mirror leaning against a wall.

'I'm a big boy, I think I'll be OK.' He half smiled and straightened his posture. He was pretty big, actually. Of course, I'd noticed his height before, but he did have rather impressive shoulders when he stood up straight. And those biceps – I was surprised his T-shirt sleeves weren't cutting off the bloodstream to his arms, they were so tight around them.

'Yes, well!' I announced, shaking myself from my ogling. 'If you really don't mind. I have a lot of work to do so that would be great, if you definitely don't mind...'

'You can say it as many times as you want, I really *don't mind*,' he mocked, his arrogance suddenly overruling his impressive muscle definition.

'OK, well, let's do a walk-around so I can show you what our top priorities structurally should be. Once I get a good feel for it, I can draw up some proper plans and send ideas over?'

A thought sprung to mind and I double-checked the day on my phone.

'It won't be tonight though. It's Thursday.'

'What happens on a Thursday? Is that the night you see your boyfriend?'

'None of your business,' I teased.

Zack didn't answer. Instead, he just pursed his lips and turned away. 'We can walk around now, and then just send the starting plans and priorities over whenever you can. I'll concentrate on the basic stuff first – clearing the mess and cleaning the space up,' he replied. 'Any excuse to go to the tip.' He beamed, and his enthusiasm for the tip made me giggle.

'What about money? For skip hire and anything else you need to buy so you can get going?'

Zack flapped a hand at me. 'Just leave it with me. I'll sort it.'

'How?'

'None of your business.' He tapped his nose, teasing me back in equal measure.

'OK. Well, great.' I clapped my hands together. 'So I'll just see you in a week or so?' I said, as I tentatively stepped over the mess and discarded bits of waste, holding on to my handbag for dear life – and perhaps in the hope it could double up as a weapon to fend off ghosts.

'Sure, yeah. A week, whenever...' he said distractedly, examining a crack in the wall and waving me off as I headed through the front door.

I tried to shake off my nagging hunch and reassure myself that it'd all be fine. He was only clearing things up, anyway. But I had a bad feeling about it, and I couldn't put my finger on why.

FIFTEEN

I'd been conned.

You know when you read those stories in the paper about women who join online dating sites and meet a prince from a faraway land, and they promise everlasting love and marriage, as long as you transfer £10,000 to a random bank account in the next forty-eight hours? Well, I appeared to have discovered the Liverpool version.

I'd fallen for it. The scam.

I'd given a scammer my life savings – my *only* savings. I'd bought a house with a man who had disappeared off the face of the earth. Between the bouts of fury, I couldn't believe how stupid I'd been. I mean, *who* in their right mind buys a house with a *complete stranger*?

Clearly, I was going through some sort of quarter-life crisis. Perhaps I was still working through the trauma of almost losing my business and falling out with my oldest friend. It wasn't impossible, but either way, I'd obviously lost my marbles. I wondered if The Priory accepted mere mortals, and not just celebrities with widely reported substance abuse issues and fast-working PR teams. This was going to be a Netflix documentary one day. I knew it – just like that guy who met women on Tinder and swindled them out of their life savings so he could gallivant around on private jets and enormous yachts. This was the Merseyside equivalent! People were going to watch my story, turn to each other and ask how anybody could be so silly.

I mean, the warning signs had been there. The whole idea was a ridiculous plan. And when he said that blatantly fake name at the bank? I had just nodded along with it. I wondered if he saw me coming; perhaps he targeted me on purpose? I felt furious with rage every time I thought about it – every time I thought about his stupid face, with his stupid dimple, and his stupid freckles, and his stupid green eyes, and his stupid little button nose, and...

I'd had no reason to worry at first. Our first step was deciding on the top priorities for the house (primarily getting rid of all the junk and cleaning it up so we had a blank canvas to work with). And in those early days, after I'd sent him mountains of sketches and ideas, he messaged me back too, sending photos of his DIY work and the random, bizarre things he'd found inside the house. But then, everything suddenly stopped. My texts went ignored, my calls unanswered. Work had been so busy that I hadn't been able to go to the house as much as I'd wanted to, but I'd stopped by twice and he hadn't been there either time. Stupidly, I'd let him take my key as a spare so he could give it to the tradespeople doing the work in the house, which meant I couldn't get inside either time I popped by.

But now, it'd been two weeks – a week longer than we'd originally agreed – and he had disappeared. Completely vanished into thin air. The yoga studio wouldn't give me any information about him, citing employee privacy, even though I explained he was supposed to be my housemate. He wasn't on social media. Of course he wasn't. Zack Bamford (if that was his real name) was *much* too deep for superficial things like Instagram and Twitter. I rolled my eyes every time I thought about him. And the fact that all I really knew about him – his enthusiasm for yoga and meditation, and his love of pancakes aside – was his unnecessarily long, surprisingly posh-sounding name.

There might've also been a teeny, tiny part of me I couldn't ignore that was genuinely concerned over his whereabouts. Just a small part, an almost unnoticeable part. But what if he'd been kidnapped? Or robbed and left for dead? What if he was stuck in the outdoor toilet? I was feeling ninety per cent furious and ten per cent worried.

The only solution I could think of was to wait it out. Literally wait it out, outside the house. My plan was to take my laptop, sit on the doorstep and get on with some work until he came back. Then, ah-ha! I'd catch him in the act. I'd hand him over to the police. Although, that might've been a little extreme, so maybe the consumer watchdog on *This Morning*? Either way, I would not be a victim of a house-buying scam, no matter how much the scammer looked like Harry Styles. I owed this to other women who might've been taken in by him. I mean, who knew how many other houses he'd bought under false pretences?

I strode purposefully towards the house, feeling like one of those detectives in a primetime ITV drama. I was dressed for the role too. I was wearing my wax Barbour, a stripy shirt tucked into jeans, and black, flat boots which were just *perfect* for running after criminals. There was a moody, atmospheric soundtrack playing in my head. I felt just like Suranne Jones!

The house, *my* house, came into view as I rounded the corner, and I saw there was movement outside. Squinting a little (perhaps I should've also bought glasses to complete my look), I noticed that the front door was open and there were people coming and going. Were they in on his plan? Were they backup for him? Were they going to help him barricade me out of my own home?

'Not today, sunshine,' I mumbled to myself, because that

was exactly what a detective in a primetime drama would say at this point. I sped up, feeling grateful for my sensible, crime-fighting boots.

There was an enormous skip on the driveway that hadn't been there when I last visited, its width taking up almost the entire garden. It was overflowing with rubbish, mounds of broken furniture, heaps of plasterboard, and there was a broken bath and an old toilet in the middle of it too. It was a tight space, between the skip and the gatepost. But this wouldn't have stopped any detective worth their salt. So, I decided to be brave and try to squeeze past the side of it, through the tiny gap.

And then I spotted him.

'Hey!' I shouted from my position between the skip and the brick post. I tried not to panic as the corner of the skip started digging further into my stomach the more I moved.

Zack turned around and spotted me. 'Lucy!' He beamed merrily, before clocking my location. 'Why did you try and squeeze through that gap? Why didn't you just come round the back of the house?'

'You're here!' I shouted, my eyes wide, both with anger and alarm that I was now completely stuck between the skip and the gatepost. And why on earth didn't I go around the back, like he said?

'Yeah, I'm here,' Zack replied casually, with a hint of caution at my tone of voice. He was wearing a hole-ridden chequered shirt, thrown haphazardly over a dirty white T-shirt, and paired with scruffy, ripped jeans. It was the first time I'd seen him wearing anything except linen, and I hated to say it, but he looked kind of – *hot*?

'Are you actually stuck?' he asked, eyeing me up and down with concern.

'I'm fine!' I raged. Without thinking, I threw my laptop bag down to free up a hand. 'Shit!' I cried, after it thudded against the ground as it landed. 'Shit, shit, shit.' My panicked breathing quickened.

'Calm down,' Zack said beside me. 'Let's get you out of here.'

'Don't touch me,' I snapped, as he tried to wrap his arms around my shoulders in an attempt to manoeuvre me out.

'Sorry.' He stepped back and held his hands up. 'I was just trying to help.'

'Well, you're not,' I barked, feeling my eyes well up. I swivelled uselessly. I was stuck, thanks to the buckle of my leather belt. This would never happen to Suranne Jones.

'What's the matter with you? Why are you so prickly?' Zack asked. 'Even more so than usual,' he added quietly under his breath, thinking I couldn't hear him.

'What's the matter with *me*?' I glared at him. 'What's the matter with *you*, is the question.'

'I'm fine,' Zack replied quizzically, shrugging. 'Why?'

'Where have you been?' I yelled, giving up the struggle and accepting my fate as Skip Woman. Would Liverpool City Council accept this as my new permanent address?

'Where have I been? When? I was in the house before I saw you,' he said questioningly. He pushed his hair off his forehead, but the curls immediately fell back, framing his face.

'No, not *now*,' I snapped impatiently. 'Where have you been for the last two weeks?'

'Oh...' Zack put a hand to his chin. 'I had something I needed to deal with.'

'And you didn't think to tell me?' I leant forward and forced my hands either side of the skip to try and push myself out. I was now at eye level with the old toilet. Yuck. I really hoped those stains were rust.

'Didn't I text you?' he asked innocently.

'No! No, you didn't, Zack!' I felt like a teacher telling off a naughty child. 'You didn't text me. You didn't tell me *anything*. You ignored my calls, my messages...'

'I switched my phone off. Don't you ever do that?'

'No!' I shrieked, aghast. '*Who* switches their phone off, in this day and age?' My phone hadn't been turned off since the day I bought it. I didn't even know *where* the off button was.

'What's the big deal?' Zack asked quizzically.

'What's the big deal?' I repeated, breathless with indignation, but also a little bit from the pressure of the skip squeezing into my stomach.

'Come on, Lucy, let me help you...' Zack moved towards me again.

'I don't need your help!' I shouted, batting away his hands. 'I'm an independent woman, OK? I don't need *your* help. I don't need *any* help, especially not from a *conman*.'

'A conman?' Zack stifled a laugh. 'Lucy, I think that skip might be cutting off the circulation to your brain.'

'Don't patronise me,' I said. 'You take my money – my only savings – and you disappear. What the hell am I supposed to think?'

'I honestly don't understand how your mind works sometimes...' Zack scratched his head.

'Everything OK out here?' a man dressed in a navy uniform with a wrench embroidered onto the pocket, and a toolbox in his hand, shouted from the doorway, obviously having heard the commotion from inside the house. So, I might've been wrong about Zack's 'backup' – they were tradespeople instead.

'Yes, we're fine!' I replied while glaring at Zack, and silently communicating with him not to ask for help in getting me out. I was mortified enough as it was.

'Why on earth would I be *conning* you?' Zack's eyelashes fluttered as he blinked in what seemed to be complete confusion. 'We bought a house together. We agreed you'd take some time out while I made it a bit more liveable. I honestly don't understand the problem here. I thought I was doing you a favour, I thought I was doing something nice for you.'

My cheeks flushed red. Perhaps I had overreacted a little bit. Maybe I wasn't cut out for detective life. With hindsight, watching reruns of 24 *Hours in Police Custody* probably wasn't the best idea. It might've sent me on a bit of a misguided mission.

'I just thought...' I said, trying to twist myself around again. 'I don't know. It freaked me out when you went AWOL and didn't reply, I guess. And you weren't here whenever I popped by.'

'Do you always assume the worst of people?' Zack asked, with his calming, meditation facilitator voice. 'Don't you trust anyone?'

I snorted. 'Trust is overrated. Where has trust ever got me?'

Zack smiled cautiously. 'Wedged into the side of a skip?'

The frosty atmosphere between us thawed a little, as we stood in silence beside each other for a moment.

'This side of it is stuck on my belt.' I sighed defeatedly. 'I can't squeeze myself out.' I pointed towards the buckle.

'Can you undo it?' Zack asked, peering closer.

'It's pretty wedged in.'

'Shall I have a look?' he offered gingerly.

'OK,' I said, in a whisper that was barely audible.

Zack stepped closer tentatively. The next moment, he was beside me and it was the closest we'd ever been to each other outside of the yoga studio. His muscular body leant over, and his scent overpowered me (and thankfully, the awful smells wafting from the skip too). His freshly washed curls smelt like coconut, and there was that heady, fresh aroma of lemon and wood again.

My body trembled as his fingers lightly skimmed my hips. My stomach fluttered as his hand moved across, over to my belt buckle. He was looking away from me, focused on the belt. But the energy between us was charged. He touched the buckle with one hand and undid it. Every movement felt like it was in slow motion. Then, the belt clasp opened.

'Thanks,' I breathed, as he pulled the leather belt from the hooks, and it left my jeans in one swift movement that really shouldn't have turned me on as much as it did.

'No problem,' he whispered, his breath hot on my cheek. Our eyes met, our faces just inches from each other, with his arm still wrapped around me.

Then a high-pitched siren pierced the air and Zack jolted backwards in shock, pulling me with him and releasing me from my spot between the skip and the brick pillar.

'What the hell is that?' Zack covered his ears.

I copied him and covered mine, but the shrill, ear-piercing noise stopped as soon as it started.

'Sorry about that!' a voice shouted from the doorway – it was the workman who was there earlier. 'Just installing the new fire alarm. It's definitely working!'

Now that everything was quiet again, I didn't know if my rapid heartbeat was from the shock of the loud alarm, the relief of getting out from potentially being trapped forever beside a skip, or the moment between Zack and me.

SIXTEEN

'Shall I put my hands over your eyes, and we'll do it like one of those surprise reveals in the movies?' Zack grinned mischievously. We were standing outside the front door to my house – *our* house.

'Do I have to? It'll smudge my eye make-up.'

'God forbid,' he mocked, holding a hand to his chest. 'Where's your sense of fun, Clark?'

I blushed. He wasn't wrong; I supposed I didn't really have much sense of fun. The last time I'd had fun was the Marbella hen party, and look what happened there. Besides, I didn't need Zack Bamford to try and bring a hidden fun side out of me. But at least his teasing, and the fire alarm, had distracted us from the undeniably charged moment between the two of us when I was wedged into a skip – the setting of all great modern romances.

'Fine, no movie-style surprise.' Zack pushed the front door open. 'I'm guessing it'd be a no to carrying you over the threshold too, right?' he joked cheekily. My cheeks flushed pink again. Fortunately, he was in front of me, so he didn't see.

From the outside, the house didn't look like much had changed at all. The weeds were still overgrowing, claiming the garden as their own. The paint was peeling like confetti from the yellow front door, and there were still cracks growing slowly across the windows like delicate spiderwebs.

My expectations for the inside of the house were low. But as I stepped into the hallway, I felt my eyes widen and my jaw drop as I took in the sight. The disgusting carpet and broken floorboards had been replaced by the gorgeous oak floors I'd sent him photographs of. There was no graffiti on the walls now either. Instead, they were painted in flawless magnolia, which brightened the entire space. It wasn't permanent because we were doing the decorating together over time (budget allowing), but it was an amazing start.

'A bit better, don't you think?' Zack stood back with his arms crossed.

'You did all this?' I stumbled over my words.

'Mostly, yeah. I mean, I had a little help from my friends. Plus, I followed all your plans and ideas. It's nowhere near finished. But you know what it looked like before – it's a definite improvement.'

'Certainly is,' I agreed. 'At least we have more of a blank canvas to work from now.'

'It's true what I said about going AWOL, you know. I did have a situation to deal with.' Zack turned around, avoiding my eye. 'I'm sorry for worrying you. I can be a little thoughtless sometimes.'

'I'll forgive you, considering how busy you've been.'

'It's amazing what you can get done when you avoid distractions and turn your phone off.' He looked back towards me and grinned.

The house was the same, but different. Memories of my childhood here, and learning about what I loved the most, flooded me. Experimenting with paint mixes and textured wallpaper. Learning about scale and balance. The importance of juxtaposition. All those memories, all under the watchful eye of my grandmother. Those memories were still happily preserved by what the house looked like back then. The house now was new – a fresh start – for me and this stranger.

'Come on,' Zack said. 'Come and have a look in the lounge.' He tiptoed around the huge, rubbish-filled bags and various work tools that were strewn around the floor. 'Watch your step,' he said, sweetly pointing out the obstacles as I followed him.

The last time I was in the lounge, black sheets acting like blackout curtains were pinned to the bay windows. And a bird had flown into my head – either angry that I'd entered its home uninvited, or grateful that the door was open and it finally had an escape route. Today, all of that was gone and bright sunshine was pouring through, illuminating the living space.

I surveyed the room and all the memories it held. The spot where my nana would make me a 'Lounge Picnic' – chopped chunks of apple, grapes and cubes of cheese, which I'd nibble on while watching the TV or doing my homework. The space where the sofas once were, which we'd sit on together, while eating her legendary Scouse. We'd revel in the shared knowledge that, wherever they were living, my parents would never have allowed me to eat a meal anywhere in the house that wasn't the formal dining room.

Zack stood back proudly. 'I think this is my favourite room,' he said. 'Why on earth they had that window covered, I have no idea. The light makes the room feel five times the size.'

Although it was empty, and the walls stripped bare so we could decide how to put our stamp on it together, it was still unrecognisable from the state it was in the last time I saw it. The damp tang had gone, replaced by the smell of varnish, paint and bleach.

We smiled at each other as our eyes met. He held my gaze for a moment before turning away, running a hand through his hair.

'Obviously it's still a bit of a work in progress, but it's an improvement, at least,' he said.

'It is.' I nodded. 'I can't believe how much you've done in the space of a couple of weeks.' I felt a pang of guilt for my anger over his absence, when really he was just working hard to transform the house. My mistrust of men after my ex-boyfriend's lies and sketchy behaviour had come back to haunt me. 'I'm sorry for overreacting and thinking the worst.'

'I'm sorry for going AWOL too,' he said diplomatically. 'Shall we put it down to a mutual misunderstanding?'

I nodded in agreement at our peacekeeping pact. 'I didn't think you'd manage to do everything you have though. How did you even know where to begin?'

'My family are in property—' He stopped himself awkwardly and cleared his throat. 'That was how I managed to get some good deals for the work that the house needed. I have friends who owe me a favour. Plus, I have a bit of a love for architecture and property renovation – old houses especially. I can't tell you how many episodes of *Homes Under the Hammer* I've watched over the years.'

'Same,' I chuckled. Finally, something we had in common.

Walking around the room, I breathed a sigh of relief. At last, I was seeing the potential of the space – what I was supposed to be able to see, as an interior designer.

'I was thinking I'd use this room as my yoga studio,' Zack said as he wandered around, looking up at the ceiling. 'The acoustics are perfect for sound therapy at the end of the practice, and the walls seem pretty soundproof, so it'll be quiet and peaceful, even if the neighbours are noisy.' He knocked a wall and the sound echoed quietly. 'Plus, the lighting in here is perfect.'

'Sorry, your what?' I shook my head, the reality of what he'd just said sinking in. 'Your yoga studio?'

'Yeah, it's ideal, isn't it?'

'For you, maybe. But what about me?' I put my hands on my hips.

'Of course, you'd be welcome to use the studio any time you like,' Zack said innocently. 'I could even give you private lessons, if you wanted.'

'No, thanks.' I shook my head distractedly. I wasn't a natural yogi, despite my attempts to improve my very basic skills during the spiritual well-being course. I still couldn't even touch my toes. 'I meant, what you said just now about turning this room into a studio... This is my house—'

'*Our* house,' Zack interrupted me.

'Our house,' I relented. 'So, shouldn't I have a say in a decision like that? This is the biggest room downstairs. What if I want to use it as my home office?'

'I'm sure we can work something out,' Zack replied, in the overly calm tone that grated on me.

'We're going to have to, aren't we?' I said as we locked eyes, neither one of us backing down.

Perhaps this wasn't going to be as simple as I kept telling myself.

SEVENTEEN

'You look like a real-life Build-A-Bear.'

We'd been in the same room together for less than ten minutes, and we'd already fallen out twice. It was taking all my willower not to chuck my paintbrush at him.

'I do not.' I frowned as I checked my reflection in the antique mirror I'd leant against the wall – the mirror we'd been arguing about for days. I wanted it in the hallway to open up the space. He wanted it in the lounge because he thought it was perfect for checking his form when he practised yoga.

'You do too.'

I surveyed my reflection. I was wearing my favourite Lucy & Yak organic dungarees. I owned a pair in every colour, and these were my oldest ones that I couldn't bear to part with. They were my standard, paint-splashed uniform for DIY projects. My hair was neatly tucked into two braids down either side of my head, and I was wearing a super cute polka dot headband.

'Why on earth do I look like a Build-A-Bear?'

'Who, over the age of ten, wears dungarees?'

I glared at him and stomped away to grab a paint tin. What

did he know about fashion? My dungarees were totally adorable. 'Nice to see you out of linen again,' I mumbled snarkily.

Zack held my eye and pulled off his hoodie, lifting his T-shirt up in the process and revealing those impressive abdominals, sculpted by the plank gods.

'Perv,' he teased, throwing his hoodie at me. It landed on my head and my sense of smell was overpowered by Zack's signature scent. I breathed it in, before dramatically pulling it off me.

'Eugh, gross,' I mumbled, shooting a glare at him. 'You know what colour we're going with for the walls, don't you?' I eyed Zack as he propped the ladder up by the first wall.

'I still think it should just be cream.' He sulked like a moody teenager.

'Zack! We've talked about this.' I rubbed my fingers against my temples. My hands were already covered in splatters of paint. 'It isn't a dominant enough colour for the proportions of the room.'

'I don't see why it matters,' he grumbled.

'Your memory is awful! Are you sure you don't have short-term memory loss from too many headstands?'

He glared at me. I glared back.

'Remember I told you about the golden ratio for colour schemes? Every balanced room needs to have a proportional representation of colours—'

'Yeah, yeah, yeah. Blah, blah, blah.' He put his fingers in his ears, but with a wink and a twinkle in his eye.

'Oh my God. How *old* are you?' I mocked, conscious of my flushing cheeks matching the colour of the pink paint pots surrounding us. 'Anyway. It's sage green on the walls for sixty per cent of the ratio, and forty per cent blush pink as the secondary colour. OK?'

'Yes, boss,' he answered, with a sarcastic salute and a stand to attention. 'I didn't realise I'd be living under a dictatorship when I suggested we lived together.'

I scowled at him, as he climbed the steps of the ladder. 'Careful that ladder doesn't *accidentally* fall over.'

'If it did, then how would you be able to reach the top of the wall to paint it, eh, shorty?'

Argh. He was *insufferable*. Inside, I was screaming. But I wouldn't give him the satisfaction. Instead, I rolled up my sleeves and opened the tin of paint I'd had custom blended by my favourite decorator. Zack was calling in favours and helping hands from friends, while I was maximising the goodwill of my contacts and suppliers. We were using every favour and every penny of spare cash to put towards getting the house in a decent state, and I was buzzing with excited thoughts about how the finished space was going to look.

The minute I touched the wall with my paintbrush, I felt the tension begin to melt from my shoulders. There was something so relaxing about the brushstrokes...

'Allllllllll night!'

I jumped and turned around. I was so startled by the sudden noise that I almost knocked the tin of paint over.

Zack was standing at the top of the ladder, his eyes closed, big headphones covering his ears. His voice boomed as he sang along to David Bowie's 'Young Americans' and shook his hips as he bellowed out the lyrics. I pursed my lips to stop myself from giggling. Not that he would've noticed if I did – he was totally in the zone as he sang, half danced (as much as he could, given he was at the top of a ladder) and painted the wall.

How did he look so good in his DIY scruffs? Self-consciously, I stole a glance at the big mirror I'd found in my favourite vintage market. The glass was cracked and the frame was falling apart, so they'd given it to me for a total steal – as well as a few other things I'd rooted out. I was probably their most loyal customer during my shopping jaunts and research trips, when I needed inspiration for a design. Studying myself more closely, I patted my dungarees down. The denim fabric was artistically stained in a rainbow of colours, thanks to all the splashed paint over the years. I didn't really look like a teddy bear, did I? Not that I cared what Zack thought.

'The top half of the wall is officially done!' Zack announced, pulling his headphones from his ears as he climbed down the ladder.

'You can't be finished. You've been painting for about five minutes.' I looked up at his slapdash paint job. 'You're not serious, are you? Please tell me you're winding me up.'

'It's only paint, Lucy. Who's going to be looking at it that closely?'

I crossed my arms over my chest and tapped my foot impatiently. 'Why wouldn't you *want* to take more care? This is our home. The details matter.'

'Details, shmetails.' Zack batted my concern away. My frustration was rising like fire in my belly.

'It might not matter to you, but it matters to me.' I grunted and picked up my paint pot and brush, placing them precariously on the top step of the ladder.

'Wait. What are you doing?' Zack asked, clocking me concernedly.

'What does it look like?' I stomped up the aluminium steps from the borrowed ladder.

'Hey, wait.' Zack darted over. 'Be careful.' He held the wobbling ladder steady as I climbed the steps to the top.

'I think I can manage standing on a ladder.'

'I'm not saying you can't.' Zack looked up and smiled.

I turned my back to his grinning face, and had a proper look at his botched paint job. Most of the time, I felt like I was single-handedly bringing my signature cosy but elegant, classic town-house-style vision for the house to life. Zack was great at the

DIY jobs when he actually focused on one task at a time, but he always started things and left them unfinished.

Zack's phone started ringing and he pulled it from his pocket. 'I have to take this.' He beamed up at me with a sparkle in his eye as I looked down at him. I nodded, and he answered the call with a warm greeting and hearty laugh as he left the room and closed the door behind him.

I was alone, just me and my trusty paintbrush for company, while Zack swooned over his girlfriend, who obviously didn't look like a Build-A-Bear. It was fine. *I* was fine. Totally. Fine.

EIGHTEEN

Things were picking up. *Life* was picking up.

I practically skipped around the co-working space I was holed up in as I put the finishing touches to my presentation. Zack was doing a few final projects at the house over the next couple of days, and then I was moving in at the weekend. But before that, I was pitching for a huge interiors project. And by huge, I mean *gargantuan*. As in, this project could put my business back on the path to where it was heading before everything went wrong. It could be the start of how I'd always envisaged life as an interior designer – bringing a vision to life and making a room the very best it could be – rather than never-ending admin and gulps of cold coffee at 2 a.m.

The client, or potential client, was Dale Street Developments, and they were the bees' knees of Merseyside property development. They were practically a *celebrity* in Liverpool. Trendy new food market? Theirs. Swanky apartment building? Theirs. Swish office block? Theirs. They were the company behind the revitalisation of some of my favourite areas in the city. And better yet, they'd invited *me* to pitch for *them*!

I did a double take and almost dropped my pain au chocolat when the email landed in my inbox. I was used to scrolling through endless tender opportunities with one eye open. They were usually on the dull side – all corporate and no creativity. But I jolted as if I'd had an electric shock when I saw it. The CEO, Josh Barron, had personally invited me to pitch for them. He said he'd been following my career for a while and was impressed by my work. It didn't seem as though he was aware that everything had gone a little awry recently, thank goodness.

There was a new spring in my step, one that had nothing to do with my limping from a pulled hamstring, thanks to a yoga move gone wrong. It was the same excited spring that was there when I first started my business, and everything was ahead of me. The days when I felt wide-eyed with optimism and had constant butterflies in my stomach about what the future might hold. When I was spending every day losing myself in the magic of interior design. I just knew things would go right for me if I bought my grandmother's house. I *knew* it. Perhaps Zack was right with all the 'positive thinking' and 'visualisation' and 'manifestation' he was always wittering on about. Perhaps he was right about the vibes of the house now too, especially as it was looking more homely than haunted with every day that passed.

I ran a hand over the A2 pieces of card that made up the presentation. I'd asked Josh if I could present to them while we visited the space together. I always found that clients responded better when I could show them my vision, and they could physically see and touch mood boards, rather than watching another predictable PowerPoint. Successful pitching in interiors was all about stirring emotions and making the client really *feel* something for the idea. I'd glued swatches to the cards so they could touch the materials with their own hands. And the printed 3D CAD visuals were stunning, if I did say so myself. Every single element had been designed to maximise the natural light of the rooms.

It was an enormous project, and I felt giddy at just the thought of them appointing me. It would mean I was the lead designer for all their Merseyside properties – every project, from homes to offices, hotels and nightclubs. Every single one. The commission alone would set me up for getting back on track with my business, in the hope that one day I'd have my own office, and perhaps I could even think about taking on a team of staff (though bearing in mind the lessons I'd learnt from last time about trying to grow too quickly). This was the contract that could change everything. My eyes lit up as I looked over the mood boards again. I had *such* a good feeling about it.

———

It was the day of the pitch. My heart was pounding so ferociously behind my crisp shirt that I was surprised it wasn't popping in and out, the way they do in cartoons. I was trying to control my breathing – one thing that, to his credit, Zack's meditation sessions had helped with. I just needed to ignore the veil of sweat on my forehead, my grossly clammy hands, the nauseous feeling that wouldn't relent, the churning sensation in my stomach, and my legs that felt as wobbly as jelly. If all those symptoms could magically disappear, I'd be OK.

'You're fine. You're totally fine,' I murmured to my unconvinced reflection in the mirror. I leant against the cooling porcelain sink with one hand either side, and dipped my head down so I could focus on my stiletto-clad feet in an attempt to try and calm my nervous mind. There was a time when I wouldn't have batted an eyelid, when big pitches were as routine as brushing my teeth. My usual reaction was a natural high from the heart-pounding adrenaline, but I was always calm and collected during a pitch. However, my confidence had undoubtedly taken a hit lately. Not to mention that I knew what was at stake with this contract. I knew that it had the potential to transform my business and get me one step closer to the level I was at before the Marbella hen party. I'd learnt from past mistakes; surely I deserved a second chance?

'You know what you're doing,' I said to myself, stealing a glance at my huge portfolio leaning again the wall of the toilets. I hoped I knew what I was doing. I hoped my design vision was strong enough to impress them. 'You are a strong, capable and intelligent woman,' I said again to my reflection. 'You have great vision; you know good design inside out. You know *exactly* what you're doing.' I surveyed my surroundings again. The unisex toilets at Dale Street Developments were still a work in progress, with half of the empty ones closed off with tape. But that was the reason why I was there – the company's new, currently empty offices would be my first project if I won the contract, and I wanted to show them my vision for the space.

My flustered appearance was distracting me. This would never happen to someone with bags of confidence, who was in potentially nerve-inducing situations like this all the time. Someone like Taylor Swift. I needed to channel my inner Taylor power. What would Taylor do? When she played to stadiums filled with thousands of people, or when Kanye ruined her acceptance speech at the VMAs, did she let it get to her? No, she shook it off, which was exactly what I needed to do.

I started whispering 'Shake it Off' to my own reflection, before looking around the empty room self-consciously again. I was mortified, but part of me wondered whether it had anything to do with being in carefree Zack's presence? Was he making me loosen up?

I shook my hands out in tune to the lyrics. Then, I stood in a couple of the 'power' yoga poses I'd learnt. I needed to summon all the power – all the confidence and all the luck. Weirdly, I did feel a bit of the tension alleviate. Standing taller, with my shoulders out and back straight, just like I'd learnt in yoga, I picked up my portfolio and headed out to meet the CEO, Josh Barron, who would hopefully become my biggest client.

NINETEEN

'When I look at this room, the first aspect that draws me in is the natural light.' I gestured to the windows with views over Liverpool. 'So, my priority would be making the most of the light, and potentially knocking one of the walls down to improve the flow of the space. Then we can partition off different zones using open dividers for meetings, collaborative working and breaks. Wide wooden bookshelves would work nicely, or we could build a suspended whiteboard using reclaimed wood inside the meeting room.' I stood back and motioned around the room, which was essentially a building site.

The nerves and nausea had gone. I was in my element. Excitement fizzed in my stomach as I walked the clients around, bringing my vision to life.

'The bones of the room are in good condition, so we'd want to maximise what we're working with instead of overhauling its structure completely.' I gestured to my sketches and the mood boards I'd created for them to really understand the sophisticated but functional space I'd imagined. 'It's a mid-century building and I think that should dictate the colour palette – I'll pair earthy hues with neutral tones, and plenty of natural, organic materials, so there are layers of texture and colour that will really warm up the room.'

I guided them around, my imagination running wild as I pictured everything coming together. 'We don't want to block the different zones off completely, because we want to encourage collaborative working. So, the whole idea is to make it cohesive. It needs to be functional as an office, but enjoyable for the people working here.'

'Does enjoyable mean a ping-pong table and a ball pit?' one of the staff members asked. What was the big obsession with table games and ball pits in offices these days? I once had a client beg me to install a slide so he could get to his printer quicker.

'Erm, sure. That's certainly something we can look at, if it's what you want,' I answered, as politely as I could muster. It wouldn't quite go with my Scandinavian-meets-mid-century vision for the office, but it was up to the client, after all. Good, honest communication and an open dialogue was key for every client-designer relationship.

'Leave it to Ms Clark. She's the expert.' Josh, the CEO, grinned at me, as he stood back with his hands in his pockets. 'Besides, how would we get any work done if everyone was playing ping-pong?' He offered a subtle wink in my direction, and I smiled back. This was going well. I always had a feeling, deep down, if I was going to win a pitch or not. You could tell if the chemistry was right with a client – if your vision and their expectations aligned. I felt a flip in my stomach as I sensed that this time, they did.

'Office design doesn't have to be boring. The core of my ideas is rooted in standing back and looking at the room as a whole – and how to get the best out of it to make a space your staff will enjoy working in, and where you'll be proud to bring your clients. The idea is to create an environment that's inspiring, but that also represents your brand.' I nodded to the smiling faces as I breathed a sigh of relief at the end of my pitch.

I looked over at Josh. He had classically handsome good looks that'd make most women go weak at the knees, and I was suddenly aware that I was wearing an enormous hard hat and high-vis jacket that was about five sizes too big. 'Thanks for coming and pitching to us today, Ms Clark,' Josh said.

'Call me Lucy, please.'

'Thanks for coming today, Lucy,' he repeated kindly. He smiled again and his soft wrinkles rose along the sides of his sparkling blue eyes. 'We've seen a lot of these pitches lately. And, well, yours was certainly impressive.' He leant back against the bare wall, and it was easy to see that his expensive suit was tailor-made, hugging his body perfectly.

'My pleasure. Thank you for inviting me.'

The rest of the staff started exiting the room, some smiling and thanking me, others looking bored and staring down into the open email inboxes on their phones.

'I mean it, Lucy. It really was amazing to see your ideas for the space come to life.' Josh grinned again. Given he was the CEO, I was half expecting he wouldn't even be at the pitch, despite inviting me personally. Most of the top management of the huge corporations I'd worked with over the years didn't get involved in details like interiors. There had been too many occasions to count when I'd had to bite my lip after a director made a joke about me simply faffing around with flowers and rearranging cushions, when the truth was, the interiors were a vital selling point of a space. Especially for property developers – they could be the difference between a company making a profit, a loss, or breaking even. It was simple: if the interiors were wrong, there was a high probability the spaces wouldn't sell.

'We've had a lot of the same ideas when we put this tender out. Everything is black and white and chrome.' He rolled his eyes. 'It's a standard working office, like every other one in the city. There's no personality, no soul.'

'I know what you mean.' I nodded. 'It's part of the reason why I wanted to set up on my own. When I worked for a big interiors company, there was a very corporate mentality. And when that goes too far, it can be like taking a hoover and sucking up every bit of character from a room.'

'See, I had a good feeling about you.' He said it flirtily, and his mouth inched up the side of his face in the beginning of a smile. 'Can I tell you a secret?'

'Go on.' I chuckled. This was the friendliest post-pitch conversation with a potential client I'd ever had.

'Your pitch is the one I've been the most excited about.'

I pursed my lips as I tried not to grin, or cry, with relief. There was still an element of playing it cool. Let's be honest, I was desperate for the business – this contract could change everything for me – but he didn't need to know that.

'I don't usually get too involved in the details of our projects,' Josh said, tracing an invisible line between us on the pop-up table that was covered in plans and sketches. 'But things are changing, and since our rebrand, we want to do things differently. I think you could be the perfect person for us.'

'Really?' I said, my heart leaping in my chest.

He put his hand over his mouth in a mock-whisper. 'You've got it,' he breathed.

'I have?' I cried, clapping my hands together.

'Shhh...' He grinned, looking around him. 'It's not official yet, but I can't sit through another predictable PowerPoint presentation of the same old stuff. You're the only one who actually wanted to get out and visit the space – to see it with your own eyes instead of looking at the plans on a screen. The contract is yours, if you want it.'

'I do, I do!' I shouted, as if I were an enthusiastic bride bellowing her wedding vows. I held a hand over my mouth to try and contain my excitement, but Josh just laughed. I tried to ignore how his smile brightened his face.

'I'll tell the team and my assistant will send over our standard contract.' Josh fastened a button of his suit. 'Well done, Lucy,' he said. He held his hand out to shake, and I wasn't sure if it was my imagination, but it felt like he held mine in his for a little longer than he needed to.

'Thank you, Josh,' I replied, grinning from ear to ear.

Josh turned and walked away, looking back at me with a smile. 'Sometimes you've just got to shake off those nerves, haven't you?'

I met his eyes perplexedly. Then my stomach lurched as his words started to have meaning. Did he mean what I thought he did?

'Got to shake it off, right?' he said with a mischievous grin, before he pushed the temporary wooden door open and walked out of the room.

My mouth dropped open; had he been in the toilets? Had he heard me giving myself a melodic pep talk? *Oh God.* I cringed and threw my hands over my face. But then I remembered that it didn't matter, not really. I'd done it – I'd won the pitch! Unable to stop myself, I jumped up and down, and gave a silent, joyous scream. Then I smoothed my outfit down as if nothing had happened – just in case anyone was watching, *again.* But I couldn't stop the enormous smile that took over my face.

TWENTY

'To you, Lucy.' Mine and Zack's plastic glasses clashed together (just like us) as we sat side by side on cardboard boxes and raised an exhausted toast.

I sipped the cheap fizz (now I was a homeowner, I was too skint for champagne) while Zack drank his sparkling water. Despite my insistence that he should've been celebrating properly with me, he refused to drink alcohol whenever he had a class to teach the next day.

'Thanks,' I said, before taking a gulp of the warm bubbles, feeling them fizz and melt over my tongue.

'Here's to a night of celebrations,' Zack stated. 'Not only did you land a new client, but it's our first night in our new home together.' He raised his glass again and I blushed. I didn't expect my first night in a home I owned with a man to be this unusual situation with Zack.

'Who's the client, anyway?' Zack asked, interrupting my thoughts.

'Just this property company.' I waved my hand to bat away the question. 'You probably wouldn't know them.'

'I see.' He nodded, accepting my answer. 'You know, I wanted to be an architect when I was younger.'

'No way,' I replied, feeling my eyes widen in surprise. 'My parents are architects.'

'Are they really?' Zack asked, his eyes lighting up. 'I love everything to do with architecture.'

'Well, that explains how great you are with DIY and house transformations.' I gestured to the space around us. 'Though I can't imagine you as an architect.'

'Oh, thanks,' Zack replied with a half-laugh. He looked so out of place sitting on a small cardboard box, his long limbs balancing over it.

'Not like that,' I quickly added. 'I just mean, I can't see you—'

'Wearing a suit and working in an office?'

I nodded and chuckled as I clocked his ripped jeans and grubby-looking T-shirt combination, which weirdly worked so well for him when he wasn't wearing linen.

'That's pretty much why I didn't go for it in the end. Well, some other things too...' His voice trailed off. 'But I was all set to study it at university.'

'Really?'

He gulped his water, mumbling 'mm-hmm' as he swallowed. 'Yeah, but I dropped out pretty quickly,' he added cagily.

'Why?'

'Top-up?' he asked, pretending he hadn't heard me. A floppy curl dropped across his forehead, where there were still remnants of white paint from his day spent painting.

'Was that when you decided you wanted to be a yoga teacher?' I asked instead, taking pity on his unease.

'My primary title is meditation facilitator,' Zack corrected me – as he always did, because my subconscious refused to believe that it was a real job.

'Sorry, a *meditation facilitator*,' I relented, though he did also teach yoga, so technically I was right.

'Yeah, sort of,' he said. 'I'm going to be such a gap year cliché if I tell you about it though...'

'Hang on.' I held my hands out. 'Please tell me you "found yourself" while backpacking around South-East Asia. And *please* say you did this while wearing nothing but harem trousers and low-cut vests, and getting elephant tattoos from dodgy tattoo parlours.'

'Got it in one.' Zack smiled and I took a bow. 'Minus the tattoos though, I'm too much of a wimp. But yeah...' He sighed as he moved to lean backwards, but quickly remembered he was perched on a box and there was no wall behind him. 'I mean, I guess it started like that – all wild parties and island-hopping – but then the more I travelled, the more people I met, the more I broadened my horizons...'

I rolled my eyes at his clichéd backpacking spiel, and he noticed it.

'It's a story for another time, I think,' he said guardedly again, and I felt a sudden pang of disappointment in the pit of my stomach.

My disheartening relationship history, primarily consisting of my cheating, alpha male ex-boyfriend who was so overly confident and sure of himself, meant I wasn't used to Zack's humbleness and sensitive side. I kicked myself every time I did something harsh like rolling my eyes.

'Shall we carry on unpacking a bit before we stop for the night?' Zack suggested, changing the subject and clapping his hands against his jean-clad knees.

I surveyed the sea of boxes; the handwriting was ineligible, and I couldn't remember what I'd packed in most of them.

'I guess we should,' I said, pushing myself to my feet. I was a little wobbly, thanks to being the only one drinking the bubbly.

'What shall we eat tonight?' I asked as my stomach grumbled greedily.

'Hmm, good point. The fridge is still getting going.' He pointed towards the kitchen, where things were still messy and disorganised, but it was practically a palace compared to the wreck it had been at first. 'Shall we get a takeaway?'

Those five words were always the way to my heart. Especially on a Friday night when all I wanted to do was stuff my face with comfort food, wear my comfiest pyjamas, take my make-up off and slather my face in overpriced moisturiser.

'I'll take that enormous smile as a yes.' Zack laughed. He scooted over to the shelf and picked up a pile of leaflets. 'A different menu has been pushed through the letter box every day,' he said as his eyes scoured the bright paper, dotted with text. 'Ladies first. You choose.' He handed them to me.

'Ooh, sushi!' I said with glee, as I spotted the first one on the pile.

'Mmm,' Zack answered, while distractedly examining a crack in the wall. 'Raw fish isn't very vegan friendly.'

'Oh, good point. Sorry,' I replied. He held up his hands in a polite 'no worries' gesture.

'Pizza?' I held another leaflet up and my stomach rumbled again.

'Do they have gluten-free?' Zack asked.

'I didn't know you're a coeliac,' I said, as I examined the menu for any GF symbols.

'I'm not. I just prefer to eat less gluten if I can.' He pointed to his stomach, which was impossibly flat.

'No, sorry, I don't think they have gluten-free.' I shook my head as I scoured the pizza options, my mouth watering and stomach growling.

The leaflets flashed in a rainbow of colours as I flicked through and tried to find something that was both vegan friendly and gluten-free.

'Burritos?' I suggested.

'Too spicy.' He shrugged.

'Ramen?' I offered.

'Too soupy.' He sighed.

'That's not a word, but OK,' I mumbled, through slightly gritted teeth. 'Ah!' I exclaimed suddenly, as I held the winning menu up victoriously. 'Let's skip dinner and go straight for dessert! Pancakes and waffles!' I beamed with glee, while also remembering his enthusiasm for pancakes at our brunch together. 'They do vegan and gluten-free options,' I interrupted as Zack opened his mouth.

'I'm just not really feeling something sweet,' he said nonchalantly. 'I think I want savoury—'

'How about you decide then?' I snapped, and shoved the leaflets into his hand.

'Just get the sushi if you really want it,' he said, ignoring my snippy tone. But honestly, how hard was it to decide on a takeaway? 'I'm sure I'll find something on the menu.'

'We could just get two different orders from difference places?' I suggested diplomatically.

He wrinkled his nose. 'That isn't very good for the environment, is it? If they're driving here twice?'

'They deliver on bikes!' I barked. 'Jeez, Zack, can't you just, like, let loose a bit?' I pushed my palm into my forehead.

'Says you,' Zack sniggered.

'And what's that supposed to mean?' I said, feeling my heartbeat quickening. I knew exactly what that meant. Suddenly, I felt like I was back at Ocean Club in Marbella, surrounded by Katie's hen party posse, with Katie threatening to drop my laptop in the pool.

'Nothing,' he said adamantly, wrapping his arms around himself defensively.

'No, go on. You say what you want to say.' I necked the final gulps of the warm fizz in my plastic flute. 'There's no point hiding anything from each other now that we live together. If you have something to say, say it.' I stood up, but quickly sat down again as I realised how wobbly on my feet I was. I really needed to eat something.

'Look, let's just get some dinner and we'll talk about it another time, OK? Plus, you seem a little tipsy...'

'I'm not tipsy!' I said, open-mouthed and swirling my flute with a clumsy flourish. Perhaps I was a bit. 'And even if I was – which I'm not.' I pouted like a petulant child. 'What's it to you? Why are you so judgemental?'

'Me? Judgemental?' Zack huffed. 'Are you kidding me?'

I copied his previous standing position, with my arms folded over my chest defensively.

'You just order your sushi—'

'I think I'll have steak, actually,' I said childishly. 'A big, fat, juicy steak.'

'Lovely,' Zack said, pursing his lips together. 'I hope you enjoy eating the flesh of a poor animal, slaughtered purely to satisfy your taste buds.'

I wrinkled my nose. When he put it like that...

'Fine!' I relented, stomping my foot on the floor. 'You just order whatever takeaway for us both – a tub of pumpkin seeds, stalks of celery, a bottle of fresh air. Whatever. Shout me when it's ready. I'm going to unpack my stuff.'

Without looking back at him, I stalked out of the door and stomped upstairs. I headed into my bedroom, slammed the door and leant against it, feeling my pulse throbbing through my body.

———

'Lucy...'

How strange. I was dreaming, but I could hear somebody calling my name.

'Lucy!'

There it was again. In a sleepy haze, I stretched out on the mattress until the door opened, abruptly waking me from my dreamlike state and making me shriek.

'Hey, sorry to wake you.' Zack's face floated alongside the door as he peeked his head around.

'It's fine,' I garbled, wiping the line of drool from my lip and smoothing down my hair. I blinked my eyes back to reality and remembered that my mattress was completely bare because I hadn't yet unpacked my bedding, and the room was still covered in an endless sea of cardboard boxes.

'Food's here.' He smiled. Thankfully, the atmosphere between us had calmed a little bit with our distancing – me upstairs and him downstairs.

'I'll be right down,' I said with a yawn. My nap had done me good and helped me sober up a little; I was such a lightweight these days.

Zack closed the door behind him, and I yawned and stretched out again. It was such a weird feeling, being back in the bedroom where I'd spent most of my childhood. I still expected to see my old posters on the walls and schoolbooks scattered on the floor. The posters were long gone, but I could pinpoint exactly where I'd plastered the walls with shrines to the Spice Girls.

My bedroom here was the opposite to any room that my parents would earmark for me on rare visits to Abu Dhabi, Shanghai or Singapore, or wherever they were calling home at the time. My grandmother always let me do what I wanted to my bedroom, experimenting with paint combinations and mural illustrations. Whereas anywhere my parents lived was always soulless, with a boring, neutral colour scheme and everything perfectly matched, with no character or colour.

Zack slept in the spare room because he preferred the light and the birdsong (eye-roll) in the morning from that side of the house. It left my grandmother's old bedroom free, and it was currently being used as our storage room before we decided what to do with it. I was a little relieved, as it would've felt strange to have Zack call that room his own, and truthfully I wondered if that was the real reason why he hadn't claimed it.

Fighting the tear that was battling its way out as I thought of my childhood here and memories with my grandmother, I rubbed my eyes and crawled off the mattress, onto the floor. I yanked off my work clothes and replaced them with my cosiest pyjamas. Tying my hair up into a messy bun, I took my make-up off and covered my face in moisturiser, with some dots of spot cream on my blemishes. I was too tired to care what Zack thought of me.

As I headed downstairs, the smell of food wafted up the staircase. I pushed open the door to the kitchen, and the wobbly old table that I'd found in a charity shop was covered in brown paper bags, all filled with food.

'Oh, wow,' I said as I took in the scene. 'How much did you order?'

'I thought you might be hungry,' he replied with his back to me.

'I am, I'm starving,' I said, before sneaking a peek into one of the bags where food boxes made of brown card were stacked inside.

'Oh,' Zack said as he turned around and faced me. His head flopped to one side. 'Do you know you have a bit of...' He gestured to his chin.

'Yeah, it's spot cream,' I replied, suddenly feeling self-conscious.

'Ah! I could use a bit of that myself,' he said kindly. His complexion was as clear and glowing as ever, so I appreciated his attempt to make me feel better. 'Nice PJs, Clark,' he added, raising an eyebrow and ruining his previous kindness.

My pyjamas *were* nice – they were covered in alpacas wearing sombreros; what wasn't to love?

'What do we have here, then?' I asked, secretly hoping he'd relented and ordered the greasiest, junkiest, naughtiest, *meatiest* takeaway for us to enjoy. 'Smells good.' I sniffed up the aromas from the bags.

'I thought I'd get us a bit of everything, given that we're celebrating our first night!' He grinned.

I knew we were both quietly hoping the evening was still salvageable after our earlier disagreement, and it was sweet that Zack was making the effort.

'This is mac and cheese.' He pointed to one box. 'Three bean chilli.' He gestured to another beside it. 'I can't really remember what's in the rest of the bags. I might've got a bit carried away.' He scratched his head and smiled. 'There's definitely sweet potato fries, garlic mushrooms, creamy spinach, seitan wings…'

'Wait, what? *Satan* wings. Satan, like the devil?' I eyed him curiously and confusedly.

'*Seitan.*' He laughed. 'S-e-i-t-a-n. It's made from wheat gluten, so not for me, but you should tuck in. Apparently, the wings are amazing.'

'Hmm. Yum. They sound it,' I said, grimacing. *Wheat gluten?* What was wrong with good old-fashioned *chicken* wings?

'You take these through to the lounge.' He gestured to the plates. 'I'll grab the rest.'

I picked up two of the mismatched plates and walked from the kitchen to the lounge, my unicorn slippers making squeaky noises on the floor with every step. As I pushed open the door to the lounge, I saw the half-painted wall was dappled with fairy lights. There was a low table in the middle of the room, with scattered cushions and cosy blankets surrounding it. On the table were two flutes, filled with sparkling bubbles.

'You like it?' Zack said from behind me.

'It looks great in here,' I whispered, with a cough to clear my throat and gather my thoughts. 'Lovely and... cosy.' It was certainly cosy. Cosy and intimate – romantic, even.

He swished around me, placed the bowls he was carrying down on the table and took the plates from my hands, repositioning our feast so that everything was visible. As he stood again, he gave one of the glasses to me and held the other in his hand.

'I'm sorry about before,' he said sheepishly. 'I think it's only natural that we're going to have some teething problems, right? It'd be weird if we didn't. This is quite a unique situation.'

I nodded.

'But I do think we can make it work.' He grinned and tilted his glass against mine, just as we'd done earlier with our plastic flutes. I couldn't help my surprised giggle as he took a big gulp.

'You're joining me in the bubbly now, are you?' I asked.

'Why not, hey? Maybe you're right, maybe I do need to loosen up a bit.' He held eye contact for just a touch longer than I could handle, and I looked away. 'Just a warning though, I'm not used to drinking, so I might be a bit of a lightweight. You may have to carry me up to bed.' He winked.

'How strong do you think I am?' I mocked before taking a sip.

His flirtatious comment, combined with the romantic setting, was confusing. We'd skirted around the subject of relationships previously. He'd been vague, in his typical Zack way, saying that his soul was free and his heart was open, and he didn't believe in 'traditional conventions of marital status'. Which I'd taken to mean either he wanted privacy for his relationship, or he was using it as an excuse to sleep around, under the guise of spiritual discovery of the mind and body – but primarily the body.

He certainly acted like there was a significant other, with

his constant texting and phone calls he'd leave the room to take. Not to mention the picture-perfect photograph that was his phone wallpaper, and the hairbrush covered in platinum hair that always seemed to be peeping out of his bag.

I wondered if he and his girlfriend (or whatever he called her) had an open relationship. Maybe she was doing the same thing? And to be fair, I'd been elusive about my dating – past and present – too. I didn't want him to know the truth about my knack for picking dreadful men. Or how my last relationship led to me concluding that I'd lost all trust in monogamous relationships forever. No, clearly Zack and I were opposites when it came to relationships. Just as we were opposites in every other possible way.

'Let's eat!' Zack said enthusiastically.

'Yes, please.' I licked my lips in agreement, sitting down beside him and taking an empty plate from the table, ready to pile it high with all the delicious takeaway delights in front of me.

'I can't believe this is all vegan!' I said, looking over the amazing dishes – the perfectly crispy edges of the dairy-free mac and cheese, the vibrant tomato sauce of the veggie-packed chilli. 'I honestly would never have guessed.'

'It's my favourite place in Liverpool,' Zack said, as he loaded up his plate. 'It's incredible. Seriously. Prepare to have your mind blown with every dish you try.'

I nibbled the seitan wing, glazed in sticky barbecue sauce – it was nicer than any chicken wings I'd ever had in my life. I couldn't stop myself as I picked up another handful of sweet potato fries, dipping them in the garlic sauce of the mushrooms. How was the sauce so rich and sumptuously creamy when there was no cream?

I made an audible groan as I ate, and Zack laughed. 'I know, right?' he said as he tucked in beside me. 'Better than that steak you wanted? And the sushi?' he teased playfully.

'No comment,' I replied. I wasn't going to make it too easy for him.

The blanket we were sharing fell off my leg, and my hand met his as I pulled it back over myself. 'Sorry,' we both mumbled apologetically.

'Shall we put some music on?' I asked, tapping my phone's Spotify which was connected up to the Alexa we'd listen to as we decorated. We hadn't yet set up the TV, and I needed something to fill the silence.

'Absolutely, what are you in the mood for?' Zack asked as he wiped sauce away from his mouth.

'Hmm. What sort of music do you like?'

'Old stuff mainly,' Zack said. 'I'm not really into modern music.'

'Well, I know you love David Bowie, after your ladder show.'

Zack turned to me, politely covering his mouth that was full of food but smiling. 'I can't deny that – I worship him, in fact. Do you like him?'

'Of course,' I stated, popping a chip in my mouth.

'We have that in common, at least.' Zack leant closer to me and nudged my arm playfully with his elbow.

'I've actually been wondering whether your "spiritual name" being Ziggy has anything to do with your love for Bowie.'

'Yes, but don't tell anyone.' Zack smiled. 'I think everyone assumes it's the alliteration with Zack and "Zen" – it's very on-brand.'

I gave a silent celebration. I *knew* it. Perhaps Zack and I actually had more in common than we'd thought.

'I can't wait to get the TV sorted. I've missed Netflix.' I sighed, before popping a sweet potato fry in my mouth. Even though I was getting full, I couldn't resist their crispy and fluffy deliciousness.

Zack shrugged. 'I don't really watch much TV.'

'What do you do to relax then?'

'That's what yoga and meditation's for,' he said cheekily, nudging me gently with his elbow again.

'But that's your job.' I took a sip of bubbly. 'Surely you need to do something else to relax. Like, properly relax.'

'That's funny coming from you,' he mocked. 'I find my work very relaxing,' he stated with a shrug.

'Is there anything you *don't* find relaxing?' I teased. 'Or are you just in a constant state of chilled zen-ness?'

'Hmm, what don't I find relaxing?' He pretended to stroke a long beard. 'Maybe when someone from my class starts an argument in the middle of a meditation lesson, then storms out of the room?'

'Does that happen a lot?' I joked, remembering the second time we met.

'No, not usually.' He shook his head. 'Just this one time. The heart rate monitor on my watch didn't know what'd hit it – it's never spiked that high. I even got an alert on my phone.' He laughed and shook his head again. 'Then there was the incident when someone was trying to steal my house from me. That wasn't very relaxing either.'

'Excuse me.' I held a finger up sassily. 'Let's not get carried away here. You'd only put an offer in – it wasn't *your* house.'

'Details, details...' He flapped a hand. 'And another alarming heart rate was when said woman accused me of being a conman. In fact, all these situations have one thing, or should I say, *one person*, in common.'

Zack held my gaze, and I took in every inch of his face as the soft light flickered romantically around the room, subtly highlighting his features. The cheekbones, dimples, a gentle graze of stubble and his jade-green, soulful eyes. He looked back, almost studying me too, and we were silent together.

'Want any more food?' Zack said suddenly, his words cutting through the moment between us like a knife. He slapped his hands against his jeans, wiping them and standing to his feet, leaving me sitting alone on the cushion.

'I'm OK, thanks,' I said quietly, feeling weird and confused. As he walked out of the room, I ran a hand over the warm bobbly blanket where he'd been sitting just seconds before. Was I imagining that moment between us? Just like the one outside when I was stuck beside the skip? Was it all in my head?

TWENTY-ONE

ONE MONTH LATER

If the opportunity to buy a house and live with a stranger ever arises, take it from me, *don't do it.*

A month had passed and clearly this whole idea was one huge, expensive mistake. I was allergic to Zack. Literally, I was *allergic* to him. Ever since we'd started living together, all I'd done was cough and sneeze. Zack suggested perhaps it was from the dust because it was an old house, but I'd dusted every surface until it was gleaming. Yet my nose was still a permanent pink and my eyes were dry, as if someone was throwing sand in them. And given how much Zack and I clashed, I wouldn't have been surprised if he'd been doing it in my sleep.

But it wasn't just my new and very annoying allergy. Our communal areas were constantly filled with his stuff. He was the messiest person I'd ever known. Everywhere I looked, his washing was hanging up to dry, or there'd be piles of books he'd pick up to read, but then abandon after a few pages. The kitchen surfaces were a conveyor belt of half-filled water glasses and half-eaten nut-based energy bars. And don't even get me started on the ingredients, preparation and *noise* that went into making his daily matcha lattes (not to mention the time he forgot to secure the lid on the juicer and our kitchen was fluorescent green for the day).

Financially, he was actually *costing* me money too. Aside from our shared pot of renovation costs for the ongoing house projects, we split the bills equally. However, he still insisted on taking baths instead of showers (despite my reminders that showers were more environmentally friendly). Not only that, but he also *meditated* while he was in there! One time, he was in there for two hours. *Two hours!* Who takes a two-hour bath? Surely the water would be cold, so you're just lying there, wallowing in your own dirt. I'd never even taken a two-hour lunch break, never mind a two-hour bath.

Oh, and there were some *weird* noises coming from his room throughout the day and night. Kind of guttural, but *grunty*. It was insane to think that a month ago, I didn't even know his official relationship status, whereas now I knew far too much about his (incredibly active and incredibly vocal) sex life. He wasn't joking at the bank when he told our mortgage advisor about tantric sex. Those noises coming from his bedroom were at *all hours*. I honestly didn't know where he got the stamina (though perhaps it explained all the energy bars). And, I know I shouldn't have done this, but I sneaked a peek into his bedroom when he left his door open once, and I found...

Oh God, I don't think I can even say it.

OK. I found a sex swing. He had a *sex swing* in there!

Holding my hands up, yes, I might be what you'd call *vanilla*. But – and call me naive – I thought sex swings were the sort of things you found in swingers' clubs and at seedy orgies. Not in a nice, respectable townhouse in Liverpool!

But that wasn't even the worst thing about our living situation. I actually walked in on him naked yesterday. Absolutely starkers. I made eye contact with his willy and everything. He wasn't even that apologetic. While I yelped and covered my eyes, he just said 'whoops' and attempted to shield his bits with his cup of chamomile tea, before making a joke that a mug filled with boiling hot liquid probably wasn't the best cover-up for exposed genitalia. He was so casual about the whole incident, you'd have thought we were commuters having a polite chat on the train about the weather.

So I'd decided enough was enough. We were going to have to lay down some rules – house rules. I couldn't live this way any more. Granted, he did spend a lot more time in the house than I did. Work was insanely busy now that I had officially started my contract with Dale Street Developments. But in a way, that made it even worse because Zack had taken over the whole house as if it was his. And when I rolled home at 9 p.m., bleary-eyed from work, I either had to listen to him chanting to himself or grunting with whatever company he'd taken to bed that night.

Today was the day it all changed. It was the day I was going to broach the subject with him. I knew his routine, so I knew he'd be up and making his antioxidant-packed, beloved matcha latte at 8 a.m. before his first morning class. When I woke up at my usual internalised time of 6 a.m., instead of lazing around in my pyjamas and dressing gown, I put on jeans and a cute jumper, a little bit of make-up, and twirled my hair up into a messy bun. I was treating this like a work meeting, and I knew I'd feel more confident if I felt better about myself. Nothing to do with caring how I looked in front of Zack. It was just a self-confidence thing.

Right on time, at 8 a.m., while I was clearing up the messy kitchen, I heard him slump down the stairs and open the kitchen door.

'Good morning,' he said sleepily, stretching out his limbs and yawning so widely I could see his tonsils.

'Morning,' I said, as I sprayed Dettol aggressively onto the kitchen counters. Clearly he'd been experimenting with another of his elaborate recipes last night, and the leftovers were stubbornly stuck on the surfaces. It wasn't much to ask to have a clean and tidy home, was it?

'You OK, Clark? Sleep well?' he said, rubbing his cheek which had the imprint of a pillow on it.

'Mm-hmm,' I answered, while using the same rubbing motion, but against a particularly permanent-seeming stain on the counter.

'Want a matcha latte?' he asked politely, even though I'd never said yes to his offer of the ghastly-looking liquid.

'No, thanks. I need—'

'You seem stressed, Luce. How about a peppermint tea? Or maybe a chamomile? Something nice and calming...'

'I'm fine!' I squeaked, my voice two inflections higher than usual. 'Actually, Zack, I'm not fine.' I yanked off a yellow rubber glove. 'I really need to speak to you.'

'Chat away,' he said. 'I'll just make my matcha.'

'Could you sit down first?' I asked, pulling a chair out from the kitchen table and gesturing to it. 'Please?'

'Sure,' he said with a sleepy shrug.

'We need to talk.' I eyed him and clasped my hands together firmly.

'Why do I feel like you're breaking up with me?' He grinned jokingly.

I would if I could, I answered silently.

'We said at the start that there were probably going to be teething issues...' *Achoo!* I let out a huge sneeze. 'Sorry,' I said, as I pulled a crumpled tissue from the pocket of my jeans and wiped my nose. The sneezing and sniffing had happened so much over the last month that it was second nature to me now.

'It's all right.' Zack eyed me concernedly and nodded along. I could tell he was trying to concentrate on the conversation, but he was always so distracted and ditsy. I'd learnt he could never focus on anything for longer than a minute or two, which explained all the abandoned books around the house.

'This isn't working for me. We need to make a change here if this living arrangement has any chance of being successful. I think we need to lay down some house rules.' I said it calmly yet firmly, just as I'd rehearsed in front of my mirror.

'Sorry, what isn't working?' His expression was innocent as he looked at me angelically with his big green eyes.

'This living situation.' I gestured around the room with one hand and used my other hand to rub my nose with the tissue.

'Why not?' Zack looked at me quizzically and leant back into the chair.

'Why not?' I raised my eyebrows. 'You want a list?'

Zack's lips pursed as he frowned and nodded.

'Shall we start with me walking in on you completely naked in the kitchen yesterday?'

He held his hands out. 'OK, I understand why that would make you uncomfortable, and I do want to apologise for that. But I can explain.' He took a deep breath in. 'I lived in a naturist community for a year, and sometimes – usually when I'm half asleep – I forget where I am, and that I need to put clothes on. I'm really, really sorry, Lucy,' he said earnestly. 'I know my naked body is the last thing you'd want to see.'

I shook the memory of his yoga-honed body away. I mean, it wasn't *that* bad, as far as naked bodies went. But that wasn't the point.

'Fine, apology accepted. Thank you.' I nodded, and Zack copied me. 'And your baths...'

He held his hands out again. 'I know, I know what you're going to say. I love my long baths, but I know how terrible they are for the environment. I think I've been in denial about it for a while now. The bubbles just really relax me, and there's no better place to meditate.' He nodded solemnly.

I stifled a laugh about his enthusiasm for bath bubbles.

'I promise I'll rein them in to a rare treat,' he said.

Hurrah! We were making great progress already. This was going better than I thought it would.

'I'll take showers lasting precisely eight minutes, like you do,' Zack joked.

I wouldn't be pulled into any arguments, I confidently told myself as I sat opposite him. He was just jealous of my economical water use and efficient, yet effective, personal hygiene routine.

'And the general mess of the house...' I said before pausing, in the hope that he'd simply agree to sort that out too, and we could soon declare the meeting finished – all issues solved!

'The general mess of the house?' He raised an eyebrow and tapped his fingers on the table. 'You think it's messy?'

'Err, yeah?' I said, semi-calmly.

'I don't think it's messy,' he answered nonchalantly.

I coughed before I spoke, giving myself a few seconds to gather my thoughts so I wouldn't cause an argument. We were adults. We could handle this like adults.

'It *is* a little messier than I would like,' I said, impressed by my diplomacy. 'And it's my house too, so I think it's only fair if you meet me halfway.'

Zack nodded slowly, staring at me. 'It's my house as well,' he said, a little more combatively than I expected.

'It is.' I mimicked his tone, and spoke a bit more sternly than I meant to. 'But why would you want to live in a messy house? Why wouldn't you want to live in a nice, clean and tidy house?'

'Jeez, I'm not that bad,' Zack scoffed.

'You are, Zack, you are!' The volume of my voice climbed up and I couldn't stop it, despite promises to myself to keep calm (and carry on). 'You have no bloody idea how messy you are because I'm the one who picks everything up after you! It's like living with a teenage boy!'

Then my nose started to stream again, my mouth itched,

and I blinked rapidly to try and bring some moisture back into my dry eyes. Our fight paused as Zack watched me. His brow wrinkled as his expression switched from annoyance to concern.

Achoo! 'Excuse me,' I said again, as I blew my nose after another sneeze. I made a mental note to make a doctor's appointment. Surely a cold shouldn't last a whole month, and it felt like it was getting worse rather than better. I made a second mental note not to google it, because obviously Google would tell me I had a very rare disease and didn't have long to live.

'You really are sneezing a lot, aren't you?' Zack touched my arm as he watched me anxiously.

'I'm probably just a bit run-down,' I said with a sniff, and a glance at his hand resting gently on my arm.

A flicker of guilt flashed across Zack's face – he must've thought it was from the stress of us living together and our ongoing DIY projects to restore the house to its former glory. Either way, at least it cooled our heated debate.

'And I don't like the grunting,' I said, seizing my opportunity as we both temporarily waved our white flags.

'The what?' Zack looked perplexed.

'The grunting! I hear it all the time.'

'I don't grunt.'

'Well, we must have a ghost then, mustn't we? A grunting ghost!'

Zack rubbed his chin thoughtfully. 'What do you want, Lucy?'

'I just want you to be a good housemate, OK? Neither of us wanted this situation, not really, but we're in it now, we're committed, and we have to make the best of it.'

Zack nodded but said nothing.

'The grunting, or whatever you get up to with God-knows-who, is none of my business, but I'd appreciate it if you could keep the volume down, especially at night.'

Zack paused and looked at me strangely for a moment. Only for my eyes to start streaming as I sneezed again for what felt like the hundredth time that morning. I wiped the tears from my eyes and rubbed my nose again. The skin around it felt red-raw and dry, even though I'd been constantly slapping on the Elizabeth Arden Eight Hour Cream.

Zack shifted awkwardly in his seat as he watched me suffer what felt like the worst cold of my life.

'Anyway,' I said defeatedly. 'I think it would be a good idea for us to set some rules that will help us both be happy here, while respecting each other's personal space and boundaries.'

'OK,' Zack replied. 'Sure.'

I grabbed a pen and paper from the side of the table.

'Oh, wow. You're actually writing them down? Will they be official then? Are they legally binding?' he said jokingly and looked pleased with himself.

Usually, I'd appreciate him making light of the situation and the tense atmosphere, but now, I wasn't in the mood.

Rule #1, I wrote. *Nakedness reserved for the bedroom only.*

Zack looked up at me and I felt my cheeks glow red.

'You know what I mean!' I said quickly.

'Sure.' He laughed, casually leaning backwards into the chair and resting his hands over the back of his head. 'Sure thing.'

Rule #2 Limit of one treat bath per person, per month.

'Does that sound reasonable?' I looked up at him from my spot leaning over the paper. 'More showers and fewer baths? Cheaper water bills? Do our bit to save the planet?'

Zack nodded his formal agreement in silence.

Rule #3 Leave each room as you find it. Pick up your mess and keep it tidy.

'Fine,' Zack relented. 'I'll try to be as clean and tidy as you.'

Rule #4 No loud noises after 10 p.m.

'Does that go for your loud laughing at that TV programme you love so much?' he said with a glint in his eye.

'I don't laugh that loudly!'

'Sure you don't,' he said.

'I know you say you're not grunting, but you are. Maybe you're doing it subconsciously,' I offered.

'OK,' Zack said quizzically. 'I'll try to consciously not grunt. Especially not after 10 p.m.'

Rule #5 Clear overnight guests with each other before they stay.

Zack's brow was furrowed as I looked up at him after I wrote it. 'Oh,' he said, sounding disappointed. 'Yeah, I mean... OK.' He wrapped his arms around his chest.

My heart sank a little at his reaction, which was a confusing feeling. He must've really liked the person he was doing his grunting with.

'Sure thing,' he added coolly.

Rule #6 No going into each other's rooms.

Zack frowned. 'I've never been in your room,' he said.

'I know, I know. I've never been in yours either, obviously. Never,' I garbled. 'It's just there so we know to respect each other's privacy.'

'Fine,' he huffed impatiently.

'Happy?' I said victoriously.

I put the pen down and inched the paper forward, so it was right in the middle of us – The Peace Treaty of 8 Falkner Avenue.

Zack looked down at it and nodded, but he didn't look happy. It was probably because he'd been awake for too long without his beloved morning matcha and was struggling to function.

'This is a great start, but we can always add to it. We can pin it to the noticeboard so we can see it clearly.'

'Mm-hmm. Great,' Zack mumbled. He got up and wrapped

his dressing gown around himself, before pulling the blender out from the cupboard.

I walked out of the kitchen and up the stairs triumphantly. I gave myself a victorious little pat on the back – *I think that went well?*

TWENTY-TWO

Living with Zack had improved drastically since the introduction of our house rules, which were now pinned, pride of place, to the noticeboard in the kitchen. The piece of paper and my unruly handwriting looked messy, so I'd typed the rules up, added some fab graphics to the page, and then printed and laminated it. Now, it was perfect.

Despite allowing myself a rebellious brief peek in Zack's room that one time, I was grateful of the rule we'd set not to go into each other's rooms. It gave us our own space and privacy, and I wanted to remember the spare room (now Zack's room) the way it was when my nana and I lived in the house together, when it doubled up as a library, filled with books. Certainly minus Zack's sex swing, which I was desperately trying to erase from my memory.

The other new house rules were working too. Zack was clearing up after himself a lot more, our water bill had been cut in half, I hadn't walked in on him naked again, and the grunting had quietened down. He'd even been leaving little care packages filled with all sorts of natural flu, cold and allergy remedies outside my bedroom door for me, which was sweet. The only thing – a small detail – was that I'd seen Zack a lot less. He'd been staying with his girlfriend, or lady friend, or whatever relationship title (or non-title) they were. It was fine, of course. It was just a bit lonely in the house sometimes, that was all.

Those lonely feelings didn't shift when he was home either. When he wasn't with his other half, he was texting her incessantly. Or running out of the room and shutting the door for privacy when she called – clearly they were into some sort of kinky pillow talk and didn't appreciate eavesdropping. Whenever we tried to watch a couple of TV shows together, I couldn't concentrate because he refused to put his phone on silent. So, all I could hear was the little typing sound effect constantly, and the bing-bing-bing every single time he got a message from her. But I was happy for him. Truly, I was! He was a good guy and deserved a good, yoga-loving, meditation-practising, matcha latte-drinking, vegan-eating girl, just like him.

Between the two of us, we were doing the house up, and room by room, brushstroke by brushstroke, it was looking better every day. We'd agreed to a compromise when it came to the rooms. He'd won the lounge because I really wanted ownership of the kitchen (I had some incredible design ideas in mind to really make the most of the stunning original features). And the lounge couldn't go *too* wrong – at least I'd already given him the colour scheme, when we'd painted the walls during the early days of living together and he treated me to his Ziggy Stardust-style dance at the top of a ladder. Plus, we'd agreed it would be a shared home-working space for us both – his cosy home studio, and my office area.

Between seeing his mystery girlfriend and teaching his classes, Zack had been busy fixing up the room, and tonight was the big reveal. I'd offered to cook a nice dinner for him as thanks for his hard work. The only problem was, it had been a while since I'd last cooked anything good. Forget that – it had been a while since I'd last cooked *anything*. I hadn't ever cooked in the kitchen at the house (except using the microwave), so I guessed I'd been living off convenience food without noticing – grabbing the odd takeaway, the occasional ready meal, a meal deal for a quick and easy lunch between meetings.

My teenage memories in the kitchen were my grandmother teaching me the basics, and later, my attempts at perfecting her incredible recipes. Now, my memories in the same kitchen, just over a decade later, were pure mayhem. I'd burnt my first and second (and potentially my third) attempts at dessert. Already, I'd had to rush out for replacement ingredients. And I didn't want to break it to Zack, but there was every chance that I might've broken his beloved juicer (in my defence, was it necessary for a single piece of kitchen equipment to have *so many* settings?).

I even nearly re-enacted one of my favourite scenes from *Friends*, when I spilt wine (don't judge) on the cookbook and the pages mushed together, so I almost put cayenne pepper in my vegan brownies. OK, full disclosure: I *did* put cayenne pepper in my brownies, but if Zack asked, I was just going to say they were supposed to have a spicy, slightly eye-watering, mouth-burning kick to them.

The fact that everything I was trying to cook was free of meat, dairy and eggs was making it more challenging. At first, I'd thought it was going to be straightforward. Easy-peasy. *A doddle.* I'd simply adapt my grandmother's old recipes to be Zack-friendly. How hard could it be, right? *Wrong!* Truthfully, I was on the verge of giving up and ordering a takeaway from that amazing place Zack had introduced me to on our first night in the house. However, as he was confined to the lounge, he'd see it being delivered from his view out of the big bay window. Plus, I couldn't bear the thought of his smugness if he knew I was eating yet another takeaway.

Take a breath, Lucy, I said silently, urging myself to take a leaf out of Zack's book. *Just breathe.* I closed my eyes and concentrated on my inhales and exhales, and immediately began to feel a little calmer.

But then that calming feeling was replaced by the piercing sound of the alarm screeching through the kitchen.

'Ahh!' I cried, as my hands darted to my ears.

The door swung open, and Zack ran in. He moved too fast for me to warn him that I'd spilt almond milk on the floor. It was too late. Zack fell to the floor in a bundle of limbs.

'Zack!' I shouted as I sprinted over, kneeling beside him. 'Are you OK?'

He was lying on the floor, looking up at the ceiling. 'I think so,' he replied. 'I mean, I hope so.' He grimaced, positioned an elbow to one side and leant on it as he slowly pushed himself up.

'I'm so sorry, it was the almond milk. I meant to mop it up, but I got distracted and then I completely forgot it was there...' My words faded from shouting over the alarm to complete silence as I held on to Zack's arm and helped him up. My instinctual panicked reaction was confusing, as it made me realise how much I cared about him being all right.

'I think I'll live!' Zack shouted over the alarm. As he stood, he rotated his torso and bent his back, rocking backwards and forwards slightly, stretching it out. 'Let's turn this alarm off.' He reached upwards to the white plastic system on the ceiling. He tiptoed as he pressed the buttons on the side, stopping the ear-piercing noise.

Zack and I looked at each other victoriously when it was blissful silence again, and our ears were no longer ringing. But he broke eye contact as he stopped and sniffed the air. 'Something's burning,' he announced.

'Oh shit!' I shouted, completely forgetting the reason why the alarm went off in the first place. I peered into the oven, and I immediately didn't want to open it. I turned back to Zack. 'Is the alarm definitely switched off?'

He nodded.

'And please could you open the back door?' I gestured towards the door that led to the small garden.

He nodded again and turned the handle. A breeze of fresh air wafted through the kitchen, but I knew it'd soon be overpowered by the smoke that was circling like clouds in the oven. I pulled open the oven door, and immediately used the oven gloves I was wearing to fan away the swirling smoke that flooded out. Zack and I both coughed and wafted away the grey clouds as the burning smell filled the small kitchen.

Feeling brave, I forced my protected hands forward into the heat of the oven. I was fighting the urge to close my eyes as I saw what was in the overflowing casserole dish, and I immediately wished Zack wasn't standing behind me, because he was about to see it too.

'What in the world...' Zack said, as I pulled the tray out and placed it on top of the stove. The bright orange sweet potato had turned muddy brown. It resembled a chocolate cake better than what it was supposed to be – a meat-free shepherd's pie.

'Ohhh!' I cried in frustration. 'This is not what it's supposed to look like.'

'Don't judge a book by its cover,' Zack said sympathetically. 'It might be lovely underneath the... brown bits...' He peered into the dish curiously. 'I'm sure we could try and scrape them off?'

'OK,' I whimpered.

We both grabbed two knives and stood side by side as we worked our way from one side of the dish to the other, slowly scraping off the charred remains of the dish that was my grandmother's speciality. Well, almost, given hers was made with lamb mince and this was vegan Quorn. I really wanted to impress Zack with it – just to prove a point that I could cook, not for any other reason.

'See, it looks much better already,' Zack said. Our knives met together in the middle, the metal touching.

We hesitated, and I pulled mine away first. 'I'm not going to make you eat that.' I shook my head. 'It looks terrible. You're just being polite.'

'I'm not, I promise,' Zack said. 'Come on, let's sit in here to eat.'

'What about the lounge? I want to see what you've done with it.'

'About that – do you mind if I show you tomorrow?' Zack said. 'I need a little more time on it, and I want to relax and enjoy eating our romantic meal for two tonight,' he joked.

I ignored the fluttery feeling in my stomach – obviously, he was joking. Wasn't he? 'Sure,' I said. 'But you have to promise not to judge me and my cooking skills on this meal. It isn't my best work. I'm a little rusty...'

Zack held both hands up. 'No judgement. I promise.' He cleared the mess away from the table and started rearranging it so we could sit opposite each other.

Turning around, I faced the kitchen counter again and concentrated on salvaging the meal. Maybe it would look a little more appetising if I dished it up and made it look pretty, like the way the contestants on *MasterChef* did, although I was pretty sure we didn't have any edible flowers or fancy herbs in.

Feeling a little more confident with my plan, I placed two of our nicest plates side by side. I artistically positioned a wedge of the sloppy pie on one side, saving the wayward peas that rolled around the plate. Then, I grabbed the HP Sauce and tried to do an artistic little squiggle beside the portion. But it glugged out in a runny brown mess, so it was less squiggle and more splash. It was fine though, I told myself, because I could cover it with some fresh herbs. I cut a sprig of thyme and popped it in the middle of the HP puddle. Brushing my hands together, I smiled. Much better!

Turning around, I realised I was so distracted by my plating up, à la Marcus Wareing, that I hadn't fully appreciated what Zack was doing. So, I was surprised to see how he'd transformed our shabby little kitchen table. There was a pretty tablecloth draped over it, with a cluster of candles lit in the middle. He'd popped a couple of cushions on the chairs and poured us both a glass of kombucha (now he'd given up on trying to make me drink a matcha latte, kombucha was his next project).

'Ta-da!' he said, beaming with pride.

'This is lovely.' I grinned. I picked up the plates and moved them from the countertop over to our places at the table.

'Mmm,' Zack said as he surveyed his plate. 'Delicious.'

I knew he was lying. We'd had to remove all the burnt sweet potato remnants at the top, and obviously there was no lamb in it. So it was less shepherd's pie, and more a messy gathering of melted, mushy legumes, coupled with burnt chunks of Quorn. The sprig of decorative thyme had toppled over and now lay in the brown sauce like a branch in a muddy, swampy puddle.

'Bon appetit!' I said, quickly mixing the food on my plate around with my fork, and forgetting any dreams of ever entering *MasterChef*.

I watched as Zack moved the fork from the plate to his mouth slowly. He was braver than I was, taking the first bite. He chewed and he chewed. His brows knitted together as he examined the sludge on his plate.

'Lovely,' he said eventually, before taking a speedy swig of kombucha when he swallowed.

'It can't be that bad, can it?' I said, as I watched him gargle the amber-coloured liquid around in his mouth as if it was mouthwash.

My turn. I took a forkful. I was pleasantly surprised as I chewed, tasting the flavours that were working their way around my mouth. Gosh, this wasn't half bad. It's just that... Well, it tasted a little like... I looked down at my plate again. It was filled with vegetables, so why on earth did it taste like a dessert?

'It's a little sweet?' I said, questioning Zack as if he'd have the answer.

'Yeah, a bit.' He mixed the food around his plate with his fork. 'Maybe it's supposed to taste like that?'

'But it's shepherd's pie. It's savoury.' I took another bite and there were definitely far too many dessert-like flavours for it to be a main course.

'Maybe it's the sweet potatoes?' Zack suggested kindly, but I noticed him wince as he braved another bite. 'They're called *sweet* potatoes, aren't they? So that might be why?'

I sat back and mentally pored over the ingredients and the recipe. I'd followed the recipe word for word, measure for measure – it was my grandmother's recipe, but I'd just adapted it a little. Where did I go wrong?

'Oh,' I mumbled as the answer dawned on me.

'What?' Zack wiped some brown sauce from the side of his lip.

I stood up and opened the fridge door. There it was – the almond milk. The *vanilla*-flavoured almond milk. I held up the white carton to Zack.

'I take it that's not supposed to be vanilla?' he said with an amused smile.

I shook my head.

'Oh no,' I groaned. 'I used it to make the mashed sweet potato topping.'

'Easy mistake,' Zack said. 'You know, it's not too bad once you get your head around it. It's much better if you close your eyes so you can't *see* the vegetables. Then it just feels like you're eating a dessert.' His long lashes fluttered as he adorably continued to tuck in with his eyes closed.

'It's not just that,' I continued, eyeing up the spice rack. 'I'm pretty sure I got some of these mixed up with the dessert. I think I might've put cinnamon in.' I picked up one of the tiny glass jars. Not all of them were labelled – it was one of the tasks on my to-do list for the house. 'There's a chance I might've put sugar in too...' I eyed up the identical jars of salt and sugar.

'Honestly, Lucy, it's really not that bad if you keep your eyes closed.'

'You don't have to do that.' I giggled. 'You really don't have to eat it.'

'It's so delicious. Look!' Zack opened his eyes. 'My plate is clear.' He held it up and it was true, his plate was clean and sparkly, as if food had never touched it. 'I promise you, I loved it so much, I'll even eat yours.'

'No, don't!' I said, laughing again.

He reached and pulled my plate over so it was in front of him, dramatically closing his eyes and tucking in.

'This reminds me,' he said, after swallowing a big mouthful and flinching. 'Remember the restaurant that opened years ago, where everyone ate in the dark? I bet you they served them something like this.'

I was glad Zack's eyes were closed because I couldn't help but grin as I watched him eating my terrible dinner, smiling with his eyes shut, just to make me feel better.

TWENTY-THREE

So, that dinner was a bit of a wake-up call when it came to cooking. If my grandmother had witnessed it, she would definitely have been tutting at me, arms-crossed, toe tapping the floor, while also having a good giggle.

The dessert wasn't much better than the sweet shepherd's pie-cake hybrid. My cayenne pepper-flavoured brownies melted. They were 'no bake' – which I assumed meant you could just leave them out on the table, but it transpired that you were supposed to put them in the fridge for a few hours so they could at least mould together.

But things could only improve, and today was the day I was going to see how Zack had transformed the lounge into our shared home-working space.

'Lucy!' Zack shouted from downstairs as I worked from my bedroom.

I found myself skipping gleefully down the stairs in my slippers. I began to push the big oak door open, and instinctively closed one eye in anticipation of what I was going to find on the other side.

'Surprise!' Zack shouted.

The room was a little blurry at first, through my one eye that was tentatively open. But as I took in the surroundings, I saw that the lounge had been divided into two, with rustic wooden open shelves that acted as a partition down the middle. The entire space was bright and airy, with light flooding in from the huge bay window as the morning sun shone down on the house.

Zack's side – the yoga studio – was covered in what looked like wedding veils. There were transparent sheets of different pastel colours draped across the walls, hanging from the ceiling. In the gaps between the draping sheets, quirky artwork added splashes of colour. The wooden floor was covered in colourful, beautifully embroidered rugs. Burning incense masked the smell of fresh paint.

'Sorry,' Zack said quickly. He darted across the room and blew on a smoking stick. 'That smell is the incense, it can be a bit strong.' Suddenly, he took my hand, which weirdly made my tummy flip. 'Come here,' he said, as he led me around the wooden partition to my designated space.

There was a wooden desk in front of the window. The desk looked old and grand, full of character; worn down by the people who'd sat at it for years, but expertly refurbished enough for it to be the statement piece of the room. On the walls beside it there were empty shelves, with a few plants dotted along, and a couple of picture frames filled with beautiful landscapes, swirls of blue and green where the sky met land.

'What do you think?' Zack leant against the wall with his arms folded. 'Isn't this much better than working in your bedroom? Not to mention how bad it is for your spine if you don't have a proper desk and chair in your room.'

I nodded in agreement, speechless at the effort that he'd gone to for me.

'I know you don't love being at that co-working space in the city, so at least you have somewhere here at home now too that doesn't mean sitting on your bed.'

'Thank you,' I stuttered. 'This is lovely, it's...' I took in the airy space, flooded with natural light, and the window that looked out onto the small front garden and the road outside. 'It's perfect. And I love the photos.' I gestured towards them.

'Ah yes, the Lake District. My favourite place.'

'Did you take these?' I picked one up and examined it.

'I did.' He smiled. 'I hope you don't mind me printing them for you. I know that whenever I'm stressed, if I look at them, I feel immediately more relaxed.'

'I can understand why.' I ran a finger over the glass frame. 'I've never been there, but I've always wanted to go.'

'Really?' Zack's eyes widened. 'We'll have to go – *you'll* have to go one day,' he said, correcting himself.

I fought the feeling that I didn't want him to correct himself, I wanted him to finish his original thought – using the word *we*, instead of *you*. 'And this desk...' I said.

'It's second-hand.' He grinned proudly.

Distractedly, I ran my hands over it. Every chip in the wood offered a quirk – a story of a past owner. It was even nicer than the custom-made one I'd had in my old office, which I'd had to sell when I moved out.

'Where did you find it? It's beautiful.'

'That vintage shop you recommended to me – you were right, it was full of pre-loved treasures.' We looked at each other across the space. I was so lost in appreciation for everything he'd done – it was, without a doubt, the nicest thing a man had ever done for me.

Zack opened his mouth to say something, but was interrupted by the sound of his ringtone. He pulled the phone from the pocket of his jeans, looked at the display and smiled. 'Sorry, I have to get this,' he said with a sparkle in his eye.

'Of course,' I replied.

He walked past me, out of the room, and closed the door, just as I heard him cheerfully answering the call with a laugh. I knew from the tone of his voice that he was smiling. It must've been his girlfriend – the woman he'd been spending all his spare time with. But it was none of my business. He was just my housemate.

TWENTY-FOUR

My new home office was perfect. When I was home, it was so much easier to work there than balancing my laptop on a pillow in bed. And my back was definitely thanking me, now that I had a desk and a chair to work from – not to mention all of Zack's posture techniques and the stretching breaks that he liked to remind me about at thirty-minute intervals whenever he was also working from home. Usually, his reminders were timed to coincide with an important client email I'd spent ages mulling over – only for him to interrupt me at the exact moment I'd thought of the perfect wording. Still, he meant well, and I was trying to be patient.

Zack only took one-to-one or small group sessions from his half of the room when he freelanced alongside his classes at the studio. So far, the timing had been perfect. We'd managed to work around each other's schedules, thanks to the timetable that was displayed next to our house rules poster in the kitchen. But today was the first day that we were working in the room together. I had my AirPods in to block out any noise, even though it was a meditation session, so generally pretty quiet. And the room divider meant any movement didn't distract me.

Plus, I had my back to them anyway, as my desk faced out towards the window.

The only problem today was my appearance. I looked a complete mess. I mean, most people don't *love* looking at themselves on Zoom at the best of times. But the natural light in front of me was just so *naturally light* – so unforgiving. Had I always had such dark bags under my eyes? Did I always look so tired? Not to mention the awful cold I'd been battling since moving into the house. I still couldn't stop sniffling or sneezing, but I'd become so used to it that it was starting to feel like a normal part of my life now.

'Eugh,' I groaned. To my surprise, Zack appeared at my side. He waved at me to take my AirPods out. My moan must've been louder than I thought.

'You OK?' he asked, a concerned eyebrow raised.

'Yeah, I'm just having a bit of a crisis of confidence for this meeting, I think,' I said sheepishly. I hated admitting vulnerability, especially when it came to work.

'Why? Big client?' He leant against the wall next to me.

'My biggest. Plus, I look terrible.'

'You definitely don't,' he said kindly, making me blush. I would've placed a confident bet that Zack Bamford wasn't used to insecure girls. He probably only dated secure women, with endless body confidence, buckets of self-esteem and solely zen mindsets.

'I feel it.' I shrugged, clocking my reflection in the Zoom camera.

'I for one definitely don't think you have any reason to. But you know that you can put a filter on, don't you? It's like a "touch-up" setting on the camera.'

'I didn't have you down as a tech-whizz.' I leant back in the comfy old leather armchair.

'I'm definitely not.' Zack chuckled. 'In fact, I'm terrible. But the studio once went through a period of teaching classes for people at home, so they gave us a bit of a crash course. I used the setting whenever I felt a bit tired. Want to see?'

'Sure,' I said, wheeling my chair away from the desk to give him room.

'Hmm,' he mumbled, scratching his head. His curls were still damp from his shower, and they left little wet patches on his blue T-shirt. 'I hope I can remember how to do it. It's been a while...'

As he leant over the computer, clicking and tapping, I gazed out at the view from the window. The front garden was still a work in progress, with its overgrown lawn and persistent weeds. But I knew what it could look like when we finally got round to reviving it to its former glory – the way my grandmother once had it – and I was so excited for when that day finally arrived.

'What time's your meeting?' Zack asked next to me.

I tapped the screen of my phone. 'It's at 10 a.m.,' I confirmed. 'Ten minutes, but I need to log on in five.'

Zack said nothing, just clicked the mouse a little quicker and jabbed the letters on the keyboard more urgently than before.

'Why?' I asked nervously.

'No reason, just give me a minute,' he said uneasily.

'Why?' I demanded, and I scooted from my place to the side of the desk. I peered closely to look at the monitor, but he pulled it around, out of my way.

'Hey!' I shouted.

'Just give me a minute, Clark,' Zack repeated impatiently, as he continued prodding the keyboard, punching the keys.

I started to panic. What had he done? This meeting was really important. It was with the Dale Street Developments marketing team to talk about the different tenders we could put the new buildings forward for. My work with them was still early days, so I was proving myself to the whole team – apart from Josh, who was being as encouraging and charming as ever.

But I knew I had to fight for my place, to prove I could handle such a big project as an independent contractor.

I checked the time again. 'Zack, I need to log on!' I grumbled. I swung the monitor back around to me. And on the screen was my face. My face, but inside a... hot dog. A *dancing* hot dog. 'What the...'

'I'm sorry,' Zack said behind me, shaking his head. 'I don't know how to turn it off.'

'I'm a sausage, Zack! I'm a dancing sausage!'

Zack bit his lip, his mouth fighting against a smile.

'It's not funny,' I wailed. I had one minute to log on – in human form, not as a heavily processed piece of meat, doing some sort of samba dance.

'It is *kind of* funny.' Zack chuckled.

'You must know how to turn it off,' I murmured, my eyes desperately scanning the settings. 'What did you press? How did you turn it on?'

'It was here in the filters, but it's as though it's completely frozen.' Zack pointed. 'It could be worse—'

'How, Zack? How could it be worse?' I barked.

'There are loads of filters – you could've been a skiing carrot, or a singing cat, or—'

'Argh!' I garbled. I was hitting the keys at random, clicking on anything that might fix it.

'Here, let me try again.' Zack leant over me.

'No, you'll make it worse, *again*,' I snapped, batting him away.

'I'm sorry, Lucy, I was only trying to help.' Zack looked hurt.

'Well, you didn't, OK? Please just leave me alone.'

Zack sloped away and I felt a pang of guilt, but it was OK for him, wasn't it? His whole life was fun and games. It wouldn't matter if he taught a class through a food filter; in fact, his adoring fans would've probably found it hilarious! But it was different for me. With just one wrong step, I could've lost everything I'd fought for. Again.

I logged on to the call and heard Zack quietly close the door behind him as I apologised for my appearance, my eyes darting with embarrassment as my panicked appearance inside the hot dog looked back at me.

The temptation to make my coffee an Irish one was huge after that terrible meeting. How would my biggest client take me seriously if I was trying to have critical conversations about brand awareness, competitive tenders and market share, with my face inside a dancing sausage?

Shaking my head, I told myself it was done now. I couldn't change anything; there was no point dwelling. Some of them saw the funny side, and at least Josh wasn't in the meeting. I finished making my coffee and plodded defeatedly back to my desk. Zack's class was starting soon, so I had to stay on my side of the partition for the next hour. I checked my calendar again. It was Thursday, which meant that afterwards, I'd be heading to my favourite weekly appointment.

I popped my AirPods back in my ears and turned to the report I was working on. It was complex, for a demanding client, and it required my full concentration. I clicked my favourite working playlist on Spotify, stretched out my tired hands, and powered through the endless rows of numbers.

That was, until Zack's face to the side of me made me jump.

'Hey,' he said, as I took my earbuds out. 'I'm sorry to disturb you while you're working.' His tone was sheepish after the filter incident earlier. 'But would you mind typing a little quieter?'

'What?'

'Yeah, I'm sorry, I don't mean to be awkward.' He shuffled uncomfortably. 'It's just you're quite an aggressive typer and it's all I can hear. I don't want it to put my students off when they arrive.'

'An aggressive typer?' I said in shock. 'That's a new one.'

'You just really *jab*.' He did an impression, pointing his fingers through the air and making a face I did not appreciate.

'I'm efficient,' I said. 'I type quickly. I touch-type.' *Unlike you*, I added silently – Zack was the slowest typer I'd ever seen. Carefully and slowly pressing each button one by one.

'If you could be a teeny bit less *efficient*, just for the next hour, I'd really appreciate it.' He smiled sweetly, and I was sure I could detect a hint of sarcasm.

'Fine,' I said, turning back to my screen.

'And another thing,' Zack said gently, to my sigh. 'Any chance you could sniff a little less?'

'*Sniff?*' I said indignantly. 'Are you serious? Next thing you're going to ask me to breathe quieter.'

'Now you mention it...' Zack swayed his head to one side.

'Urgh.' I huffed and held a hand out to stop him nagging me any further. 'Fine, I will watch the volume of my typing and my sniffing and my breathing, and my general existence. OK?'

'Thank you,' he said sweetly again, drawing his hands to a prayer position and bowing forwards, like he always did at the start and end of a class.

I turned my attention back to my report, switching the volume of the music playing in my AirPods up as I heard Zack's class shuffle inside. The sound of jackets unzipping and trainers being yanked off was only just audible over the hushed musical tones.

Every moment that I thought I was typing *aggressively*, I made a conscious effort to try and slow down. And every time I went to sniff, I'd rub my nose with a tissue instead. This damn cold was one of the reasons for the hot dog filter fiasco, anyway. My nose looked even more inflamed in the harsh light of day, no matter how much concealer I used.

Now wasn't the time for the report, I decided huffily; I was feeling too riled and unsettled. I'd deal with it later. Instead, I opened up WhatsApp. I wasn't sure what the time difference was in Thailand. But to my relief, there was a little green button next to Katie's profile picture – she was online. Finally, someone I could openly vent to.

I clicked the settings so that I could type to her and listen to her voice note replies (Katie could never resist a voice note), while scrolling through my favourite trashy celebrity gossip news site and trying to regain my composure.

Lucy: How's the honeymoon?

Katie: Just terrible. Totally not living my best life, I swear.

A selfie of Katie sunbathing with a cocktail in one hand and a book in the other filled the screen.

Lucy: Oh, stop it. Is it bad I now want to get married just for the honeymoon?

Katie: You never know... it might be you and Zack travelling around the world together. They have great yoga studios here in Koh Samui. Wink wink.

Lucy: OMG, don't even joke about that. Living with him is hard enough, never mind travelling around the world together. He's driving me insane. It's making me question whether it's worth being back in my beloved house. Can I please move back in with you?

Katie: That would be rather difficult, given we've sold the flat and our new house is still a building site. Speaking of which, did you check in with the builders?

Lucy: Yes, it's all going swimmingly. I'm just waiting for the bespoke pieces to be delivered, and I need to catch up with the joiner about a few bits. But apart from that it's all fine. The tradespeople all seem to be getting on with it and I think the architect is keeping an eye on things.

Katie: YAY! I can't wait to see your genius vision come to life. So anyway, why is Hot Hippy so bad? What's he done now?

Lucy: Eugh, just our shared living space has now expanded to a shared working space too. Among a long, long list of many other very annoying things. We're just too different.

Katie: I bet he isn't as bad as you say he is – you're always so harsh, babe! Any more funny stories about his sex life? Aren't you tempted to have a go on the sex swing?

Lucy: No, my house rules managed to put a stop to that, thank goodness. And never mind HIS overly active sex life – I have a date tonight!

Katie: A date? Oh my god, finally! Who with? Is it after your regular Thursday engagement? Tell me everything...

'Lucy?'

I jumped at Zack's voice beside me unexpectedly, while I was lost in a guilty blur of celebrity gossip and a much-needed catch-up/venting session with Katie.

'Aren't you teaching your class?' I whispered, taking my AirPods out of my ears.

'Trying to,' Zack said, and I noticed his jaw was clenched, his eyes intense.

'What's the matter?' I asked, puzzled.

'We can hear you.'

'I'm trying to type quietly, OK? And I'm not even sniffing. I've taken an antihistamine, so I'm all bunged up and—'

'No,' Zack interrupted. 'We can hear your conversation with your friend.'

'What? What friend?'

'The friend you're talking to – the one you're offloading to about me...'

I looked from Zack to my screen, and back to Zack again.

'I thought it was hooked up to my headphones.'

'Well, it isn't.' He huffed impatiently. 'It's coming out of the laptop speakers. *Very* loudly.'

'Oh.' I felt my cheeks flush. I'd got used to that muffled, bunged-up sensation in my ears, thanks to this darn cold. Part of my ranting to Katie was so that I wouldn't take it out on Zack. I didn't necessarily want him to *know* my angry frustrations.

'Mm-hmm,' Zack mumbled. 'Perhaps you could check the settings?'

'Don't worry, I'll go and work up in my room.' I yanked the wire from my laptop and pushed the screen down. I needed privacy, I needed to be able to type and sniff without him breathing down my neck. But I also felt embarrassed that he'd heard my not-so private rants to Katie.

'Enjoy your date tonight,' Zack whispered, so quietly I hardly heard him. I wasn't even sure he'd said it or if I'd imagined it, as I shuffled past him. The glares of Zack's adoring students/fans followed me as I tiptoed around the sea of yoga mats, where they were all gathered, cross-legged and waiting for their meditation master to return.

TWENTY-FIVE

The date that night was a failure, as they always were whenever I pointlessly made time for one. It wasn't quite the same level as the man who wanted to share an Uber ride, only for him to be dropped off outside a lap dancing bar. Or the guy who dumped me while I was in the toilet, with a note on the back of the receipt for the evening I'd paid for.

The weirdest part, however, was the realisation that *I* was the disappointing half of this date. That the entire time we sat together, as I tapped my fingers on the table and stared at the passing minutes on the clock, I was aware of my mind wandering to how I could've been spending my time instead. I could've been at home watching Netflix or catching up on work. *Or hanging out with Zack* – the thought popped into my head, completely random and unwanted.

Besides, Zack would probably have been out, anyway. Off somewhere with his girlfriend. And on the bright side, the time away from the house gave my terrible cold a brief reprieve, at least. It was always worse in the house, and I was starting to wonder whether there might be something wrong there. Hopefully nothing serious, like asbestos. I made a mental note to google how to check for anything like that, just in case.

The drive back from the city centre to the house was a beautiful route, passing by the magnificent buildings that lined the Georgian Quarter. The dull yellow, soft glow of lamps and fairy lights inside the lounge framed the big old windows of our house as I parked. It looked so pretty from the outside. I couldn't stop the smile creeping over my face as I got out of the car, opened the little gate, and walked through the small, still shabby, front garden. Even if it was a bit up and down with Zack and me, at least I had my home – and not just that, it was the most special house I'd ever known.

The old front door creaked open as I put the key into the lock. There was quiet music coming from the kitchen, but it wasn't the gentle tones that grabbed my attention. It was the sounds of fumbling and the muted mumbles of, 'Shit, shit, shit.'

Feeling puzzled, I put one foot precariously in front of the other and slowly tiptoed towards the kitchen.

'I'm home!' I shouted in warning.

'I... I thought you were out for the night,' Zack stammered from behind the kitchen door.

'I came home early,' I answered. My curiosity was killing me. 'I'm coming in.'

Full of anticipation, I put my head around the door as I opened it.

Zack was standing there, looking disappointingly normal for someone who was clearly up to something, but there was no doubt he looked flustered. 'Hey,' he said with a wave. 'Hello. Good evening,' he stuttered.

'*Good evening?*' I giggled. 'How retro of you.' I took another step into the kitchen and Zack's eyes widened as I moved closer.

'What? What are you up to?' I said, looking around. I peeked behind the door. Was he hiding his girlfriend? Were they into some sort of weird kitchen sex fetish? Did they use *utensils*? I shuddered, remembering his tantric taunting at the bank, the sex swing in his bedroom, and the constant guttural grunting noises that haunted my sleep before I'd imposed the rules. A weird kitchen fetish wasn't totally impossible.

'I'm not doing anything,' Zack said, his eyes wide with innocence, his arms confidently open, as if he was a man with nothing to hide.

I squinted at him, but he was giving away no clues as to his night-time activities. 'Fine,' I relented, but with a plan, and hoping my cunning smile wasn't so obvious that I'd give it away. 'Want to watch a movie?'

'Not right now... soon though,' he said sketchily.

'It's OK, take your time, I'll just see you in the snug when you're ready?'

'Sure.' He nodded. 'I'll be right there.'

Hurrah! He was falling for it. My plan was working.

I headed out of the door, but instead of going into the snug, I waited outside the kitchen. The side of my face was pushed up against the door as I listened carefully, wishing I'd swiped a glass to put against my ear so I could hear better.

'You're such a good girl,' I heard Zack whisper.

Gross! If any man ever called me a *good girl* I think I'd be sick in my mouth.

'You're so beautiful,' he murmured, and my stomach did a weird spin.

'I love you so much,' he said. My heart flipped unexpectedly. Right, that was it. I'd have to enforce the rule he was breaking: *Clear overnight guests with each other before they stay.* I couldn't have some strange woman making herself at home in my house – in *my* kitchen – without meeting her. No, I was being perfectly reasonable.

'Ah-ha!' I shouted victoriously as I swung the door open again.

Zack's mouth dropped open as he saw me. And my face

mirrored his as I saw what was in his lap. Not a woman, but a tiny, fluffy dog. It made a little *yarp* sound – somewhere between a bark and a yawn – as I stood in the doorway, before it crawled out from Zack's lap, stretched into a downward dog, and trundled lazily over to me, its tail wagging from side to side.

'A dog?' I stumbled over my words. 'What on earth is a dog doing here?' I tried to be stern, but my heart melted as it balanced on its back legs, planting two tiny paws on my thighs, and looked up at me. Its little mouth was panting, making it look like it was smiling, and its big, puppy-dog eyes were unwavering in its friendly gaze.

'She's, erm, she's...' Zack nervously pushed a hand through his mop of curls.

'What?' I shook my head at him. Why did he take so long to get his words out? Why did he do everything so slowly? 'Did you find her on the street? Is she a stray?'

'She's mine,' Zack said eventually, resting his hands on his knees.

'She's what?' I said in astonishment. 'You've never said you have a... a – *achoo!*' I let out a huge sneeze, which gave the poor little dog a fright, and she jumped up at my legs again to make sure I was OK. I took a tissue out of my pocket, and as I rubbed my stinging nose, everything fell into place.

'Oh my God,' I said. I held the snotty tissue up as if it was a fount of knowledge – as if it held the answer to everything. 'You.' I pointed to him. 'Her.' I pointed to the pooch, who wagged her tail with glee. '*She's* the reason why I can't stop sneezing! *She's* why my nose is always running. *She's* why I thought I had a dangerous mega-cold that was going to turn into some sort of imminent death virus!'

'Imminent death virus?' Zack said quizzically. 'Do you always have to be so dramatic?'

'That's not the point!' I said. 'That is not the point, and you know it.' I felt like we were back in teacher and naughty pupil mode, the standard role-play of our relationship. 'How could you not mention this? Especially when you knew what effect it was having on me?'

'I'm so sorry, Luce,' Zack said. The dog, sensing the atmosphere, curled back into her position, in the safe cocoon of Zack's crossed legs. 'Honestly, I am. When we first moved in together, I had no idea you were allergic to dogs, otherwise I would never have brought her here, I promise.'

'But you did keep her here,' I said, in a contemptuous tone that I wasn't proud of, but that I couldn't stop. 'And you still didn't tell me when you knew what a bad reaction I was having – *achoo*!' I sneezed again and felt the familiar stream of my nose, and my relentlessly itching eyes.

'I really am sorry.' Zack winced. The little dog rested her head on his knee and gazed at me pleadingly. 'The first time she stayed over, you were away on a work trip. Then, when you started sneezing all the time, I thought there was a chance you were allergic, so I had friends look after her, or when they couldn't, I kept her hidden in my room.'

'Hang on,' I interrupted. 'Do you mean to say she's been living here this whole time?'

Zack nodded and I swore she did too. 'Well, not all the time, but yeah, a lot,' he said.

'In your bedroom?' I asked.

They nodded again.

'I knew there was something sketchy going on!' I cried, still feeling victorious from catching him out, but equally worried about my dog allergy and how it was going to manifest. Hopefully my face wasn't going to swell, or my throat close. I coughed to clear it, just in case.

'She's my family's dog,' Zack said reservedly. 'It's a bit complicated...' He hesitated. 'Basically, I share custody of her, and she's always dropped off with me sporadically...' His words tailed off again. 'I tried putting her in kennels for a night, but she was absolutely terrified. She has separation anxiety, you see.' He looked at the pooch adoringly.

'Separation anxiety? That can't be a real thing.'

'It is, I swear!' Zack said, looking to the dog for silent agreement.

He turned back to face me again. 'Honestly, I am genuinely so sorry, Lucy. I hoped my natural remedies would help with your allergies. I mean, give them time – they still might.'

'Hmph,' I grunted. 'What's her name, anyway?' I asked.

'She's called Kat,' he said with a bright grin, while tickling her under her chin.

'Kat.' I scowled. 'Bit of a cruel name for a dog.'

'Family humour.' Zack rolled his eyes with amusement. 'But she's also named after Katniss Everdeen. Big *Hunger Games* fan.'

'Ah,' I nodded.

'I mean, I am. Not the dog. Although she does have a penchant for action movies,' he confirmed light-heartedly. He looked down at Kat lovingly, to which the little dog rolled over, and he gave her a big tummy rub while she wagged her tail enthusiastically in approval.

'She can't stay here, Zack.'

'Are you sure? But I don't know what will happen to her otherwise,' Zack said, his eyes filling with sadness. 'It's not like we're renting, and we're not allowed dogs. We own the house together.'

'Exactly,' I agreed impatiently. 'We own the house together, you and me, and you didn't think to ask me about this? To see whether I wanted a dog?'

'Every time I tried to speak to you about it, you brushed me off and said you were too busy with work.' Zack's sad eyes remained fixated on the bundle of fur.

'How do you even know if I like dogs?' I tried to be firm, but I couldn't stop myself from going all gooey-eyed at her gorgeous eyes, fluffy eyebrows and smile-like panting mouth. *No, don't make eye contact with the dog, Lucy,* I instructed myself. *Don't be taken in by her adorable little face. Be strong.*

'Who doesn't like dogs?' Zack wrinkled his nose. 'To be honest, that would've been a bit of a deal-breaker for us living together, anyway. Never trust somebody who doesn't like dogs.' He tapped his nose knowingly, and Kat wagged her tail in agreement.

'Fine.' I rolled my eyes. I wasn't going to win this when they were both ganging up on me, looking all cute in their tangled cuddling position on the kitchen floor. 'But only if your allergy remedies work.' I offered a sniff in justification. It was true; it wasn't as if I was making it up. And even if – *if* – I wanted her to stay with us, I really missed life without constant sneezes, a streaming nose and itchy eyes.

'That's totally fair,' Zack said, tickling Kat behind her floppy ears. 'Thank you, Lucy, seriously.' Kat's tail was brushing the tiles so enthusiastically, it was going to save us from cleaning the kitchen floor. 'You're the best,' he added quietly, and for a second, I wasn't sure if he was talking to me or to Kat. Surely it was to Kat? I told myself it was to Kat, it must've been.

'I'm guessing your date didn't go so well then, if you're home early?' Zack didn't make eye contact with me, instead rubbing Kat's tummy again as she rolled around on the floor.

'It wasn't great,' I said, which was the understatement of the century.

'I know what will cheer you up,' Zack announced, jumping to his feet, with Kat following his long legs as he darted out of the room. He reappeared again, holding a board game.

'Scrabble?' I asked, an eyebrow raised. 'That's seen better days.' I took in the battered box, torn at the edges, the once-bright colours faded.

'I found it in the loft.'

'Oh,' I said, taken aback. 'Wow. That might've been my

grandmother's.' I remembered playing board games with her, usually around Christmas time when my parents, if they were in the UK, had done their duty with me and headed off to a cocktail party with their friends, leaving me to eat Quality Street, watch all the festive specials on TV, and play board games with my nana. 'We should have a look up there tomorrow, see what else there is.'

'Definitely.' Zack beamed. 'Fancy a game now? And maybe a glass of wine?'

'Sure.' I smiled, as Zack reached for the glasses. He opened a Malbec and it glugged messily into the glasses, releasing a deliciously fruity and spicy aroma. One glass for me, and one glass for him. It wasn't how I'd expected to spend my evening, but I wasn't complaining.

TWENTY-SIX

Naturally, I thrashed Zack at Scrabble. Usually, I'd find someone who could only conjure up four-letter words an instant turn-off, a dating deal-breaker, even. But there was something so adorable about him, the way his brows furrowed as he concentrated on the letters, sighing as he shuffled them around. He'd catch me looking at him every now and again, and our eyes would meet over the board while my score topped two hundred and his was a third of it. We polished off the wine while we bartered over whether certain words were actually words – they weren't most of the time when they were Zack's, but I surprised (and frustrated) him with my Scrabble know-how, especially the easy-win ones that didn't sound like real words (*xi* provoked a particularly passionate argument between the two of us).

Kat was happily snoozing at our feet, and every now and again she'd roll over to expose her tummy, so I would rub it with my foot, and Zack would have the same idea. Our accidental footsie would end abruptly with apologies to each other and pulling our legs back under our chairs. Although I was a little sceptical, Zack's natural remedies had started to take the edge off my allergies to Kat. And my initial anger faded a little at the relief that I finally knew what was causing them.

The grunting that had occasionally peppered my sleep ever since Zack and I moved in together woke me up again that following morning after our Scrabble session. I assumed he'd sneakily invited his secret girlfriend to stay for a late-night sleepover and was again feeling frustrated at his blatant disregard for our house rules.

In a repeat of last night, when I arrived home and knew something wasn't right, I followed my instinct to find out the truth. I followed it right to his bedroom, where I stood in front of the door, in my fluffy pink dressing gown and matching slippers.

I knocked and the grunting stopped.

'Yeah?' Zack said breathlessly from the other side.

'Just wanted to see if you fancied a tea or a coffee?' I offered innocently.

'Erm...' Zack mumbled behind the door. 'I'm just on the swing, come in.'

What? Come in? While they were on his sex swing together? Was he kidding?

'I think I'm OK, thanks,' I answered nervously.

'Come in, Luce!' Zack shouted breathlessly again. 'It's great!'

I cringed. 'Are you on your own?' I asked timidly and curiously.

'Of course not!'

God, this was definitely getting weird. I could've maybe turned a blind eye to his tantric enthusiasm and his sex swing, but was he into some sort of strange voyeurism too? Did he and his equally adventurous partner like it when people watched them on it? This was all getting a bit too *Fifty Shades* for me.

'It's not really the sort of thing I'm into,' I said.

'You won't know unless you try!'

Ew. I was all for doing what you want – live and let live, and all that – but this was going too far.

Before I could answer that I really didn't want to try swinging on a swing, or swinging otherwise, Zack opened the door. He was bare-chested and wearing his tiny yoga shorts that only just covered his modesty, even though I'd seen it all (briefly) before, thanks to the naked kitchen incident.

'Hey,' he said, wiping the beads of sweat from his forehead.

'Hey,' I said nervously.

Kat tootled over, brushing herself against my feet. 'Good morning, beautiful girl,' I said as I bent down to stroke her. I snuck a peek into the bedroom. I expected to catch sight of his beautiful, impressively flexible girlfriend, but she wasn't there. However, there was a big, framed photograph of the two of them in pride of place on his wall. But the room itself was surprisingly empty, just the swing swaying gently from the breeze of the open window.

'I thought you said you weren't on your own?' I asked, pretending not to care.

'I'm not, Kat's here.' He did a 'duh' face, which was pretty cute when it was combined with his half-asleep face.

'What were you doing? I know you've denied it, but I could hear that grunting noise again, which is fine, but I just wanted to let you know I could hear it...' I rambled.

He stood in the doorway watching me with an amused grin as I wittered on.

'I was on my swing, like I said,' Zack answered.

'Mm-hmm,' I mumbled.

'My *aerial yoga swing*,' he confirmed.

'Oh,' I said, feeling a bit silly. 'I see.' I breathed a subtle sigh of relief – phew, not a sex swing, after all!

'Want to give it a go?' He opened the door wider so I could get a closer look at it.

'It's all right, I'll pass, thanks.'

'I'm sure we can bend the rules,' he said flirtily.

What rule did he mean? There was only one related to the bedroom and that was number one: *Nakedness reserved for the bedroom only.*

'Erm.' I shuffled from one foot to the other. My heartbeat felt like it had moved from my chest to my cheeks, which I was sure that if I looked in the mirror would be tinted pink.

'*Rule number six: No going into each other's rooms,*' Zack said, matter-of-factly.

'Of course.' I nodded profusely, stumbling over my words, and hoping my physical reaction wasn't too noticeable.

'Why? What did you think I meant?' Zack asked innocently, but with an undeniable sparkle in his eye.

'Nothing, nothing. Anyway. Yes. No,' I garbled. 'Best to keep the rules in play. They're rules for a reason.' I tightened the belt of my dressing gown. 'So, did you fancy a tea or a coffee?'

———

At least the sex swing (or aerial yoga swing) mystery – and with it, the mysterious grunting – had been solved.

It was Saturday and I had set the day aside to finally finish the report I'd been working on. But as procrastination was my best friend when it came to numbers and statistics, I decided instead that I'd update mine and Zack's new shared calendar.

After 'Zoom-gate', we'd concluded that sharing the studio space at the same time wasn't the best idea. So, at least if we could essentially 'book' the times, then we could each use it on our own. It would work fine, really, because I could either go to the co-working space in the city centre or one of my favourite coffee shops (or even just my bedroom) if he needed it for a free-lance class. And he'd make himself scarce if I needed it for work. Usually that would mean spending the whole day or night away, something he was still doing at least once a week.

I clicked onto the calendar – organised as pink for me and 'calming ocean blue' for him (his description, when I asked him what colour he'd like it to be). I wasn't being nosy, looking through everything he was doing, because it was a shared space. If he didn't want to put it there, then he didn't have to; he knew I had access to it. The clue was in the name – *shared* calendar, I reassured myself. I wasn't doing anything wrong.

Chewing my thumbnail, I clicked through the weeks. Mine were boring – all work meetings, project deadlines and over-seeing Katie's house interiors. And of course, my Thursday appointments. Then, I looked at Zack's. Every Tuesday and Wednesday, and alternate weekends, were blocked out with the name Molly. That explained where he went on the days that I didn't see him, and who he was always texting and calling. My feelings were torn. I was glad I finally knew that he had a girl-friend, but I didn't understand why he hadn't told me, or talked about her, or why he acted so strange about it.

I clicked on and on, before going back to this month and the remaining days left in the calendar. *Hang on.* What did that weekend say? I peered closer to the screen to read it properly. It was in two weeks' time. Saturday and Sunday were blocked out. It said 'Lake District – Venue Visit'. A *venue visit*? A venue for what? Zack wasn't getting *married*, was he? He'd never mentioned officially being with someone, not to mention *engaged*. And to be honest, I didn't have him down as the marrying type. When it came to relationships, he'd always said he didn't believe in 'traditional conventions of marital status'. But a venue visit? In the Lake District, of all places? It was probably the most romantic place in the country; surely that meant something.

Shaking myself back to reality, I pushed the laptop lid down and sat back in my seat. Why did I care, anyway? We were just housemates.

TWENTY-SEVEN

I'd finished pitching my final vision for the Dale Street Developments offices to the team. There were no ping-pong tables, slides or ball pits, thankfully. It was an airy space, where light flooded in from the windows, drawing attention to the natural materials that separated the different work zones. The entire office was a beautiful combination of classic Scandinavian with mid-century touches – perfectly complementing the building's heritage, and hitting the brief of an inspiring workspace they could be proud of.

Standing back from the boardroom table, I smoothed down my suit and looked around at the faces in front of me. At the end of the table, Josh was sitting back in his chair. His outstretched palms were resting on the back of his dark hair, which was tousled perfectly into place with hair gel. He looked around and then sat forward, resting against the table. His eyes met mine and I felt my cheeks redden. I told myself it was nerves rather than anything else. It was as though somebody had picked up a remote and pressed pause for the entire room. Until Josh lifted his hands and slowly started to clap. And the whole room copied him.

'Oh wow, thank you,' I whispered, self-consciously tucking a loose curl behind my ear.

Josh stood up as he carried on clapping and walked closer towards me.

'This is amazing, Lucy. This is exactly what we wanted.' He was standing so close to me that I could smell the spice and leather of his cologne.

'Thanks. I just wanted to get it right.' I stuttered over my words. This was it. All of my hard work was finally paying off. I'd given every waking hour to this design, and they liked it.

'You've more than got it right.' He smiled widely and held our eye contact, before he turned back to address the boardroom. 'Thanks, everyone,' he said. 'What a great start to the day! You can all head back to your desks now.'

The noises of the staff members closing their laptops and gathering their belongings peppered the room. I smiled and nodded at the ones who told me what a great job I'd done before they got back to work. Then the room was silent, but the atmosphere was charged.

'Wow,' Josh said. 'Honestly, you've well and truly blown me away – blown us all away, I should say.'

I shrugged modestly, but inside I was dancing.

'So was it another Taylor Swift pep talk today? Or do you also branch out to other pop singers?' Josh flashed a mischievous grin. 'A bit of Ariana Grande, perhaps? Some Katy Perry?'

'Stop it,' I said, covering my eyes as I cringed at the memory. 'I can't believe you heard me! Why on earth were you in there? I thought the toilets were empty.'

'It's the only place I can get peace and quiet.' He grinned. 'Where I'm not being pulled in for meetings every ten minutes, or being yelled at by my assistant to answer an urgent call. It's quite handy that the place is a building site, and half the toilets are taped off – nobody would ever know.'

'I certainly didn't,' I said with a chuckle. At least he didn't

see my power poses that went with my melodic pep talk.
Unless, of course, he was also peeping through a gap and
watching me.

'This might be inappropriate,' he said, his eyes sparkling,
'but I would really love to take you out to celebrate, if you
would like to?' It was a question, but he said it with a level of
confidence that told me he rarely heard a no to that
invitation.

I was torn as I considered my reply. The adrenaline was still
rushing through my body after the success of the presentation.
And there was no doubt Josh ticked a lot of boxes – handsome,
successful, ambitious and charming. But it would be unprofessional to agree to a date with a client, and there was no way I
was going to potentially jeopardise what I'd worked my bottom
off to build for my business again.

'That does sound wonderful,' I said, and the start of a smile
crept slowly over his mouth. 'But I'm going to have to say no,
I'm afraid.'

Josh's smile faltered. He crossed his arms over his chest,
before pushing his hands into his pockets. 'I see. May I ask
why?' He was rocking subtly backwards and forwards on his
heels and toes.

'I'd rather keep it professional,' I said, with an apologetic
smile that I hoped conveyed my internal wish that I could take
him up on his offer.

Josh pursed his lips and rubbed his chin. He definitely
wasn't used to the word 'no'. 'OK,' he said eventually. 'Keeping
it professional, I understand.'

'Thanks.' I nodded. 'I'm glad you do. I mean, if things were
different...'

'Say no more.' Josh nodded too, with a hint of a smile. 'Message received.'

I picked up my laptop and unplugged it from the big screen
in the boardroom, just so I had something to do with my hands,

and something to distract myself from the way Josh was looking at me.

'Great job again today,' Josh said as he walked towards the boardroom door. 'You're surpassing my expectations in every way.' He turned around and grinned before pushing the door open. The scent of his expensive cologne lingered in the room after he left. It was definitely the right decision. Or was it?

———

'I told you you'd smash it,' Katie said through the speaker of my phone. She was the first person I'd called after my presentation. Even though, weirdly, the idea to call Zack had flashed across my brain, just like all my thoughts of Zack that worked their way inside my mind – they were always uninvited and confusing.

'I know you did, thank you,' I replied as I walked down the road, away from the Dale Street Developments headquarters. I tried to ignore that she'd now moved on from Thailand on her globe-trotting adventure, and was living it up in sunny Bali. Meanwhile, it had just started to rain on a grey, windy day in Liverpool, and I wrapped my jacket around myself as I felt the chill of the breeze. Still, I loved the city, come rain or shine.

'Of course! I knew you'd get back on your feet again,' Katie said proudly.

'It does feel like everything is going well. A little too well, maybe.'

'Oh, don't be so bloody cynical, Lucy! Things can go well in life, you know. Stop thinking of the next thing to worry about.'

'I know, I know.' I rolled my eyes. She knew me better than I knew myself.

'How's the honeymoon, anyway? How's Bali?'

'Fine.'

'*Just* fine? Bloomin' heck, Katie. Fancy swapping places with me?'

'How's my house coming along?' Katie cut me off. 'Did the architect give you the new floor plans?'

'Certainly did.' I smiled. Of all the design projects I'd worked on, Katie's house was already cementing itself as one of my favourites. The best projects are when you really understand the client, and I knew Katie as if she was my sister.

'Good. I have that to look forward to at least.'

'What do you mean?'

'Anyway, tell me what's new with you,' Katie interrupted. 'Aside from smashing your pitch, of course. How's the house? How's Zack?'

'The house is great. Zack is...' How to describe Zack? 'Zack is Zack.'

'At least it's all working out OK though.' I heard Katie sip the dregs of her margarita. 'Any news on the romance front?'

'Yes, in fact. I think my boss – well, my client – just kind of... asked me out?' I wrinkled my nose as I said the words. It sounded a lot sleazier saying it out loud.

'Ooh, Josh? The super sexy CEO?'

'Yep,' I mumbled into the phone as I walked down Castle Street.

'And what did you say?'

'No, of course! How unprofessional would that be?' I shook my head even though she couldn't see me. 'Besides, imagine if it all went wrong. I can't lose them as a client, they're my biggest one.'

'Imagine if it went right though?' Katie, the old romantic, pleaded. 'What's he like? Apart from being the super sexy CEO, obviously.'

'He's... well, he's perfect, really. On paper, at least. He's got this corporate Liam Hemsworth sort of look going on.'

'Ooh, stop!' Katie said teasingly.

'He's charming, he's successful, he's ambitious, he's nice to his staff...'

'Well, why on earth did you say no?'

'Didn't you hear me? He's my boss!'

'He's not really though, is he? He's your client, not your boss.'

'Still...'

'If you want my expert opinion—'

'You're just going to give it to me anyway, aren't you?' I interrupted her.

'Obviously. But I know you. I know you well...' Katie hesitated. 'And I think you're just looking for an excuse to say no.'

Dammit. Again. Katie did know me well. I turned the corner and clocked that I was close to Zack's yoga studio. Perhaps I'd check in on him and see if he fancied grabbing a coffee. We were friends, kind of. Nothing unusual about friends getting a coffee together, is there?

Rounding the corner with a sudden skip in my step, I spotted the studio as the busy crowds along the street parted ways. Weirdly, I felt my stomach flutter as I saw Zack standing outside, leaning up against the wall. He was wearing his favourite khaki beanie hat and earphones. I was just about to shout and wave, when a pretty blonde woman walked up to him. It was the same girl who was in the framed photograph hanging on Zack's wall, and on his phone wallpaper. Her legs were clad in pastel yoga leggings with a baggy hoodie, and her platinum hair was almost completely covered by a matching beanie. His face lit up as he saw her, his smile stretching the dimples in his cheeks. I bit my lip as I watched them hug and then walk down the street together, his arm comfortably across her shoulders.

'Hello? Lucy?' I was shaken back to the present moment, a lesson I'd learnt, ironically, from the studio in front of me. I heard Katie shouting down the phone, which had floated away from my right ear without me even noticing.

'Sorry, I'm here,' I said, ignoring the quiver in my voice.

'Did you hear what I said? Why don't you call Josh and tell him you've changed your mind?'

'Do you know what?' I replied, ignoring my thumping heart. 'I think I will.'

TWENTY-EIGHT

Josh's reaction wasn't quite what I expected when I told him I'd changed my mind about the date. I'd even go so far as to say it was a rejection. He said he agreed with my initial answer, that we should keep things professional. Instead of the cocktail bar I'd suggested when I texted him, he asked that I meet him at the office after work instead, as he wanted to talk to me about the project again.

Pacing my bedroom, I reassured myself everything was fine. *But what if he's going to fire me?* I couldn't shake off the thought that kept popping into my head. Kat was sitting on my bed, and her big eyes followed me from left to right as I stalked up and down.

It was as though she was a furry little spy for Zack. She'd watch my every move and listen to my mumbles as I talked to myself like a crazy person. Albeit she wasn't the best spy, as she could be easily distracted by one of her squeaky toys or chicken-flavoured biscuits.

'What do you think, Kat?' I asked, and she tilted her head to one side. 'Do you think I've blown it?' She adorably tipped the opposite way. Then she dipped her fluffy little head, tucked her chin between her paws, and looked up at me with her big choco-late-brown eyes.

'That's what I think too!' I cried, and shook my hands in front of me as if I were drying my nails. I was definitely getting fired, I could feel it in my bones. I had far too much anxious energy inside me and nothing was helping.

Tapping my phone, I noticed Zack had exactly five minutes to get home so that Kat wouldn't be on her own when I left for my meeting with Josh (her separation anxiety was actually a real thing, I'd discovered). The nerves were getting worse with every minute that went by.

Taking in my reflection in the mirror, at least I looked good if he was going to fire me. Every cloud. After the presentation, I'd treated myself to a gorgeous Ted Baker shift dress. I'd reasoned that even though I couldn't afford it, it would double up as workwear and weekend wear – not that I ever did anything with my weekends, but still.

Smoothing my hair down, I leant closer to the mirror so I could inspect my eye make-up for the hundredth time. I was overthinking it. If Josh hadn't asked me out, and I hadn't rejected him, then I wouldn't have thought twice about meeting him. In fact, he'd probably forgotten he'd even asked me out. How many women did Josh Barron ask out on a regular basis? The figure was probably big, and I would've placed a bet that nobody said no to him.

Anxiously, I checked the time again. Zack was late, of course. I made a mental note to myself to always tell him times thirty minutes earlier – so he'd be on time when he was inevitably late. Obviously, he couldn't be torn away from the gorgeous blonde I'd seen him with outside the yoga studio.

'Men, eh?' Kat said to me with her deep, soulful eyes.

I nodded at her in agreement before jabbing at my phone. *Where are you?* I texted Zack, trying to calm my shaking hands. As long as I left in the next ten minutes, I'd get to the meeting on time. Although part of me thought, why did it matter? If he was going to fire me anyway, then bad timekeeping wasn't my biggest problem.

Why on earth had I let Katie convince me to tell Josh I'd changed my mind about a date? I'd handled it professionally when I politely declined. And my decision to say yes to Josh had absolutely nothing to do with seeing Zack and his girlfriend together in real life. Absolutely nothing. In fact, I'd hardly thought about it since I'd seen them. Hadn't given it a second thought. Not one. Not a single thought.

My phone buzzed. *Sorry, nearly home! Be two mins! *hands together emoji**

Oh, thank God. At least now I'd be on time to lose my biggest client. I gave myself a final once-over in the mirror, which mainly consisted of brushing off all of Kat's hair with a lint roller that Zack had presented to me, together with his various allergy relief remedies.

Kat looked at me again with her big eyes, the whites just about visible around the deep hazel surrounding her black pupils. 'Sorry about that.' She was communicating to me, as I brushed the fur from my dress.

'Can't be helped,' I replied, giving her a tickle behind her ear – I couldn't believe how attached I was getting to her. 'Unless we shave you. But somehow, I don't think you'd be as cute without your lovely fur.' Her long blink conveyed agreement, and that she'd definitely look like some sort of bald and oversized guinea pig.

The front door opened, and Kat excitedly leapt off my bed to greet whoever was home, or breaking in. It was a good job that we didn't rely on her as a guard dog. She literally never barked (hence why I hadn't known she was our secret house guest for so long), and all she wanted to do to visitors was lick and sniff them, and rub her tummy against their legs.

I picked up my laptop, phone and handbag, and followed

Kat's path from my room and down the stairs. Already from the midpoint of the stairs I could hear Zack's cooing and cuddling of Kat. Her little nails made scratchy noises on the wooden floors as she jumped around excitedly. I took the last step down into the hallway and saw that she was wagging her tail so much her bum was wiggling like a Zumba instructor.

'Hey,' I said to Zack's bent position, his arms wrapped up around the little dog.

'Hey,' he replied before looking up. He stood slowly as he saw me. 'Oh, wow,' he breathed, and I felt his eyes taking me in, from the top of my head down to my stiletto heels. 'You look incredible, Lucy.'

'Don't be daft,' I said modestly.

'I'm not,' Zack said, shaking his head, but not before surreptitiously looking me up and down again. 'You look amazing.'

We were silent for a moment. The only noise was Kat playing with her favourite squeaky toy, a hot dog that Zack had bought as a joke after Zoom-gate.

'Where are you off to tonight? Another date?' Zack avoided my eye and leant against the wall. He looked like he was pretending to inspect a non-existent stain on the paintwork.

'Not a date, no. A business meeting.'

'A business meeting?' Zack raised an eyebrow. 'That's what you wear to a business meeting?'

'You're making me feel self-conscious now!' I said, smoothing the luxurious fabric down. It felt good to dress the way I used to again. 'Is it too much?' I twirled around slowly, knowing exactly what I was doing. His girlfriend might've looked good in leggings and a hoodie, but I knew how to do workwear chic.

'It's not too much. Not at all.' He gulped and cleared his throat. 'It's perfect. You look perfect,' he repeated before he coughed again, pushing his fist into his Adam's apple. 'The dress, I mean. The dress looks perfect, perfect for a business meeting—'

'Got it.' I held a hand up to stop his rambling. He was obviously feeling a bit guilty about complimenting another woman when he was a taken man, and I suddenly felt guilty for encouraging it.

'What time will you be back?' Zack asked. 'Just so I know you're home safe,' he quickly added.

'I won't be late.' I shrugged. 'I don't think it'll take very long, depending on how it goes, I mean. There's a chance I might need a glass of wine when I get back, and some chocolate, and any delicious, calorific carbohydrates.'

'Oh no,' Zack said. 'That kind of meeting?'

'Maybe.' I forced a deep breath. 'Hopefully not, but I'm not sure.'

'Well, good luck,' Zack said, rubbing his hands together. 'I'm sure you'll be fine, Lucy. You're...' He hesitated. 'You're... just. Great.'

I nodded slowly. What girl doesn't want to be told she's 'just great'? Compliment of the century.

'Thanks,' I offered neutrally, hiding my disappointment. 'See you later, Zack.'

TWENTY-NINE

Most of the lights in the Dale Street Developments building were out except for a few late workers, and the soft glow of the lamps that illuminated Josh's sprawling corner office. I looked up at it from the pavement as I walked closer towards the building, just in time for our meeting. He'd given me the passcode for the main entrance, and my footsteps echoed against the marble floors as I walked through the reception to the lift and pressed the button for the top floor.

My emotions were jumbled together like a pile of laundry. Zack's neutral compliment earlier was in contrast with the way his eyes looked me up and down when I walked down the stairs. And why did Josh suddenly change his mind after asking me out? At least I'd know the answer to my second question sooner rather than later. Who knew when I'd figure out what went on in Zack's head.

The lift doors pinged open, and I was thrown back to that memory of my first pitch with Dale Street Developments. The nerves were probably about the same level tonight. I held my hand against my stomach as I stepped out. The office was quiet, with only the sounds of the staff who were working late; frantic keyboard typing and tired voices, half yawning on phone calls. Weirdly, as I walked towards Josh's office, I could hear the gentle notes of jazz music guiding my way.

Turning the corner, I stopped when I took in the sight of his office.

'Hey,' Josh said, as he got up from the makeshift table in the middle of the room. He was a distracting sight, with his tie long gone and his top button undone. There were candles everywhere, and what must've been at least twenty bouquets of velvety red roses with bushy green leaves.

'Hi,' I murmured as I looked around, taking in the scene.

'I know it might be a little over the top,' Josh said. It was the first time I'd heard a hint of self-deprecation in his tone.

I opened my mouth to agree, but was distracted by the open bottle of Dom Pérignon champagne on the table.

'But *technically*...' He emphasised the word as he walked towards me. It only took him a couple of strides, thanks to his long, suit-clad legs.

'Technically...' I repeated in a dreamy haze. I felt like the star of a romantic comedy movie on Netflix. Although there were definite *Fifty Shades of Grey* vibes, the way he was looking at me so hungrily.

'Technically, we're keeping it professional.' Josh was standing in front of me now, and our eyes were locked, taking each other in.

'I'm not sure what's professional about this.' I laughed, trying to defuse the heated atmosphere between us.

'We're still in the office,' he stated smoothly, taking my hand and running it under his mouth as he kissed it, his warm breath giving me goosebumps. 'And this is in my calendar as a meeting. *And* we can discuss work, if you want. It's just a complete coincidence that there happens to be champagne and food.'

'Food too?' I said, momentarily distracted by my rumbling tummy. All day, I hadn't been able to stomach food. I was too worried about the meeting – the meeting that was now a date, and a rather romantic date at that.

'Hungry?' he said, in a way that shouldn't have been as attractive as it was.

'Starving,' I replied. Our eye contact hadn't broken, until he gently dropped my hand, which slowly fell to my side, as if I was floating weightlessly in water. The entire situation felt surreal, like I was dreaming.

Josh swooped around and neatly poured the bubbly into the pair of crystal flutes on the table. 'Here you go,' he said, handing one to me.

'What are we toasting to?'

'To technically being professional.' He smiled, gently clinking his glass against mine.

'To technically being professional,' I repeated, before we both took a sip.

The bubbles tingled against my lips. So *that* was what champagne tasted like. It had been so long since I'd last had a glass, I'd almost forgotten. Not since Katie's disastrous hen party, when we'd lived on a diet of Veuve Clicquot morning, noon and night. And after the hit my bank account took when I bought the house – well, let's just say I missed some of life's luxuries that I'd taken for granted when I could afford them.

'Shall we sit?' Josh said, stretching his arm out to the table, beautifully set for two, covered in a white tablecloth and complete with a silver candelabra. He pulled out a chair for me, before sitting in the one opposite.

'Do you do this for all the girls?' I said with a healthy dose of cynicism.

'Only the special ones.'

If this had been a date and he'd been pulling these lines, I would've rolled my eyes, but there was something about Josh. The way his shirt fitted tightly over his muscular torso and gym-honed arms certainly helped. But really, it was the way he

carried himself – the confidence he had in every subtle movement and every word he spoke.

'If you're hungry, we'd better tuck in.' He lifted the silver
cloche in the middle of the table to reveal a feast of caviar,
cheese, olives and meats.

'This looks amazing,' I said, my mouth watering at the filled
serving dishes.

'Tell me about yourself, Lucy Clark.' He picked up a blini
and it looked tiny between his fingers. He delicately spooned
soft cheese and a cluster of caviar onto it.

'Well, I'm an interior designer, I run my own business—'

'I know that,' he interjected. 'Tell me something I don't
know, tell me something about you. Something surprising.'

I paused as I desperately tried to think about something
interesting. Something other than the automatic spiel I'd say on
a first date with somebody. 'I guess my living situation is a little
unusual,' I said eventually.

'Hmm,' Josh said. Our fingers brushed as he passed me the
blini he'd made up. 'Go on.'

'I bought my house with a stranger.'

'That *is* interesting.' Josh picked up another blini and
created a second miniature masterpiece, with soft cheese and
caviar layered perfectly. 'How did that happen?'

Why did people always ask questions when you had your
mouth full? I smiled and pointed to my mouth apologetically as
I chewed the delicious food.

'It's a bit of a long story, really,' I said, the moment I swallowed the last mouthful of the blini. I didn't want to go into the
nitty-gritty details of mine and Zack's arrangement – the way
my deposit and his monthly income had brought us together.
And nothing said mood-killer like me being a complete control
freak and writing a list of dos and don'ts that hung like a shrine
in our kitchen. 'It's been a bit of a journey, shall we say. But we
came up with an arrangement that suited us both.'

'What's she like, your housemate?' Josh dabbed the side of his mouth gently with a napkin.

'*He,*' I started, before taking a sip of the champagne. 'He. Zack. He's...' I pondered. 'He's just great.' I remembered what he'd said earlier and couldn't ignore the tinge of bitterness when I repeated his words.

'Wow, that's lucky,' Josh said, topping my glass up like a gentleman. 'Imagine how wrong it could've gone.'

'What do you mean?'

'Well, it could've been a disaster, couldn't it? Imagine if you didn't get on—'

'Oh, don't get me wrong,' I interrupted, spurred on by feeling tipsy, thanks to alcohol on an empty stomach. I hoped the tiny blinis were more filling than they looked, or I'd soon be drunk. 'We've certainly had our differences, but we've found our rhythm now. It's good. It works.'

'Good job it doesn't work *too* well.' Josh sipped his drink. 'Imagine if you ended up dating your housemate.'

'Mm,' I mumbled. It wasn't as if that thought *hadn't* ever crossed my mind. But just out of curiosity, more than anything. What Zack and I would be like together... Nothing to it, though. Nothing at all. Purely curiosity.

'You'd be trapped together in that house. Jesus, the pressure. The *commitment.*' Josh took an audible gulp of his drink that was so big I could see his Adam's apple shift. So, perhaps Mr Perfect's flaw was that he was a commitment-phobe.

'True,' I said, covering my mouth as politely as I could, given I was mid-bite of the next blini, one that I'd piled impressively high. One must always make the most of free caviar, after all.

'And then if it all went wrong,' Josh continued, 'you'd have to sell the house. Or one of you would have to move out and get bought out. And how would you decide who would do what?' He shook his head.

It was as though Josh was reading my mind and suddenly

had access to all the reasons I'd always told myself that I couldn't have a minor, tiny, harmless crush on Zack. Not when he got adorably frustrated at Scrabble. Or when he bought my favourite chocolate treats for me when he knew I'd had a hard day. Or the way he'd always leave my coffee mug out for me in the morning.

'True,' I said again, wiping some remnants of caviar from the side of my lip. 'But he'd have to move out. It's my childhood home.'

'Oh, wow.' Josh's brows drew together in confusion and intrigue. 'The plot thickens! How did that happen?'

'Like I said. It's a long story, and I promise it isn't very interesting.' I took a big gulp of champagne. Suddenly, I felt a bit weird. I didn't want to talk to Josh about Zack, and I could tell my blinks were getting longer and my speech was a little slurry. 'Actually, could I have some water, please?'

'Of course.' Josh took to his feet. 'Let me get a jug of it.'

I cursed myself – why on earth hadn't I eaten anything all day? Well, I knew why. I'd been riddled with anxiety. But at least now I knew I wasn't going to be fired. I looked around to make sure Josh wasn't in sight and quickly spooned more caviar onto blinis, loaded them with smoked salmon, and ate as many as I could.

'Here we go.' He arrived back in the room with a full jug and two glasses. 'Lightweight,' he teased.

'Sorry,' I said. 'I was so nervous today, I couldn't eat—' I stopped myself. I couldn't tell him that I'd thought he was going to sack me – that was oversharing, and I still wanted to be professional. As professional as I could be, given that we were lit only by flickering candlelight and the room smelt like a florist's.

'Nervous? Why?' He leant back in his chair and ran his fingers around the long stem of the glass. 'Not about coming here, surely. You've been here a hundred times now.'

'No, I know. It was just after last time...'

'When I asked you out and you rejected me?' He gave me his best puppy-dog eyes as he held a hand to his chest, over his heart.

I nodded.

'What made you change your mind?' he asked.

The image of Zack and that gorgeous woman together flashed into my head – uninvited and unwanted – again.

'Nothing in particular,' I said, feigning a smile. 'I don't know. I still want to keep things professional. Well, as professional as things can be when we're surrounded by roses and champagne...'

'Why do you want to keep it confined to professionalism, anyway? In case things go wrong and I fire you?' Josh half laughed, but it struck a nerve deep down inside me. The power balance was all wrong in this situation.

'It's not like that couldn't happen,' I said defensively.

'Why on earth would I? You're doing an amazing job for us. You need to relax, Lucy Clark.'

I bit my lip. 'Thank you. And maybe you're right, maybe I do. Enough people tell me I need to. My life has been about work and only work for so long. I've kind of forgotten how to live, I guess...' I sipped the final dregs in my glass.

'I'm exactly the same.' Josh nodded. 'So, let's do it. Let's live a little.' Josh pushed himself up from the table and stood next to me. He held a hand out, which I took, and stood so we were facing each other. Before I had time to register what was happening, his other hand was holding my waist. His arms were so broad, I felt tiny as I stood in front of him.

'Look, I have to go away on this business trip tomorrow,' he said softly. 'I'm going to be gone for a little while, probably a week, but maybe more. When I get back, I really want to pick this up again.'

My mind was whirring, taking in what was happening. It

felt like a dream. This was Josh Barron, and he had his arms around me.

'I think you're... incredible.' He whispered it so closely I could almost taste the champagne on his tongue. Being called *incredible* definitely beat being called *great*. And incredible was probably how Zack described his beautiful girlfriend. So, when Josh lowered his head to kiss me, I let him.

THIRTY

As I headed home, I was still in a surreal bubble of decadence – of champagne, caviar, and my kiss with Josh. I hoped I wouldn't regret our passionate kiss in the morning, although my judgement was clouded by Dom Pérignon. I'd been in such a dream-like state that I hadn't realised my phone was out of battery until the taxi pulled up outside the house.

Holding my lifeless phone in one hand, I took my house key from my bag and tried to put it in the lock. I was still a little tipsy, so I kept missing. The door swung open, and my delayed reactions meant I had to work extra hard not to fall through it.

'There you are,' Zack said immediately, as I set foot inside the house. He was standing in the hallway and his face was tinted red with anger.

'What?' I said, his solemn expression sobering me up. 'What's wrong?'

'Where the hell have you been?' His eyes were wide and wild, his jaw tensed.

'I told you. I was at a client meeting.' I shuffled past him and towards the kitchen for a glass of water. 'Sorry, *Dad*.'

'I've been out of my mind with worry,' Zack said, his eyes darting, looking me up and down.

'I'm a big girl,' I retorted, a little more snarkily than I meant to. I kicked my heels off clumsily, as Kat watched from the top of the stairs. It wasn't like her to keep her distance; obviously she was cross with me too.

'It's late,' Zack said angrily, crossing his arms over his chest.

'Jeez, it's only...' I tapped my phone, forgetting it was dead.

'It's gone midnight,' Zack confirmed.

'It's only gone midnight,' I said, slurring a bit. 'What's the big problem?'

'You told me it might be a bad meeting and you weren't going to be long, Lucy. I've been worried sick. I've called you a million times, but your phone kept going straight to voicemail. I thought...' He brushed a hand through his hair. 'I don't know what I thought, just that something bad had happened.'

'Why do you care?' I sneered drunkenly.

Zack instinctively jolted back, as if my words were an electric shock. 'What do you mean, "why do I care"? Jesus Christ, *of course* I care.' He hit the wall with his fist, making me jump. It was the first time I'd ever seen Zack as anything other than laid-back and calm. Before this, the closest I'd seen him reaching anything resembling anger was mild annoyance.

'Sorry,' Zack said quietly after a few seconds, stroking the wall as if it were a person. I wasn't sure if he was talking to the wall or to me. 'It's probably none of my business—'

'You're right. It *is* none of your business,' I snapped. He was the one who went away for nights and entire weekends without telling me where he was. Why was this different? At least I'd told him the truth, that I was in a work meeting. I didn't know it was going to turn into a date.

Zack backed away slowly, pursing his lips and nodding. 'I see,' he whispered. 'I'm sorry for looking out for you. It won't happen again.'

'Good,' I said under my breath as he sloped up the stairs. I wasn't sure if he could hear, but I carried on talking. 'I don't need you to look out for me. I don't need anyone to look out for me. I'm fine on my own.' I stood in the hallway, glued to the spot, as I heard Zack's door slam shut upstairs.

———

The high-pitched beeping of my usual 6 a.m. weekend alarm felt like someone was sitting in bed with me, prodding my temples sharply with their fingernails. My mouth was so dry, my body so dehydrated, it was as though I'd eaten a plate of salt for dinner.

Wincing, I forced myself up on my elbows. Had last night really happened? The gorgeous bachelor that was Josh Barron had invited me to a romantic dinner for two in his office? Had we really kissed? I'd crossed the strictly professional boundary with a client for the first time. I lay back down, pulling the cover over me for comfort as I considered it with a sober mind.

There was something else too. Something deep down in the pit of my stomach, bubbling angrily away like a witch's cauldron. Zack and I had fallen out. The volume of alcohol I'd drunk had flooded my body by the time I'd got home. I hoped my snarky, snippy remarks to him weren't as bad as they were in my hazy memory. I felt embarrassed and ashamed at the thought. As he said, he was only looking out for me.

A strong coffee was what I needed. A mug of piping-hot Americano and food of any description slathered in butter. Then back to bed for a nap, and I'd be fine by the afternoon.

Forcing myself to my feet, I peered out of my door, over at Zack's room. His door was closed, but I knew his routine. He was probably out for his usual morning walk with Kat. Every step down the stairs thudded my entire body, and I rubbed my forehead to try and soften the mind-numbing headache.

Blinking my sleepy eyes awake, I moved around the kitchen on autopilot. The coffee grinder rumbled to life, and the smell of the freshly ground beans momentarily revived me from my zombie-like state. Zack had kindly left the last crumpet for me, thankfully. I popped it in the toaster and grabbed the butter from my designated shelves inside the shared fridge.

In an attempt to distract my mind, which felt like it was melting while I waited for my crumpet to pop out of the toaster and inevitably make me jump, I clicked the radio on and tidied around the kitchen. There were a few things in the fridge that were well past the expiry date, so I put them to one side, before pushing the bin lid open with my foot using the lever at the bottom.

As the lid opened, I saw it. It was everything I'd told Zack I might need when I got back from my meeting last night – when I thought I was being fired, instead of wined and dined. My favourite chocolates, a big packet of sweet and salty popcorn, the crisps I loved, the jelly sweets for kids that I pretended I didn't like as much as I did. I put the food I was holding in my arms down to one side and went back to the fridge again. I hadn't noticed it before, but there was my favourite bottle of rosé on the shelf, right next to Zack's oat milk.

Zack had been out and bought everything to cheer me up after my potentially awful work meeting. That was why he was so annoyed last night. That, and being worried about me. I leant against the kitchen counter as I considered it. Why would he do that? Why did he care? The toaster made me jump as it announced the crumpet was ready, in the dramatic fashion that toasters do. But I'd lost my appetite. My confusion and my hangover were swirling together like a whirlpool. I went back up to bed and pulled the cover over my head, hoping everything would be clearer after a few hours' rest.

THIRTY-ONE

It was 6 p.m. and Zack still wasn't home. I knew he was probably giving me a taste of my own medicine, but that wasn't really like him and I was worried. I bit the bullet and texted him, apologising and saying if he could just let me know he was OK I'd appreciate it, but that I understood if he was still angry at me. I was pacing around my room, something I'd grown used to doing lately. The cloud of my hangover had lifted, but this feeling was worse than anything alcohol-inflicted.

At the exact moment I was thinking of Zack as dead and buried, my heart flipped as I heard the familiar sound of the front door opening. I could've cried with happiness at the sound of Kat's nails grazing along the wooden floor of the hallway, and the keys jingling as Zack hung them up on his usual hook. Next, I knew he'd be taking his jacket off and hanging it on the stand over his beanie. Then, he'd be kicking off his shoes without undoing the laces and putting them in their spot by the front door.

Suddenly, I was overwhelmed with happiness. Not just because he was home, but that I knew his routine as if it were my own. I knew exactly what he would be doing and when. And he was doing it in this house – *our* house.

Fuelled by relief, adrenaline, and perhaps some of last night's booze, I threw myself from my room and down the stairs. Zack was standing in the hallway, and before he could breathe a word, I ran up to him, pushed myself onto my tiptoes and threw my arms around his neck.

We stood there in silence. Our bodies fitted perfectly together like jigsaw pieces. It was the closest and longest physical contact we'd ever had.

After some time passed, which could've been seconds, minutes or hours, I whispered, 'I'm sorry,' in his ear. I held my cheek close to his, feeling his soft skin. It was a loaded apology, and there wasn't one definitive issue that I was sorry for. Last night was our most recent fallout, but every time we were at loggerheads, we also had snippets of good times together when we couldn't stop laughing or smiling. Usually when we were playing Scrabble or trying to complete another DIY project together.

'I'm sorry too,' he said, his breath lingering on my neck. Less than twenty-four hours earlier, I'd been this close to Josh. I flinched when I thought about it. Somehow, it seemed disloyal to Zack.

We pulled away from each other slowly, but his eyes were still locked with mine. He opened his mouth while his eyes searched my face, but then he closed it again without saying a word. I couldn't help the feeling of disappointment. I didn't know why, but I desperately wanted him to say the words that he didn't say – the ones that lingered on his tongue.

There was nothing but silence between us, until a little dog interrupted with a silent message. Kat wanted us to say what was lingering in the air between us too. She balanced on her back legs, as she put one front paw on Zack's leg and the other on mine. Her fluffy face looked from me to Zack, and back to me again.

Mirroring Zack's earlier movement, I opened my mouth and closed it again. What did I *want* to say? What *could* I say? It was complicated. He had a girlfriend, or whatever she was in Zack's easy, breezy, non-conventional world. And Josh's words of warning about the consequences of our arrangement not working out were still ringing in my ears. It could all go so wrong. There was so much to lose.

But there was no time like the present. I took a deep breath, closed my eyes and opened my mouth. 'I—'

'I—' Zack said at the same time, and I opened my eyes again.

'You go,' we both said.

'No, you go,' we both said again.

I smiled as he pursed his lips.

'Great minds.' He grinned. 'Look, this might sound a bit mad, but what are you doing today?'

'What day is it?' I asked, feeling disorientated.

'Thursday.'

'I have that thing...' I hesitated.

'Oh, of course. Your mystery Thursday engagements.' Zack rubbed his hands together. 'One day I'm going to get it out of you. One day I'll find out where it is you go.'

I offered a half-smile. *Maybe one day*.

'What about tomorrow?'

'Sleeping off the rest of this hangover, I'm sure,' I said sleepily.

'Other than that.'

'Other than that, nothing. Except I need to send some invoices. Oh, and I need to chase up my supplier in Italy. *And* I have a mood board I could really do with finishing... What?'

'Doesn't exactly sound like nothing,' Zack said, holding his elbow and resting his chin on his fist. He had his usual mischievous glint in his eye again.

'What?'

'You just make me laugh. You always have something to do – you always have *lots* of things to do.'

'Well, yeah, of course,' I stuttered. 'Doesn't everyone? Isn't that just, you know, life?'

'To an extent.' Zack nodded. 'But you're on another level, Lucy Clark.'

I ignored the flutter in my stomach and the flip my heart did when he said my name while looking into my eyes. 'Fine,' I relented. 'What about if I had nothing to do tomorrow?'

'That would be the surprise of the century.' Zack laughed.

'Amuse me.'

'Well, I was wondering if you fancied a little road trip?'

'Sure,' I tried to answer casually. 'Where?'

'The Lake District,' Zack said. 'I have something to do there.'

My heart went from excitedly flipping to sinking as I remembered his appointment in our shared calendar. It was this weekend that he was going to the Lake District, where he was going to look at a venue for his laidback, bohemian, beautiful wedding – or non-wedding ceremony, knowing Zack and his hatred of conventional labels.

'Oh,' I said. 'Why do you want me to come along?'

'I thought it'd be fun – a nice thing to do together. I need to check out a special place. Plus, my partner can't make it.'

'Ah,' I said at the confirmation of what I'd suspected. 'I don't think I should, really.'

'Why not?' Zack looked hurt. 'I promise, it'll be great. We'll just go for the day, and we'll be back in time for dinner – or in time for you to do some work, if you really want to.' He raised an eyebrow.

'Fine,' I relented, to his gleeful, single clap of his hands.

I guessed there was no harm in going with him. We were housemates; we had to make things work. *Until he moves out*, a

little voice in my head said. *Until he gets married and leaves.*
The thought cut through me. Even though an early plan of
mine (and every time he'd driven me crazy) was to eventually
persuade him to leave and buy him out, I couldn't imagine my
house – or my life – without Zack in it.

THIRTY-TWO

'Ready?' Zack's voice boomed through the house at 8 a.m. the next morning.

'Ready!' I shouted down from my bedroom, where I was finishing up packing the essentials for the road trip. Zack laughed at me when I told him what I was doing. In typical Zack fashion, he was taking nothing more than the clothes he was wearing.

I felt I owed it to his fiancée to be the organised one. I'd packed a notebook to make notes on the venue, refreshments for the car, two phone chargers, a foldaway waterproof jacket (apparently it always rained in the Lakes), walking boots, spare walking socks, some snacks for the day, and that's not to mention everything for Kat. I had another bag filled with her extendable lead, tasty treats, two tennis balls, a little rain jacket, and an obscene number of poo bags for such a small dog.

Standing back, I admired my organised handiwork before closing the backpack and shuffling it onto my back. Crikey, it was heavier than I'd thought. I pulled my tote bag on to one shoulder and nearly dislocated it in the process, and manoeuvred the other bag onto the opposite shoulder.

'Lucy, are you coming?' Zack shouted.

My legs were wobbly from the weight. I hobbled down the hall and carefully took each step at a time.

'Oh, wow,' Zack said, stifling a laugh.

'Yeah, erm. I might've packed a bit too much.' I wobbled down the next step.

'Hang on, you're going to fall.' Zack sprinted towards me, taking two stairs at a time. He easily lifted the two tote bags from my shoulders, and my body straightened from the relief.

'Thank you,' I said, feeling pounds lighter, despite still wearing the backpack on my back.

'What do you have in here, anyway?' Zack chuckled. 'We're only going for the day, we're not even staying over.'

'I know,' I said, blushing at the thought of Zack talking about us staying over somewhere together. 'I just like to be organised. It might rain, or we might get stuck on the M6 for five hours, or Kat might need something.'

'I love that you're looking after her so much and she isn't even your dog.'

I flinched internally and followed him through the front door, which he locked behind us.

'Sorry, of course she's your dog too, she lives here with you as well. You know what I mean,' Zack said, flustered.

'I know,' I said. 'Don't worry.' I clicked the car key to open my Mini Cooper.

'Are you sure we're going to fit all of this in here?' Zack joked at the size of the tiny boot and my big backpack.

'Hey, you can get the train if you'd prefer,' I teased. 'Although knowing you, I'm sure that's your preferred mode of transport. Cars aren't great for the environment, are they?'

'Exactly,' Zack said, seeming impressed at my nod towards his passion for going green. 'I'll make an exception this once, though. And it's not as if you drive a huge gas-guzzling Range Rover, is it?' He put the bags in the boot, and without me even asking, he politely shuffled the shoulder straps on my backpack and took it from my back.

'I don't think I'd be able to reach the pedals if I did.'

'I know, it's too cute.' Zack smiled but then looked away, focusing his attention on opening the passenger door.

I sat in the driver's seat, as Zack carefully put Kat in her dog bed on the back seat, strapping her in with the dog seat belt we'd borrowed from our neighbour yesterday after realising we didn't have one; obviously, Kat was precious cargo.

Zack sat beside me and immediately adjusted the passenger seat to make more room for his long legs. I looked at them, muscly and clad in denim that was ripped from long-term wear, rather than a fashion statement. I distractedly focused my attention on the satnav instead, punching in the postcode that Zack gave me.

'Two hours and ten minutes exactly,' Zack announced triumphantly.

'Pah,' I snorted.

'What?'

'Have you seen me drive? We'll get there quicker than that.'

'Oh well, gives us more time to make the most of our day togeth— our day out,' Zack said, correcting himself. He looked out of the window, bit his thumbnail, and started fiddling with the radio.

I pretended I was adjusting the mirror and caught a glimpse of my huge smile looking back at me.

———

'Wow, is this it?' The driveway was about a mile long, surrounded by lush trees and a rainbow of colourful flowers. The setting was so beautifully picturesque, it was as if we were on the *Bridgerton* set.

'This is it,' Zack said, grinning. 'Pretty impressive, huh?'

The old manor house was covered in ivy, broken up only by big windows which were decorated with gorgeous, intricate carvings in the frames. There was a water feature in the middle of the gravelled drive, and I pulled up to the guest parking on the furthest side of the spectacular house. It was a quintessential countryside manor – the perfect wedding venue. My chest ached and felt heavy as I gripped the steering wheel.

The minute the engine stopped, Kat excitedly jumped up and rested her front paws against the window in the back seat. Her little tail was practically vibrating with happiness as she looked out. Zack's grin would've matched hers if she could smile. He was beaming as he turned to me before getting out of the car.

'Excellent timing too, Clark,' he said as he stretched his long limbs out.

'I told you I'd get us here safely and efficiently.'

'It was definitely efficient. I don't think you went in any lane other than the fast one.'

Zack got out of the car and carefully unstrapped Kat, picking her up from the back seat before gently placing her on the gravelled drive, where she did her adorable usual routine. It was as though Zack had taught her the perfect downward dog as she yawned and stretched out her stiff little limbs, before giving her fur a shake.

'Aren't you coming in with us?' He bent down so he was looking at me from the open door of the passenger side.

'I don't know, I feel a bit weird.'

'Why?' Zack said, concerned. 'Did you eat too many car snacks?'

'Probably,' I sort of lied, although I did have the sugar shakes. Car snacks were the best snacks.

The truth was that being there was too much for me. I didn't want to see the spot where Zack would say 'I do' to his beautiful fiancée, even if he didn't call her by that official, traditional title. It was easier for me to be in complete denial about the whole situation if I didn't look at the rose gardens surrounding the manor where the wedding photos would be taken. Or the ceremony room that I just knew, even without looking at it, would be intimate and romantic, with a stunning view of the lake from the windows.

'Why don't I go and have a wander around in the town, and I'll meet you a bit later?' I suggested. 'There's a great fabric shop here that I follow on Instagram. I've been dying to check it out.'

'Oh,' Zack replied. He was doing a bad job of hiding his disappointment. I supposed he was relying on me for a trusted second opinion and an eye for interiors. Plus, I was the organised one. At least I'd brought a notebook. 'Sure, we can do that. If you want?'

I nodded.

'I won't be long anyway. Maybe an hour?' he said.

'That's fine, take your time.' I smiled.

'Do you want to take Kat with you?' Zack offered.

'Sure, we'll go for a wander together. I've read that it's super dog-friendly here.'

'Perfect,' Zack said, still trying to summon a smile. 'Do you still want to do the walk I mentioned afterwards?'

'Sounds good to me.' My faux-enthusiasm and pretending everything was fine was exhausting. I had to get far, far away from this dreamy wedding venue.

'Great,' Zack said, picking up a disappointed Kat and quickly strapping her back into her seat. 'So, I'll meet you in the town in an hour? Maybe just text me where you are?'

'Will do,' I replied. 'Is your phone charged?' I asked. Zack was terrible for remembering simple things like a full phone battery.

Zack rolled his eyes jokingly, before sneakily pulling it from his pocket and checking it. 'Yes,' he confirmed. 'And hey, you were the one with no battery most recently.'

'Fair point,' I said, warming up from the stifled tension a little. I tapped mine, which was doubling up as a satnav and plugged into the USB port. 'I can confirm it's fully charged.'

'Excellent. I'll see you later then.'

'See you,' I said, aware that I was looking at him for longer than I should've been.

He nodded, hesitated for a split second, and closed the car door. I watched him walk up to the gorgeous manor, before he disappeared inside.

'Don't worry, he'll be back soon,' I said to Kat in the rear-view mirror, as I clicked the car into reverse and backed up. The setting was complete and utter picturesque perfection, but I couldn't get out of there fast enough.

THIRTY-THREE

Kat and I wandered contentedly around the chocolate box village of Grasmere. She tootled along at my heels as we explored the daffodil garden, visited Wordsworth's grave, and peeked into the windows of the gorgeous shops dotted along the road. The fabric shop had been a complete fabrication (ha ha) to get out of visiting the wedding venue, but Kat and I didn't run out of ways to pass the time until we met Zack for our walk. I even loaded up on delicious, world-famous treats for it: Grasmere Gingerbread for me and vegan-friendly Kendal Mint Cake for Zack.

We perched on a bench with a dramatic view of the surrounding fells, and watched the world go by while we waited for Zack to walk over from the manor house to meet us. There were tourists excitedly taking photographs, walking groups either venturing out or arriving back from a hike in the hills. There were families on days out and locals taking a coffee break. Kat's little tummy rhythmically rose and fell on my thigh as she happily panted away while she sat with me. She was taking it all in and enjoying the occasional cuddle from a passer-by. I couldn't believe how much love I had for her so quickly after meeting her that time in our kitchen. Thank goodness Zack's allergy solutions had been a success – I couldn't imagine life without her.

That sudden flip of excitement erupted in my stomach when I saw Zack walking through the crowds. Like Kat, he was taking it all in too. He walked along cheerfully, as he always did, wearing a smile that was as warm as sunshine. Even strangers gravitated towards him, as he politely stepped out of the way to let people pass along the narrow pavement, and stooped down to pick up a toddler's hat they'd thrown out of a pram.

His smile grew even wider when he spotted me and Kat, and waved, quickening his pace towards us. 'Hey!' he said, marking his arrival with a hug that took me by surprise. Until yesterday's lingering hug, we'd never really had any proper physical contact. Aside from our accidental table-footsie when we were each wanting to rub Kat's belly with our feet, and, of course, when he corrected my positions in his yoga classes.

'Hi,' I said, taken aback by the show of affection. Kat let him tickle her under her chin and rubbed her furry head against his arm as he did it. 'How did it go?' I asked gingerly, not really wanting to know the answer if it went well.

'Amazing,' he said, beaming. 'Absolutely incredible. Jeez, that place is out of this world.' He shook his head in amazement. 'Honestly, it could not be any more perfect—'

'Great,' I said, cutting him off. 'That's good. I'm glad.'

'You should've come with me,' he replied. 'You would've loved it. The interiors were even more impressive than the outside, if that's possible. The building dates from 1903, and they still have loads of the original features inside. Honestly, Lucy, it's the dream.'

'Well, I'm sure I'll see it on the day. If I'm invited, that is,' I added quickly.

'You want to come?' he asked quizzically.

'Only if that's OK, obviously. I wouldn't want to just invite myself along,' I said. Not that I actually *wanted* to go. I couldn't think of anything worse.

'Yeah?' he stammered. 'Yeah, absolutely. You're more than welcome. I just didn't think... Anyway, no, of course you can.' Zack shook his head and zipped up his jacket. 'Ready for our walk?'

'We certainly are.' I slapped my hands onto my knees and stood up.

'Excellent. You're going to love it. It's this way.' Zack pointed along the road that headed away from the village. We walked together side by side, with Kat alongside us, heading down the narrow pavements and drystone walls.

We passed Wordsworth's Cottage, and the path started to get wider as we started an ascent. I quickened my pace, in part spurred on by Kat and her gentle pulling on the lead. For a small dog, she was surprisingly speedy – and strong. As we walked upwards, the village got smaller in the distance, and Grasmere Water came into view from above, surrounded by the jagged edges of the fells.

'Wow,' I breathed, as we looked down over the landscape.

'I know.' Zack nodded, taking in the beautiful scenery. 'And it gets even better.'

'Oh, are we going much higher?' I asked, as casually as I could muster.

'Yeah, of course we are.' Zack chuckled. 'We're right at the start. That's OK, isn't it?' He flashed me a concerned look.

'Absolutely, yes. Totally fine.' I rested my hands on my hips and tried to catch my breath as I panted. I furtively wiped the sweat from my head and stretched out my calves, which were already starting to ache. It had been a while since I'd properly worked out. I used to run miles every day, usually before work, and follow it up with a spin class at lunch. Surely exercise was like riding a bike; you'd quickly pick up your cardio fitness level again, wouldn't you?

'Onwards and upwards,' I said, in a more high-pitched tone than I'd intended. 'Literally,' I murmured quietly, surveying the continued incline in front of us.

'Tell me if you need a break,' Zack said. 'I don't mean that in a patronising way. I just mean that you're doing your first Wainwright, so needing to take a break is understandable.'

'A Wainwright? What's that? I thought we were just going for a nice, gentle ramble.' Kat led the way ahead of us as we plodded along the leaf-lined path.

'The Wainwright fells,' Zack explained. 'Named after Alfred Wainwright. He was a fell walker and a writer; he wrote about the different hills in the Lake District. And lots of people use his guide and try to do all of them.'

'Is that what we're doing?'

Zack stifled a laugh. 'Erm, I think we'd need a little more time.'

'Why? How many are there?'

Zack closed one eye as he took a moment to think. 'Pretty sure it's two hundred and fourteen.'

'*Two hundred and fourteen?*' I repeated, aghast and also out of breath. 'Bloody hell. Yes, let's definitely *not* do all of them today.'

'You know, you might find it a little easier if you slowed down,' Zack said. I turned around and he was a few feet behind me. 'Hey, I'm not telling you what to do,' he said, raising his hands defensively. 'But you've spent most of the walk so far looking down at your feet and stomping full-charge ahead.'

'I have not,' I said.

Kat turned and looked at me as if to say, *Well, you have.*

'It's fine, I'm used to it with you.' Zack stifled a laugh.

'What do you mean?' I purposely slowed my pace, as if I were like Zack, wandering without a care in the world – not that I could imagine how that would feel. I shifted my eyeline from down at my feet and looked upwards.

'We're in no rush,' Zack said calmly. 'Just take your time, take it all in. Enjoy it.'

'I *am* enjoying it, arghhh—'

I felt Zack's arms quickly grab on to my shoulders as he hoisted me up.

'See, that was your fault!' I said, flustered.

'How?' Zack said, mock-outraged.

'The reason why I was looking down at my feet was because all these leaves hide big stones and massive tree roots! So I looked up, as instructed, and almost rolled my ankle.' I huffed. 'There's a reason why you should keep your head down, concentrate and be cautious.'

'On a walk, or generally in life?'

'I was talking about the walk, but yeah, in life too.'

'Hmm,' Zack mumbled, unconvinced at our different views of life. 'Can I ask you something?'

'Mm-hmm,' I replied, skirting around the potential ankle-rolling obstacles of nature, while also trying to ensure Zack could see me looking up and around – *taking it all in.*

'Do you ever just try to let go and live in the present moment?' he said.

'Pfft,' I snorted, expertly dodging another hidden tree branch on the woodland route. Hurrah! I was getting the hang of this. 'Could you sound any more condescending?'

'I'm not trying to be,' Zack said, a hint of hurt behind his words. 'I'm just asking—'

'I know,' I said. 'Sorry.' My apology was tinged with regret at my combative attitude – my usual go-to mood when it came to mine and Zack's disagreements.

'We're quite different, you and I,' Zack stated. He nodded slowly, as if he was trying to figure out a complicated maths equation.

'Just a tad,' I agreed.

'Let's give something a go when we get to the top,' Zack said, with a clap of his hands.

'Why does that sound terrifying? You're not going to make me do some sort of wild nature dance or something, are you?'

'You'll see.' Zack smiled.

'How far to the top now?' I asked, as nonchalantly as I could muster.

'We start a descent again now, along Rydal Water and Rydal Cave, and then we head upwards again, until we get to the trig point of Loughrigg Fell.'

'So, not long?' I said through gritted teeth.

'It'll be worth it.' Zack smiled at me again.

I hoped so.

The backs of my calves burned with every step I took upwards. I'd taken off each layer I was wearing, to the point that taking off any more would've been inappropriate. I'd given up on making conversation long ago. Survival was now my priority. I, Lucy Clark, was not made to climb mountains. I was trailing behind Zack and Kat, who had turned into small figures in the far distance as they happily strode on upwards, struggle-free with every step.

It felt like my chest was on fire, and I tried to dispel the image of what I looked like from my head. All I knew was, it wasn't pretty. I was a lobster-red, sweaty, panting mess. I knew without looking in a mirror that my hair had turned to frizz and my eye make-up was splodgy and smeared.

'Nearly there!' Zack shouted behind him, and I waved in a non-verbal response.

The two of them climbed the final stretch upwards and disappeared from view. The end was nigh, thank God. And if I was going to die, if this really was the end, then at least it was somewhere pretty. Although, at the moment, everything was such a blurry haze that I hadn't appreciated the surroundings or the view. It was as though the weather forecast had changed entirely the moment we started our ascent. The cold wind was stinging my eyes and my breaths felt difficult as I drew in the chilly air.

Forcing myself forwards, I knew there were only a few more steps upwards to go. I gave myself an internal pep talk. *Come on, Lucy. You've got this, you've run a marathon, for goodness' sake.* My optimal fitness levels felt like a dream in the far, far distance. Just like the view around me, where everything in my life felt far away from this present moment, and the vast rural landscape of mountains zigzagging through the sky on the horizon.

One foot in front of the other. I panted and pushed on. *Come on. One foot in front of the other.* And then...

Wow.

The view from the top was so spectacular it didn't look real. It was as though I'd stepped out of my real life and into a painting.

'Told you it was worth it,' Zack said, as he stood beside me.

'It's...' Luckily, I could pretend I was lost for words at the beautiful view, rather than being out of breath from my squeezed lungs. 'It's...'

'I know,' Zack said. He leant against the trig point, a small dry-stone pillar decorated with a plaque that signalled our accomplishment. 'Do you see why I love it so much now?'

I nodded.

'I knew you would. I saw your face when I put those pictures by your desk at home.' He looked around, his eyes hungry for the view, taking in every inch of it. He turned to me, beaming. 'Shall we get a photo?'

'I'm not sure I want to immortalise forever how bad I look right now.' I used the sleeve of my jacket that was tied around my hips to wipe my forehead, and I smoothed down the frizzy bits of hair that were sticking out over my head.

'What are you talking about? You look great!' Zack smiled. 'You're glowing!'

'Glowing with sweat,' I huffed.

'Don't be silly,' Zack said. 'Come here.' He pulled me close to him. How did he still smell so good after climbing an actual mountain? In fact, how did he *look* so good after climbing one? He looked like a model for an outdoor wear company, whereas I was all flustered and sweaty.

'Kat!' He whistled, and Kat scurried over after sniffing something interesting – though it was probably sheep poo; she was obsessed with the stuff (dogs were so weird sometimes). Kat wagged her tail as she stood in front of us. Even she looked less tired than I was, and her legs were only about ten inches long. She panted a couple of times and followed it up with a big yawn. I swore it was only to make me feel better.

'Family photo!' Zack declared as he picked her up.

What? I thought. *Family photo?* Just like the one of him and his fiancée stood at the top of a mountain with Kat?

'Smile!' Zack held the phone out; his long arms meant we were all perfectly captured in the frame of the camera. 'Perfect!' he declared, after peering at the old screen.

'I'm surprised that thing can even take photos,' I teased, as I frowned at the shot of me, wide-eyed and windswept, with a sweaty face and bright red cheeks. *Not* my best look. I didn't look anywhere near as good as his fiancée.

'It's just as good as your fancy phone,' Zack said. 'See.' He showed me the photo filling the screen again. I looked at it closely. There we were – in his words – a family. 'But I'm putting it away now.' Zack shoved it into his pocket. 'Let's just take in the view, live in the moment.'

'Oh no. I've just remembered. You're going to make me do that thing you said...'

'Mm-hmm.' Zack nodded.

'Can we have a snack first?' I pleaded.

'Absolutely.' Zack rubbed his hands together.

There were two big rocks perfectly positioned beside the trig point, like deck chairs on a beach. We sat, nestled side by side, resting our bums on the ridges. I unzipped my backpack as Kat sat down in front of me. She did her party trick, lifting her paw as if to say 'please' whenever there was the prospect of food. I patted her head and gave her a Dentastix – her favourite treat.

'What's on the menu?' Zack said. 'It's a good job you're the organised one. I didn't pack a thing for today.'

'I know you didn't.' I rolled my eyes.

'You know what they say,' Zack said, looking out at the mesmerising scenery.

'What?' I rummaged around the bag.

'Opposites attract.' He smiled a joyous grin, his dimple dotting his chin. We looked at each other, before I forced myself back to the important task at hand. Snacks.

'Here we go!' I announced. 'Kendal Mint Cake for you. Grasmere Gingerbread for me...' My mouth watered as I lifted them from my bag.

'Have you tried the gingerbread before?' Zack asked.

'Never.' I shook my head. 'I've heard it's the best though.'

'I've heard it is too.' Zack grinned. 'My friends and family are totally obsessed with it. I have to pick some up for them whenever I come here, or they threaten to disown me. You're in for a treat.'

The Grasmere Gingerbread was wrapped up tightly in white and blue paper packaging. I took off the elastic band and unwrapped it layer by layer. 'Wow, that smells *so* good,' I said, sniffing the mouth-watering scent that was released from the packaging. I broke the chunky slab of gingerbread in half – but knowing I had every intention of eating the whole thing, anyway.

'Cheers,' Zack said. His piece of mint cake looked so tiny in his big hands. He tapped it against my gingerbread piece as if they were champagne glasses.

'Cheers,' I replied happily, batting away the memory of doing that with Josh, only with actual champagne in his office. Thankfully, he was away on a business trip, so I could try to ignore the memory of it.

We both took a bite at the same time, and another and another. We were completely silent, watching the view as if we were watching the TV. The only noise was the groans from our full mouths, as we mumbled greedily about how delicious each of our snack choices were. Mine, with its crumbly texture, was sweet but a bit spicy, and soft but chewy at the same time.

'OK, now I understand why everyone says this gingerbread is the best in the world.'

'Told you you'd love it,' Zack said. 'See, I can be right about *some* things.'

I stubbornly ignored him as we sat in silence, completely enchanted by the view in front of us. The inky blue lake and the pastel-coloured ombré sky, with the swirly clouds that looked like brushstrokes on a painting. The jagged edges of the surrounding fells, and the candyfloss-like smudges of white that were flocks of sheep, happily grazing on the hills.

'Another piece of mint cake?' I offered Zack.

'Absolutely,' he replied, taking it from my hand.

'I'm glad I got the big pack of gingerbread,' I said, before taking another large bite from a fresh slab after quickly polishing off the first one.

'You're a girl after my own heart.' Zack looked away from the view at me, and I looked back at him. His eyes seemed even greener than usual, with the deep hues of the sky and the water reflected in them. And his skin was glowing with the fresh air, his cheeks adorably flushed.

Then, he slowly leant in towards me, his eyes closed.

It felt like everything around us stopped – the wind wasn't blowing any more. There were no ripples in the distant water. But my heart was thudding in my chest; every hair on my body was standing on end. I closed my eyes, and his finger lightly traced the outline of my jaw. He moved closer. His lips brushed against mine, softly and carefully.

Then reality hit.

'Stop,' I said. I put my hand on his chest, gently pushing him away.

Zack jolted back to life. His eyes opened and he pulled away. 'What? What's the matter?'

'I can't do this. I'm not that kind of girl.'

'What do you mean?' His eyebrows drew together in confusion, and his eyes searched my face for clues.

I rubbed my face with my hands and rested my elbows on my knees. 'I know you have a girlfriend. Not even a girlfriend, Zack. You have *a fiancée*,' I said quietly, with my fingers covering my eyes.

'I don't have a girlfriend, or a fiancée,' he answered perplexedly.

'Well, whatever you call her – your soulmate, your *spiritual wife*. I know you don't like labels, but I know you're *with* somebody.'

'Lucy, what are you talking about?' Zack gently took my hands from my face and positioned me so I was facing him. 'I'm not. I'm not at all.'

'You are! You're... you know, *betrothed*.'

'Betrothed?' Zack stifled a giggle. 'Have you been binge-watching *Downton Abbey* again? I can tell you, Lucy, I'm absolutely not.'

'But you must be.' I felt myself frowning as I tried to put all the clues together and present them to him like a solved case. 'You're away all the time. And when you're home, you're always distracted on your phone. You have photos of her in your room and on your phone. You're always carrying that hairbrush around. Your calendar is blocked out with "Molly", who I'm assuming is your other half.' I was breathless, the words falling out of my mouth in confusing muddles of information. 'I know you looked at a *wedding venue* today, and she couldn't make it which is why I'm here. Come on, I'm not stupid. Actually, I even *saw* you with her – I saw you both together, with my own eyes.' I pulled my hands away from him as I rambled.

Zack bit his lip but didn't break eye contact with me. 'There's a chance you might feel a little silly in a minute.' He brushed a hand through his windswept hair. *How* did it still look so good? 'There's definitely been some sort of miscommunication, or a misunderstanding here.'

'What do you mean?' I tried to ignore the fizzy feeling throughout my body, as if my blood was sparkling and bubbles were coursing through my veins.

'I don't have a fiancée, or a girlfriend.' He raised his fingers and air-quoted me teasingly. 'Or "a spiritual wife or soulmate" – I'm free as a bird. I always have been.'

'Wait, what? I don't understand...'

'There is somebody *significant* in my life, shall we say. Except we're not romantically attached. We are attached though, very much so. She *is* called Molly, you're right. And she's my sister.'

'Oh,' was all I could manage. 'But I still don't—'

'It's a bit of a complicated situation.' Zack shuffled on our stone seats.

Kat was still merrily chewing her Dentastix, lying in front of us with all four legs stretched out as far as they'd go. Mid-walk bliss.

'Hang on. You said you share custody of Kat with your family – is she your sister's too?'

'Yes,' he answered. 'That hairbrush I carry around everywhere might have something to do with a blonde-haired shedding dog.' He offered a half-smile. 'And there are a few things I haven't told you about my family. Well, family by marriage, not by blood...' Zack grimaced. 'And kind of linked to how we met and our current living situation. But perhaps I should start at the beginning.'

'Take your time, it's OK.' I could tell how uncomfortable he was. Zack was never jittery or unsettled. He was always calm – calm and composed, bright and breezy – that was the Zack I knew. I didn't recognise the man sitting next to me, his leg twitching as he anxiously chewed his fingernail. It broke my heart seeing him like that. Needing to comfort him somehow, I put my hand over his, and his skin warmed mine as he held it tightly.

'My parents got divorced when Molly and I were teenagers. We were from a traditional family, an old family. We were farmers, right here in Cumbria.'

'You're *from* here?' I raised my eyebrows. 'That's why you know it so well?'

'Yep.' Zack nodded.

'Your family are farmers? I didn't have you down as a farmer.'

'Yeah.' Zack gave a chuckle. 'For generations, actually.'

'Hang on, does that explain your name?'

'My name?' Zack looked at me bewilderingly.

'When we were in the bank to sort out the mortgage. The advisor asked your name and you answered...'

'Ah.' Zack smiled at the memory. 'Yeah, we have a bit of a tradition when it comes to middle names. Plus, I'm the third Zachariah in the family, after my dad and grandad.'

'I see.' I grinned. 'I thought you were some sort of secret millionaire, landed gentry, Old Etonian type.'

'Pah!' Zack let out a laugh. 'No, well. Still no. I'll get to that.'

I looked at him quizzically, before we both turned our gazes towards the amazing scenery again.

'When my parents got divorced, my mum met someone else pretty quickly. And he wasn't...' Zack shook his head and stopped, almost physically shaking the words away. 'He wasn't a nice person. Mum and Dad's money was always tied up in the farm. We had an amazing childhood, my sister and me, and we never wanted for anything. But we never really had *money*. Whereas Mum's new partner was a successful businessman with a bottomless bank account, and Mum was swept away by it all. Suddenly, it was all country houses in the Cotswolds, holidays in the Caribbean, city breaks and shopping, first-class flights, champagne and caviar for breakfast.'

He sighed and leant backwards, still not meeting my eye and just looking out over the view. 'Mum had custody, so we had to slot in with her new life, and that included her new husband, Dominic, and his two kids from his first marriage. The kids were so awful, they made Dominic seem like the nicest man on earth, let's put it that way. He and Mum were away all the time, so it was just us and them in this big old country house. One time, they tricked us into going in the cellar and locked us in for twenty-four hours. We were terrified, we genuinely thought we were going to be left there forever. They seemed to find their joy in terrorising us, bullying us constantly and making us feel worthless – Molly and I had to fend for ourselves.'

'I'm sorry,' I said quietly, touching his arm.

'That's not even the worst of it,' he said, his words weighing heavily. 'Molly was younger than me. She took the whole situation badly; she just couldn't cope with the change and the upheaval. And things got worse when Dad died.' Zack's voice croaked. 'Molly's life was turned upside down all over again. She'd gone from a happy, grounded family, growing up in Cumbria, to a living nightmare. Our stepfamily might've been rich, and on the outside our life was extremely privileged, but all the money in the world can't help you when you're suffering inside.'

I rested my hand on his as I listened, appreciating every second of how open and vulnerable he was being.

'Molly had a breakdown. She got in with the wrong crowd, dropped out of college. Things were... things were bad,' Zack said firmly. I knew he wasn't going to go into the details. 'Mum just didn't care. They shipped Molly off to rehab a couple of times, but that was a plaster over the problem. A temporary fix so they could pretend they were doing something about it, but really, they were just carrying on gallivanting around the world with their friends.' He laughed incredulously.

'Molly got pregnant, and the father wasn't exactly the best character, so they essentially cut her off from the family. They wanted nothing to do with her. They basically wiped out her very existence.' Zack's jaw clenched as he pulled out bits of moss from the gap in the stones. 'Mum was brainwashed by her new husband; she was completely taken in by it all. But still, what kind of mother does that to their own child, and grandchild? I still can't believe it, even to this day. And Molly still feels the effects of it. She's doing better, but she still has bad days. *Really* bad days.'

'I can't even imagine what you've both been through,' I said delicately. I thought my childhood without my absent, workaholic parents was challenging.

'You don't want to imagine it,' Zack said. 'We felt like we were alone in the world with nobody, no family and no friends either – our lovely stepbrother and stepsister turned everyone at school against us because we didn't fit in at their posh private school, and nobody would stand up to them. They made our lives complete and utter hell.'

Sensing the heightened emotions, in that unique way dogs do, Kat sauntered over towards us, licking her lips after finishing her bone. She nestled in between both of our legs for a cuddle and ear tickle.

'When Mum and Dominic cut Molly off, I told them to cut me off too. I dropped out of my architecture course at university and got a job instead. I gave most of my money to Molly and her daughter, Tilly, so they could get settled in a flat with some money to get by, so at least Molly wouldn't have to worry about money on top of everything else.'

'Is that why you didn't have any savings when we bought the house?'

Zack turned to me and smiled. 'Yep. I didn't have any money for a deposit because I still give any money that I can spare to them. It makes saving difficult, I guess.'

'I see.' I smiled back at him. 'So, that was how fate threw us together?'

'It did,' he said with a grin. 'But yeah, before all of that and before they cut us both off, I had a gap year before I went to university, while Molly was in rehab. I just booked a flight and didn't come back for a while. I travelled around the world, I met people from all walks of life, I saw places I couldn't even have imagined – I experienced everything I possibly could.'

I nodded slowly, wanting him to carry on. Now he – Zack Bamford – made sense.

'I've never been into money or material things. Not since meeting my stepfamily. I wanted to see the world for the experiences money couldn't buy. That was why I got into yoga and meditation. I accidentally booked a class when I was in India, and it was like an itch that was finally being scratched. Everything fell into place. It sounds so cheesy, but I knew immediately that it was my calling.'

'It's not cheesy at all. And this explains a lot...' I said jokingly, to lighten the mood. 'I feel like I know more about who you are now.'

'Yeah.' Zack half smiled. 'Sorry, jeez. I'm sure you didn't want to know my entire life story while we're sitting at the top of a mountain.'

'I did. I mean, I do. I want to know everything,' I said.

We looked into each other's eyes. I knew what I wanted to ask, again. I needed to know, again. 'So, there's no girlfriend or fiancée?'

'No girlfriend or fiancée, I can assure you.' He gazed back at me. 'Which means I can do this.' Then, he leant closer. Our kiss: take two. His soft lips touched mine, planting my mouth with gentle kisses, before he pressed his lips against mine firmly, wanting more. He held me in his arms and his heat warmed my body all over.

'Do you have any idea how long I've been wanting to do that?' he said, his mouth just inches away from mine when we finally came up for air.

'How long?' I giggled, nuzzling my face into his warm neck.

'Ever since the day you stormed out of my meditation class,' he murmured between kisses.

'We're going to have to make up for lost time then, aren't we?' I whispered. He kissed me deeply again and it felt like my whole body melted into his, as we sat together at the top of the mountain.

THIRTY-FOUR

The pub we were in was like one of those snug sanctuaries you see in a Hallmark Christmas movie. Complete and utter cosy perfection. A checklist of everything you might want to be as warm and comfortable as humanly possible. And better yet, Zack's arm was wrapped protectively around me, with Kat snoozing at my feet. Zack had ordered us two pints of a local craft beer to sample, and we'd just polished off a portion of triple-cooked chips. It was an English countryside dream.

'So, the manor house isn't a wedding venue?' I questioned him. We were still dissecting our long, and now funny, misunderstanding. I was trying to comprehend the reality of the day – that Zack and I had kissed, and that we were now snuggling up together, looking like one of those ridiculously loved-up couples on a date. Zack's explanation had caused a seismic shift between us. I was still mulling over everything he'd told me – about his upbringing and his sister, the bond they had – but at least now I had a better insight into why he acted the way he did and his outlook on life. My heart broke a little every time I thought of everything he'd been through, and how he was still such a positive and happy person.

'Yes, I mean, I'm sure the manor house *is* a wedding venue,' Zack said, as he pressed a crumb from one of the chips onto his thumb and put it in his mouth – the mouth I wanted to spend all evening kissing. 'Just not for me.' He laughed. 'I still can't believe you, thinking that.' He shook his head.

'What was I supposed to think?' I admonished, sipping my golden pint. 'All the signs were there. And we're in an insanely romantic part of the world. Plus, you yourself said it was a *venue* visit.'

'A venue for a yoga retreat!' Zack chuckled, mimicking my movement and taking a sip from his glass too. 'Why on earth didn't you just *ask* me?'

'I did!' I said loudly and a little tipsily, putting the glass back down on the paper beer mat. 'I did.' I giggled again quietly. 'You were so vague! Saying you didn't believe in "traditional conventions of marital status",' I air-quoted. 'And some other sort of hippy dippy doo-dah nonsense *about your heart being open, your soul being free.*'

Zack shook his head as I flirtily mocked him.

'You were definitely acting like you had a significant other!' I insisted.

'"Hippy dippy doo-dah nonsense"...' He shook his head again. 'You're a little rude, you know that? Just because you like to put an official label on everything in life doesn't mean everyone else has to.'

'Me? Rude?' I turned to him in mock outrage.

'Don't tell me you haven't been called rude before.'

'There's a difference between being *rude* and being *direct*. If I were a man, I'd never be called rude, or bossy, or a bitch. Or any of those words reserved for ambitious women in business.'

Zack grimaced. 'Sorry, I didn't mean to hit a nerve.' He rested his hand over mine.

'I don't mean it like that, it's fine.' I sighed. '*Sorry for being rude,*' I teased, before sipping the final dregs of my beer.

'Hang on,' Zack said. He touched my chin to turn my head towards his, and the new and sudden contact was like a jolt of electricity through my body. 'You're so pent-up all the time,' he whispered, as he gently wiped the froth of the beer away from my lip. 'See, look what happened when I touched you just then. You need to relax, you need to unwind.'

I rolled my eyes but was distracted by the thought of him unwinding me. 'Speaking of relaxing, you said we were going to do something when we were at the top of the mountain, but we didn't. What was it?'

'We did do it,' he stated victoriously, leaning back into the comfy chair and resting his head against his open palms.

'What?' I said, confused.

'Well, *you* did it. You lived in the moment. Finally. That was all I wanted.'

'Huh?' I raised an eyebrow.

'It was the first time I'd seen you without either your laptop tucked under your arm, or your phone glued to your hand. Or looking like you were on the verge of a nervous breakdown. You actually just let go and enjoyed the present moment.'

His comment brought back memories of what other friends and acquaintances had said in the past. It was a deal-breaker, and most recently, it was the deal-breaker that almost destroyed my friendship with my best friend, Katie.

'I'm not that bad, am I?' I asked hesitantly, but knowing the answer.

'Like I said on the walk,' Zack said, ignoring my question, 'I'm not saying it to be patronising or preachy, not at all. But ever since I met you, all you've talked about, cared about – and I'm pretty sure, thought about – has been work.'

I slumped into my seat. Here it was, happening again.

'I'm not saying it like it's a bad thing,' Zack added quickly. 'There are certainly worse things you can be than a workaholic. And it's amazing that you're so passionate about it. Scratch that, it's *incredible* and *admirable* that you love what you do so much. Not everyone finds their calling in life. And there's no doubt that you're insanely talented.'

The roaring fire had already tinted my cheeks blush pink, but I was almost certainly verging on deep crimson by now.

'Don't get me wrong, Clark.' Zack took a sip of his drink. 'I have my own shortcomings – to be honest, I have too many to count. I'm completely disorganised. I struggle to focus on most tasks. I don't take certain things seriously when I really should. I'm terrible with money. I'm too laid-back for my own good, really. Not to mention my lateness...'

'I'm not arguing with you there. Your awful punctuality is one of the reasons why we butted heads when we first met.'

'I have to say, I'm surprised you never gave me a little kick during Warrior pose.'

'It's not like I didn't fantasise about it...' I teased him. My fantasies about Zack had changed somewhat now. Though they still involved twisty positions.

'I think what I'm trying to say is that, in my opinion, life is about balance,' Zack stated. 'And yes, I agree that maybe I'm too laid-back and I don't care enough, I accept that.' He nodded meaningfully. 'But after what I went through, and seeing how miserable people who seemingly have it all can be...' His words trailed off. 'You kind of think, what's it all for? What's it all about? Life is short. You just need what you need – and in my view, that's inner peace, feeling generally content and having a sense of purpose.'

There was no doubt that he had a point. It just wasn't some-thing I'd ever considered before. Not with the relentless pres-sure of matching up to my parents' high-achieving standards, and the idea that your self-worth was based on your salary and bonus. So far, I'd rushed through life, measuring my happiness purely though numbers. It was a ruthless hurricane of profit and loss – of working hours and ambition. But when I was enjoying every moment at the top of that mountain, I didn't give it a second thought. Really, what was the point? I'd sacrificed almost every aspect of my personal life for my work; I only had Katie as a friend, and I'd come scarily close to losing her.

I matched Zack's laid-back slouch into the seat. I wasn't sure if it was the beer or the post-hike exhaustion, but for once, I was relenting. Perhaps Zack Bamford had a point? I wanted and needed to concentrate on my purpose and my passion again – what my grandmother had always drummed into me.

'Another drink?' Zack said, slapping his hands on his knees and breaking the silence, signalling the end of our intense conversation.

'Better not, I'm driving.' Suddenly, I remembered where I was – in a Lake District bubble that didn't feel like reality.

'Of course, I completely forgot. I've been so caught up in all this...' He turned to me and looked at me delicately, as though disbelieving that I was *really* there. That this was really happening, that we really were in this love bubble of perfect unreality together.

'I've been caught up in it too.' I matched his dreamy smile. 'I don't want to go home. I want to stay here forever.' I looked around again at the cosy, homely surroundings.

'You know, we could... No.' He corrected himself before finishing the sentence, and shook his head, making his curls fall around his face.

'What?'

'We could maybe stay the night? I'll be a perfect gentleman, I swear,' he added quickly, holding his hands up as if he was surrendering. 'But I really don't want this day to end.'

'It isn't the worst idea,' I said, and stifled a yawn. 'Plus, I'm shattered. And also terribly embarrassed by my pathetic cardio levels.'

'Pah.' Zack flapped a hand. 'You climbed your first Wainwright today. That calls for a celebration. So, shall we?'

'Go on then, why not?' I nodded.

Zack kissed me on the lips as if it was the most natural thing in the world, then went to the bar and asked if they had a dog-friendly room available for the night. I wrapped my arms around myself. All I wanted was to stay in this warm cocoon of Zack forever.

THIRTY-FIVE

It was our second night in the Lake District. We both meant it when we said we didn't want our time together in our lovely bubble to end, and we'd moved on to another chocolate box town called Kirkby Lonsdale. Being here, only a couple of hours away from our home in Liverpool, felt like we'd stepped out of our normal lives and into a dream.

For the first time in my life, I felt as if an invisible weight had lifted from my shoulders. It was as though the time away was a full body massage that had worked out every knot of tension in my body. We'd had a lie-in before a long and leisurely breakfast; a morning smorgasbord of weekend papers, fresh orange juice, steaming mugs of coffee and delicious sustenance for the day. I couldn't remember the last time I'd done that, if I ever had.

Zack had kept his word about being a perfect gentleman and we'd slept side by side in the luxurious double bed, with Kat snuggled up at our feet. I woke first and watched him while his long eyelashes fluttered in his dreams. When he started to stir, I closed my eyes too, in the hope he wouldn't think I was verging on crazy with my sleep-watching. But there was something about being with Zack. It was as if he radiated sunshine.

After breakfast, we had another wander around before setting off in the car to explore. We'd accidentally stumbled on the market town of Kirkby Lonsdale when we were supposed to be heading home, and it was me who suggested staying another night this time. But I wasn't being totally selfish; it was Kat who'd found her paradise. The town was the most dog-friendly place you could imagine – she was treated like a VIP in all the homely pubs, cute cafes and chic boutiques visited.

A cosy inn that dated back to the seventeenth century was to be our home for the night. Kat thoroughly approved when she was presented with a welcome pack on arrival, with treats and her own fluffy towel, blanket and bowl. Our gorgeous room looked out onto St Mary's Church, which was surrounded by clusters of blooming flowers in the tidy gardens.

We'd wandered around the town, visiting the famous Ruskin's View, before slowly meandering along the River Lune and down to Devil's Bridge. Kat was in her element, running freely off the lead, sniffing all the interesting smells and making fellow doggy friends. We lived up to the photo (in Zack's words, the 'family photo') we'd taken on top of the mountain on our first day in the Lake District that marked the shift in our relationship. To look at us from the outside, you'd think we were a happy little family. I didn't want it to end, and I knew Zack didn't either.

'That bath was amazing!' I shouted from the gleaming white bathroom as I towel-dried my soaking wet hair. I padded from the en suite into the bedroom. The fact I was completely starkers underneath the fluffy robe demonstrated how comfortable I felt in Zack's company.

'I might have one too,' he said as he lay on the bed, flicking through the welcome booklet that had been left in the room.

'My feet are sore, and I've been wearing proper walking boots. I can't imagine how yours are feeling.'

'My old boots have served me well,' I lied. I was still allowed to be stubborn about *some* things. I curled my big toe underneath my foot so he wouldn't notice the massive blister forming on it.

'You're going to have to get some decent boots if we're going to make this a regular thing.' Zack grinned.

Did he want to make this a regular thing? The thought sprung into my head. What even was this? It was easy to forget our situation while we were in our loved-up Lake District bubble, but what about when we went home, back to reality?

'What's the plan for this evening?' I shook my hair and the wet ends left tiny damp dots on the super-soft dressing gown.

'I figured we could go for a couple of drinks in the town. I really want to try the local brewery's beers, and maybe eat back here? Probably easiest with Kat and the dog-friendly dining room.'

Kat looked up at us from her position, little limbs spread out on the blanket, and wagged her tail in agreement.

'Sounds good,' I agreed, shuffling onto the bed next to the two of them. I let out a yawn that held years of fatigue – early mornings and late nights, weekend projects and high blood pressure – fuelled by coffee and convenience food, served with a side of adrenaline.

'Or if you're tired, we can just stay in?' Zack said as he stroked my hair softly. It was those moments and tiny gestures that still felt surreal. I was lying on a bed, *naked*, with Zack Bamford, and he was stroking my post-bath, damp hair.

'Hmm, maybe,' I murmured. My skin was hot from the steaming bubble bath, and my temperature rose again when he leant his head down closer to me, and his lips met mine.

There had been burning tension between us from the moment we met, and it was presenting itself tangibly in this moment. I kissed him back, hard, pressing my mouth against his. It had been a long time since I'd wanted someone so badly.

'Hey.' He pulled away and whispered in my ear, before kissing me softly on my neck. 'Slow down.'

'Is that your favourite thing to say to me?' I breathed, my skin tingling with anticipation.

'If we're going to do this, we're not going to rush it.' His body, strong and protective, was pressed over me now. Between his words, he was still delicately kissing every inch of my skin that the dressing gown left exposed. His big hands made me feel tiny as he held my waist, delicately teasing at the belt that held the fluffy gown – and my modesty – together. 'We're going to take it slow. Really, really slow...' He looked at me, bit his lip and smiled, before moving his attention to the other side of my neck.

For the first time in my life, I was happy to slow down.

THIRTY-SIX

I thought the bubble was going to burst when we arrived back home from the Lake District, but it didn't. We were playing house, as if we'd skipped past the dating stage and had gone straight to the fully-fledged, can't-keep-our-hands-off-each other, honeymoon stage.

Zack was unlike anyone I'd dated before. He'd wake me up in the morning after a lie-in with a drink and a kiss. Coffee for me, matcha latte for him. My laptop remained shut for days after we got back. My phone was on silent. An out-of-office automatic response was hastily written and set indefinitely, while Zack moved my hair to kiss the back of my neck. The strength of my feelings for Zack had taken me by surprise, though deep down I knew they'd been simmering away since the moment we met. The Lake District break had simply let them pour out, like the water in the lakes we'd admired together.

But today was the day I had to leave the beautiful little life we'd created – where nothing went wrong, and we could spend every minute of every day making up for lost time. As reality loomed, I was determined not to overthink our new normal. I was keeping the promise I'd made to myself during our getaway – I'd live in the moment and not worry about what might happen if it didn't work out between us, though just the thought of that filled me with a dark and gloomy dread.

To make matters a little more complicated, Josh was back at Dale Street Developments after his business trip, and it was the pin that eventually popped mine and Zack's love bubble. The last time I'd seen Josh was when he'd filled his office with candles and red roses, and wooed me with champagne and caviar. Of course, I hadn't told Zack what had happened with Josh. At first because I was ashamed of how thoroughly unprofessional it was and how much I regretted it. But now, for obvious reasons, I thought it was better to stay quiet for the time being. Zack and I hadn't had the official conversation about our relationship status, but there was no doubt that we were 'together' – in every sense of the word.

'I hope today goes well,' Zack said, sipping his matcha latte as he leant over the kitchen counter.

'Thanks, me too,' I answered a little nervously. I scooped the freshly ground coffee into the AeroPress. It was a two-scoop and a two-coffee morning. I needed all the help I could get. I was knackered – in a good way, thanks to Zack's impressive stamina. 'I'm sure it'll be fine. The CEO has been away on a business trip and today's the day he's back, so we're all in for a briefing.'

Zack nodded. 'This is your biggest client, isn't it?'

'Yeah.' I stirred the water. 'The biggest by far. It's a long story, but winning the contract with them essentially saved my business.'

'So it's a bit of a "we say jump, you say how high" situation?' Zack said, lowering his voice and pretending to straighten a tie, in what I assumed was his impression of the corporate world.

I giggled. 'Mm-hmm, you could say that. They're great though, really, and they trust me. I just have a lot of work to catch up on because I've been somewhat distracted...' I turned and raised an eyebrow.

'Oh,' Zack said, feigning innocence. 'What has possibly been distracting you?'

'You know what.' I laughed. 'How's your day looking, anyway?'

'Good,' Zack replied, before gulping the fluorescent green drink that I still refused to get on board with, despite Zack's persuasions. We might've been getting on better than before, but we still disagreed on ninety per cent of things – the ideal morning drink being the main one.

'I haven't been to the studio since the venue visit, so I need to tell my partner – my *business* partner, Nigel' – Zack mocked my mistake again, one of his favourite pastimes – 'about the place in the Lakes. I think it'll be the perfect venue for the new retreat.'

'Yeah, I think you'd even get me back into yoga and meditation if it was there.'

'That's saying something.' Zack stretched his arms and broke into a big, dramatic yawn. 'Then I'm going to visit Molly and Tilly after work.'

'That'll be lovely,' I said. 'Don't forget the Grasmere Gingerbread and Kendal Mint Cake for them.'

'Oh yeah, they'd never forgive me.' He laughed. 'You'll have to meet them sometime,' he added shyly.

'I'd love to,' I said.

'What are you doing tonight?' he asked.

I knew my answer without having to check my calendar. It was Thursday. The day of my only immovable weekly appointment. 'I'll be out after work, but I won't be late.'

'Good,' he answered, with a flirtatious grin. 'We can carry on where we left off this morning.'

I stood on my tiptoes and gave him the quickest kiss I could manage. If I kissed his soft lips properly, I'd never make it into the office. 'I'll see you tonight,' I said, looking up at him.

'You tease.'

'Bye!' I used every ounce of resolve and quickly scooted away, grabbing my laptop bag and handbag from the hallway, and giving Kat a quick stroke before heading out of the door for the first time in days.

———

During the drive and brief walk to the Dale Street Developments office, it was like I was seeing the world in technicolour. It was as though before my trip to the Lakes with Zack, everything had been in standard definition, and now it had been upgraded to high definition.

Usually, I'd sprint through life in an impatient flurry. Every day would rush by in a hasty haze of early alarms, caffeine, deadlines, invoices, pitches and client calls. But today, the sun was shining down, illuminating the city in a golden glow. I admired the incredible architecture around me, remembering Zack's words to look up, not down. My work–life balance felt right, for the first time. There was a spring in my step, as if I'd taken a sip of what life was really about, and now I wanted to finish the bottle. It was intoxicating and I was addicted, desperately wanting more – more of Zack, especially.

When I walked through the doors of the boardroom, my co-workers on the design team asked if I'd been on holiday, and a couple of the women asked if I'd had a facial and where. I was glowing from the inside out and I knew it. A real change had happened. It was all thanks to my time spent with Zack, and bolstered by my own realisation – the promise I'd made to myself to re-evaluate my priorities and try to remember that life is for living, not just working.

As I settled into my seat, my shoulders felt lighter than ever before. But then the weight returned to them when Josh Barron walked into the room. His eyes lit up when he saw me, and he smiled in a way that I was sure many women would've loved Josh Barron to smile at them. To me, it spelt trouble that I was trying to ignore. I smiled politely back. I knew what I had to do. I had to come clean to him and explain that my situation had changed now. Besides, a lot could happen in a couple of weeks. My world had turned upside down in the best way possible, and if I was honest with myself, I hadn't thought about Josh for one fleeting moment when I was with Zack. The memory of our brief and tipsy kiss, which I knew had been a mistake (spurred on by flattery and champagne), had faded away to dust.

Turning back to my laptop, I pretended to be engrossed in emails. In reality, I'd only opened twelve of the hundreds that sat in my inbox, gathering since I'd set my out-of-office and switched off *properly* for the first time, probably in my entire life.

'Good morning, everyone,' Josh said, clapping his hands together. He addressed the room, but I could feel his eyes lingering on me. I shut my laptop and swivelled my chair to face him and Roger, the operations director.

Although I knew what had happened between Josh and me had been a mistake, part of me could still see why it had happened. His tanned skin was glowing golden against his crisp white shirt; he'd obviously been somewhere warmer than here. His eyes glistened with energy – he had the kind of hunger and ambition that I thought I wanted in a man, before the Lake District where everything changed.

'Thanks for coming to this meeting, I know it's been a bit last-minute.' Josh stood tall next to Roger. 'But we have some incredibly exciting news to announce. I've been keeping it quiet in case it didn't happen, but...' He looked at Roger who grinned back. 'We've won the Lexington Towers contract.'

Audible gasps and murmurs were the immediate responses

flooding the room. Hands flew to mouths, while others punched the air in delight, before everyone started to whoop and cheer. I sat there, oblivious to everything. What was Lexington Towers?

'I know, I know,' Josh said, gesturing with his hands in a silent request for everyone to calm down. 'It's so exciting and it's something we've been working on for the last year. Of course, not everyone here has been involved as we've had to keep some resources behind.' He glanced apologetically at me. 'But I can say with certainty that everyone in this room will be coming with us to work on the project.'

More bursts of cheers and hushed whispers of 'oh my God' filled the boardroom.

'Going where?' I said, looking around me. Seemingly, it was only me and a few others who looked as confused and clueless as each other.

'Our first international project!' Roger confirmed to the room, which was buzzing with excitement.

'Where?' I asked again, to nobody in particular, but was ignored. Everyone was too busy celebrating.

'To New York!' Josh said, raising his arms victoriously. 'Dale Street Developments goes global!' He matched the cheers of everyone else in the room.

The energy and excitement in the room was overpowering, for everyone except me. Not long ago, this would've been my dream come true. I'd missed out on my dream interiors project in New York when I sent that stupid email and lost Lavinia as a client, but this was my second chance. My heart started to race.

Josh shuffled past everyone, politely excusing himself from joining conversations, as the whole team celebrated. I was staring out of the window, my whole body wobbly with confusion.

'Hey, you,' he said, leaning close to me. 'Long time, no speak.'

'Yep,' I answered distractedly. A messy jumble of thoughts

swirled around in my mind. My limbs were a strange combination of stiff, but also wobbling like jelly.

Josh kept a seemingly professional distance in front of everyone, but I could feel his intense eyes on me, and he was standing so close I could smell the shampoo he'd used on his hair that morning.

'Sorry I couldn't tell you,' he said. 'I've just been out there to confirm everything and sign the contracts. I think part of me didn't believe it was really going to happen.' He shook his head in elated disbelief. 'Most of the team here have been working on it for a while, but I wanted to get my external team right too, and you're the best consultant we've ever had.'

I nodded numbly. A compliment like that would've made my heart sing a couple of weeks ago. I'd have been joining in with the others, who were now popping champagne bottles, even though it was 9.30 a.m.

'You will come with us, won't you?' Josh said cautiously, in a rare display of a lack of confidence.

'Erm,' I murmured, still looking out at the Liverpool skyline. My imagination was now drawing over it – I was picturing myself wandering along the streets of Manhattan. And just like that, I was the Scouse Carrie Bradshaw, prancing around in a designer tutu and dramatically hailing taxis while wearing fabulous, yet totally inappropriate, footwear.

'We can't do it without you, Lucy,' Josh said firmly, interrupting my daydream and giving me a sudden craving for a Cosmopolitan. 'It's a massive development. You'd be working on all the interiors in the apartments and offices. Of course, we'll confirm your contract and your fee, but I can tell you now, there will be no problem with the money. You're going to be very happy with it. And of course, it's all expenses paid.'

'Sounds good,' I whispered shakily. 'How long will it be?' I added without thinking. I couldn't go to New York – not now, but still...

'About three months initially,' Josh confirmed, taking two glasses of champagne that were thrust into his hands by Linda from accounts. 'Then probably around eighteen months, as an estimate. It might be longer.'

I held the champagne glass in my hand, watching the bubbles fizz in the golden liquid. I imagined what life would be like in the Big Apple, what it would mean for the business and everything I'd ever worked for. But then reality hit me.

'I can't go to New York, Josh.' I shook my head decisively. 'What about my life here? My business, my clients...'

'You won't need any other clients with this contract. Trust me.' Josh arrogantly took a sip of his champagne.

'But they've been loyal to me,' I replied. 'I can't just up and leave them. Plus, I've just bought a house...' It was like a vocal brain-dump of the thoughts that were whirring around my head. But the most important fact was the one I wasn't saying out loud – what about Zack?

'Can't your housemate just look after the house for you? Get another tenant in?' Josh shook his head impatiently, like it was the most obvious solution in the world. Of course, he didn't know how things had changed between Zack and me. 'If it's about the money and you need to cover some expenses back here, as I said, we'll renegotiate your contract—'

'It's not about the money.' I sighed impatiently.

'Hey,' Josh said, touching my elbow gently after looking around and making sure nobody was looking. 'What's the matter? The last time I saw you, things were great—'

'I just can't do it,' I said. I was frozen with panic at the thought of leaving Zack, of bidding farewell to the life we might have together. 'I can't go to New York.'

Josh's posture stiffened next to me. I looked up at him and his jaw clenched as he eyed my face intensely. Why couldn't he understand what I was saying?

'Well, you have to. You don't have a choice,' he said through gritted teeth.

'What do you mean?' I could feel my pulse quickening.

'Part of the reason why we won this contract was the idea, the vision, and that includes the interiors, which is you, Lucy. Besides, isn't this what you've always wanted? I thought you and I were on the same page. I thought you were ambitious, I thought you wanted to grow your business.'

'I do,' I snapped instinctively. 'I do, or I don't, I don't know,' I mumbled, and held my fingers firmly against my temples. 'Why on earth didn't you tell me before now? If I was so important to the project, don't you think I should've known?'

Josh shrugged. 'We're too alike, you and I. Work is everything. I knew when you came here that night that this would be a good partnership.' He touched my elbow gently again. 'I knew that you lived and breathed work. I knew you had nothing here to stay for.'

I took a step back, and looked at him and his cocky stance. I was outraged that he could be so arrogant as to think he could make these huge decisions for me, and I'd just go along with it, no questions asked.

But at the same time, I couldn't fight the nagging thought – the tiny voice in my head – that said he was right. I'd been in a bubble, but that bubble had burst. Reality had hit, and this was a once-in-a-lifetime opportunity to achieve my dream.

Besides, how long was it going to be before Zack and I couldn't stand each other again? We were so completely and utterly different – opposites in every way. Could we really be happy together? And was it worth losing my business, which meant everything to me? To take a chance on the idea of happy families? The questions in my head made me nervous.

'I need to get some air,' I said, handing Josh my untouched glass of champagne.

'Of course, I know I've sprung this on you,' Josh said, half apologetically. 'Go away and think about it.' He moved closer to me and lowered his tone. 'But remember, we can't do this without you. And I know a lot of business owners in this city. Word travels fast when you let someone down.' The tone in his voice made me shiver, and his words lingered with me as I hurled my belongings into my bag and darted out of the office.

THIRTY-SEVEN

'Wow, Lucy, this is incredible!' Zack said, picking me up and spinning me around the kitchen.

'I know, I know.' I giggled as my legs flung around like a doll.

'New York!' Zack breathed excitedly. 'It doesn't get much better than that.'

'Yeah, I suppose,' I said, pulling out a chair and planting myself down on it before kicking off my high heels. After leaving the office, I'd walked what felt like the length of Liverpool as I paced nervously, manically texting Katie, before heading back to my car. She'd told me in no uncertain terms that I absolutely had to do it – it was the opportunity of a lifetime!

'Why aren't you more excited? This is amazing. It's your dream, isn't it? To do a project in New York?' His eyes sparkled as he sat down opposite me and squeezed my hand, which always felt so tiny in his. 'I'm so happy for you, Luce.'

His enthusiasm made me like him even more, adding further confusion to my feelings about my choice. I didn't want to leave Zack, and I couldn't ignore my unease at Josh's thinly veiled threat, but these thoughts were paired with the nagging voice in my head that told me I couldn't turn down New York. I was still traumatised from the episode in *The Hills* when Lauren Conrad chose her boyfriend over going to Paris, and that was well over a decade ago.

'How long is it? How long would you have to go for?' Zack smoothed out the interiors magazine on the table, not meeting my eye. I knew he was trying to ask the question as casually as possible.

'Three months,' I replied. He clapped his hands together, but I held my hand out to stop him. 'Initially,' I continued. 'Then maybe eighteen months to oversee the entire project.'

'Oh...' Zack's face dropped. 'Wow, OK.' He nodded. The cogs were turning in his head as he processed the new information, trying to find a solution. The tables had turned – that was usually my role in our relationship.

'We can do long distance.' He looked at me hopefully.

'Do you think so?' I couldn't ignore the optimistic flip in my stomach. It was an idea I wanted to suggest, but the fact it came from him first was even better. After all, we weren't even 'official' yet. I knew Zack didn't like traditional labels, and we hadn't yet had *that* talk – although I hoped we were leading up to it soon.

'Absolutely, we can do long distance.' Zack nodded resolutely. 'I'll come visit you out there, you can come back here. There's FaceTime, there's Zoom. We can make it work.'

I stood up and nestled myself into his lap, cosying into his shoulder and resting my forehead against his neck as we snuggled with Kat at our feet. 'I think we could make it work,' I said softly.

'There's no doubt about it,' Zack said.

'Well, this has been a lot easier than I thought it would be,' I said. 'I didn't want to tell you.'

'Why? Because I'd tell you not to go?'

'I don't know. Things with us are fresh, aren't they? They're new.'

'It's not as if we're strangers, Luce. We've lived together for a while now. We probably know each other better than most married couples.'

I nodded. 'What shall we do about the house?'

'I'm sure I could find somebody to come and live in it while you're away.'

'I'll still be able to help out with the bills though,' I quickly added. 'I'm not going to leave you in the lurch. This house is ours.'

Zack leant backwards to look at me closely, while still supporting my weight against his arms. 'Do you know, that's the first time you've said *our* house without any bitterness or teeth grinding.'

'What? I'm not bitter.'

Zack wrinkled his nose. 'Mmm. You kind of have been. Just a smidge. But I've been under no illusion that your claim on this house is stronger than mine.'

'That doesn't matter now. It's just as much yours as it is mine. It's ours. And Kat's, obviously.'

Zack leant in closer and kissed me as I wrapped my arms around his neck.

'It's going to be officially announced at the Dale Street Developments annual gala, if you want to come as my guest?' I asked. I knew I still had to tell Josh that my relationship status had changed, but I wanted to include Zack in this part of my life.

'I'd love to,' he said, and kissed me again.

What had I been so worried about? Now, I finally had the best of both worlds. I had Zack and I had my career. And, eek, I was going to New York!

THIRTY-EIGHT

The Dale Street Developments annual gala was held in a rooftop restaurant, high up above the Liverpool skyline, with floor-to-ceiling windows that offered panoramic views of the city. A live jazz band played in one corner, and waiting staff dressed in tuxedos worked their way around the room, holding plates filled with either glasses of champagne or delicate canapés. Sumptuous evening dresses brushed the floor, while the men looked dapper in formal dress.

Zack was arriving later on, which was perfect, as it gave me enough time to chat with Josh. I'd been trying to talk to him all week, but he'd been in back-to-back meetings. However, tonight I could formally tell him my decision. I was going to New York! And also, that we had to keep things strictly professional. Even if nothing had happened with Zack and me, that would've been my decision anyway. Mine and Josh's kiss had been a huge mistake.

The room was buzzing with excitement and anticipation. The New York team members were sworn to secrecy, as Josh was going to announce it officially tonight. Everyone who meant something to the business was there. Every staff member and stakeholder milled around, and even the press had turned up.

It was the perfect redemption for me and my business. Josh had emailed me my contract so I could look it over while I made my decision. He was right; thanks to the fee, I wouldn't need any other clients alongside the project. It would be hard work and long hours, but enough to elevate my business way ahead of where it was before everything went wrong. Plus, having the Lexington Towers project in my portfolio, and the potential networking I could do through it, would ensure I'd never be in that position again. And after two years, when the project was finished, I could come back to Liverpool and open my own office, hire staff and grow the business as I'd always planned to. I just had to ignore the nagging feeling in the pit of my stomach that told me I was risking going back to my workaholic lifestyle, before my realisation of wanting a better work–life balance.

Still, my whole body was giddy with anticipation; I was fizzing like the bubbles in my glass that never reached half empty, thanks to the attentive waiting staff. I circulated the groups of people, keeping one eye on the doorway, waiting for both Josh and Zack.

After what felt like hours of small talk, the excited sounds and hushed whispers marked Josh's arrival. Everyone in the room was either clapping, whooping or cheering. The gentle sounds of jazz were drowned out by the energy. *Wait until you hear what he has to say*, I thought to myself, feeling a little smug that I was one of the chosen few who already knew what was to be announced.

I made my way through the crowds, self-consciously smoothing down the satin of my plum-coloured dress. It had been a long time since I'd worn something so elegant. My hair was tousled into a neat chignon and my high heels were already digging into my toes – always the sign of a fabulous pair of shoes.

'Lucy!' Josh said brightly as he saw me emerge from the crowds.

'Hi, Josh,' I answered politely. I let him kiss my cheek as he lowered his body down to greet me. But he lingered there a little longer than was necessary. 'I need to speak to you,' I said, subtly inching away from him.

He nodded to the man next to us, who patted Josh on the back. 'Hey, thanks for coming,' he said to him, before turning his attention back to me as he scanned my face. 'Do you have an answer for me?' he asked, with a glimmer in his eye.

'Yes,' I replied.

He gestured at another guest eager to talk to him. 'Two seconds,' he said to the guest. 'Sorry.' He raised his eyebrows at me apologetically. 'Please just tell me it's a yes and that you're in?'

I nodded. 'I'm in.'

'Yes!' he cried and punched the air, but without any hint of surprise. Something told me Josh Barron was a man who always got what he wanted.

'But there's something I need to tell you,' I added quickly, aware that there was a crowd forming around us, and I urgently needed to remind him that this was a professional partnership, nothing else.

Before I could say anything, he pulled me in closer by the waist, and lifted a curl to expose my ear. He was too close, as he opened his mouth to whisper, but he stopped abruptly. I felt his body freeze as he held the lock of my hair in his hand, with his other one firmly gripping my waist.

'What?' I said, and turned to face where his eyes were locked – the door to the function room.

Zack was standing there.

He was dressed in a tuxedo, his unruly curls smartly tied back into a short ponytail at the nape of his neck. I quickly pulled away from Josh, but it didn't matter; his complete attention was on Zack. And Zack's was on him, as he slowly stepped closer towards us.

The energy between them was palpable. It was like an electric current running from one to the other. Their eyes were locked onto each other, as if it was just them in the crowded room. Josh's body was tense, his shoulders stiff and square, while Zack's jaw was clenched and his hands were curled into fists, tucked in his pockets.

'Zack?' I said quietly as I stepped away from Josh. 'Do you two...' I looked between them both. 'Do you two know each other?'

The intense staring continued. They looked like they were going to come to blows, and judging by the fire in both their eyes, I wasn't sure who was going to throw the first punch.

'Zack?' I asked again, inching away from Josh's side and closer to his.

'Yes, yes, we do know each other.' Zack cleared his throat.

'Good to see you again, brother.' Josh held out a hand.

'What?' I cried.

Zack's jaw tightened even more, before he forced a hand out from the pocket of his suit, and he shook Josh's. Both of their knuckles whitened with the tension.

'What do you mean, *brother*?' I said again. 'You're related?'

'No. No, we're not,' Zack said, his nostrils flaring.

'We're stepbrothers,' Josh confirmed with a smug smile. 'Aren't we? Zack Bamford-Barron?'

Then it dawned on me. Everything Zack had told me about his childhood and growing up with the stepsiblings that had made his and Molly's lives hell. The family they were both estranged from.

'I don't go by that name anymore,' Zack muttered through gritted teeth.

'Well, this night just got a whole lot more interesting,' Josh said arrogantly, ignoring Zack. 'Lucy and I have some good news to announce, don't we?' He leant towards me and put an unwelcome arm around my waist again, as if I were some sort of trophy on sports day and he was the winning team. I tried to yank it away behind my back, but his grip was too firm.

'I didn't know Dale Street Developments was your company,' Zack said to Josh, his voice shaky but firm.

'It certainly is,' Josh said haughtily, standing tall. 'Finally branched out from the family property firm and started my own.'

'How commendable,' Zack said coldly. 'I suppose it helps when you have Daddy's credit card to fall back on when things get tough.'

Josh's posture stiffened as he locked eyes with him. 'At least I work for a living, and don't prance around chanting and doing headstands all day.'

Zack half laughed and shook his head. 'They're really your client, Lucy?' He turned to face me. 'Really?'

'Yes,' I answered, as I finally escaped Josh's vice-like grip and stepped away into a neutral position in between them.

'We certainly are,' Josh said with a smug smile. 'And even better, lovely Lucy's coming to New York with us... with me.' He shot a glance at Zack before turning and grinning at me. 'Aren't you, Lucy?'

I looked between Josh and Zack again. What was I supposed to do? My heart was in my throat. Someone had clearly turned up the heating in the room because my whole body felt like it was on fire, and my heart felt like it was thudding against my cheeks.

'Erm, yes, I am,' I mumbled. My mouth was dry, and my words were lodged in my throat.

'I know they say never to mix work with pleasure, but rules are made to be broken, aren't they?' Josh winked.

Zack stared at him, considering his words. He turned to look at me, his eyes ablaze with a cocktail of emotions – a messy mix of anger, shock and sadness. 'Can I have a word with you, please?' he said, before he stalked away.

Still wordless, I followed Zack out into the hallway silently. Josh's eyes didn't leave either me or Zack, and his gaze felt stronger with every step we took, until the door closed behind us. Zack walked down the hall and I followed him. His pace quickened, until we got to the end of the long corridor – a distance Zack seemingly deemed far enough away from Josh, his *stepbrother*. I still couldn't believe it. My hands felt like they were glued to my hot and rosy cheeks as I held them there, trying to slow my thoughts and calm my anxious mind.

Zack leant defeatedly against the wall. 'I can't believe Josh – Dale Street Developments – is your client.' He shook his head in disbelief.

'It's not as if I've done it on purpose,' I retorted. 'I didn't know. I mean, how on earth was I supposed to know you two are related?' I stumbled over the words falling out my mouth. 'I've worked with them for a while, practically for as long as I've known you. It's not my fault.'

All Zack could do was shake his head and stare down at the floor. 'Lucy, what did Josh mean when he said "never to mix work with pleasure"?' he asked slowly, his words loaded with uneasiness.

'I don't know,' I answered, halfway between defensive and stubborn. I couldn't tell Zack that Josh and I had kissed, not now I knew their connection.

'He said it, Lucy, you know he did. You heard him,' Zack said softly, but with a growing frustration in his voice. 'He said that, and then he said, "but rules are made to be broken" – what the hell did he mean?'

I bit my lip as my eyes darted around, looking at everything in the hallway except Zack in front of me. 'It was nothing,' I offered weakly, struggling to find the words.

'Stop lying to me, Lucy. For God's sake.' Zack ripped the

bow tie from his collar and shoved it into his pocket. 'I can take it. I can take the truth. I can take anything, except you lying to me.'

'OK, I'm sorry.' I took a deep breath and closed my eyes. 'We kissed.' I blurted the words out. 'But it meant nothing. It was completely unprofessional; I've regretted it ever since it happened and I wish more than anything that I could take it back, but I can't.' My desperate explanation tumbled out of my mouth urgently, before I could even properly register what I was saying. I just needed Zack to know the truth.

'You kissed him?' Zack's eyes landed on me, but I looked away guiltily. 'You kissed *him*?' he repeated incredulously.

I shuffled from one foot to the other on my spot. We were so close but so far away.

Zack shook his head and started pacing the floor. 'Was it when we were together?'

'Of course not!' I cried. 'You really think I'd do that?'

'Well, *why* would you kiss him, Lucy?' he answered, ignoring me and asking his own questions.

'I don't know now,' I whispered. 'I was in a weird place with myself. I was confused about my feelings for you. And I thought I was going to be fired.'

'What? And he came on to you instead? Did he force himself on you?' Zack practically spat his words through gritted teeth as his jaw clenched and his fingers balled into a fist again.

'No!' I shouted. 'Bloody hell. It was nothing like that. It was just a mistake, Zack, that's all it was.' I shook my head at the memory. 'And anyway, you and I weren't together – we weren't even a tiny bit together.'

Zack's flushed face calmed a little as he considered my words and rubbed his chin with his hand.

'How can I fix this? What do you want me to do?' I asked pleadingly. All my emotions were pouring out and I didn't know where to put them; they were landing like hits on Zack, and I couldn't stop myself. I felt completely powerless.

Zack opened his mouth and closed it again. 'There's nothing you can do,' he said quietly. 'What's done is done. And I'm not going to ask you not to work with him.'

'Good,' I said. 'You can't ask me that.'

'I know.' Zack nodded slowly. 'It's your life. It's your business. It's nothing to do with me.'

I said nothing. Instead, I kicked off my heels; my throbbing feet needed a break and I couldn't think straight.

'But I can't be with you if you do work with them – with *him*.' Zack wouldn't meet my eye again. His gaze was fixed downwards, on the carpet.

'So, you're *not* asking me to *not* work with them?' I clarified. 'But you're saying you can't be with me if I do?' I could feel the red tinge of anger reddening my already flushed cheeks. 'Do you know how manipulative that is?'

'Manipulative?' Zack said, aghast, finally meeting my eyes. 'Manipulative?' he repeated. 'You have no idea.' He brushed his head with his hand, pulling out the ponytail and releasing his curls to their rightful position, tumbling over his broad shoulders. 'You have no idea, Lucy. You have no idea at all,' he said.

'Do you know how hard I've worked?' I fumed. 'Do you know how long I've been dreaming of this moment? And the opportunity to work on a project like this? It's my dream, Zack.'

Zack pursed his lips, watching me. 'Of course I do,' he said eventually. 'I'm not denying that. I'm not denying you anything.'

'But you're making me choose,' I said impatiently. 'You are. You know you are.'

Zack shook his head. 'I've told you about my history with him, what he's *really* like. If you don't believe me – or if you don't believe how bad it really was back then, fine. Perhaps you're willing to take the risk so you can achieve your dream, but please trust me, Lucy. Josh is bad news. I can't help how I feel and I'm not going to change my mind about this.'

'Well, me neither,' I said stubbornly. I remembered Katie's hen party in Marbella, and the 'Loosey Lucy' chants and how it all went wrong. I had to choose work this time. I wasn't going to let it happen again. 'Someone once asked me to make a decision like this, and it got me nowhere. In fact, it meant I lost everything, and I had to start over. Do you know how that feels? I made a promise to myself I'd never do that again.' I wasn't missing a second opportunity to live my dream, to go to New York and to grow my business. 'I'm not doing it again,' I said firmly, and a little more decisively than I was really feeling, deep down.

'OK,' Zack said gently. 'If that's your decision.'

'It is,' I replied, ignoring the wobble in my voice.

Zack looked at me pleadingly, as if he knew he had one last shot to convince me. 'Lucy, you're brilliant. You're gifted at what you do. I've seen your passion and how you come alive when you're designing. You can be a brilliant designer anywhere and achieve everything you want in life. You don't need Josh for that, you can do it on your own. I truly believe that.'

I opened my mouth, but the words were lodged in my throat – they were caught between a choice, feeling stubborn and unmoving. Was this really what it came down to? Choose Zack or my ultimate career dream?

'I need some headspace,' Zack said before I could answer. 'I'm going to go away for a bit. I won't be home when you get back.'

'Fine,' I said, swallowing the words and crossing my arms across my chest like a stubborn child.

Suddenly, I was worried I'd gone too far. Surely this was just a fight. Our first proper fight since our new normal, but we'd work it out. We had to work it out.

Zack didn't say anything. He just stood in complete silence, as if his limbs were frozen in the moment. His only movement was when he clicked the button for the lift. Within seconds, which felt like hours of painful, stomach-churning silence, the doors opened, and he stepped inside.

I opened my mouth to tell him to stop, to wait, but the words didn't materialise. Something was holding me back. I knew what it was, and it was work. I knew it had to come first this time, or I'd regret it forever.

'Please be careful with him, Lucy,' Zack said.

The doors closed, and he was gone.

THIRTY-NINE

I had everything I'd ever wanted. I'd finally reached the ultimate goal of my career. But it was as though there was a hole in the middle of my soul. The house was empty of life without Zack. A week had passed, and he hadn't been home. His phone was switched off and I had no idea where he was.

My suitcase was packed, and I was leaving for America next week. I'd transferred money to Zack's account to cover my side of the bills, but even that hadn't led to a response from him. I was glad to be getting away from the house because without Zack and Kat in it, I felt like I was drowning in memories of our life here together.

Every inch of the house offered a memory of the life we'd built, on top of those precious memories with my grandmother. The walls were made up of brushstrokes I'd painted. The wooden floor he'd laid. The pictures were hanging on nails we'd hammered into the wall together. As I was packing up, I tried to pack my feelings away too – to stuff them tightly into a cardboard box, seal it up, label it as fragile and then put it away somewhere to be forgotten about.

Had I made the right choice? To choose work over Zack? I

was going to live my dream and go to New York, but at what cost? I paced around my bedroom. I'd closed the door to Zack's because I couldn't bear to see his unmade bed without wanting to get in it and pretend that he was next to me, to smell him on the pillows. I was going so stir crazy and verging so close to stalker territory that I'd even had to stop myself from sniffing his shampoo, just to remind myself of his scent, which was fading from my memory with every day that went by without him.

Surely Zack was overreacting about Josh. Family dynamics were difficult; even I could relate to that. I hardly spoke to my parents and was used to them living abroad for my entire life, thanks to their high-flying jobs. But to carry it on for this long? Couldn't he let it go? Even for me? He said he wasn't making me choose, but we both knew he was.

I had so much pent-up frustration in my body, I wanted to scream. I needed to speak to him, but I didn't know where he was, and he wasn't replying to me. The only alternative was to distract my anxious mind. I needed to lose myself in my favourite world – the world of interior design. Luckily, there was a big task at hand that would hopefully take up the majority of my brainpower and stop me from thinking about Zack during every waking hour. I had to finish Katie's house before she returned from her honeymoon and I left for New York. So, I tucked all my sketches and notes into my briefcase and walked out of the house, for one of the last times before my temporary move to America next week.

———

'You're home!' My jaw dropped at the same time as the door opened, leaving the key I was using to unlock it inside the keyhole. 'Yay!' I dropped my briefcase and put the boxes and bags I was holding on the floor. I threw my arms around Katie. 'Tell me everything. How was the honeymoon? How's married life? Did you eat a scorpion in Thailand? Did you do a bungee jump?' My questions went unanswered, and I realised Katie was stiff, her body rigid with tension.

'What's the matter?' I asked as I stepped backwards, onto the paving stones of their freshly landscaped driveway.

'What was the one thing I asked of you, Lucy?' Katie's eyes were pink, her cheeks tear-stained.

'When?'

'While I was away. What was the one thing you were going to do for me? The only thing I've ever asked you to do for our entire friendship?'

'To do the interiors of your house,' I answered perplexedly.

'Exactly,' Katie stated, pinching her lips together as she stood back and folded her arms across her chest.

'I don't understand, Katie. I was just coming round to finish it off for you. I have all the final touches here with me.' I gestured to the packed boxes and bursting bags I'd carried from my car.

'When was the last time you were here?' Katie's nostrils flared as she ran a hand through her beachy, sun-kissed waves.

'Not that long ago,' I answered quickly. Although now I came to think of it, when *was* the last time I'd checked in on the house? I'd been so swept up in my Zack love bubble, and so consumed by Josh's dream project proposal, perhaps it'd slipped a bit in my order of priorities. 'Why?' I asked desperately, my heart thudding, the guilt washing over me.

'Come and see for yourself.' Katie stepped back, still in her flip-flops, and opened the door for me.

I followed her in, and gasped at the state of their dream house – the one they'd designed from the ground up. There was a dull, heavy sensation in the pit of my stomach as I took in the sight of what was supposed to be the farmhouse-style kitchen. Hole-ridden walls and unfinished carpentry were left abandoned. There were no wooden planks laid on the floor – the

planks I'd carefully designed widely so they looked like a quintessential farmhouse floor. The shaker-style units were half
finished, and oak slabs for the worktops were piled up in a
corner. Instead of the glass hanging pendants, the ceiling was
dotted with wires poking out of holes.

'What on earth has happened?' I said shakily. Had I really
dropped the ball that badly? Had everything gone wrong under
my watch – or what should've been my watch?

'You tell me.' Katie's arms flew up as she kicked a screw-
driver across the floor. 'I thought you had this under control.
Yes, we're back early, but literally by three days. Did you really
think they were going to finish all this in three days?'

I shook my head. I didn't know what to say.

'I thought you were keeping an eye on all this,' Katie said,
her eyes bulging between the tan lines her sunglasses had left. 'I
thought you were doing this for me, to show you cared about our
friendship and that you were sorry for what happened at my
wedding.'

'I was. I am...' I stuttered.

'Well, it doesn't look like you care very much, does it?' Katie
half laughed in disbelief as she took in the state of the space.
'Upstairs is even worse. Did you do *anything* the entire time I
was away?'

'I did! Of course I did!'

Katie simply shook her head. Perhaps in the chaos of my site
visits, I hadn't taken in exactly what a state the house was in. I'd
been asking for updates from the architect and nagging the
tradespeople, but I'd assumed they were on top of everything. I
should've been more on it, I knew that now.

'This is all my fault.' My lip quivered. I thought my eyes
were dry from tears after those days and nights spent crying
over Zack, but I brushed one away as I looked at Katie's disappointed expression.

'Yes, it is,' she said coolly. 'I know we were half joking about our friendship ultimatum. But honestly, Lucy, I thought you wanted to make it up to me when you nearly missed me saying "I do" at my wedding. I thought you cared enough about me that you wanted to do this.' Her voice broke too. 'But clearly you don't.'

'I do, Katie. Of course I do. You're like a sister to me. I wouldn't do anything to hurt you.' It was as though there was a brick wall between us, and my words couldn't penetrate it.

'Sisters or friends don't treat each other like this – like they're the bottom of the priority list.'

'Please let me make it up to you,' I begged. 'I'll do it right now. I still have some time before I go to New York.'

Katie said nothing, she just shook her head. 'I think you should leave, Lucy. I need some time and space.'

'I don't want to leave. I want to help.'

'I don't want you here, Lucy,' Katie shouted. 'Please, just go.'

Accepting her answer, I shuffled out of the room. The abandoned remainders of my vision were dotted across the floor. I sloped past the bespoke pots of paint I'd mixed to get the perfect colour for the rooms, the rolls of wallpaper I'd carefully curated and the tiny details I knew Katie would love – like the secret wine cupboard that was supposed to be filled with her favourite rosé, and the hand-drawn etching of a family of chickens we'd giggled about, subtly painted onto the bottom of the pantry door.

Tears stung my eyes as I stepped out into the fresh air. I'd let Katie down and I'd let Zack down – two of the most important people in my life. But I knew what I had to do and where I had to go. I needed to speak to the third – the person who'd have the answer of how I could fix everything before I left for the airport next week, and it was too late.

FORTY

It was time for afternoon tea at the White Dove Care Home.

Pushing open the front door, the warmth of the home and the familiar smells hit me all at once. Freshly baked biscuits and lavender laundry detergent. Coming here wasn't easy. It never was, even though I did it every Thursday – it was the one immovable appointment in my diary. I knew my grandmother, Dotty, was the one person who would have the answer.

The residents sat in their usual places, in the comfy, mismatched armchairs that lined one wall of the lounge area. Some of them were watching the daytime TV programme that was showing on the big television, the sound turned to almost full volume. Others were snoozing, and a group was chatting animatedly while knitting.

I walked through the lounge, learning my lesson to dip down underneath the TV or they'd huff and groan. I waved at the ones I knew, who recognised me as Dotty's granddaughter.

'Hi, Lucy!' my nana's carer, Penny, greeted me, while she took a plate of scones out from the wheelie trolley and poured a cup of tea for one of the residents.

'Hey, Penny,' I said. I tried to fake a little bit of happiness and positivity, even though my mind was blank and I was chewing my lip to stop my tears. I knew this visit could go one of two ways. It could make me feel better, or even worse.

'She's in her room.' Penny gestured towards the bedrooms at the back. 'She didn't fancy afternoon tea today,' she said sympathetically.

'How's she been?' I asked.

'Much the same,' Penny answered gently.

I nodded and shuffled through the tables already set for dinner time. The big canvas-style framed pictures on the wall were individual collages of each resident. Their name was in big letters in the middle, and surrounding it were photographs of them in times gone by, with little descriptions of the memories.

There were black-and-white photographs and colour ones, all telling the tale of something significant in their lives. Fred's displayed a young man about to go off and fight in the war. Ivy had twenty-four grandchildren! Gladys was once a famous ballerina. Arthur had won a gardening award and was interviewed by the BBC. Mabel married her childhood sweetheart.

And there was my grandmother. Dorothy Walsh. Her name was surrounded by photos of two things: me and 8 Falkner Avenue. My parents featured in smaller snippets, but there was no doubt everything she did in her life centred around me and that house – her pride and joy. My heart swelled as I thought of how the house and I had serendipitously come back together again.

My pace slowed as I rounded the corridor that led to her room. It was an instinctual reaction, as if my body was telling me not to go. Gingerly, I set one foot in front of the other and traced the steps of the weekly visits I'd made for years, no matter how many times my heart shattered with every minute spent here.

Knock, knock.

'Come in,' a fragile voice said from behind the door.

I opened the door and plastered a smile on my face. 'Hello,' I said.

'Oh, hello dear!' My grandmother was sitting up in bed, reading a book. I tried not to look at the cover, but I knew it would be the one she'd been reading for as long as I could remember. The bookmark was always set in the same spot, in the middle, as if it was glued to the page.

I pulled up the chair, as I always did, and moved it so I could sit next to her bed. I held her hand in mine. Her skin was like tracing paper, so thin and translucent, all her blue and green veins visible. But her hands were always warm, just like her. She grinned at me and held my hand tightly in hers.

'How are you?' she asked, her eyes still with the same sparkle.

'I'm good, thank you.' I nodded.

'How are you settling into your new job?' she said. 'It's so lovely here, isn't it?' She looked around her cosy room, decorated in her favourite shade of sunshine yellow – the same colour as the front door at 8 Falkner Avenue. If there was one colour that represented Dotty Walsh it was a sunny yellow that cast light and warmth on the world.

'Yes, it's wonderful here,' I said, the lump in my throat getting bigger with every word.

'Why aren't you wearing your uniform?'

'I thought I'd have a change today,' I said gently.

'That's why I like you, you're a rebel.' She winked. 'I like rebels. Reckon you could smuggle me in some brandy?'

'I'll do my best.' I giggled.

'Don't tell Agnes in room twelve if you do.' She eyed me sternly. 'Or you'll have trouble. I bet you she'll nick it for herself.'

'Noted,' I said, happy for the distraction from the sadness of seeing my grandmother here, and in her confused but content state of dementia, which had gripped her for the last few years.

'The stories Agnes has told me...' Nana shook her head, but smiled. 'You wouldn't believe what she got up to, back in the good old days!'

I made a mental note to check out Agnes's picture board outside before I left.

'So, dear, are you here to take my dinner order?' The innocent, childlike way she asked me simple questions like that broke me even more than the days when she couldn't place my face at all. Though at least today she'd recognised me, even if she did think I was a new carer at the home.

'No, that's not me today, but I'll ask the lady who is to pop by later on,' I said, and she nodded and tapped my hand gratefully.

'I was looking at the photographs on the corridor outside,' I said. 'There are some amazing stories here, aren't there?'

'Ooh yes.' Dotty nodded her head enthusiastically. 'Wonderful stories, dear. We have story time after dinner sometimes, when we talk about our lives and reminisce for a little while. I'm sure you'll be here for it one of these days, depending on your shifts, of course.'

'I'm sure I will.' I smiled. 'Why don't you tell me a bit about your life? So I can get to know you better?'

'That sounds lovely.' She grinned, putting her book on her bedside table. It looked too heavy for her fragile arms. 'First things first. I'm a Scouser through and through.' She lowered her gaze and eyed me seriously. 'There's nowhere like Liverpool. Never moved from here since the day I was born.'

'That's amazing,' I said. 'And where did you live?'

'I'll tell you where I lived.' Her twinkling eyes lit up. 'Oh, it was the most beautiful house. It was on...' She paused and scratched her head. 'It was on...' Her lip started to wobble nervously. 'I can't remember the name of the road. My memory's not what it used to be,' she said apologetically.

'That's OK,' I coaxed her gently. 'I don't need to know the name of the road; you just tell me about this beautiful house.'

Her smile returned as her worry disappeared. 'It had a bright yellow door, and I can tell you now, it caused quite the stir back in the day when I painted it that colour.' She winked cheekily. 'Some of the neighbours were all, "Don't you think a more *neutral* colour would be more appropriate for the area?"' She pursed her lips and mimed somebody pushing their glasses down their face. 'Neutral?' She giggled like a schoolgirl. 'Bloomin' boring, more like. No, I stood strong, and that yellow door stuck out from all the others. Loud and proud, a bit like me, I suppose.' She giggled again.

My heart squeezed in my chest as I listened to her talk like this. It was as though the old Dotty was coming back. The wit and the mischievousness.

'My garden was like another child to me,' she said. 'I could pass away the days planting, pruning. Pulling up the weeds and tending to the flowers. I loved it. It was my little sanctuary. A piece of paradise, just for me.' She sighed wistfully. 'The house wasn't a mansion; it wasn't the sort of house the rich and famous would live in. But it was a palace in my eyes. I loved every inch of it. I adored every brick in those walls.'

'It sounds incredible,' I replied, matching her dreamlike state. I felt exactly the same way about it.

'And even better...' She grinned. 'My granddaughter lived with me most of the time.'

'She did?' I was heartbroken but overwhelmed with love. At least she could remember me there, even if she couldn't remember me here.

Dotty nodded eagerly. 'We had a wonderful time together. Her parents were always very busy people. My daughter, her mother, had an important job and they travelled a lot. They were going to put her in boarding school.' Her mouth was wide, aghast. 'Can you believe that? I said "absolutely not", and so she lived with me a lot of the time.'

'That sounds so special. I'm sure she felt lucky to have you.' It was taking every inch of me not to let my voice break completely. *Lucky* didn't even come close to how I felt about my grandmother and our relationship – and growing up at 8 Falkner Avenue.

'I was lucky to have her,' Nana said gleefully. 'She was everything to me.' Her brow furrowed and she looked out of the window. 'I haven't seen her in a while,' she said quietly.

It was a punch to the gut. 'I'm sure she'll come and visit you soon,' I offered shakily.

My grandmother's eyes turned back to me, and she smiled. 'I'm sure she will. She's very busy. She has her own business, you know?'

'Really?'

She nodded. 'She's an interior designer, works with clients all around the world. Oh, you wouldn't believe the messes she's got herself into. The things her clients have made her do.' She giggled again. 'You'll have to meet her some time.'

I took a deep breath. 'Definitely, one day,' I said.

'She works far too hard though.' Dotty tutted and shook her head, in that way I was so familiar with. 'I don't know how many times I've told her that life is for living. She's going to make the same mistakes that her parents made.'

'What do you mean?'

'They spent their lives working. They missed most of Lucy's childhood.' She shook her head again. 'And what was it for? What was the point? Yes, they bought their fancy houses and silly sports cars, they wear all their fancy clothes.' She waved her hand dismissively. 'But when you get to my age, you learn none of that matters.'

She took my hand and squeezed it again. 'None of that matters,' she repeated.

Our eyes met and she peered more closely at me. Our eyes were exactly the same.

'You look...' she whispered, taking in every inch of my face.

Was it going to happen? *Please let it happen*, I urged silently. I didn't say anything; I just held her gaze, willing her to remember. Inside I was shouting, 'It's me, Nana! It's Lucy, your Lucy!'

'Sorry, dear.' She sighed deeply and shook her head, looking out of the window again. 'You reminded me of someone.'

My heart sank, but her words rang like song lyrics stuck in my head.

None of that matters.

What on earth had I been thinking? Not only the idea of leaving Zack, but leaving the house that meant so much, and leaving my grandmother too, albeit temporarily? I knew the care home did Zoom calls for residents who lived far away, but that wasn't enough. I had to continue my weekly visits, and make the most of whatever time we had left. I had to hold her hand and look into those blue eyes.

'Thank you so much for chatting with me...' I hesitated, the word 'grandmother' lingering in my mouth. 'Ms Walsh,' I said. I stood and gave her delicate hand one last gentle squeeze. 'I'd better get ready for dinner service, and I'll ask my colleague to come and take your order.'

'That'd be wonderful, thank you,' Dotty replied with a grateful smile. 'I'm in the mood for Scouse tonight. You can't go wrong with a good pan of Scouse.'

'You definitely can't,' I replied, remembering weekends when she'd cook her legendary Scouse and I'd sit cross-legged on the sofa, watching TV and burning my tongue because I'd be trying to eat the mouth-watering meal far too quickly.

I opened the door and looked back at her, all warm and

comfy in her bed, surrounded by super-soft throws and cosy cushions. If she couldn't be at 8 Falkner Avenue, which the doctor had said in no uncertain terms she couldn't any more, then this really was the best place for her.

'See you soon,' I said.

'See you, love.' She offered a weak wave, but a strong grin. 'Hey, don't forget my brandy.' She winked.

'I won't.' I smiled. I'd sneak it into a hip flask for her next week.

As I closed the door, she picked up her book again, starting it from the same page she was reading earlier – the same page she was always reading during my Thursday visits.

FORTY-ONE

I had my answer, thanks to my grandmother. The scales of my priorities had tipped in the wrong direction for too long. I knew what mattered now and what didn't. I'd found a glimmer of it in the Lake District, but then I lost it again when I had the chance to go to New York and pursue what I thought was my dream. However, now I knew my priorities had been wrong, and I was going to make them right. I wasn't going to New York. I was staying in Liverpool. I was going to grow my business the way I wanted to, with the balance right, and with clients who didn't blackmail me – who respected me enough to ask me before making life-changing decisions on my behalf.

But first, I had to make it up to Katie, and then I had to track down Zack. Katie had finally responded to my begging messages. I asked her to give me a week, that was all. Just the time I would've had before I moved to New York, so I could give her the dream home she deserved. Then it was up to her if our friendship could be saved, but I hoped that it would be enough to show her how much I cared and how sorry I was.

Stepping back, I surveyed my work. It was by no means

perfect, given the time constraints. But I was trying to loosen up when it came to perfectionism. Nothing in life was perfect, but that didn't make it any less good or worthy. The main thing was, I'd done my best. Every single aspect of the house that I worked on, I did it with Katie in mind. She was the most important interior design client, and best friend, I'd ever have. If she forgave me for dropping the ball and letting her down.

Taking one last look, I left the card and bottle of champagne on the oak countertops, brushed off the final specks of sawdust from the table, and walked away. I closed the door behind me and hoped that I wasn't closing the door on our friendship, that I'd be sitting at that kitchen table with her one day. Evenings when we'd drink homemade cocktails; mornings nursing hangover-curing breakfast; afternoons spent sipping steaming mugs of Yorkshire Gold, while talking about our favourite memories of Dotty.

———

Today was the day I was supposed to be going to New York. Now that I'd hopefully made it up to Katie, Zack was next on my list. The only tiny problem – a minor detail – was that Zack was still nowhere to be found. I'd popped home again, just in case, but there was no sign of him even dropping by over the last week. I'd visited the coffee shops I knew he loved; I went to the cafe on Bold Street that was his favourite place for food.

Already, I was getting some strange looks as I showed the staff his photograph and asked if anyone had seen him. At first they were helpful and sympathetic, but that turned to bemusement as I tried to explain the situation. He wasn't actually a missing person; he was just avoiding me.

I was on the verge of printing out massive photographs of him and leaving them around Liverpool, asking anyone who might have information to call me. But was that a step too far? I couldn't say I wasn't seriously considering it. Perhaps I could wear a big sandwich board on my body and walk around the city with a booming megaphone.

Before I considered doing that, my next stop was the yoga studio, again. I'd already called them and they weren't very forthcoming, but I figured if I stopped by, it was much harder to say no to someone's face. Plus, I was bribing them with delicious vegan doughnuts. So even if they could say no to my face, they couldn't say no to doughnuts. Who could say no to doughnuts?

But my heart sank when I saw who was sitting behind the reception desk. Each of the yoga teachers and meditation facilitators took turns in manning the desk when they didn't have a class to teach. Today, it was the woman who hated my guts more than anyone I'd ever met before. Mainly because she had the biggest crush on Zack, and he'd let slip about us being together when we were in our happy, hazy bubble of love, and she'd texted him to ask if he could cover a class.

Yikes. I was going to need more than doughnuts. Even if they were coated in dairy-free chocolate.

'Hi, Adriana!' I said brightly, as I walked towards the desk.

She raised her eyebrows and looked me up and down coldly in reply. I gulped. This was going to be harder than I thought.

'I called earlier. I was hoping to find out where Zack was. Do you know if he's teaching a class?'

Nothing. Just a death-stare from her.

'Oh, and would you look at that?' I said, feigning shock. 'I happen to have these amazing, incredible, delicious doughnuts with me.' I pulled the pink cardboard box from under my arm and placed it right in front of her on the desk. If the looks alone weren't enough to tempt her, I opened the box in the hope that the sweet, sugary smell might help.

I could tell she was about to relent, as she cast her eyes over them and licked her lips. But then it was as if the reality of who'd brought them hit her.

'I'm on a diet.' She rolled her eyes and slammed down the flimsy cardboard lid. She accidentally squished a doughnut, and surreptitiously licked the cashew cream from her hand when she thought I wasn't looking.

'Please, Adriana,' I begged. 'Please, please, please. Just tell me where Zack is. This is urgent.'

I caught sight of my reflection in one of the studio mirrors when a door opened. I looked crazed and manic. The sleep deprivation had got to me, and in my rush, I'd forgotten I was still wearing my loungewear set that had two significant wine blotches and various chocolate stains on them: my comfort eating (and drinking) duo of choice. I shook my head and tried to ignore my appearance. 'I'm begging you, Adriana. I will do anything. I just need to find Zack.'

She rolled her eyes again. 'I don't know where he is.'

'But you have to know. There's been this whole thing.' I stammered over my words. 'I can't explain it all now, but I had to make a choice. I made the wrong one and I don't know what I was thinking.'

My phone vibrated and my heart squeezed. Was it him? My heart sank again. No, it was Josh. Again. We were supposed to meet in the British Airways lounge at the airport.

'I'm supposed to be going to New York right now,' I said.

'You are?' It was as if somebody had recharged Adriana's battery and now she had come to life. 'You're moving to New York?' Her eyes sparkled with glee.

Hmm, could I use this to my advantage?

'Yes, yes I am,' I said diplomatically. 'I'm moving to New York. And I'm late, very late.' This was a lesson in thinking on my feet. 'But in order for me to go – *forever* – to America, never to be seen again...'

Adriana was lapping up my every word, her eyes hungry

with the idea of having Zack to herself and me out of the picture.

'Then it's imperative I find Zack. He has...'

I considered desperately what he could have of mine that was so essential.

'My passport!' I shrieked. 'He has my passport.' I shook my head and matched her eye-roll. 'I need it. I need to find him and get it from him. Or I can't go away. *Forever.*' I emphasised it again.

Adriana pursed her pillowy lips and leant forward as she listened to me. If she was a cartoon, I would've been able to see a massive beating heart throbbing in her chest as she considered a newly single and lonely Zack Bamford.

'Sorry.' She sighed, disappointed, as she sat back in her seat. 'I still can't help you. I genuinely don't know where he is.'

'Really?' I sulked.

She nodded. 'I'd help if I could. *Trust me.*'

I tapped the box and turned to walk away, mumbling polite thank yous under my breath.

'Oh, I know he's gone abroad though!' she shouted after me.

'What?' I said, practically breathless as I turned around. 'Abroad? He's gone *abroad*? How do you know?'

She shrugged her tanned shoulders. 'It's what he does when he loses himself; he goes away travelling.'

'Where?'

'Could be anywhere,' she said indifferently. 'We have studios in Spain, Thailand, Bali, Mexico... I know he loves the one in New Zealand.'

'New Zealand?' I shrieked, my mouth flying open, my eyes wide. 'You don't really think he's gone to New Zealand, do you?'

She shrugged again, and I was sure the reason why her upper body was so toned was all the shrugging that formed her primary mode of communication.

I turned on my heel again. He couldn't have gone to *literally* the other side of the world. What about his sister? His niece? What about Kat? What about the house? There was no way he'd just up and leave. But *where* was he?

'I hope you find your passport!' Adriana shouted after me as I closed the door.

FORTY-TWO

There was a low mist on the streets, making everywhere look like it was a setting for a scary story. The truth was, my story *was* scary. Questions darted around my mind, my panic deepening with every step I took as I mindlessly roamed the city.

What if I'd lost him forever? What if I'd made the wrong choice, *again*? I couldn't imagine my house – *our house* – without Zack in it. I couldn't imagine my life without Zack in it.

My phone buzzed in my pocket again, but I ignored it. So far, Josh had called me ninety-eight times, and left at least thirty-three voicemails that I could imagine were getting angrier and angrier, judging by the random one I accidentally clicked on, when he'd promised to ruin me and my reputation, and that I'd never work in this city again.

But that was the ironic thing. His threats felt meaningless to me. Everything paled in comparison to losing Zack. I knew I was resourceful and resilient – I'd find new clients somehow. But there was only one Zack for me.

The house was like a magnet drawing me home. It always had been, throughout my life. While I was walking, I realised I was on my way there. I'd been so lost in my thoughts, I had no idea how long I'd been walking for. I didn't know if I could handle going home and it being empty of Zack and Kat again, but where else could I go?

The sunshine-coloured door stood out from all the others, as it always did. I loved that about it. I loved that Zack had managed to find the exact shade of yellow, sanded the neglected wood and repainted it again. He'd brought it back to its original splendour, back to life again. Just as he'd brought me back to life again.

Flowers were blooming in the garden. The weeds were long gone. It didn't look exactly the way my grandmother had it, but it still had her spirit. The house was a nod to her, but we'd put our own stamp on it – Zack and I.

I pulled the key from my pocket and put it in the keyhole, lifting the door handle and jiggling the key to the right, just as I'd done so many times before. Except this time, I could feel the tears rolling slowly down my cheek. The lump in my throat was so big that all I wanted to do was crawl into bed and sleep for days. I was pushing back the question in my mind. It was a problem that was impossible to solve. How could I live here without Zack? First, I couldn't stand to live here with him, and now I couldn't bear the thought of living here without him.

Slipping my jacket off, I balanced it on one of the arms of the old coat stand. I put my shoes in the wooden shoe holder by the door where Zack had once put his, back when everything was simpler. The little hook that Kat's lead usually went on was empty, and it was that sight that sent me over the cliff-edge of my feelings. He must've taken her to his sister's. When would I see her again? Would I *ever* see her again?

Standing in the hallway, it was as if years of emotions were let out like a tidal wave, flooding me. My vision was blurry as I cried and walked through the house, padding over the floors he'd laid, my hands brushing the walls he'd painted. I pushed open the kitchen door and jumped as I realised someone was sitting at the table. Someone with a small fluffy dog in their lap. It was Zack.

'You're here,' I whispered, hardly able to control the ocean of emotions I was swimming in at that moment. 'You're here,' I murmured again, hoping that the more I said it the more real it would feel. His presence was like a life raft, keeping me at the surface.

'You're here,' Zack said, in the same disbelieving tone as me. His eyes were red and swollen. Kat jumped off the chair and gave me a quick, adoring welcome, before leaping back onto Zack's knee and resuming licking his tear-stained cheeks.

We stared at each other. Our small kitchen was filled with so many words unsaid.

'I thought you'd gone to New York,' Zack said eventually. 'Adriana phoned me. She said you needed your passport. I didn't realise you were leaving so soon. I thought it was too late...' He shook his head in disbelief. 'I've just got back from Manchester airport.'

'What? You went all the way there?'

Zack nodded. 'I couldn't just let you go. I even had to pay for a ticket to get through to the gate.'

I bit my lip. I couldn't believe he'd done that for me.

'Yeah. It's not like how it is in the movies. You can't just run through the gates without attracting the attention of security.' He half smiled. 'I tried calling you, but it kept ringing out or going to voicemail.'

'Oh, yeah.' I touched the outline of the phone in my pocket. 'After not hearing from you, and getting *a lot* of other missed calls, I've been avoiding my phone.'

'That's not like you,' Zack said, his expression warming as he took me in, realising that I was really there, standing in front of him.

'You're right, it isn't. There are a lot of things that I wish weren't like me.' I shook my head. 'I should never have chosen to work with Josh over choosing you.'

'Lucy, please,' Zack said. 'You didn't choose. It was unfair of me to say, and I put you in an impossible position. I'm sorry.'

Zack carefully placed Kat on the floor and stood up. He took two slow strides towards me, and as he got closer, I could see there were dark bags under his eyes, his cheekbones were visible, and his stubble was rough and overgrown.

'I've been a mess without you,' he said, explaining his appearance.

'Tell me about it,' I answered, gesturing at myself.

'If you do work with him' – Zack's jaw clenched as he said 'him', unable to say Josh's name – 'I can live with it. I'll find a way to deal with it.'

'I don't want to,' I said. 'I've made the wrong choices before, and I'm not making the same mistake again. My priorities have been wrong in the past, but I want balance now. I want to run my business and live my life with a better grasp of what matters and what doesn't.'

I stepped back and looked at Zack, taking in the sight of him entirely. I remembered my grandmother's words – *none of that matters* – and how, for the first time in my life, I realised how true they were. I'd spent years sweating the small stuff and getting swept away with things that really didn't matter in the grand scheme of things. I loved my work, but I loved my life too, and I wanted more of it.

Zack's face melted with relief. He stepped closer to me and wrapped his arms around me gently and graciously, as if it was the first time he'd ever done it. 'There are some things I'm going to work on too,' he whispered.

'Oh yeah?'

'Punctuality being the first one.'

'Finally.' I laughed, almost breathlessly.

'I need to learn how to focus. I want to work on my ideas for the new yoga retreats we're running in the Lakes.' He tucked a loose curl behind my ear. 'So, you're going to have more of a work–life balance, emphasis on the *life*. Whereas I'm going to take *work*, and myself, a little more seriously.'

'Sounds like a plan to me.'

We were body to body, nose to nose.

'You know, at first I couldn't live with you, Clark,' Zack said softly.

'I might've had the same thought.' I grinned.

'But ever since your first, and potentially dangerous, attempt at a headstand... or when you stormed out of my class... and even that first night here together, when you walked in with those ridiculous sombrero-wearing alpaca pyjamas, with spot cream all over your face...'

I blushed.

'To now.' He held my face delicately in his big hands. 'I've realised that I can't live without you.'

We sealed his words with a kiss, his arms wrapped around me, and Kat on the floor at our feet. There we were, together, in the kitchen of 8 Falkner Avenue. Our house. Our home.

EPILOGUE

'I can't walk another step.'

'My legs are *literally* going to fall off.'

'They're not *literally* going to fall off though, are they, Clark?'

'How does Kat do it?' Katie wailed. 'Her legs are, like, ten inches tall. She's basically an oversized guinea pig and she's making it look easy.'

'It'll all be worth it when we get to the top. Plus, I have Grasmere Gingerbread and Kendal Mint Cake for everyone to enjoy when we do.' Zack marched ahead merrily with Kat by his side.

'Has he always been this insufferably smug when it comes to climbing mountains?' I asked Molly.

'Oh, absolutely. If anything, he was even worse when we were teenagers. He'd run up them sometimes.' It was easy to see the family resemblance in those green eyes as she rolled them while stealing a glance at Zack.

'Just a little bit longer!' Zack shouted back to me, Katie and Molly. To be fair to him, he did insist he wasn't going to be walking anywhere near the three of us, with our matching pink walking boots. Even Kat was keeping her distance.

'Why didn't Matthew come with us?' I asked Katie.

'He's still sorting out my walk-in dressing room.' Katie grinned. 'It's the least he can do after our disastrous honeymoon.'

Katie had forgiven me for the house situation, and we'd sat in her fabulous new home, drinking wine at the kitchen island, while she told me about how awful her honeymoon had been. Matthew had spent the entire time tracking down sports bars so he could watch every match his beloved Liverpool played. It was why she always sounded less than enthusiastic whenever we spoke, and why her pictures were all selfies of her drinking cocktails on her own.

Katie had apologised profusely to me for the day she'd arrived back to her new, unfinished home. I wasn't blameless because I'd undoubtedly dropped the ball and let her down. However, she insisted she'd massively overreacted. She was still reeling from a huge argument with Matthew, paired with recovering from terrible food poisoning after some dodgy prawns they'd eaten in Phuket.

We'd hugged it out before cracking open another bottle of rosé, eating our body weight in pizza, putting the world to rights and dancing to ABBA until 3 a.m. I'd reassured her that we all had our meltdowns every now and again – look at what a frazzled hot mess I had been at her hen party and on her wedding day. The main thing was that our friendship had recovered and was stronger than ever.

'How much longer?' Molly panted, as she wiped her forehead. 'I can't believe we grew up doing this. I'm so unfit now. Thank God I didn't bring Tilly – she would've made me carry her and her toys all the way up. Is my face the colour of a tomato? Tell me honestly.' She turned to me and grimaced.

'You look great!' I reassured her and her rouge-tinted cheeks

– always the sign of a good walk. 'You always look great, Moll. And you always looked good when I saw you on Zack's photos!' I giggled. 'Back when I thought you were his girlfriend.'

Molly shuddered dramatically.

'A few more steps now, guys. I can see the trig point from here!' Zack shouted. At least I had a good view of his lovely bottom while I staggered slowly behind him. It wasn't the reason why I always hiked slowly. Promise.

Kat turned and looked down at us. She wagged her tail and gave us a knowing look, as if to say, 'You probably wouldn't be that slow if you hadn't insisted on a big pub lunch before we set off.' To be fair, she had a point.

Zack and Kat disappeared from sight, as Katie, Molly and I – the three musketeers we'd become – forced our tired legs forward to tick off another Wainwright fell together. At least I'd invested in new walking boots for our regular trips to the Lake District, even if they were pink (when they weren't coated in mud).

We took the final few steps up the grassy verge, and the view opened out in front of us. The spectacular landscape of the Lakes from the top of a mountain never failed to take my breath away (even if it was partly due to being exhausted from the climb).

'Look! You can see the new retreat from here!' Zack pointed excitedly, after we'd all taken a silent moment to appreciate the memorising view.

Zack pulled his arm around me. I was so proud of him for following his dream of opening his own yoga retreats. He'd put his love of property to good use, as he worked closely with architects on bringing the old buildings he'd scouted out back to their former glory. I had designed the interiors and had taken on an assistant to deal with the admin side of my job, leaving me to concentrate on what I loved best – researching, designing, curating and creating. Most importantly, bringing visions to life through interior design, and making people feel something when they walked into a room.

My new mission statement for the business was *Purpose and Passion*. It was inspired by Dotty, who taught me to always have purpose and passion in life. And it perfectly encapsulated my interior design ethos – every room had a *purpose*, which would highlight my client's individual style and *passion*. I'd also landed a big new client, who just so happened to be Dale Street Developments' number one competitor. Liverpool was a small place in the grand scheme of things, but luckily we'd only bumped into a sheepish Josh once. He'd left endless threats on my phone (including a bitter and angry confession that our date was part of his plan to ensure I'd agree to the New York project). But being the bigger people, Zack and I had greeted him politely. However, Kat, being the perceptive pooch that she was, must've picked up on the awkward vibes. She tootled over, lifted a fluffy leg, and peed all over his expensive leather shoes. Dogs are brilliant judges of character, aren't they?

Zack was happy to finally find out where I was going every Thursday evening, and he was a hit during afternoon tea at the White Dove Care Home. He'd sat and eaten cake, drunk endless mugs of Yorkshire Gold, and watched *Casablanca* (my grandmother's favourite) with her countless times. Although she thought he was a new carer too, every now and again, I caught her looking at him with a twinkle in her eye. I knew she knew – somewhere deep down – who he was and how important he was to me.

Zack and I still bickered fondly, of course. We wouldn't be us if we didn't. But I'd stopped wanting to give him a little kick whenever we did yoga together. I was even getting better at meditation, clocking up a three-minute record. I couldn't do a headstand yet, but I'd definitely had some good practice with a few other positions...

And, as for the house rules? Well, rules are made to be broken, right?

Rule #1 Nakedness reserved for the bedroom only.

A lady never kisses and tells...

Rule #2 Limit of one treat bath per person, per month.

Does that still count if you're having one together?

Rule #3 Leave each room as you find it. Pick up your mess and keep it tidy.

Zack is still working on this one. But it's a bit less frustrating when the mess is our shared mess.

Rule #4 No loud noises after 10 p.m.

I sometimes have Zoom calls with my parents after 10 p.m., thanks to the time difference, but I do try to keep the noise down. We're trying to improve our relationship, and Zack and I are flying out to their new home in Sydney soon so they can meet him.

Rule #5 Clear overnight guests with each other before they stay.

The only overnight guests we have are Molly and Tilly, plus Katie and her husband Matthew, so that's a simple rule to stick to.

Rule #6 No going into each other's rooms.

Well, we only have one bedroom now, so that's easy.

A LETTER FROM DANIELLE

Dear reader,

I want to say a huge, heartfelt thank you for choosing to read *Stuck with Him*.

If you enjoyed Lucy and Zack's story of making a very special house their home, I would be incredibly grateful if you could write a review on Amazon or Goodreads. I'd love to hear what you think, and as a new author, it makes an enormous difference in helping readers to discover one of my books for the first time.

If you would like to be the first to know about any of my book news, just sign up at the following link. Your email address will never be shared, and you can unsubscribe at any time.

www.bookouture.com/danielle-owen-jones

I love hearing from my readers – you can get in touch through Facebook, Twitter, Instagram, Goodreads or my website.

Love,

Danielle

KEEP IN TOUCH WITH DANIELLE

www.danielleowenjones.com

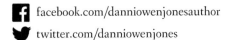 facebook.com/danniowenjonesauthor

twitter.com/danniowenjones

instagram.com/danniowenjonesauthor

ACKNOWLEDGEMENTS

Firstly, I'd love to say a big thank you to the readers who have bought my books. This is my second novel and I'm still absolutely giddy with happiness at the idea that I can call myself a published author! The reason why I write is to tell stories that I hope offer some uplifting escapism from everyday life. So, thank you for reading this book, and I hope you enjoyed Lucy and Zack's rocky road to their happily ever after.

This book wouldn't be what it is without the ideas and input of my incredibly talented and lovely editor, Emily Gowers. Thank you for having so much faith in me to do this house-buying idea justice. Of course, my wonderful agent, Clare Coombes, for always being the best cheerleader of my writing. A big thank you to the Bookouture team who are a joy to work with. And an extra special thanks to my brilliant publicist, Jess.

I'm incredibly lucky to have the amazing support of my family and friends. Firstly, thank you to my mum, Colette. I could fill a book with pages of thanks for everything you've done for me!

The world's most supportive in-laws, who are always cheering me on – thank you Amanda and Trefor, Nain, and Amy and Tom Williams. And my whole family: Owen-Joneses, Howards, Gilberts, Scurrahs and Coackleys. Thanks to all my dearest friends, including Han, Loz, all my wonderful Kirkby Lonsdale pals, The Besties, Lazzle & Sazzle, The Welshies, The Journo Girls and Book Club.

Interior design was a whole new world to me as I researched and wrote this book. Thank you to Jalan for letting me into your world and for taking the time to answer my many questions about all things interiors!

Publishing is a real rollercoaster, and the best way to get through the ups and downs is by holding hands with those sitting next to you on the ride. A big thanks to my supremely talented and supportive writing buddies: Meera, Sarah, Steph and Catherine.

Finally, to Tom and our little fluffball, Pops. I love every chapter of our story, and I'd be happily 'stuck' with the two of you any time, any place.

Printed in Great Britain
by Amazon